THE TRIARCHS

Also by Derek Wilson

FICTION
Feast in the Morning
A Time to Lose
The Bear's Whelp
Bear Rampant

NON-FICTION
East Africa through a Thousand Years
A Tudor Tapestry
Sail and Steam
The People and the Book
A History of South and Central Africa
White Gold – The Story of African Ivory
A Student's Atlas of African History
The Illustrated Book of World History
The World Encompassed – Drake's Voyage 1577–80
England in the Age of Thomas More
Africa, A Modern History
The Tower 1078–1978
Sweet Robin – Robert Dudley Earl of Leicester
Francis Frith's Travels
Rothschild: A Story of Wealth and Power
The Circumnavigators
The Astors 1763–1992: Landscape with Millionaires

THE TRIARCHS

Derek Wilson

HEADLINE

First published in 1994
by HEADLINE BOOK PUBLISHING LTD

10 9 8 7 6 5 4 3 2 1

British Library Cataloguing in Publication Data

Wilson, Derek
Triarchs
I. Title
823 [F]

ISBN 0–7472–0977–4

Phototypeset by Intype, London
Printed and bound in Great Britain by
Mackays of Chatham PLC, Chatham, Kent

HEADLINE BOOK PUBLISHING LTD
A Member of the Hodder Headline PLC Group
Headline House
79 Great Titchfield Street
London W1P 7FN

THE TRIARCHS

PROLOGUE
A private view

The determined beating of rain on the windowless attic roof confirmed that outside there was no let-up in the autumn storm. Within, all was dryness. The dryness of antiquity. The dryness of massive hand-hewn oak and of dust seldom disturbed in four centuries. There was a click, and an almost solid shaft of light probed the gloom.

'I've come better prepared this time.' The young man stepped through the doorway. The beam from his powerful torch ranged over the miscellany of discarded objects. Utilitarian, fanciful, some grotesque – they had all been at one time or another important in the daily life of the Cranvilles, only to be dismissed as useless by some later generation, then consigned to this cavernous mausoleum.

'Oh dear, the thought of having to sort this lot out is too depressing for words.' The woman peered past her visitor, light from a naked bulb on the landing behind making a halo of her fair hair.

'Well, don't worry yourself about the pictures. I should be able to separate the wheat from the chaff for you on this visit.' He directed the beam towards the end wall, where ornate gilded frames gave back a dull gold gleam.

'Will you be OK? Can I do anything?'

'No thank you, Miss Cranville. Just leave it to me. I'll sort out any items that seem interesting, and bring them downstairs so that we can have a closer look. If there's anything comparable to the one we found last time . . .'

'You're sure about that one?'

'Well, as I explained in the letter, I've got more research to do on it, but the quality is indisputable. So, who knows what other treasures may be lurking here?' He advanced into the attic.

There were a dozen or more paintings stacked unscientifically, one atop the other, in three piles against the wall. He felt a tingle of excitement as he carefully lifted each one aside, and played his torch over the surface. What would it be? Some eighteenth-century family portrait executed by a provincial hack? An indifferent copy of an old master? Or the genuine article – a long-lost original from the atelier of one of the great Dutchmen or Italians?

Half an hour later he was engrossed in the study of a small picture. It was a Flemish 'Annunciation' – that much was obvious. But an original or a copy? The highlights, flesh tones and the silver-grey of Gabriel's wings, penetrated the discoloured varnish. (Strange about the varnish, he thought. The other one had had just the same coating.) When he turned it over, the oak panel on which it was painted gave every appearance of venerable age. Yes, this one certainly merited close scrutiny.

He lifted the unframed picture to place it carefully on top of the four others he had already selected. As he straightened, he heard – or thought he heard above the drumming of the rain – a soft footfall.

'Miss Cranville?'

He half turned. Something flashed in the light of the torch. Then his head exploded with sudden pain. He sagged to his knees. The painted panel clattered to the floor. His body fell across it. Again and again the silver candlestick struck the back of his skull. It did not stop until the point of impact was a mess of flesh, bone, hair and blood.

PART I

GODS AND MEN

'Those who possess such gifts as Raphael are not mere mortals but rather mortal gods'

Giorgio Vasari:
Lives of the most eminent
Painters, Sculptors and Architects

CHAPTER 1

Big Ben chimed 2.45, as Tim Lacy strolled along the Embankment. This was the time he liked London best – at night when he had it to himself. Especially after an evening that had abundantly satisfied all the senses. He had just spent such an evening. The English Opera's performance of *Idomeneo* had been both profound and scintillating. Dinner had been well up to Cyrano's usual superlative standard. The companion upon whom he had lavished these delights had, in her turn, been equally generous. Now, having torn himself from the lady's enthusiastic embrace, he was enjoying the nocturnal charms of *his* city.

There was a dank October chill in the air, but Tim wore no topcoat over his thickset frame. Hands deep in pockets, he sauntered across Parliament Square, past the silent black bulk of the Abbey, and turned into Great Smith Street. A couple more blocks and he would be in his warm, comfortable apartment. A glass of the very special Armagnac he kept exclusively for his own consumption would, he assured himself, appropriately round off an excellent day. He crossed the street to enter the familiar Victorian portal, let himself in, and climbed the steps to the first floor.

There was a woman sitting with her back to his front door.

That was the first shock.

The second came when she looked up. Recognition douched his sense of well-being like a bucketful of ice-cold nitric acid.

'What the hell are you doing here?'

Venetia Cranville uncoiled stiffly and stood up. She brushed the long hair from her face and stared back unapologetically, almost defiantly.

5

'Tim, I don't like this any more than you do, but I need your help.'

' "I need. I need." I seem to have heard those words rather often.' He tossed his key-ring from hand to hand.

'Tim, *please*. Just let me come in and explain.'

He did not move. For several seconds he looked deep into her Judas-blue eyes. Beautiful, as always. He read anxiety and fear in them. Little girl lost, reaching out for acceptance, reassurance, comfort. He had to make an effort to remind himself of the lies those eyes had told during the sixteen months and three days he had been under their spell. He reached past her and jammed the key into the lock.

'Keep it short.' He let her precede him into the flat. 'It's late and I have to be in Paris by lunchtime.'

'Business is good, then?' She sat on the edge of a deep settee and stretched her long legs before her.

Tim subsided heavily into an armchair opposite. 'Since this is painful for both of us, let's get it over quickly.'

Venetia nodded. But the words would not come. She had rehearsed them over and over again, ever since she had, reluctantly, decided to throw herself on Tim's mercy. Now that she was face to face with the familiar, rugged, uncomplicated, no-nonsense scowl of her ex-lover, baring her soul was suddenly hard and painful. When she did find something to say it was not what she had intended.

'I'm sorry. It wasn't such a good idea after all.'

'Whatever it was, spill it. Then we can both get some sleep.'

It came out in a rush. 'Tim, I need somewhere to hide – no, rest . . . stay . . . get myself together. Oh, I don't know! I've got the police on my back. Oh God, it's awful. They think I've murdered someone.'

'Well you have – our child. Or had you forgotten?'

Now the blue eyes lasered anger. 'Not again, Tim. Not now. This is deadly serious.'

'And aborting my baby isn't?'

Venetia sprang to her feet. 'I should've known you wouldn't listen!'

'You certainly should!' Tim made no effort to rise. 'After what we've been through, you pitch up here in the dead of night. Unannounced. Looking for a shoulder to lean on. Did you really expect me to say "OK, Venetia, move back in. Let's go on as if nothing has happened"?'

He gazed at her, trying to catalogue objectively what he saw. She was beautiful; there was no denying that. Beautiful in a distracted, fay sort of way. Her shoulder-length hair straggled in gold wisps, and constantly needed to be pushed back by a fluttering hand. The blue, full-length coat and loosely-knotted scarf seemed to have been donned hurriedly. '*A sweet disorder in the dress kindles in clothes a wantonness.*' Not for the first time, Venetia brought Herrick's lines to mind. She was a wayward, wilful spirit, and he could not be dispassionate about her. Deep wounds took longer than ten months to heal.

He watched her standing indecisive in the middle of the room, knuckling away her tears. Genuine or for effect? It didn't really matter. He sighed and shook his head. 'Sit down and tell me a tale of police and murder.'

She resumed her seat. The story came out jerkily at first, then gathered pace until the words gushed forth incoherently.

'Three months ago Uncle Ralph died. He was quite gaga towards the end, poor dear. In a nursing home. He hated it.'

Tim reflected that Uncle Ralph had probably never been what anyone would call 'sane'. He remembered that spectral figure with the gaunt face and shambling gait, who insisted on being known as 'Rafe de Cranville', showing him round his magnificent Wiltshire home. Tim loved the cream stone and jumbled roofs of the part-Plantaganet, part-Tudor mansion. He loved the way it still dominated its downland hollow, as it had done for well over four centuries. He was sorry to hear that the old house had now lost its dedicated caretaker.

'So you became the proud owner of Farrans Court?'

Venetia pouted. 'Yes. He kept his promise – or, rather, his threat. He left the ghastly place to me – the "last of the Cranvilles".'

Tim, whose ancestors had never even risen to the rank of sheep-stealers, found it hard to understand the annoyance, even bitterness, with which Venetia regarded her heritage. She had, presumably, absorbed it from her father during their brief relationship. Hugh Cranville, eldest of two surviving brothers (a third was killed at Tobruk), taking to extreme the maxim that 'simple faith' is more than 'Norman blood', had refused to have anything to do with the family estate, which he regarded as a millstone. He had simply given Farrans to Ralph, and gone to Italy to paint. His egalitarian principles had not prevented him marrying into a wealthy Milanese family and living off his wife's income. By her he sired two daughters, Venetia and Firenze (heaven preserve offspring from the romantic whims of their parents), thereby cocking a final snook at the proud family name. Tiring of *la dolce vita*, he had one day taken off into the wild blue yonder, and never been heard of again.

Thereafter, the girls had divided their time between schools in England, where their uncle Ralph kept an eye on them, and holidays with their mother in the sunnier clime of Umbria. Apart from his nieces, Ralph's life had been devoted to Farrans. Saving it, preserving it, passing on his inheritance intact had become an obsession. Everything, literally everything, had gone into restoring the house and keeping it in good repair. The farmland had been sold off, to be followed by all the best furniture, silver and pictures. Farrans had sucked up every last penny the old man could lay his hands on. But he had succeeded in his purpose. The house was in splendid shape as he neared his end. Ralph had the satisfaction of knowing that he could deliver to the next generation the torch of an ancient family, burning brightly.

It mattered not that the hand into which that torch was to be thrust was extremely reluctant to receive it. Venetia had told her uncle often that she did not want the burdensome responsibility of Farrans. He never listened. She would, he assured her, feel differently when she actually came to live in the house and bring up her family there (the family that Ralph himself had never had the inclination to engender).

'Of course, it took simply aeons to sort out his affairs. God! I wouldn't have believed lawyers and accountants and people could be so slow. We had to get everything valued – down to the last doormat. That's how I found the pictures.'

'Pictures?'

'Yes. In the attic. I suppose I should've remembered them. We used to play up there as kids – murder in the dark. Oh!' She stopped suddenly, again tugging strands of blond hair away from her cheek. 'Only now it's real murder, isn't it?'

'Is it?'

'You're not being very helpful.'

'It's your story.'

'Sorry. I'm not telling it very well, am I?'

'Not very.' Tim looked at his watch. 'I presume you are going to get to the point of it this side of dawn?'

Venetia scowled, part anger, part concentration. 'There were a lot of old paintings stacked up there, covered in dust and cobwebs and bird droppings. Obviously they'd hung in the house once, till people had got tired of them and had them stacked away. I got a local dealer in from Marlborough to have a look at them. It was too dark for him to see much. There's no light up there, and the canvases were all grimy. The first time, he took one of the smaller pictures away. He said he'd come back with a torch and sort out the rest later. I had to go to Italy for a couple of weeks, but when I got back and phoned him to make another appointment, he sounded very excited. He said he'd done some preliminary cleaning on the painting he'd taken away, and it was quite valuable. Perhaps some of the others might be good, too. He took a photograph of it, and did a report for me.'

From a large tapestry bag she took an A4 buff envelope, and laid it on the low table between them.

'We fixed another visit for Tuesday afternoon, just a couple of days ago. Oh, God, it gives me the creeps to think about it.' She looked at him appealingly. 'Tim, I wouldn't mind a drink. Would that be asking too much?'

Silently he poured an Irish whiskey the way she liked – no ice and a dash of water.

She gulped it down, took a deep breath, and went on with her story.

'I took him up to the attic and left him there, while I got on with various tidying-up jobs. It got dark early. It was a rotten day. He didn't come down and I didn't want to disturb him. It was almost six before I went up to the attic to fetch him.' She paused, took another deep breath. 'At first I could only see his torch lying on the floor. I called out, and there was no answer. I went to pick up the torch and almost fell over him.'

'Him?'

'Yes, the dealer. I shone the torch down, and there he was. I thought he must have been taken ill. Until I saw his head. It was caved in. He was lying across a painting and there was blood all over it – glistening. And splashes over the other pictures. Oh, Tim, I was terrified. I knew there must be someone else in the house: a madman, a murderer, lurking in the shadows, hiding in some empty room. I rushed out, got in the car and drove into Marlborough. Then I realised I'd have to go to the police. But when I went to the station, they said they already knew. They'd had a telephone tip-off, and would I come with them back to Farrans.

'But why . . .?'

'There was no trace of anyone else having been in the house, and the murder weapon had only one set of fingerprints on it. Mine.'

'What *was* the weapon?'

'A heavy Victorian candlestick – all florid and knobbly. I'd been cleaning it, along with the few other bits of silver Uncle hadn't sold off.'

Tim sat back, eyes closed, scarcely able to believe what he was hearing. Trust Venetia to get herself into a mess like this – and then run away from it. He said: 'It certainly doesn't look good, but it'll look a hell of a lot worse if you do a bunk. Fingerprints don't prove anything, and then there's the mysterious telephone call. Your best bet is to go and face it out, with a good lawyer if necessary. From what you've told me, I'd say the police will be hard put to it to make out any sort of case.'

Venetia looked more miserable than ever.

'There are supposed to be three points to be proved in the conviction of a murderer, aren't there – means, opportunity and motive?'

'Exactly. And you certainly don't have a motive.'

'Yes, I do. Or they'll think I do if they see that.' She pointed to the envelope. 'Grosmith – that's the dealer – thought the first picture he found in the attic might be worth a great deal of money. Normally that would go into the estate, and be calculated for death duty. But if no one else knew about it, I could spirit it away and sell it off privately. So, on paper, I had a very good reason for silencing poor Mr Grosmith.'

'So the police haven't seen this letter?'

She shook her head. 'No! And they mustn't!'

Tim knew what he had to advise, and he also knew Venetia would not listen. Her only way of extricating herself was to be absolutely open with the police: to tell them everything. But because she was scared – and, more importantly, because she had never learned to be honest with herself – she would find that very difficult. He said, 'OK, Venetia, you've had a terrible shock, and I'm sorry. You can unwind here – for tonight. But tomorrow you'll have to face up to reality.'

'Thank you, Tim. I knew you'd help out. I won't be a nuisance. I'll sleep on the sofa.'

'You certainly will! You vacated my bed ten months ago, remember?'

Twenty minutes later Tim Lacy lay in that same bed – a Carolean four-poster with headboard inlaid in bog oak and boxwood – and knew he was unlikely to sleep. He had given Venetia blankets and pillows, and thought she would be reasonably comfortable. She looked exhausted. Probably she would slip easily into unconsciousness. But he was now wide awake, dormant emotions raked savagely into painful life. Old quarrels re-running themselves in his head.

To take his mind off past agonies, he opened Venetia's buff envelope. He tipped out its contents on to the counterpane. A single sheet of typed notepaper and a 6 × 4 photograph.

The letter, on heavy cream bond with a pretentious embossed heading – 'Grosmith Gallery, Antiques and Works of Art, Downs House, Marlborough' – was written in a florid hand.

Dear Miss Cranville,

Further to our telephone conversation, here is my report on your painting, together with a photograph taken after preliminary cleaning.

We have removed a layer of discoloured varnish and this has brought to light a fine Renaissance work in very good condition. The colours are vivid, the composition excellent and brushwork is of a particularly high quality.

I am not yet in a position to advise you as to approximate value, but I can assure you that this is an important work of art. It is North Italian, early to mid-sixteenth century. Unrecorded items of this period and quality very seldom come on to the market, and when they do they are much sought after. This makes

11

it particularly important to find out all we can about your painting. May I ask you to leave it in my hands a little longer so that I can research it thoroughly?

I look forward very much to examining the rest of the pictures at Farrans Court. Who knows what other gems we might find?

Yours sincerely

Arthur Grosmith

Tim laid the letter aside and picked up the black-and-white print. He held it to the lamp to get a better view.

The next moment he sat up straight. 'Good Lord!' He stared at it. Blinked. Tilted it in case the light was playing tricks. It wasn't.

He jumped out of bed, grabbed up his dressing-gown and strode to the door, shouting, 'Venetia! Why didn't you tell me what this picture is? It changes everything.'

She sat up on the sofa, hugging a large pink blanket around her.

He tossed the photograph on to the seat beside her. 'How long has *The Triarchs* been at Farrans?'

Venetia gazed at the picture vacantly. She shrugged. 'I don't know. It could have been up in the attic for ages. Why do you call it *The Triarchs*? It looks like a run-of-the-mill religious picture. Pretty, though.'

'Pretty!' He went to the black lacquered chest on its elaborate, gilded stand. He opened the door and removed a bottle and a glass. He would have that Armagnac after all. He needed it. 'Pretty! I'm sure Raphael would be over the moon with that accolade!'

'Raphael?' Venetia's eyes opened wide. She looked more closely at the photograph. She could see now that its subject was the Adoration of the Magi, though not handled in any conventional form with cattle and straw all over the place. In the centre of the composition the Madonna, in a very relaxed seated pose, cradled the Christ child in her arms. The stable, if stable it was, was a stone structure in the middle distance, set in a sparsely-wooded landscape, with a river and far hills merging into a hazy sky. The painting was perfectly balanced by the figures of the three kings who made up the foreground.

'Well, yes, I suppose it could be a Raphael, or more probably "School of", but Mr Grosmith—'

'Huh!' Tim waved the letter contemptuously. 'Mr Grosmith of "Grosmith Gallery Antiques and Works of Art" is . . . was nothing but a general-purpose provincial dealer. He wouldn't know a Turner from a Tintoretto, a Picasso from a pizza. He'd certainly never handled anything like this.' Tim pointed to the picture. He sat down beside Venetia and swirled the brandy round in its balloon glass.

Venetia frowned at him. She knew him far too well to question his judgment about old masters. 'So what you're saying is that this . . . *Triarchs*, or whatever it's called, is a well-known, authenticated Raphael?'

'Yes and no.' He sipped the Armagnac and let the rivulet of smooth fire run down his throat. 'It's well known to those who specialise in such things. In the art world *The Triarchs* is a legend.'

'You haven't told me why it's called *The Triarchs*.'

'It's because of the three kings. The word means three rulers: three men who had divided up a territory between them. In this case Europe – or, I suppose, more accurately, north Italy.'

Venetia shook her head and brushed the hair away from her face. 'You've lost me.'

He picked up the photograph and moved closer to her, totally mastered now by his enthusiasm. 'These three figures,' he pointed to the men grouped in a semicircle round the Virgin, 'they really are rulers. The bareheaded one here, on the right, is Pope Julius II – Raphael's patron, and the patron of Michelangelo.'

Venetia pouted. 'I know that. I'm not a complete dunce. He commissioned the painting of the Sistine Chapel and had a stormy relationship with Michelangelo, and they called him the "warrior pope" because he spent more time on his horse than at his prayers. Who are the other two?'

'The massive, athletic ox of a man on one knee – that's Maximilian I, Holy Roman Emperor. And this other kneeling figure is Louis XII of France. A more bellicose bunch it would be hard to imagine. They all spent most of their lives fighting for land and power. Round about 1506–10 – I'm not sure, because I'm not very good on dates – they came together in the League of Cambrai. It seems that Venice was getting too big for its boots. Not content with being a great commercial power, controlling the trade of the eastern Med, it ruled a sizable

chunk of the mainland between the Alps and the Po. The state was
fabulously wealthy because of the galleys laden with spices, gold,
ivory and precious stones from the Levant, so the doges could afford
to pay *condottieri* whose mercenary armies gobbled up still more
territory.'

'And that didn't suit Pope Julius and Co?' Venetia was fascinated
despite herself. It had been partly Tim's ability to catch her up in his
own enthusiasms that had frightened her off their relationship.

'Exactly! Give the lady a prize! Hence the League of Cambrai –
formed to put the Venetians in their place. If I remember rightly, Spain
came in as well.'

'So what happened?'

'Oh, what usually happened in Renaissance politics: a few battles,
a few conquests, and then, when the contracting parties had got all
they thought they could get out of the military conflict, the alliance
fell apart and the allies went back to fighting each other.'

'So it was all a waste of time?'

'These affairs usually were. A few towns captured. A few thousand
acres of peasant holdings, transferred from one ruler to another. It
signified little. Unless,' he added bitterly, 'you take account of dead
soldiers and grieving widows and orphaned children. But men like
Julius, Maximilian and Louis didn't bother themselves with such trifles. Statesmen and generals never do.'

Venetia recognised the hobbyhorse breaking out of its stable. Tim's
years in the SAS had left him heartily disillusioned about the politics
of war. She quickly pointed to the photograph. 'And where does this
come into the story?'

'Raphael can't have been in Rome long.' Tim went over to the floor-
to-ceiling shelves where his books stood in ordered rows. He selected
the appropriate volume of Bryan's *Painters and Engravers* and
turned the pages. 'Yes, here we are: 1508. Julius collected men of
talent, and he recognised something very special in this precocious
twenty-five year old. Raphael was painting with a fluency and inven-
tiveness rare in men twice his age. So Julius grabbed him to do a
huge series of murals for the papal apartments. Then, on an impulse,
he deflected him from that project to paint *The Triarchs*.'

'To mark the League of Whatsit?'

'The League of Cambrai.' The slightest frown of impatience flitted across his face. 'I guess it was a diplomatic gesture, probably designed as a gift for the Emperor. Maximilian fancied himself as a great patron and a man of taste. He surrounded himself with artists and scholars – Altdorfer, Cranach, Dürer.'

'But the picture wasn't finished before Julius and Maximilian fell out?'

'Ah, now that's the first of many various mysteries about *The Triarchs*.' Tim, without meaning to, poured another brandy. Venetia diffidently picked up her empty glass from the coffee table and Tim refilled it. How quickly the externals of an old routine slipped back into place, even when the soul had gone out of it.

'Mystery?' She gulped the spirit in a very masculine way.

'I can't remember all the details.' Tim crossed the room again. 'There was an article about it in *Apollo* a few years ago.' He rummaged through the bound copies of the magazine in the bottom row of the bookshelf, talking as he searched. 'There were a couple of letters in the Vatican Archive referring to it, but the painting itself disappeared. It's been an enigma ever since. It's come to light three or four times in the intervening centuries . . . Ah, got it!' He returned and laid the open volume on her lap. She saw a full-page version of her painting, this time in colour, illustrating an article by an American expert. She raised her eyebrows at the very unscholarly title of the feature.

'*The Bloody Triarchs*?'

Tim laughed. 'Sounds a bit over the top, doesn't it. But it seems to be a fact that this picture has often been associated with violence. It started life commemorating a rather cynical military alliance and, according to the legend, death and destruction have accompanied it ever since. It's acquired the reputation of being unlucky, cursed. Nonsense, of course, but it may explain why it's been hidden from view most of its existence. Hardly anyone's ever seen it.'

'Then, how do we know what it looks like? And how come there's a photograph of it in this magazine?'

'In the seventeenth century a copy was made of it. Some scholars think it was done by Rubens, but I doubt it. It's in the Kunsthistoriches Museum in Vienna. I've seen it there myself. But, as far as I know, the original hasn't been heard of since before the last war. I think it was in Austria then.'

He sat beside her on the sofa once more, and some moments passed in silence. Venetia stared at the *Apollo* article with its gory title.

'*The Bloody Triarchs*! Well, it certainly seems to be living up to its reputation. Oh, Tim, what are we going to do?'

He frowned. 'Well, the first thing is to think the whole thing through. Unless poor Arthur had a secret life which could have provoked a *crime passionnel*, it's reasonable to assume that his murder is connected with *The Triarchs*. Now, he didn't realise what he'd found. But someone else obviously did, and knew that he had a goldmine within his grasp.'

'But who?'

Tim shrugged. 'One of Grosmith's cronies, perhaps. The dealers' world has more than its fair share of unscrupulous people.'

'Unscrupulous enough to kill?'

'For something as valuable as this? My God, yes!'

He jumped up and began to pace the room excitedly. 'The more I think about it, the more obvious it all seems – I could almost write the script. Grosmith shows the picture to one of his friends, or sends him a copy of the photo and talks on the phone: he says he is going to do some research. "I've found this sixteenth-century Italian Adoration of the Magi," he says. "Hidden away for yonks in the attic of an old country house." His chum recognises it instantly. His heart misses a beat – just as mine did, when I saw the photo. Immediately he sees this is his chance, not only to make a fortune but also to have his name written into the history books as the man who finally located a long-lost Raphael. The only problem is how to get his hands on it. "This is very interesting," he says. "Who does the painting belong to?" "Oh," Grosmith replies warily, "some lady whose property I'm valuing." "Does she know what the painting is or where it came from?" "No, it's been stored away for years with a pile of other pictures. I didn't realise what it was, myself, till I'd cleaned off the varnish." "And you haven't told anyone else about it?" "No, only you." "Good, well look, keep it under your hat and let me have a really good look at it."

'Does young Arthur begin to smell a rat at this point, I wonder. "I can't let it out of my sight without the owner's permission," he says. "But I'm seeing her again on Tuesday, and I'll ask her then." So our unscrupulous friend has until Tuesday to plan how to get Grosmith out of the way – permanently. Then all he has to do is pinch the picture, lie low for a few months, then produce it with a fanfare of publicity – along with a phoney story of how he discovered it. And there's no one around to contradict him.'

He looked down at Venetia. 'How does that sound?'

She stared back moodily. 'Plausible. But the Farrans picture could be just another copy.'

'Could be. Unlikely though. Not that it really matters. Sometime or another, that painting is going to turn up on the international market. When it does, it will point straight to the murderer.'

'But, even if you're right, that could take months.'

'That's right . . . unless.' He stopped pacing. He ran a finger along the bridge of his nose – a gesture Venetia knew well and found rather irritating. His brown eyes were half closed in concentration. 'Unless, unless, unless. There's just a chance. The murder happened on Tuesday. It's now Thursday – or, rather, very early Friday. Grosmith's gallery will have been swarming with police since the murder.

'Come on!' With a sudden darting movement, he grabbed her hand and pulled her to her feet. 'Get your clothes on! We're going to Marlborough.'

'At this hour in the morning? Tim, don't be silly!'

He glared at her, and she saw in his eyes the familiar pig-headed truculence she had always found impossible to handle.

'You came here of your own accord. I didn't invite you. I could have slammed the door on you. Perhaps I should have, but I didn't. You asked me to do something. Well, I'm doing it. Don't you dare tell me I'm being silly.'

An hour and a half later, after a journey of frigid silence interspersed with monosyllables, Tim steered his Porsche 356B Roadster off the M4. Venetia felt as though she was wrestling in mud with a bevy of slippery emotions which she could barely recognise, let alone grasp. Fear, she realised to her surprise, was now the least aggressive of them. Her more turbulent feelings all centred around Tim Lacy.

Damn the man for his self-confidence and assertiveness! For Tim everything was always very clear cut. Issues were black or white, right or wrong. No room for doubt. No compromise. If Tim proposed something you either fell in with it, hook, line and sinker, or you stood aside and watched him make a success of it without you. He was a bundle of enthusiasms. He had thrown himself wholeheartedly into a military career, earned quick promotion, then just as determinedly turned his back on the SAS and, using certain Middle East contacts he had already made, started a business which flourished just as rapidly. 'Failure' was a word which had no meaning for him. She knew exactly what he must have been like as a little boy – the local gang leader, the kid who owned the football and made the rules. He had simply never grown up; never reached the debilitating adult conviction that life is, in fact, complicated and bewildering. His certainty was infuriating. It made her feel inadequate, stupid – the weak and feeble woman who could not exist without a male prop.

But, then, it was because of Tim's strength and clear-headedness that she had gone to him. It had not been easy to push aside all the pain of the past, to swallow her pride and say 'Please, help me.' No, to be fair, it was not just because he was good in a crisis. Tim was also generous. Venetia knew that, despite all the bitterness of their parting, he *would* help her. He could not resist the knight-in-shining-armour rôle.

That was how they had first met: she a struggling artist anxious to sell her work, not convinced it was any good, whether she could ever find customers; he a self-made entrepreneur with his own security firm and many contacts in the world of dealers and wealthy collectors. He had offered to make some introductions, and the result had been her first exhibition. In those early days their relationship had been an adventure, each exploring the other. It did not seem to matter that they came from different worlds. In fact those worlds had seemed complementary. Only as the months passed and their relationship became more intense had Venetia realised that her life was being directed, channelled, taken over. Tim was trying to turn her into 'the business wife', someone to show off at parties, to impress prospective clients, give glittering dinner parties. Suddenly, when she got pregnant, she had seen Tim's vision of her future: the smart home in Surrey or Berkshire, the children at the right schools, the lonely days and nights waiting for him to return from foreign business trips. The baby was a trap. It would close for ever the door of her own life, and lead inevitably to the one Tim had chosen for her. At twenty-seven she had not been ready for that, and she probably never would be.

'You're very quiet.' Tim glanced across briefly, then returned his attention to the empty, winding blackness of the road ahead.

Venetia shook her mind back to the present. 'I was wondering whether you might tell me exactly what we're doing roaring through Wiltshire at dead of night.'

Tim slowed for a double bend, then put his foot down as the A4 straightened out for the run into Marlborough. 'Oh, didn't I say? We're here for a wee spot of burglary.'

'Tim, you can't mean you're intending . . .'

'To break into the Grosmith Gallery? That's exactly what I mean. Don't look so shocked. I'm not going to steal anything. I'm just going to look for your property and try to get it back for you. That's all.'

'But, Tim, it's nearly dawn, and there's bound to be a burglar alarm.'

'You're forgetting that security systems are my speciality. I fit 'em, and I can sure as hell break 'em. I'll be very surprised if the late lamented Arthur got round to installing anything very sophisticated at Downs House. Speaking of which, how do I get there, and what kind of a place is it?'

Venetia gave directions and explained: 'It's a big, Georgian town house. The shop part is on the first two floors. Above that I suppose there's a flat or storerooms or something.'

'That's where *The Triarchs* will be, then, if we're not too late.'

'Why's it so important to get it back.'

'Because, if I'm right, it's the key to the mess you've got yourself into . . .'

'*I've* got myself into!'

'Sorry, sorry. I should have chosen my words more carefully. This mess which you find yourself in through no fault of your own. You've no idea how or when your uncle got hold of that picture?'

'I've been thinking about that since you told me the story of *The Bloody Triarchs*. You said it was last seen in Austria around 1939. I know Uncle Ralph was in Austria with the army at the end of the war. I seem to recall him once saying something about being involved with the allied commission for the restoration of works of art looted by the Nazis. But I could be wrong; he never spoke much about his wartime experiences. Unlike some soldiers, I think he found the whole thing pretty hateful. That's partly why he was so delighted to take over Farrans. It represented everything that was old and secure and peaceful and traditional and . . . permanent.'

'I can understand that.'

'Poor Uncle Ralph; he could never see why I didn't share his feelings for the place. For me Farrans is just a big, draughty, damp old house that must be a nightmare to maintain. Perhaps that's because I spent most of my childhood in Italy.'

Tim broke in on her reverie. 'So he could have obtained the picture in Austria?'

'I suppose so.'

'But he never hung it up in the house?'

'I never saw it. And I'm sure I would have noticed if it had been there.'

'Odd, isn't it? He has the painting, and he must have some idea of what it is, yet he never displays it and he doesn't sell it either. If he'd ever sent it to auction, it would have solved all his problems about restoring Farrans.'

They were silent for a while, then Venetia voiced the suspicion that had been growing steadily in her mind. 'Tim, why are you really pulling this crazy burglary stunt? Is it to help me, or just to recover some famous work of art and get your name in the papers?'

'Well, here we are.' Tim turned the car into a side street close to the market square. He pulled into the kerb and parked. 'I'll do the rest on foot.' He opened the door. 'I shouldn't be more than half an hour. I'll leave the key in the ignition. If for any reason I'm not back by . . .' He checked his watch. 'By six, get back to London and wait in the flat.'

'Like hell I will!' Venetia flung the passenger door open and leaped out. 'I want to know exactly what you're up to, Tim Lacy. After all, as you pointed out, it *is* my property.'

He glared at her across the car's soft top. 'Suit yourself,' he grunted. 'But don't get in my way! Don't make a noise! And don't offer any comments or advice! Now close your door – *quietly* – and lock it!' He set off along the street without waiting for her to catch up.

Apart from the nearby clinking of bottles indicating the local milk-man on his round, Marlborough was enjoying its last hour or so of nocturnal calm. The two visitors passed no one as they made their way, by back roads, to the Grosmith Gallery. The tall house, like all its neighbours, brooded, quiet and lampless, over the narrow pavement. A gate in the high wall at one side was, surprisingly, unlocked. They passed through into a small enclosed garden or yard.

'Wait there!' Tim ordered and disappeared round the back of the house.

Venetia hugged her coat around her. The air was heavy with a pre-dawn dampness that seemed to penetrate to her very bones. She shivered, and knew that it was not just the cold that made her long for the cosy interior of Tim's car.

He seemed to take an age. She shifted from one foot to the other, hands deep in her coat pockets, and thought: what the hell's he up to?

Then he reappeared around the corner of the building, carrying a torch with one hand over the glass to cut its light to a minimum. 'This way,' he whispered.

He led her into the house through the back door, across a small kitchen, and thence to a wide hallway. She remembered the layout of the building, the tables and chests tastefully arranged with small pieces of porcelain and glass. In the darkness she could only make out rough shapes. She clung to Tim's arm, terrified of stumbling into some delicate piece of furniture and sending its contents crashing to the stone floor.

'Tim, how on earth did you get—?'

'I said no questions! Come on, quickly!'

She hesitated and he added, 'The only alarm system is a set of infra-red sensors. I found the control box and switched them off. It's pathetic; almost an insult to the intelligence of any self-respecting thief.'

He led the way up the wide staircase, lighting the way with his half-masked torch. On the top landing they were confronted by two doors. One of them had a Yale lock.

'That must be it. Here, hold the torch.' Tim produced an implement from his pocket and inserted it in the key slot.

Moments later there was a click and the door swung inwards. Tim took the torch and went first, into what seemed to be a large junk-room. It had two windows and Venetia noticed with alarm that the first light of the new day was creeping over the roofs opposite. Tim crossed the room and pulled heavy curtains across the glass.

'Find the switch,' he ordered, coming back towards her. 'We can risk some light now.'

As she felt along the wall beside her, Venetia sensed a familiar mingling of smells: paint, varnish, spirit. When she had clicked the tiny plastic lever and filled the room with light from a single, unshaded bulb, she was not surprised to turn around and see an artist's studio. Or, at least, a chamber that was part studio. In fact the room was neatly divided into two by a four-fold leather screen set at an oblique angle across the middle. The right-hand side seemed to be the office. There was a Victorian roll-top desk and, in front of it, a very twentieth-century typist's chair. Beside the desk was a heavy safe. To her left was a large table cluttered with the paraphernalia of a painter or restorer: brushes, paint-streaked rags, cotton swabs, pots and jars of various solvents, and tubes of paint.

Tim glared at the untidy jumble. 'Seems the late Arthur fancied himself as a restorer. I only hope to God he knew what he was doing. Renovating a Raphael isn't a job for an enthusiastic amateur. Now, where do you suppose . . .?' He glanced at the safe and muttered, 'Too small!' He looked around the room's perimeter. Frames and canvases in profusion were propped against the faded Victorian wallpaper. He began a hurried examination of the pictures, some of which were turned to show their stretchers.

'It's obviously not here, Tim.' Venetia advanced nervously into the room, ears straining for the sound of anyone else in the house, frantically wishing herself a thousand miles away. She stepped round the edge of the screen. There she saw an easel occupied by a fairly large canvas. It was turned away from her, facing the window. A cloth was draped loosely over it, and a chair with a broken back stood in front of it. This was, obviously, where Arthur Grosmith did – had done – his work. She reached out a hand towards the grubby piece of old curtain covering the painting.

In the second before the material fell to the ground, she knew. Even so, the revelation was a shock.

Tim! her mouth formed the word but no sound came. She cleared her throat and called again as her trembling knees gave way and she sank on to the chair.

Instantly Tim was at her side, a hand on her shoulder. 'My God! Oh, my God,' was all he could find to say.

CHAPTER 2

'Hey! Saint!' The swarthy Florentine with the knotted black beard hammered on the red-painted door. Although it was almost noon, and sunlight had only just begun to seep into this narrow street in Rome's Borgo district, foetid heat already surged up from the cobbles like the clouds of flies disturbed from gorging themselves on the refuse and stagnant puddles.

'Come on, holy man! It's late to be still at your prayers!' This time Valerio Balbi applied a foot as well as his fists to the unyielding oak.

The street was busy with people: wives returning from the river with baskets of wet laundry; priests scurrying from cheap lodgings towards the piazza which separated the Borgo from the Vatican palace and its attendant sprawl of buildings; liveried servants dawdling about their masters' business and finding time to try their luck with the local girls. There was even a steady toing-and-froing of stonemasons, labourers, carpenters and other artisans working on the new St Peter's. After half a century in which other popes had tinkered with Constantine's decaying basilica, Julius II had finally ordered the ancient building to be swept away. Now all that could be seen was an immense crater, from which clouds of white dust drifted across the Borgo. The work brought hundreds of foreigners to the city, who daily filled the air with the clamour of hammering, sawing and shouted orders, and who nightly got drunk in the local taverns. Amidst this bustle, no one paid any attention to the dishevelled sculptor with the wine-stained shirt and patched, russet hose, trying to rouse his late-sleeping friend, young Santi from Urbino.

With a surname like Santi, it was inevitable that the young artist's friends nicknamed him 'the Saint'. Later ages would call him 'the divine Raphael', but for now he had to be content with mere canonisation. And content he was. What artist would not be? At the age of twenty-five he had found himself summoned to Rome to work for the mightiest prince in Italy – the pope himself. Grasping this amazing opportunity, Raphael worked hard to win the approval of his patron. Not that it was difficult: Julius, who prided himself on his ability to recognise talent, was generous with his praise, his encouragement – and his money. But he did expect value for that money. So, for eleven months, Raphael had spent all the hours of daylight on the frescoes in Julius's private apartments, and often laboured deep into the night on additional commissions given him by the pope. Work consumed him entirely, and he was oblivious to all else. It was his friends who showed that concern for his welfare that Raphael himself had no time to indulge.

'Val, what are you trying to do; raise the dead?'

Balbi turned to look at – and admire – the young woman who had come up unnoticed behind him. Margherita Luti was nineteen and beautiful in a dark, intense, almost tragic way. Her jet hair was tightly coiled at the back of her neck. Her large brown, wide-set eyes seldom shared the smiles and laughter of her lips. She had a fashionably plump figure, accentuated by the wide, yellow sleeves tied to her full-length green over-dress.

'Worse than that, Grit. I'm trying to raise that indolent lover of yours! His apprentice told me, up at the palace, that the blessed Raffaello hasn't been seen today. I've come to tell him he's wasting good drinking time.' Balbi brandished the bottle of wine, and almost felled a passing cardinal. The dignitary muttered an oath and hurried on, catching up his skirts to avoid the ankle-deep filth.

Margherita untied the large key from the cord round her waist. 'You won't budge him till he's finished this wretched painting his holiness is in such a hurry for. It was supposed to be done last week before Julius went north to join his army, but Raffaello couldn't get it right. You know what a perfectionist he is. Now he's working at it every night, and won't let anything distract him. He told me to go home until it's finished. I'm sure he's not getting any sleep.'

'Our beloved Julius isn't content with talent. He has to have blood.'

'Oh, it's not just the pope who's making such cruel demands. Raffaello is punishing himself. He's obsessed with this particular painting.' She unlocked the door and stepped first into a wide, simply furnished, chamber. A bed in the far corner had not been slept in. A loaf and some fruit on the plain table lay untouched. Balbi entered behind her.

It was then that they both smelled smoke.

They looked across to the narrow staircase against the facing wall. A blue-grey cloud hovered round the top step.

With a roar, Balbi flung the wine bottle from him and ran up the narrow steps. He threw his weight against the door at the top: the door to Raffaello's studio. He fell into the room and immediately had to retreat, coughing. Pausing only to take a deep breath, he went back. Through a dense haze of smoke he made out the figure of his friend slumped over a table, head resting on his arms. On the floor beside him a pile of paint-soaked rags was smouldering. It was easy to see what had happened. The artist, overcome with exhaustion, had fallen asleep, knocking his candle off the table. Balbi rushed across to the motionless figure, threw him over his shoulder and staggered back to the staircase, lungs bursting.

In the room below he laid Raffaello on the bed. 'Water! Wine!' he ordered. 'Anything! Try to revive him. I'm going back up there to stop—'

There was a sudden roar. They looked up and saw flickering light glowing behind the veil of smoke.

Balbi took the stairs three at a time. In the studio the pile of cloths was ablaze. He tried to gather them up. They burned his hands. He dropped them. Dragged them towards the door. Flung them through and followed, kicking and stamping on them as he did so. He turned. The table was already on fire.

'Quick!' He almost fell into the room below. 'Get out! I can't stop it! The whole house will go up any minute!'

Margherita did not seem to hear. She was bent over the figure on the bed, forcing a cup to his lips. 'He's all right,' she murmured. 'Thank God, he's all right.'

The young man sat up, coughing and choking. 'What's the matter? What . . .?'

The sculptor put an arm round his shoulders and hauled him to his feet. 'You've set your bloody studio on fire, that's all. Now, come on, let's get out.'

Raffaello pulled away. 'What? Fire?' He stared up at the staircase. Flames were already snaking around the doorframe. 'The painting!' He staggered forward and collapsed at the foot of the stairs.

'Never mind the bloody painting!' Balbi bellowed. 'Get out!'

'No! No! I must save the painting.' Raffaello began to crawl up the steps.

Margherita ran to him, trying to pull him to his feet. 'Raff, come away, come away – *please.*'

Valerio helped her haul the painter upright. He was a dead weight, about to pass out again. 'Get him into the street. Drag him by the hair if you have to.'

She stared up at him. 'But, Val, what are you going to do?'

'I'm going to get his bloody picture!'

'Val, be careful!'

But he was already at the top of the stairs, stepping over the blazing threshold. One side of the room was now all fire. The heat almost felled him. But Raffaello's picture, on its easel, was in the opposite corner. Valerio grabbed the window fastening and pulled the casement open. The street below was now crowded with people. A woman screamed as Balbi briefly stared out, then stepped back into the inferno. He wrenched the painting from its stand, went back to the window and pushed it through. He called to the onlookers and felt someone take the weight. The flames were now coiling around the casement, drawn by the draught. As he grabbed the sill to pull himself through, he felt intolerable, searing pain. He let go. Looked for a new grip. There was none. The casement was now a hissing O of fire. He knew he would have to leap through and hope someone below would break his fall. Balbi took a step back to get a good jump. He braced himself. Bent his knees. At that second the floor timbers gave way. With a scream the sculptor fell back as sparks and flames billowed up to meet him.

'Master Raffaello, it is magnificent. His Holiness will be extremely pleased.'

The painter turned his back on 'The Adoration of the Magi', which was propped against the edge of a fountain. 'It's hideous and I wish to God I'd never agreed to do it.'

They were gathered in the Vatican gardens two days later – Margherita, Raffaello Santi and the tall, thin-faced Cardinal Bibbiena. The
painter – slight, beardless, usually graceful in movement and speech
(which added some point to his nickname of 'the Saint') – was showing
the signs of his ordeal. His cheeks were hollowed and grey, his red-
rimmed eyes glistening. Talking was an effort, and was interrupted by
bouts of coughing which shook his whole body. Margherita led him
to a stone bench, where he slumped, head in hands.

The cardinal was sympathetic, but distracted. While his gentle mel-
lifluous voice was directed at Raffaello, he could scarcely keep his
eyes from the painting whose colours, glowing in the morning sunlight,
seemed to have a luminosity of their own.

'Master Raffaello, you are naturally upset. This has been a terrible
tragedy and you grieve for your friend. That is good, but—'

'Best friend I ever had . . . and I killed . . .' The sentence ran into a
barrier of coughing.

'My son, to speak, even to think like that is sinful. In legal terms
Signor Balbi's death was an accident. In human terms it was an act
of great heroism. In theological terms it was an act of God. And God,
we may be sure, will reward him for his noble self-sacrifice. To have
preserved this . . .' The thought drifted incomplete among the over-
arching branches of an ancient cedar as Bibbiena surrendered himself
to the beauty of the Virgin and her royal visitors.

For several seconds the only sounds were the obbligato of a black-
bird concealed in the foliage above and the pattering of water which
gushed from the mouth of a stone griffin. Then Raphael took a deep
breath and made a great effort to string several words together.

'Eminence, when you take the picture to His Holiness, you must
entreat him to release me from his service.'

The cardinal turned sharply. 'I shall do no such thing. Anyway, he
would never agree.' The soothing tone returned. 'Master Raffaello,
he values you too highly.'

'But don't you see, Eminence.' The artist looked up with distraught,
pleading eyes. 'I can never paint again.' He held a kerchief over his
mouth to stifle another cough. 'My talent is cursed. This is the best
thing I've ever done, and it's cost . . .'

Bibbiena scowled. 'And who are you to decide such things? Did
you create the talent? No. It is a gift from God. And it isn't his gift

to Maestro Raffaello Santi. It is his gift to the world. You are merely his instrument. His Holiness has been very kind to you, because he has been given grace to recognise the gift.'

'But, Eminence . . .'

The cardinal made an impatient gesture. 'My son, can you deny that His Holiness has been generous?'

'No, but . . .'

'Do you know how many aspiring young painters, sculptors, poets and architects clamour daily for his patronage?'

Raphael shook his head.

'And why do you suppose he chose you? Gave you the grand commission to design his own chambers? Allotted those vast areas of wall? Allowed you a free hand? Is it for his own glory? In years to come, centuries to come, Pope Julius will be just a name in history books, but people will still arrive here from all over Europe for a glimpse of the great frescoes in the *Stanze*, and the name they revere will be Maestro Raffaello. All this was revealed to His Holiness in a dream, a vision. He confided in me that he had received this revelation.'

Bibbiena reached forward to grasp the young man by the shoulder. 'So you see it is not for you – or even His Holiness – to frustrate God's purpose. You and the holy father share a divine commission. That must override all mere human ideas and feelings. My son, God's will is never easy to obey. Sometimes it is painful. But all of us – popes, cardinals and even brokenhearted young artists – must obey it, or put our immortal souls in great danger.'

Raphael shook his head. He was puzzled, unconvinced. He strove to put his doubt into words.

Bibbiena forestalled him. 'Now, you must excuse me. There is much to do in organising the supply train for His Holiness's army – and, of course, in seeing that your magnificent painting has a safe place on one of the waggons. Kneel and I will give you my blessing.'

Raffaello and Margherita dropped automatically to their knees. The cardinal made the sign of the cross over the couple, and mouthed the Latin formula. 'Now, off with you. Young lady, see that this fellow gets some rest. I will tell His Holiness that I have discharged you from your duties for one week.'

The visitors bowed respectfully and walked towards the gate in the high wall which kept all but the privileged out of the pope's private garden.

'Oh, one more thing!' Bibbiena called after them. 'I have arranged for a special mass to be said in the Sistine Chapel for Valerio Balbi.'

He shook his head as the two young people disappeared through the gateway. What highly-strung creatures artists were! How impressionable. What would happen if princes of the Church were ruled by their passions – or swayed from their resolve by hastily concocted stories about dreams and visions? The great advantage with young Raphael was that he did not yet realise just how great his talent was. Pope Julius did. Clever, wily old Julius. And he was determined to extract as much as he could from the painter while he still remained in this state of ignorance. Before he started becoming troublesome, over-confident, and making impossible demands like Michelangelo.

It had been a smart move to get this young genius to paint the picture as a present to flatter the vainglorious Maximilian, although the thought of this masterpiece belonging to that barbarian seemed anathema. And, truly, it *was* a masterpiece. To think that it had almost gone up in flames! Its preservation was nothing short of a miracle.

Cardinal Bernardo Bibbiena sat down, facing the fountain in the comforting warmth of the June sunshine, and marvelled at the most beautiful painting he had ever seen.

For several seconds Tim and Venetia were silent before the sumptuous serenity of *The Triarchs*. No black-and-white photograph or magazine illustration or even an accomplished copy had adequately prepared them for the reality. Even in the dim light of Grosmith's studio-cum-office the Renaissance masterpiece glowed with an inner warmth. The hazy blue of the landscape had a numinous quality. The trees and hills were those of Raphael's native Urbino, yet at the same time they were not. They were a corner of Elysium, and they made for the foreground figures a setting that was timeless. The groupings of figures was at once restful and full of movement. The kneeling Julius stared straight out of the canvas, drawing the viewer into the scene and directing one's attention to the peasant woman more interested in her baby than in the attentions of her wealthy visitors. The line of the pope's cloaked shoulder was continued across to the left of the picture in the outstretched arm of Maximilian, who leaned forward and offered a golden casket to the Christ child. The other kneeling figure, Louis the French king, balanced the composition and set up another diagonal, which carried the eye across the picture from bottom left to top right. The painting was making several statements, yet, at whatever point the viewer began his visual journey, his gaze always rested at last in the shared tenderness of mother and child, the meeting of hearts as the baby reflected the Virgin's adoring gaze – the Virgin who was Margherita Luti.

Tim marvelled at the intricate, yet simple composition, the balanced areas of colour, the flesh tones and the painter's perfect mastery of the human figure. Never had a painting given him such a completely satisfying experience. The long years studying for his Open University degree, the visits to major European galleries, the handling of import-ant pictures in museums and private collections – nothing compared to the thrill of this clandestine meeting with the divine Raphael in the dingy, ramshackle back premises of a provincial antique shop.

He wanted this supreme moment to last for ever, but suddenly Venetia was tugging his sleeve and whispering urgently. 'Tim! I heard a noise!'

They both strained their ears.

'Yes! There it is again! Someone's coming upstairs. Tim! It's the police!'

Tim crossed the room and switched out the light. Then he was back beside her. 'Get ready to move quickly.'

'But we must give ourselves up!' Venetia was trembling with fear and guilt. 'We'd be crazy to resist.'

The sounds were distinct now: two sets of footsteps climbing the second, uncarpeted flight of stairs.

'Shut up and do as I say!'

Tim felt for the easel clamps and loosened them. He slid the picture free. 'Guard this with your life!' He thrust it into her hands.

There were muttered voices outside the door and the sounds of someone fumbling with the lock. A click. The faint creak of a hinge. A probing torchlight beam splayed over the walls and ceiling.

'Do you know where it is?' A woman's voice – not taking much care to be quiet.

'Not the foggiest. I don't even know for sure it's up here.' The man's tone was softer, less assertive.

'Well, it'd better be, for both our sakes. So start looking. See if it's one of those against the wall. And, for God's sake, hurry.'

Venetia and Tim held their breath as the voices were replaced by sounds of rummaging. Then the woman spoke again.

'Shine that torch over here. Let's see what's behind this screen.'

As light played around the edges of their hiding place, Tim counted silently to three, then shouted, 'Now! Run like hell!'

He threw all his weight against the screen. As it crashed into the room there was a scream. As Tim arched a path to the door he caught a glimpse of a sprawling female figure.

He and Venetia reached the door at the same moment. He pushed her through and slammed it behind them. They tumbled down the stairs and reached the first-floor landing before hearing any sounds of pursuit.

Tim calculated that the element of surprise had gained them several seconds, but carrying the picture would slow them down. As they turned on to the bottom flight of stairs, he grabbed a small table standing against the wall. Something on it crashed to the floor and splintered noisily. Tim pulled the table to the top of the stairs behind him, then hurried after Venetia.

Outside, the world was noticeably lighter. They reached the back gate, Venetia wide-eyed and breathless with panic. Tim grabbed the latch and pulled. The gate stuck. He tugged harder.

'Stop right there!' The pursuers appeared round the side of the house.

Looking back, Tim saw the woman – middle-aged, ample and squeezed into jeans and a tight sweater – holding both hands straight out in front of her. He wrenched the gate handle with urgent energy. It crashed open. At the same instant came another sharp sound. Splinters flew from the frame.

He pushed Venetia through. Paused to drag the gate shut. Sped after her along the street.

'Tim, did you see—?' The words jerked out as she ran.

'Save your breath!'

'But that woman had—'

33

'A gun. Yes. All the more reason to keep moving.'

They turned a corner.

Tim knew there was no way they could outstrip their pursuers. He dug into a pocket for the car keys. He pulled Venetia into an alleyway along the back of a row of houses.

'Take these and give me the picture! Get to the car and bring it to the main square. Now get down by those dustbins!' He set off along the narrow passageway like a relay sprinter taking the baton.

Venetia just had time to squeeze into the space behind the tall plastic bins, when she heard more running footsteps. They headed past the end of the alley.

Then the woman's voice screeched, 'No! This way, you fool.' Moments later both pursuers rushed on past her hiding place.

Venetia waited till they were out of earshot. Then she took off in the opposite direction. She looked up and down the unfamiliar streets, grey, empty and friendless in the dawn light. Which way now? Dear God, all these roads looked the same. Supposing she could not find the car! Supposing that crazy woman with the gun caught up with Tim! Venetia turned to her right – ran as fast as her trembling legs would carry her. Forced her mind to concentrate on seeking familiar landmarks.

It seemed an age later that she was tweaking the Porsche's engine into life. Not wasting time to adjust the seat, she perched on its edge, crashed the gears, and steered for the town centre.

Now there were signs of life in Marlborough's large market square: a cyclist who wobbled as she sped past, a lorry unloading at a greengrocers, two boys waiting for the newsagents to open so that they could start their paper rounds. But no Tim!

Venetia made one complete circuit of the empty central area that would soon be full of parked cars. Then she spotted the man and woman. They were standing by the Town Hall, looking along the street, pointing and arguing. She drove right past them as fast as she dared without drawing attention. Tim had obviously given them the slip. But where was he now?

Fifty yards farther on, he leaped from a shop doorway almost under her wheels. Her foot came down hard on the brake pedal, and her jaw slammed against the steering-wheel. Tim wrenched the side door open, twisted the painting into the space behind the seat, and jumped in. 'Go!' he yelled.

Venetia fancied she heard another pistol shot as she jabbed the car into second gear.

'Which way, Tim?'

'London!'

She had to drive round the square again, to get on to the right road. She saw the man and woman run forward as the classic convertible passed them. Were they about to shoot again? Venetia concentrated her eyes and her mind on the road.

Tim turned to stare out of the back window. 'Damn!'

'What's the matter?'

'They're getting into a Range Rover. It's not over yet. Pull over and let me drive.'

They stopped just long enough for Tim to run around to the driving side, and for Venetia to slide into the passenger seat. Then Tim sent the venerable engine whining into a racing start.

'Keep your eyes glued to the road behind, and tell me if you see a green Range Rover.'

Venetia knelt on the seat, peering around the edge of the painting which blocked much of the rear view. As they swerved around winding lanes and suburbs, they saw no further sign of pursuit. Then they hit a long, straight stretch of road, and headlights appeared a hundred yards behind.

'Tim, I think . . .'

'Yes, it's the Rover all right. You can tell by the set of the lights. Sit down and hold on tight. We'll have to give it all we've got. This beauty's fast, but she is twenty-nine years old.'

Venetia spent most of the next few minutes with her eyes closed, as Tim took bends and corners impossibly fast. Now and again she looked back along the road. The Range Rover was not gaining, but it was still there.

Then they were on the motorway. With Tim's foot flat on the boards, the Porsche flashed along the outside lane. The pursuers did the same, and slowly they closed the gap. Occasionally another car appeared in front of them, only to be flashed impatiently out of the way.

Venetia thought, what happens when they catch us up? They can't shoot at us in the middle of the M4. Or can they?

The first Reading junction was signposted. The white roadster slowed. Were they out of petrol? She checked the gauge. The needle was on a quarter. She looked back. The Range Rover was right up behind them. She glanced at Tim, but he was concentrating on road and traffic.

They were passing a TIR truck making good speed on the inside lane. For the moment the middle lane was clear. Tim glanced across. Then into his side mirror. He clenched his teeth. All a matter of timing and accuracy.

Ten yards ahead of the lorry now. Twenty. The Range Rover still breathing down his neck. Slip road a hundred yards ahead.

Suddenly he yanked the wheel to the left. The Porsche slewed in front of the truck. A horn blared. The car hit the slip road at 80 mph.

Tim braked steadily, pulled on to the roundabout, circled above the motorway and headed down the A4 in the direction of Newbury. The Range Rover and its passengers were being swept along in the traffic streaming towards the capital.

Venetia felt as though her entire body had liquefied and was seeping into the seat. 'Tim!' Her voice was somewhere between a whisper, and croak. 'Could we stop? I think I'm going to be sick!'

Tim continued at a sedate pace, turned on to the Basingstoke road and, once they reached the town, he parked in the main street. A quarter of an hour later they were seated among the commercial travellers and other early risers in the dining-room of the Royal Mail Hotel, having breakfast.

So far from being sick, Venetia discovered that she was actually hungry. Though she could not cope with the pile of bacon, sausages, eggs and tomatoes that Tim was tucking into, she disposed of several rounds of toast and three cups of black coffee. Afterwards she lit a cigarette, and discovered that she could hold it without her hands trembling.

Tim paused between mouthfuls to observe, 'I see you still haven't given up that obnoxious habit.'

She stared at him. There he was, indulging his huge appetite, and making nauseous proprietorial comments as though nothing unusual had happened. She glanced around at some travellers chatting up the waitresses, the two German tourists on the next table with their heads together over a map, the clergyman in the corner doing *The Times* crossword. It was all utterly normal, everyday, mundane. She felt like jumping up and shouting 'Listen everyone! I'm wanted by the Wessex constabulary for murder! My ex-lover and I have just pulled off a daring robbery! We've got a stunningly valuable painting in the car outside! We've been chased by another pair of crooks armed with guns! And we've nearly caused an enormous pile-up on the M4!' Then she thought, what would happen if I did? There'd be an embarrassed silence and everyone would go on eating their cornflakes. My God! The English! With an angry gesture she stubbed out the cigarette, half-smoked.

'Feeling better?' It was about the nearest Tim ever came to a really solicitous enquiry.

'Yes. No. Oh, I don't know. Tim, what does it all mean? What happens now?'

'Well, to take the second question first, I walk you to the station. There you pop on a train and go back to my flat. I'll give you my spare key. When you get there, phone up Wessex CID and give them the phone number. Say you're spending a few days with a friend, to get over the shock. Then they'll know you haven't done a bunk. Stay put until I return, which should be some time tomorrow afternoon. I, meanwhile, have work to do in Paris.'

'You're just going to carry on as though nothing has happened?'

'On the contrary, I'm going to make sure the painting is safe. Then I'm going to make some discreet enquiries of one or two of my friends in the French art world. To see if anyone knows anything about the recent history of *The Triarchs*.'

'But what about those assassins who . . .?'

'I reckon they've shot their bolt. They've failed to get hold of the painting. They don't know where it is, and they don't know where *you* are. As long as you keep your head down, what can they do?'

She stared at him. In all the time she had known him, she had never been able to come to terms with his matter-of-fact nonchalance. Whatever happened, Tim Lacy was never nonplussed. He always had a neatly worked out plan of action. 'You leave me speechless!'

'Well, there's *one* thing you might say.'

'What's that?'

'Thank you.'

'*Thank you*!'

'I took you under my wing and I got your picture back for you – in the nick of time.'

'Tim, you almost got me killed!'

He shrugged and stood up. 'All part of life's rich tapestry.'

And he sauntered towards the exit.

Pope Julius's precious supply waggons and their armed guard clattered along the Via Flaminia, which followed the valley of the Tiber before climbing to Foligno to cross the Apennines and then descend to the flatlands of the Marches. But instead of continuing directly along the highway to Fano, where it could turn northwards on to the coast road and proceed immediately to rendezvous with the main papal force camped around Ravenna, the caravan came to a halt at Calmezzo, some twenty miles from the Adriatic.

It came to a halt because Bernardo Bibbiena wanted to visit Urbino. The official reason for this ten-mile diversion was political. He needed to talk with the city's young ruler, Francesco Maria della Rovere. To gain the latest intelligence about the war and about the loyalty of the surrounding cities. To remind the nineteen-year-old duke – very gently – that Uncle Julius, who had obtained for him this jewel among Italian states, could just as easily dispossess him. But the cardinal had another motive for delaying the delivery of gunpowder, salted meat and fish, pike staves, helmets and overdue wages to the waiting troops. To him Urbino represented everything that civilised life was about.

As he urged his tired horse along the dusty carriageway at a fast trot, the ecclesiastic, who had discarded scarlet silk for more practical leather and cambric, anticipated his arrival in the hilltop city virtually created by Federigo da Montefeltro. Federigo – that man of contradictions. The violent mercenary general whose smashed-in face and empty eye-socket reminded all who met him of the warrior vocation by which he had amassed his vast fortune. Federigo who had used the spoils of war to create the most beautiful palace in all Italy and to adorn it with works by della Robbia, Piero della Francesca, Botticelli, and even to import pieces by such northern masters as Van Eyck. Federigo, not just a patron who could buy genius, but a man of genuine taste and scholarship who could converse with the finest savants of his day and who had built up a library far surpassing the Vatican's rightly acclaimed collection of books and manuscripts. Federigo the enlightened ruler who had personally met almost all the expenses of government, and virtually abolished taxation throughout his realm. Federigo who had left a well-ordered state to his heir, the unfortunate Guidobaldo, now dead from consumption. What a diplomatic triumph it had been for Julius to implant his own nephew in the affections of the ailing duke, and thus bring magnificent Urbino firmly under papal allegiance.

Bibbiena savoured in advance the sweet liturgy of the ducal chapel, the comfort of the best guest chamber, the paintings and sculptures, the decorative friezes of the palace's main rooms, the sumptuously provisioned board.

The reality did not disappoint. As the light faded outside, and the flaring torches in a hundred wall sconces fluttered the shadows of the dining hall, Bibbiena sipped dark Umbrian *vernaccia* and sighed his appreciation. He closed his eyes and enjoyed the gentle melody woven by the small band of musicians at the far end of the chamber.

'You have settled well in Urbino.' It was a statement, not a question. 'But, then, who would not? I sometimes wish my religious duties . . .'

The young man with the shoulder-length fair hair surveyed his guest warily. This velvet-tongued cardinal was yet another emissary from the head of the family, come to remind him of his duty of unquestioning allegiance to the pope. But Francesco was determined to be his own man, and was on the watch for any stratagems Bibbiena might use to draw him into his uncle's latest plots.

'There's much to be done here. The new university—'

'Ah yes, the new university. I gather you have attracted some of the best teachers in Italy.'

'In Europe. We have masters here from Paris, Oxford, Vienna. Our jurisprudence school rivals anything in Bologna or Padua.'

'To be sure, to be sure. You have made an excellent beginning.' Bibbiena beamed across the table at his host. He had asked for a private supper, and the hall, which would normally have been thronged with members of the ducal household, was empty save for the two diners and the servants who set down dishes on the polished walnut table: prosciutto cooked in wine, with capers and sugar, piles of grapes and olives, spiced cakes, roasted skylarks in lemon sauce, Ferrarese sturgeon sprinkled with gold dust, and a great variety of other delicacies.

'Urbino has lost one of its greatest sons.' Bibbiena was determined not to encourage Francesco's self-congratulation. 'I refer of course to Master Raffaello. Do you know him?'

The young man scowled. 'Your Eminence knows well how both Guidobaldo and I tried to persuade Raffaello to return here from Florence. We were outbid.'

'Forgive me, I had forgotten. I am conveying one of his paintings to His Holiness even now. A remarkable work. I believe it is his best yet – though, there is no doubt Master Raffaello will go on to even greater things.'

The conversation flowed easily around general topics, until at last the cardinal focused it on the war.

'I gather from the latest despatches that His Holiness was a little disappointed with the size of the contingent supplied from Urbino. Doubtless you are recruiting more troops to supplement it.' His expression was polite with just a hint of criticism.

Francesco wiped his fingers on a towel and tossed it to the kneeling servant at his side. 'There is no war left to fight in the north. Since their defeat at Agnadello last month, the Venetians are in headlong flight. Besides—'

'Surely it is for His Holiness to decide—?'

The duke was not going to allow Bibbiena to dominate this exchange. 'Besides,' he continued, 'I need troops to defend my own territory.'

'Your own territory!' The cardinal laughed his protest. 'What threat is there to Urbino?'

'Your Eminence cannot be unaware of the latest Venetian tactics.'

For once Bibbiena found himself without a suitable response.

Francesco continued. 'Denied a major victory, the doge is doing everything in his power to harass the allies' supply routes. There have been several attacks in the Marches. Small forces landed on the coast. Towns and villages – villages mostly – plundered and burned. Messengers, merchants, bands of soldiers attacked on the highway. I trust your own column is sufficiently protected, Your Eminence.'

Bibbiena thought of his well-guarded waggons, the important military supplies and food. Above all, he thought of the covered carts loaded with casks of coin, with personal items for the pope and his household, and with Raphael's painting. He felt a twinge of anxiety, a flicker of foreboding. The goblet of *vernaccia* paused at his lips. He stared down into the gold and scarlet swirls. Send a messenger back the ten black miles to Calmezzo with a warning? But his men were tired, and deserved better than to be despatched on a sudden errand because of the young duke's alarmist talk. Cut short the visit to Urbino? Order the horses saddled and spend an uncomfortable night in some hastily commandeered hovel?

The pope's representative offered a prayer to the Virgin for the protection of the waggon train. Then he put it from his mind as he drained the cup appreciatively.

It was a well-planned attack. Lorenzo Rossi was no grand condottiere. He only had a few score men at his command. But he had already proved his worth to his Venetian paymasters. He deployed his slender forces intelligently, bought information, planned scrupulously. He knew the convoy carried gold; knew how the specie casks were marked. The rest was ruthless simplicity.

Rossi and thirty hand-picked men arrived at Calmezzo – a collection of meagre dwellings straddling the highway – in the darkest, deadest hour of a dark, dead night. It was not difficult to locate the waggons drawn up in a single line in front of the church. Six guards sat round a brazier, throwing dice to keep themselves awake. Six of Rossi's men despatched them swiftly and silently. The leader himself crept along the row of waggons till he had located the bullion cart. He made a short, high-pitched, animal noise.

Moments later three members of the band emerged from the murk, leading a horse. Its padded hooves made little sound on the roadway. Quietly they hitched it to the waggon. Nothing to do now but wait for the next signal.

'Come on! Come on!' Rossi tugged at his beard, ears alert for any sound from the nearby houses.

At last he heard the two squeals from somewhere away to his right. It told him that the horses of the papal party had been located and set free.

'Go!' he yelled.

A whip cracked. The bullion waggon jolted forward. The horse broke into a trot along the eastward road out of Calmezzo. At the edge of the village Rossi joined the rest of his group, with the horses. They mounted and fell in behind the waggon, a rear-guard ready to deal with any of Julius's men rash enough to come in pursuit.

No one followed. The road behind remained silent and empty.

'*The Triarchs*? Now, I ask myself what interest could Monsieur Timothy Lacy possibly have in that old story? And I reply that it is sufficiently important for him to buy me this extravagant luncheon. My friend, you have succeeded in intriguing me.'

Jean-Marc Laportaire looked every inch the French patrician. At sixty plus, he was still slim and athletic of build. His eyes had lost none of their lustre and surveyed the world with intelligent curiosity. His complexion suggested that he spent several months a year in sunnier climes, which was in fact the case. As one of the world's leading dealers in Renaissance art and antiquities he travelled a great deal, and most of the clients who could afford to do business with him had their homes in very congenial locations.

Tim smiled, and watched his guest select another oyster from the ice-laden dish between them. 'I'm just taking the opportunity of keeping in touch with a highly-valued customer.'

The blue eyes flashed. 'To use one of your odd Anglo-Saxonisms, Tim, pull the other one. You want information and, since you are a businessman who doesn't believe in wasting time, there must be a very good reason for your sudden interest in the mysterious Raphael.'

Tim decided to take another tack. 'What exactly is the mystery of *The Triarchs*?'

The Frenchman paused while an attentive waiter refilled their glasses with crisp Bâtard Monrachet. He glanced round the small dining-room, which was rapidly filling with lunchtime customers. He approved his host's choice of venue. But, then, young Lacy displayed excellent taste in most things, and that, for an Englishman, and particularly a self-taught Englishman, was remarkable.

'My friend, I'm sure you know the story as well as I. *The Triarchs* is an enigma. An ace up the magician's sleeve of history – now you see it; now you don't.' He allowed himself a little smile at his own fanciful imagery.

'Have you ever seen it?'

Laportaire laughed. 'It may surprise you to know that even I was scarcely a child at its last known appearance.'

'Before the war?'

The dealer nodded and leaned back in his chair as the dishes were cleared. 'It was in the collection of Otto von Zalen, a big German industrialist. As to how he came by it . . .' He shrugged. 'But he was hand in glove with the Nazis, so anything is possible.'

'What happened to this von Zalen?'

Again the lift of the shoulders. 'Whatever it was, one can only hope that it was very unpleasant.'

'Nasty piece of work, eh?'

'As you say, a nasty piece of work. His factories supplied much of the equipment for the gas chambers of Auschwitz and Dachau. It is *incroyable* that he did not know the purpose to which those diabolical inventions were to be put. He made large contributions to National Socialist funds. He was *intime* with all the Hitler gang. He even bought a schloss at Obersalzburg, to be at hand when his beloved Führer was holidaying at Berchtesgaden.'

'And that was where he kept his collection?'

'Yes. A collection which grew miraculously as German armies plundered their way across Europe between 1938 and 1943.'

There was another pause as the next course was ceremoniously presented: *roulade de volaille* for Jean-Marc and *magret de canard* for Tim.

'What happened at the liberation?'

'Allied troops entered the area in May 1945. During the occupation, that part of Bavaria became a very popular recreation centre for British and American troops.'

'And von Zalen's schloss?' Tim leaned forward, his food untouched.

The Frenchman was in no hurry to continue his story. He savoured a mouthful of the chicken with its *farci* of wild mushrooms, herbs and garlic. 'The schloss? For two or three years it was run as a hotel for US army officers. I believe it is still a hotel today.'

'And the collection?' Tim could scarcely conceal his impatience.

'*Vraiment*, that is the question.'

'There was surely an attempt to restore the works of art to their rightful owners.'

Laportaire smiled, intrigued to see the extent of his host's interest in the lost Raphael. 'My friend, your duck – it is getting cold.'

Absently, Tim prodded at the thin, pink slices of meat and the slithers of pears cooked in Burgundy which accompanied it.

Jean-Marc condescended to take up his narrative. '*Bien sûr*, there was an Allied commission to catalogue and, where possible, return Nazi loot. They brought to light tens of thousands of objects – paintings, sculptures, porcelain, jewellery, furniture, silver – hidden in cellars, attics, barns, saltmines, or simply just buried. They reached Obersalzburg early in 1947. They made a most detailed list. I myself have seen it.' He sipped his Chablis and savoured the fruity dryness.

'And *The Triarchs*? Was it on the list?'

'The catalogue was notoriously incomplete. And, no, the Raphael was not on it. There were at least half a dozen works which were known to be in von Zalen's collection before the war, which had apparently disappeared by 1947.'

'Do you think the damned Kraut got away and took some of his ill-gotten gains with him?'

Laportaire shrugged. 'That is one theory. The Israelis have, of course, followed up every clue about von Zalen's whereabouts. There have been supposed sightings in Brazil, Argentina, even Portugal, but . . .'

'So what are the other theories? Isn't there a story of it being seen in the saltmine cache at Altaussee?' Tim was thinking about a certain young British army major, named Ralph Cranville, moving through liberated Europe with a couple of trucks and a small detachment of men, handling immensely precious objects and under no immediate supervision, but he was determined not to ask leading questions.

'You know how confusing war is – and its aftermath. Groups of soldiers wandering the countryside. Empty houses, unguarded galleries and museums. To anyone who knew anything about *objets d'art* and their value, the temptations were immense.'

'So the missing Raphael could have been stuffed into some Allied soldier's kitbag.'

A pained look came over the Frenchman's face. '*Quelle horreur!* One does not even like to think of it.'

'But lots of war "souvenirs" did find their way to America, Britain, Russia and, I suppose, to France also?'

'Certainly. But I suspect most were sold for quick profit. There was a vigorous blackmarket network in Austria and Switzerland. I can name at least three top Parisian dealers whose businesses were established or re-established after the war with works of very dubious provenance.'

'And the trail of *The Triarchs* ends there, in 1947?'

'Possibly.' Laportaire popped the last forkful of food into his mouth and chewed with elaborate care.

Tim laughed. 'Jean-Marc, you are being deliberately enigmatic!'

'I? But it is you who are being – what is the word – cagey. You have not told me why you are interested in this particular painting.'

'There's no mystery. I've simply heard a rumour that it might have come to light again.'

Laportaire fastened his shrewd eyes upon Tim's face. 'In England?'

'Yes.'

'Interesting. May one enquire . . .?'

'I really can't say any more at the moment, Jean-Marc.'

'If it transpires that there is any truth in this rumour, you will not forget your old friend, will you?'

For a few minutes Tim concentrated on his food. Then he said quietly, 'Jean-Marc, what would it be worth on the open market today?'

Laportaire shook his head in a gesture of helplessness. 'A genuine Raphael with such a story behind it? One could name one's price. There is not an important public or private collection in the world that would not want to acquire it. A hundred million francs? two hundred million?' He shrugged. 'Who knows.'

Tim visualised the canvas, with a rug nonchalantly thrown over it, lying in the Porsche's boot in the long-stay car park at Heathrow. He had thought that the painting was as safe there – in one anonymous vehicle among hundreds, albeit a rare classic vehicle – as anywhere. Now the possibility of some casual thief prying, quite by chance, into the 356B brought the perspiration to his forehead.

Rapidly banishing the image of some disgruntled adolescent searching in vain for cash or credit cards, putting a fist through twenty million pounds' worth of old master, Tim said, 'What rumours have you heard about the Raphael lately?'

'They are just that, my friend – rumours. No more likely to be accurate than the stories you have heard.'

'Nevertheless . . .'

'*Alors*. Some people believe *The Triarchs* found its way to a *very* private collection in America – you know what I mean, I'm sure. A year ago, perhaps less, perhaps ten months, there was a whisper – nothing more – that it had gone missing. A reward was being offered, very discreetly, for its recovery. There was no question of the owner going to the police or requesting an Interpol stolen art notice, of course. And that really is all I can tell you.' He fixed Tim with an intense stare. 'You will keep me informed if you come across anything more . . . tangible, won't you?'

During the short flight back to Heathrow the following afternoon, Tim pondered Laportaire's information. As the Frenchman had said, it was all rumour: mere tremors on the grapevine of the art underworld. But, if there was any substance in Jean-Marc's story, it raised a very unwelcome possibility: Venetia's Raphael might be a mere copy. He shook his head, not wanting to believe it. His money was still on wily Uncle Ralph stumbling across *The Triarchs* all those years ago in Bavaria, and salting it away against a rainy day. Perhaps he had meant to tell Venetia, and never got around to it. He certainly could not specify it in his will, and it would have been difficult even to mention it in a private letter to his sole beneficiary – 'Dear Niece, you will find a priceless work of art in the attic. I stole it over forty years ago.'

But that was in the past. Now, the first thing to do was get the painting privately vetted. Tim took a writing-pad from his attaché case and began to make notes. If it did turn out to be genuine – well, that was when Venetia's problems would really start. She would need advice and support in tackling them. The simplest thing – popping it round to Sotheby's or Christie's – was probably out of the question. The auctioneers would want to advertise worldwide. Handling *The Triarchs* would be a major coup – the most sensational sale of the decade. That would bring all sorts of interested parties out of the woodwork. Under British law the real owner of a stolen object could always lay claim to it. So, if there were von Zalen children or grandchildren around, they would make a great deal of trouble. They might not, eventually, be able to prove title, but they could certainly soak up a lot of time and money in court proceedings. Then there was the little matter of Arthur Grosmith's murder. Venetia was right that the painting did provide a theoretical motive. Even if the police were to eliminate her from their enquiries, the press would have a field day with the story. What a gift for headline writers: 'Heiress In Art Murder Probe'/ 'Framed! "I'm Innocent," Says Dealer Murder Suspect'/'Raphael's Curse – "Unlucky" Painting Claims New Victim.'

Tim gazed out at the dazzling, sunlit top of the low cloud layer. Was the answer, then, to dispose of the picture quietly and privately? That could not be right. *The Triarchs* ought to be in a public gallery; the many ghosts of its chequered past finally laid; a masterpiece at last available to all art lovers. Auction it abroad, then, where different laws applied and where the limitation period for establishing ownership had long since expired? That would involve smuggling the painting out of England, and could set a new police inquisition in train.

As the aeroplane dropped through the grey covering of cloud towards the runway, Tim Lacy gazed mournfully at the long list of 'Things to Check and People to See' that he had written. For the first time – and only fleetingly – he wished he had never set eyes on *The Triarchs*.

While Tim was arriving at an overcast Heathrow, Venetia sat in his flat, sipping hot, strong tea and wondering, not for the first time, whether she had done the right thing in involving her ex-lover. She had known of course that, if Tim agreed to help her, he would take over completely. If she was honest, she knew that was what she wanted – someone to lift the responsibility from her shoulders; someone resourceful, clear-headed and decisive. But breaking and entering? Being shot at? Nearly causing a motorway accident? Perhaps she would have been better off sitting meekly in a police cell, letting Inspector Gantry sort it all out. As it was, she was even more in his bad books. That much had become clear in the phone-call she had received a few minutes ago.

'Miss Cranville?'

'Yes.'

'This is Inspector Gantry. I was out of the office when you phoned. This is supposed to be one of my rare weekends off. You should have had a word with me before you left the area.'

'I'm sorry, I—'

'I realise you're upset, but dashing off like that . . . well it doesn't make my job any easier. You weren't thinking of going back to Italy, I hope. I don't want to be forced to confiscate your passport.'

'I just needed to go away. Rest. Get over the shock.'

'Yes, well, I'm afraid you're going to have to come back to Swindon for an hour or so. There have been further developments, and I need to ask you some more questions.'

Venetia's heart pounded faster. 'Developments? What's happened?' She tried not to sound anxious or guilty.

'There was an incident the night before last which we think may have a bearing on the murder. I can expect you here tomorrow, then?'

'Yes . . . yes, of course.'

'Good. The earlier the better. Meanwhile, I can get you on that number, can I?'

'Yes, that's right.' She added as an afterthought, 'I'll do anything I can to help, of course, Inspector.'

'So I should hope, Miss Cranville. So I should hope.'

It was after that that Venetia had put the kettle on and made a mugful of tea, deliberately using two teabags. Gantry wanted to question her about the burglary. Oh God! She would be sure to give herself away. Perhaps he'd discovered some evidence; something to fix her at the scene of the crime. Tim had insisted that they both wore gloves so there couldn't be any fingerprints, but perhaps she had dropped something.

Venetia sat coiled in a wide armchair, feet pulled up beneath her, cradling the mug of tea in both hands, going over and over again the events of the night before last. Was there anything that could have given her away. If only Tim were here: to tell her to pull herself together and stop being silly . . .

The doorbell rang.

Venetia thought 'Tim'. Only when she had turned the latch did she realise that he would have used his key.

The door opened to reveal a middle-aged woman. Venetia recognised her instantly, and saw that she was still holding a gun.

CHAPTER 3

The woman nodded and two men appeared from beside the doorway.
She motioned Venetia back into the room. Her companions followed
as she stepped inside, and one of them fastened the door.

'We've come for the painting.' Her voice was coarse and hard, like
her over-made-up features. 'But first.' She threw her left hand, heavily
beringed, in a slashing arc, and caught Venetia across the cheek.

With a squeal Venetia reeled back on to the sofa. The mug of tea
fell to the parquet floor and shattered.

The woman glowered. 'That's for all the trouble you caused us the
other night. Now, where's the picture?'

Venetia pushed the hair back from her face, and felt the trickle of
blood from a cut just below her left eye. She stared back, too shaken
to speak.

'What's the matter, dear? Cat got your tongue? I want that picture,
and I want it now.'

'It's not here,' Venetia gulped. 'He put it in a safe place. He didn't
tell me where.'

The woman leaned forward, raising her hand to strike again, as
Venetia pressed herself into the corner of the sofa.

'Don't you muck me about. I 'aven't got the time for it!'

Venetia cowered. 'It's true, I swear it!'

The woman straightened up. 'We'll soon see. OK, boys, have a
look!'

Venetia watched, horrified, as the two young men systematically
destroyed Tim's home. They pulled open cupboards and drawers,

49

strewing their contents. They wrenched a Queen Anne bookcase away from the wall and tipped the small collection of eighteenth-century bindings on to the floor. They tore the early Flemish tapestry while pulling it from its hanging rail. As their frustration increased, so did their vandalism. A Bristol Delft charger, unchipped in three hundred years, was smashed and deliberately trampled. The marauders ripped the backs from chairs, emptied out Tim's folder of old-master drawings, threw down paintings, photographs and trophies. Twice Venetia called out to them to stop. They did not even pause. When they had wrecked the sitting-room, and destroyed Tim's most treasured possessions, they moved on through the rest of the apartment.

'Not here, Jane.' One of the men emerged, at last, from the bedroom, brushing off his jumper the feathers from a ripped pillow.

The woman turned her attention back to her prisoner. 'OK, dearie, when's your boyfriend due back?'

'I don't know. He's gone to Paris!' Venetia flung the words out defiantly. She was now trembling with an emotion that was more anger than fear. 'And he's not my boyfriend!'

'Paris!' The woman was startled. 'Has he taken the picture there?' Venetia shrugged.

The woman muttered to herself, 'This is getting too bloody complicated.'

She stepped over the debris and retrieved the cordless phone from a pile of cushions. She punched in a number. Listened for several seconds. Swore, and threw the receiver on the floor. She went to the window and glared out at the glistening pavements, suddenly unsure of herself.

Then she reached a decision. 'You! On your feet.' She jabbed the pistol in Venetia's direction. She then went into the kitchen, and returned thirty seconds later.

'Bring her!' she ordered, striding towards the door.

The two men grabbed Venetia by the arms.

'You don't need me!' She struggled. 'I can't tell you anything. Tim's the only one who knows . . .'

The woman smirked. 'Exactly, dearie. Now move.' She prodded the gun into the small of Venetia's back.

One of the men opened the door and looked around the landing. He turned and nodded. 'All clear.'

That was the point at which Venetia's life took another sharp twist.

The four of them were standing in the corridor, and the woman called Jane was closing the door behind them, when the lift gates opened, a couple of yards away. They revealed a young man in a grey overcoat and a woman police constable. The man's eyes flicked to the apartment number on the wall, then to the group standing momentarily frozen.

'Excuse me, is one of you ladies Miss Venetia Cranville?'

Venetia jumped forward, almost throwing herself into the stranger's arms. 'Yes, that's me.'

He stiffened, then recited a well-rehearsed formula. 'Venetia Cranville, I have a warrant for your arrest for the murder of Arthur James Grosmith, and I must ask you to accompany me to . . .'

That was the point at which Venetia fainted.

The monotonous rhythm of the drum slowed as the galley moved across the still surface of St Mark's basin like a scurrying water beetle. Rossi was glad of it, and gladder still that in a few minutes he would be completely free of the unremitting reverberation that was making his head split. The exertions of the previous night, the lack of sleep, the discomforts of this rigidly functional vessel put at his disposal by the Serene Republic, and above all the ceaseless thumping of the timekeeper's drum, made him feel ill. His head hurt. He had difficulty focusing on the line of merchant ships moored along the Riva degli Schiavoni. And his shirt was glued to his back with sweat. Standing in the open prow helped, for it put as much distance as possible between himself and the burly Moor who was sitting under the stern canopy and crashing his bare fists down on the stretched pigskin; and it also gave him the full advantage of the offshore evening breeze.

The captain made his way along the catwalk between the two ranks of rowers. 'Docking in about five minutes, Signor Rossi. We've made good time.'

'We can't arrive soon enough for my liking.'

The sailor laughed. 'You may be a fine soldier, my friend, but you've no stomach for the sea.'

'I admit it readily. The moment you set me down on the quay, I shall be a different man.'

'Your lads are all set to unload?'

'Yes, they have their orders.'

'They seem happier than their leader, but just as anxious to be ashore.'

'They've well-stuffed purses, and they can't wait to be flashing them around in the inns and brothels.'

It had been a good venture for all of them. Remarkably good. The papal money casks had yielded much more than Rossi had expected. As was his custom, he had paid his followers their share at the earliest opportunity. It was the only way to keep them loyal and honest. Now he could trust them to deliver the bulk of the treasure to the doge's officers.

It had been an excellent night's work for Rossi also. As well as now being several hundred ducats richer, he had discovered something carefully wrapped and protected by a wooden framework. Investigation had revealed a new painting – obviously a very good one, though Rossi was no judge. Anyway, he had soon calculated that this bonus might be used to advance his career very significantly, if exploited properly.

That was why, as soon as the galley reached its mooring along the Giudecca canal and he had gained the blissful reassurance of firm ground, he took a gondola, accompanied by one man to carry the picture.

Lorenzo Rossi was thankful to sink back on the cushions. He felt more tired than usual after a raid, and was glad to watch the Venetian skyline from this oblique angle as the shiny black gondola emerged from a narrow waterway on to the broad sweep of the Grand Canal. He gazed past the gondolier, in his red and yellow parti-coloured tunic and jaunty plumed bonnet, to the darkening blue above, smeared with pink and gold by the departing sun. The city's patterned, goblet-shaped chimneypots made the roofs look like tables set for a feast of the gods. From the upper storeys of roseate walls, rising like cliff faces from the canal, protruded poles festooned with laundry like drab bunting, while from the warehouses and merchants' dwellings extended the beams and tackles used for hauling in cargo. Richly-dressed ladies sat out on marble-pillared galleries. Lamps shone in a thousand windows. Torches lit up the landing stages in front of palaces, and were reflected by the gilded paintwork of nobles' barges lying alongside. Somewhere a bell tolled for Vespers, but seemed to be ignored by the citizens strolling on the waterfront: brightly-dressed groups of young bloods looking for an evening's fun; priests walking in earnest pairs; portentous merchants in long, fur-trimmed gowns.

The gondola swept under the Rialto bridge, with its wooden walls and roof, and Rossi noted that it was still flowing with people heading towards or returning from the business area. He drew a sleeve across his moist forehead, and knew that his future lay here in Venice. Despite the setback at Agnadello, which would certainly lose the republic some of its mainland territory, this state was still far and away the richest in Italy. Rich enough to allow its citizens to concentrate on trade, and to pay others to fight its wars for it. Some said that Venice's wealth and power were things of the past, now that ocean-going ships could do business directly with China and the Indies, thus bypassing the Levantine trade and its Venetian monopoly. But let the Jeremiahs come here and see for themselves the confidence, the affluence, the gaiety, the excitement and the deliberate parading of wealth.

As they neared the Palazzo Contarini, the visitors found themselves among a throng of gondolas all converging on the same destination. The magnificent house, as they drew close, was illuminated by a hundred guttering torches. From every window hung wide banners in blue and white, the Contarini livery. Ladies and gentlemen in gorgeous apparel were stepping on to the landing stage and making their way up the broad steps. Everyone of any consequence in Venetian society was here, from the doge himself downwards – as Rossi had known they would be. As his gondola, in its turn, drew alongside, he gazed up to the brilliantly-lit interior. The sound of music and the babble of voices told him that the celebrations were in full swing. Old Daniele Contarini, a main pillar of Venice's noble élite, was putting on his best display for the wedding of his eldest son to young Maddalena, daughter of Allesandro Grimani, another member of the same exclusive establishment.

Rossi found a quiet anteroom, where he deposited his prize, and dismissed his man. Then he made his way through the throng in search of a tall young fellow with a head of tight, dark curls. How Pietro Contarini would receive him, he could not be sure. In the conviviality of the tavern, when the wine was flowing freely, the fresh-faced stripling, trying so hard to be a man, had, on more than one occasion, sworn undying friendship. Rossi knew that the boy regarded him as something of a hero. But all that took place under very different circumstances. Here, amidst all his own people, and on his very own wedding day, Pietro might well prove cooler, more circumspect.

Rossi entered the main courtyard. The central area was filled with dancers. He peered through and among the throng of leaping men and women caught up in an exciting galliard. The swaying figures, the heat, the flickering lights and the loud music from a large orchestra only a few paces away made his head swim. He clutched at a pillar for support.

When the wave of dizziness had passed, he climbed the staircase to the first-floor gallery. Leaning against the balustrade from which were suspended lengths of cloth of gold, giving the whole party a gleaming backdrop like some old religious painting, Rossi peered down at the revellers. But with all the movement it was difficult to make out faces.

It was, in fact, Pietro Contarini who saw him first.

'Lorenzo! Lorenzo!'

Rossi was suddenly aware that his name was being called from across the courtyard. The music had stopped momentarily, and Pietro's voice sounded clearly across the babble below. Rossi looked up and saw the young man waving from the gallery opposite.

'Wait there!'

Pietro jostled his way through the crowd and was soon rushing up, arms spread to embrace him. He showed all the uncontrolled enthusiasm, Rossi noted, of a hound greeting its master.

'Lorenzo, this is marvellous! I was afraid you wouldn't get back in time.'

'It was all over more quickly than I had dared hope.'

'And successful?'

'Very. The pope's troops will be going without their pay, and Venice's war chest is richer by about fifteen thousand ducats.'

'Come and have a drink, and tell me all about it.' Pietro linked an arm, sumptuously clad in scarlet slashed with cloth of gold, through the soldier's, and drew him towards the staircase.

'But your other guests. Your bride.'

The scion of a great Venetian family pulled a long face. 'All these people bore me.' He drew Rossi close and whispered in his ear. 'To tell you the truth, Maddalena bores me, too. She's such a *child*!'

He led the way through a succession of rooms until they emerged on to a balcony overlooking the canal. There he despatched a servant for drinks and, when these had been fetched, he threw one leg over the marble balustrade and sat nonchalantly astride it. 'Now, Lorenzo, tell me everything – from the beginning. God! I wish I'd been with you!'

Rossi described the recent expedition in detail, colouring his account, here and there, to impress his admiring audience even more. When he reached the point in the story at which he and his men had unloaded the waggon on the beach, he paused. 'I've brought you a wedding present. Something special.'

Pietro beamed his pleasure. 'What is it? Show me.'

'It's downstairs.'

'Come on, then!' The boy jumped down from the balustrade and rushed his friend back through the crowded palazzo.

When they reached the small room near the canal entrance, he excitedly helped to unpack the painting. At last it was clear of all its wrappings, and leaning against the wall.

'It must have been done by one of the pope's artists,' Rossi explained. 'I believe he has quite a collection now.'

Pietro stood back, surveying it quizzically. It was not quite the 'surprise' he had expected. He peered closer, then pointed to the kneeling figure on the right. 'Isn't that—?'

'Yes, that is Julius, the bloodthirsty old goat in person. And there's Maximilian – and Louis. It's a picture to commemorate their unholy alliance.'

Pietro laughed. 'And now they've lost it. Won't the holy father be furious. Lorenzo, this is splendid! Come, we must go and tell everybody. They're all gloomy because of the French victory last month, so this will cheer them up a bit.' He grabbed up the picture and rushed out of the room.

Lorenzo followed him with difficulty. The house was even more crowded now, and it was getting terribly hot. His head was throbbing again, and the pain seemed to be spreading from the back of his skull down into his neck.

When he reached the gallery once more, he found that the young bridegroom had already called for silence. In the torchlight he saw a mass of upturned, glistening faces, like a bank of wild flowers pointed towards the sun.

'Listen, everyone! Good news! One of our condottieri has just returned from making an attack on the enemy. He's going to tell you all about it – Lorenzo Rossi.' He waved the soldier forward.

Rossi did his best to give once more an account of the raid to the indistinct mélange of faces before him. He felt very uncomfortable, and the heat wafting up from the courtyard was almost intolerable. After a few sentences he seemed to become detached from his own voice, not responsible and not even understanding clearly what he was saying. But everyone cheered, and they applauded in the right places. When he reached the climax, and Pietro held *The Triarchs* aloft, there was a roar of approval from the crowd. Rossi waved, stepped back from the balustrade, and sat down on a chair by the wall.

'That was great!' Pietro clapped him on the shoulder. 'You're an orator as well as a general. You have a great future in Venice. Now enjoy the party. I've got to go – my father wants to see me. We'll talk again later.'

Pietro found his father in the banqueting hall, giving instructions to some servants. The old man turned. 'Oh, my son, there you are. Where have you been? Maddalena's feeling neglected.'

'I was talking with Rossi. You heard him just now?'

Daniele Contarini gave his son no more than a half smile. 'Yes. Very welcome news. But, Pietro, you really shouldn't appear quite so familiar with hired servants of the state . . .'

The young man blazed with sudden anger. 'Lorenzo's my friend. And while we here have all been sitting around shaking our heads about Agnadello, he's actually been doing something. I think you might try to be a bit more appreciative.'

'I am very appreciative. Rossi has done his job . . . most efficiently. And he has been paid handsomely, I suspect. And that's where the matter ends – for him and for Venice. He is now just as likely to go off and sell his services to Mantua, or Ferrara, or even to the pope.'

Pietro shouted, 'He would never do that!'

The old man stretched out a hand and gripped his son's shoulder firmly. 'Don't be upset – especially on this day, of all days. I just want you to remember that you have great responsibilities before you, as head of this family after me, and as a leader of the state. One day you may be, *should* be one of the Council of Ten. But that will only happen if you form the habit of choosing your friends wisely. This Rossi is obviously a fine soldier, and I'm sure he has many excellent qualities. But he is . . . well let us just say he comes from a different background. Tonight, for example, he has obviously been drinking heavily. Everyone could see how he was swaying about and his words were very—'

The door burst open, and the two men were suddenly aware of a strange commotion outside. A servant stood before them, obviously agitated.

'Excuse me, my lord. Could you come please? Quickly!'

The two Contarinis hurried after him. The courtyard was a scene of panic. In a shouting, screaming mass, men and women were pressing towards the main door.

The liveried retainer circled round the back of the crowd, not answering Daniele's repeated cries: 'What is it? What's the matter? Tell me what's happened!' He led the way up to the gallery and stopped at the top, pointing. The passageway was empty except for the sprawled figure of Lorenzo Rossi.

'Pietro! No!'

The old man's warning shout was too late. The boy was already kneeling beside his dead friend.

Rossi had fallen on his back, his eyes staring up, frightened. His forehead was wet with sweat. His hands were at the collar of his shirt, which he seemed to have ripped open. With horror Pietro saw the hard, suppurating lump on the dead man's neck.

That was how the plague, a periodic visitor to Europe's cities, reached Venice in the summer of 1509. It was not a bad epidemic by bubonic standards, but it did claim the lives of nearly fifteen hundred people. Among them were Pietro Contarini and his sixteen-year-old bride.

Tim stood in the doorway of the apartment, immobilised. He surveyed the wreckage and felt as though someone had kicked him in the groin, leaving him doubled up with pain and gasping for breath. He was looking at a part of himself, a large part, battered, brutalised and bleeding.

Only when the first shock wave had passed did he remember Venetia. He called her name and rushed from room to room, fearful of what he might find. What he did find was a message in red three-inch capitals scrawled across the white fronts of his kitchen cabinets: 'WE GOT YOUR GIRLFRIEND   DONT DO NOTHING TILL WE PHONE'.

He leaned back against the fridge and swore, long and hard. He felt no better for it. He needed a drink but, judging from the smell of stale alcohol which pervaded the flat, the marauders had emptied out all his bottles and decanters. He checked and confirmed this suspicion.

Tim went out, slamming the door behind him. Minutes later he was sitting in a nearby pub making short work of his second double brandy. The spirit went some way towards anaesthetising his churning emotions, while leaving his mind fully awake. It was early evening, so the bar was still quiet. Tim sat in a corner and made himself think. Slowly he sorted all the clamouring questions into their order of importance.

How had the kidnappers located Venetia? He couldn't answer that until he had talked with her.

Had they harmed her? Would they harm her? Surely not, if they wanted the picture. Venetia was their only bargaining counter.

If they offered a straight swap, what should he do? There was only one answer. They had killed once to get the Raphael. They would almost certainly kill again, if they were frustrated.

Meekly hand it over, then? He gulped down more cognac. Good God! The very idea. To have held a priceless and famous work of art in his hands. To have had the power to see this long-lost painting at last on view housed in some public gallery. And then to let it be sucked back into the anonymous stinking bog of art thieves and unscrupulous collectors. The thought was insufferable. Yet no painting was worth a human life. There was no question about it; his first responsibility was Venetia's safety.

Call in the police? That posed the dilemma faced by everyone in a hostage situation; public duty versus private responsibility. Never give in to crooks or terrorists. It was a golden axiom, and Tim subscribed to it firmly. But to risk Venetia's life in some cat-and-mouse operation that could end in a shoot-out? That was not an option either.

So were this gang of murderers, vandals, kidnappers and thieves going to get away with it? Tim drained the glass. Oh no! They were going to pay. Somehow, sometime, he vowed he would get even. He would bring them to account for Grosmith's brutal killing; for whatever suffering they had caused Venetia; for their sacrilegious invasion of his life.

Tim returned his empty glass to the counter. Then he walked back home to begin the depressing task of putting straight his flat.

It was 9.00 the following morning when the phone rang. After a troubled night Tim was sitting in the kitchen drinking black coffee. He had restored the place to a semblance of order, but this was the only room where he could feel at all comfortable. Elsewhere, broken furniture and gaps on shelves and walls met his gaze wherever he looked. He wondered how long it would take to recover from this sense of having been violated. The telephone's buzz broke in on these sombre thoughts.

'Tim?'

'Venetia! Are you all right? Have they hurt you?'

'The police?' She sounded distracted, puzzled.

'What do you mean, police?'

'Oh, Tim, I'm being held at Scotland Yard. They've arrested me for murder.'

His brain went into top gear. Pointless to try and fill in the gaps in Venetia's story, but somehow he had to find out what the hell was going on.

'Tim! Are you still there?'

'Yes. Look, don't worry. I'll come straight round.'

'Oh no, you can't.' She was on the verge of tears. 'Inspector Gantry's here. He's taking me back to Swindon. Oh, Tim, you must come down and talk to him. You will come as soon as you can, won't you? PLEASE!'

'Look, Venetia, try to relax. I'll drive down now. Meanwhile don't worry. You're not guilty, so they can't pin it on you.' He wished he really believed that.

'But, Tim . . .'

'Venetia, get one thing quite clear: you mustn't tell them anything. Don't make any statement, written or verbal. They can't force you until you've seen your lawyer. You haven't said anything, have you?'

'No. They just put me in a cell and told me I wouldn't be interrogated till Gantry got me back to Swindon.'

'Good. Stay mum till I'm there. I'll leave straight away.'

He did not drive to Swindon immediately. His first call was at his office, where he left *The Triarchs* in the safe. Only when he was satisfied that the painting was still secure did he steer the Porsche in the direction of the Cromwell Road and the M4.

All the way down to Swindon he puzzled his way through the problem. What was Venetia doing chez plod when she was supposed to be in the hands of kidnappers? What evidence had the police gathered? Did they really think they could make some charge stick, or had they merely rushed into an arrest to cover the fact they were making no progress with the case? Would it help to come clean about Tuesday night's escapade? The sequence of events at the Grosmith Gallery had made obvious the motive for the dealer's murder. Yet revealing Venetia as a burglar could scarcely help her, and Gantry might well not believe the story of the other nocturnal visitors trying to get their hands on the painting.

'Damn Venetia! Damn her and her unerring talent for lousing up her own life and other people's too.' He shouted the imprecation as he slid the car into the fast lane and took it up to 95 mph.

'Why not? You might be able to knock some sense into her.'

To his surprise, Tim found the inspector quite amenable to his request to see the prisoner. Gantry, a small, pugnacious-looking man in a dishevelled suit, seemed to be at the end of his tether – which Tim suspected was not very long in any case.

'Bloody hysterical woman!' Gantry glowered across the cluttered desk in his small office. 'Half-past bloody five! That's when I had to get up this morning – Sunday morning! – to go and collect that sodding woman. No bloody breakfast! What with the fog and a pile-up on the motorway, it took three hours to reach town. Then what do we get? Bloody hysterics all the way back in the car!'

Tim decided that sympathy was the best tactic. 'Yes, she is rather highly-strung.'

'You can say that again.' Gantry belched loudly. 'Bloody stomach always plays up when I miss breakfast.' He picked up a phone and shouted into it. 'George! Go down to the canteen and bring me a bacon sandwich and a big tea . . . What? Already? Go round the corner, then, and get something – anything.' He dropped the receiver. 'And they wonder why it's difficult to recruit policemen.'

He lit a cigarette, inhaled deeply, and seemed to be calmed by it. 'OK, Mr Lacy, just where do you fit into all this?'

'I'm a friend – a close friend – of Miss Cranville's. She is naturally very distressed by this whole business and came to me for help.'

'When was that?'

'Thursday evening.'

'What time?' The inspector watched him closely as he threw the question.

Tim improvised. 'It must have been about nine.'

'And what happened then?'

'Well she told me all about the terrible business at Farrans Court and I tried to calm her down.'

'I see. And then?'

Tim carefully returned Gantry's gaze as he stalled. 'I don't know what you mean, Inspector. Miss Cranville seemed to relax after a while. She was with me the rest of the night. I told her she could stay in my apartment as long as she needed. I also told her she ought to let you know her whereabouts. There wasn't much more I could do immediately. I had to go to Paris on Friday.'

'Ah, yes.' Gantry rummaged among the papers on his desk and found a computer printout. 'Visit the Continent a lot, do you, Mr Lacy?'

'Yes, my business involves a fair amount of travel.'

The inspector nodded. ' "Security systems adviser",' he read from the sheet before him. 'What's that when it's at home?'

'I really don't see what relevance . . .'

Gantry ignored the protest. 'I see you were in the SAS until five years ago. Was that when you started your business?'

'Yes . . .'

'Rank of major. Not bad for someone just turned thirty. BA, too? Found time for study then?'

'Open University, if you must know. I did a course on the History of Art.'

Gantry looked up with an expression that was technically a smile, but had neither humour nor goodwill behind it. 'Soldier, businessman, artist *and* scholar – very impressive, Mr Lacy. Doubtless that multitalent explains how you made a fortune so quickly.'

'Scarcely a fortune, Inspector.'

'Flat in an expensive part of London? Frequent foreign travel? I reckon that puts you in an income bracket way ahead of anything a plodding police inspector might aspire to.'

Tim decided it was time to change tactics. 'I don't know where you got all this information – or why. Don't we have laws about data protection in this country?'

Gantry was unmoved. 'I merely accessed your military record, Mr Lacy. Nothing there you want kept secret, is there? It makes impressive reading. Seems you were a devoted servant of Queen and country. Come!' The last word was shouted in response to a tap at the door.

A nervous constable brought in the inspector's belated breakfast, and ran the gauntlet of Gantry's wrath because there was too much milk in the tea and not enough mustard in the sandwiches. Tim waited patiently as Gantry dwelt on these failings with apparent relish. After several mouthfuls, the policeman pointed at him with a half-consumed sandwich.

'I have a murder to solve, Mr Lacy. A brutal, premeditated murder . . . and perhaps more than just a murder?'

'More?'

Gantry swallowed a mouthful of tea and seemed to be weighing up how much to reveal. 'On Thursday night there was a break-in at the business premises of the deceased.'

'Oh, was much taken?'

'That we shan't know till we've been all the way through the late Mr Grosmith's stock book.'

'Well, at least you can't blame her for that?' With those words Tim had crossed his Rubicon. He gave Gantry a frank stare.

The inspector's response was measured, noncommittal. 'You certainly alibi Miss Cranville very conveniently. If what you say is true, she couldn't have been in Marlborough in the small hours of Friday morning.' He paused, then continued, watching closely for Tim's reaction.

'But her confederate, Bernie Stevens, might.'

'Bernie who?'

'Stevens.'

'The name means nothing to me, Inspector.'

'That's strange.'

'Why?'

'Because yesterday afternoon Bernie Stevens was seen leaving your London flat in the company of Miss Cranville.'

'And just who is this character?'

'As nasty a piece of work as you'd ever hope not to meet. He's done time for GBH, armed robbery and extorting money with menaces.'

'I can't imagine Venetia being involved with anyone like that. There must be some mistake.'

'Oh, I don't think so, Mr Lacy.' Gantry's face creased into a slow smile. 'Let me outline for you yesterday's sequence of events. After the business at Grosmith's shop, we naturally wanted to contact her. I was off duty, so my sergeant called at her hotel. They told him she'd already checked out. That put paid to my weekend. I had to come in and apply to the magistrates for a warrant.'

'But she phoned to explain she was staying with me.'

'Indeed she did, around the middle of yesterday afternoon.'

'Well, then—'

'Oh, come on, Mr Lacy, you don't suppose I'd let myself be caught twice by the same trick, do you? I was sure she was going to do another flit – and I was right. I faxed the warrant through to a colleague at Scotland Yard and asked him to nip round to your place pdq. And what do you think he found?' Gantry paused theatrically before proceeding to his grand dénouement. 'Your lady friend was in the process of leaving the place in the company of three pretty shady customers. They didn't wait to answer questions. They made off as fast as their little heels would carry them, but not before my colleague had positively identified Bernie Stevens.'

Tim listened in stunned silence. He tried to make sense of these new pieces of information, to fit them into the tantalisingly incomplete jigsaw he had been carrying around in his head for the last few hours. As he slotted them into place, he did not like the picture that began to appear.

'And what's your interpretation of all these events, Inspector?'

The policeman opened a buff folder lying on the desk before him. 'In my experience the simplest answer usually turns out to be the right one. As I see it, Miss Cranville and her accomplices wanted something that Mr Grosmith had in his possession. They lured him out to Farrans Court. Perhaps they had an argument. Anyway, they ended up killing him. As soon as the coast was clear, some of the gang ransacked the gallery, found what they wanted, rendezvoused with Miss Cranville at your flat, and were on the verge of making their escape when we nabbed her.'

'And you reckon you can make that stand up in court?'

'There are still a few t's to cross and i's to dot, but we're getting there.' Gantry casually extracted some black-and-white photographs from the file.

'And why are you telling me all this, Inspector? If your theory is correct, I might be part of this gang.'

'If that was the case, I don't reckon you'd be here now. No, I'm very much afraid, Mr Lacy, that the oh-so-innocent-looking Miss Cranville has taken you for a ride. She needed somewhere in London to meet up with her associates, so she used you. Of course, that's guesswork. Whatever the truth of the matter, Miss Cranville's best chance now is to be as co-operative as possible. I'd like you to tell her that: persuade her to make a clean breast of it, give us the names of her partners in crime. She's got herself mixed up with some hardened criminals, and she has nothing to gain from protecting them. Tell her that, Mr Lacy. She'll believe *you*. You can also tell her that I'm going to get to the bottom of this business, come hell or high water. I don't like this sort of racket on my patch. You may feel sorry for your lady friend, but not as sorry as I feel for this poor sod.' He tossed the photographs across the table.

They were scene-of-the-crime shots. From different angles they showed Grosmith's body sprawled on the attic floor. And there were several close-ups of the dealer's head, with black rivulets running from half a dozen hideous gashes.

The phone on the desk buzzed. Gantry picked it up and swivelled his chair round, becoming immersed in conversation with the caller. Tim was glad of the chance to think. Things could scarcely be blacker. The inspector had, of course, got the whole affair totally round his neck, but there was a logic to the plot his imagination had constructed, given the fragments of information on which it was based. How could he undermine Gantry's conviction? Should he say, 'Well, actually, Inspector, it was Miss Cranville and I who burgled Grosmith's gallery'? That would be no help to Venetia, and would probably put himself straight into the neighbouring cell. And if, at this stage, he said anything about *The Triarchs*, a priceless, probably stolen work of art, that would confuse the issue hopelessly, and what then would happen to the painting? God, what a mess!

Tim stared down at the police photographs. Poor Arthur lying there on the dusty boards with his staring eyes, his sideways-turned face, and the whole area above his right ear caved in. The only thing anyone could do for him now was to catch the violent bastard who had smashed the life out of him. And that certainly was not Venetia Cranville.

Tim stared hard at the photographs – then saw the hint of a silver edge to the black clouds of confusion and despair.

When Venetia was brought into the interview room a few minutes later, she immediately ran to Tim and threw her arms round him. In the few seconds before a policewoman prised her away, he could feel the shivers that convulsed her entire body. Then she was sitting red-eyed at the table opposite him, her pallid, unmade-up face scarcely distinguishable from the skeins of fair hair which hung around it. He had seen her looking like this once before – just after she had discovered that she was pregnant. She was close to breaking point.

'Tim, what am I going to do? I haven't murdered anyone. You know that. Tell them. Tell them, Tim!'

There was no time to soothe her down gently. He had to use harsher tactics, for her own sake. He gripped her hand hard across the table. 'You're not doing yourself any good by this silly act. Drop the helpless little girl pose. You should know by now that it doesn't work with me. You've got a perfectly good brain. So use it!'

'It's all very well for you to say that. You can just walk out of here.'

'And so will you if you do what I tell you. Have you contacted your lawyer yet?'

'No.'

'Right. I'll get on to him. I presume you still use the family solicitors in Lincoln's Inn. You can now tell the inspector that you'll make a fresh statement when you've spoken to your legal adviser on Monday morning.'

'Will he accept that?'

'He doesn't have any choice. Anyway, he has other problems at the moment. Apparently there's been a break-in at the Grosmith Gallery, and he has no idea who did it. He thinks it was the bunch of criminals you were seen with yesterday evening.'

Venetia gasped. 'You mean he doesn't . . .'

Tim hurried on. 'He's a bit confused, and I intend to unconfuse him. But you've got to help me. We haven't much time. I want you to concentrate and tell me again exactly what happened when you found Grosmith's body.'

Venetia shook her head and clasped a hand over her eyes. 'Oh, Tim, I can't!'

'You must!' Almost shouting. Then quieter: 'It may be your only chance.'

She swallowed, took a couple of deep breaths. 'I went up into the attic. At first, all I could see was the torch lying on the floor.' Her voice sounded hollow, expressionless. 'I called out, but there was no answer. I went over to where Grosmith had been working and called again. I then assumed he'd gone out of the room for a minute. I picked up the torch and . . . that was when I saw him.' She shook her head, then brushed the hair away from her face.

'I know it's tough, but tell me exactly what you saw.'

She nodded. 'At first I saw the little pile of pictures on the floor. Then, beside them . . . He was sprawled across another painting. And there was blood . . . so much blood . . .' Her voice tailed away.

Tim framed his next question carefully and slowly. 'Were his eyes open or closed.'

Venetia looked puzzled. 'I don't know. I couldn't see them. He was lying face down.'

'Across a picture?'

'Yes.'

'How many paintings were in the little pile beside his body.'

'I don't know. I only glanced at them. Four – five perhaps.'

'So, you ran out and called the police?'

'Yes, I had to go into the village. The house phone has been disconnected for months.'

'When the police came, did you go back up to the attic with them?'

'No, I couldn't face it. I just showed them the way. I waited down in the kitchen with a policewoman. We had a cup of tea.'

'OK. That's good. Very good.' Tim smiled his encouragement. 'I'm going over to Farrans now to have a scout around. Can I have the key?'

Venetia's face fell. 'They've taken everything away.'

'Of course. Sorry.'

'But you can get a key from Mrs Strang at Court Farm. She and her husband keep an eye on the place. I think you met them once. They're very helpful.'

'Right, I'll do that. Meanwhile, try not to worry. We'll get to the truth. Just remember not to say anything more.' He lowered his voice. 'Especially about *The Triarchs*.'

Tim took the Roman road that branches off the A345 at Ogbourne St George and cuts, straight and little used, across the downs. Where the descent towards the valley and Savernake Forest begins, he found a quiet pub. He took his pint of bitter and plate of beef sandwiches into the farthest corner of the bar, and sat down to do some hard thinking.

He had been wrong in his whole understanding of this crime. He had assumed that it was all about the Raphael, and some crooked dealer's attempt to get his hands on it. He knew scores of men and women in the trade, from exclusive gallery owners in St James's with drawing-room manners and farmyard ethics, to the keepers of dingy Kensington emporia who swarmed in their estate cars around the sale-rooms and petty dealers of the shires, like clouds of voracious flies flitting from dung-heap to dung-heap. There were few scruples between the lot of them. Their little world might appear glamorous and chic, fronted as it was by opulent decor and 'nice' young men and women from minor public schools. But its inner reality was made up of back-room restorers paid to 'improve' pictures and fake signatures;

shady runners who unloaded valuables from their car boots at the back doors of fashionable West End premises; entrepreneurs who did not enquire too closely into the ownership of the goods they were offered; auctioneers who provided secret finance to selected buyers to keep sale-room prices high; investors and institutional buyers who acquired old masters by the yard and buried them in bank vaults; and a large army of petty thieves and conmen whose activities helped to feed the greed and vanity of this fashionable haut monde. Yes, Tim knew this world, and knew that there were some in it who would not shrink from murder if the profits were high enough.

But all that did not square with some of the events of the last few days. How had the thieves been able to locate his address so quickly? It could only have been by tracing his car numberplate. That meant access to the national registration computer. Then there was the sheer persistence of the criminals. The break-in, the killing – they were simple opportunist crimes. But attempted kidnap? He gazed out of the window across golden-headed treetops. In the distance there was a sudden flash as sunlight was momentarily reflected from a car moving up the Salisbury road. No, it did not fit together. Whatever he and Venetia were up against was big. It was vicious. It was well-informed. It could plan on a large scale. And then change those plans at a moment's notice. That meant organisation. The thought sent a flicker of apprehension down his spine.

The key to it all was – or had been – at Farrans Court. And the police photographs held the clue. Between Venetia's discovery of Grosmith lying in the attic and the arrival of the police, the body had been moved – turned over. And the pictures had been rearranged. Why? And what were they doing there? The idea of Uncle Ralph spotting an old master in Bavaria and popping it in his kitbag was one thing. But to imagine him secreting an entire cache of stolen paintings in the ancestral home . . .?

With a gulp Tim finished his beer. He waved to the only other two occupants of the bar, then strode out, leaped into his Porsche, and continued the short drive to Farrans. As the car dropped down through overhung lanes above which the sun made a gilded lacework of the thinning foliage, Tim had no eyes for the passing scene. He was now very worried, and not just because Venetia was shut up in a prison cell. In fact that was probably the safest place for her. Whichever way he looked at the facts, they always pointed to one very frightening conclusion.

CHAPTER 4

Sex in a gondola was one of seventeenth-century Venice's principal tourist attractions. The sweating Dutchman, heaving away within such a craft's claustrophobic, velvet-draped tunnel, thought it overrated. The courtesan, Teresa, was expert enough. Nestled down on the cushions she slid out of her voluminous gown and petticoats with amazing dexterity. With equal skill she divested her corpulent client of his clothing, all the time murmuring endearments in a lilting, husky voice. Daniel Nys was certainly roused by her expert caresses, the fingers and tongue that slithered all over his flaccid flesh. But the woman's heavy perfume was suffocating in the enclosed space, and he felt feverish and torpid. He had, he knew, eaten and drunk too much in Teresa's sumptuous palazzo. She had dined him on a bewildering variety of delicacies, and plied him with a sweet, thick wine that had gone straight to his head. Now that head was throbbing, and coursed by rivers of sweat which dropped on to the woman who lay beneath him, gasping with simulated pleasure. All the merchant could think about was achieving a climax as quickly as possible. That was a struggle. The boat rocked with his exertions. Teresa squirmed and simpered encouragement. Nys thrust, puffed, panted and longed for fresh air.

At last it was over. He rolled sideways and lay limp upon the cushions. Teresa pulled back the curtains slightly and the merchant felt the delicious chill of the evening air on his glistening body.

Minutes later the woman called out an order to her gondolier. She leaned over her wealthy client, dabbed his forehead with a kerchief, and lightly kissed it. Daniel Nys felt her frizzed, bejewelled hair scrape his cheek.

'Thank you, my dear,' he was able to gasp at last in his passable Italian.

'No, my strong cavalier, it is I who must thank you.' She sat up and patted the kerchief on her cheek, neck and breasts. 'What a lucky woman your wife is, you great, handsome stag. But now,' she began wriggling back into her gown, 'we must make ourselves respectable. It would never do for the great Sebastiano Contarini to see us like this!' She giggled and prodded the Dutchman's round belly with a beringed forefinger.

Nys recalled the principal object of the evening's excursion. He was a rich cosmopolitan, a dealer in furs, silks and other luxuries, with shops and warehouses in London, Amsterdam and Paris. But he was much more. His business naturally took him to the courts of Europe's kings and noblemen. Among the rich, the vain and the fashion-conscious he had built up a reputation for exquisite taste, discretion and hard bargaining. He was just the man to be entrusted with important commissions, matters involving tact and secrecy. In this spring of 1628, Daniel Nys had several such delicate errands and pieces of minor diplomacy to attend to. But by far the most important was the acquisition of fine paintings for King Charles of England.

Nys had spent an exhausting three months in Mantua, negotiating for part of the incredible ducal collection. Generations of Gonzagas had brought together the finest and most selective group of Italian masterpieces. Europe's major connoisseurs had long coveted Mantua's splendours, with little chance of being able to acquire any of them – until now. Duke Ferdinando Gonzaga and his brother Vincenzo II committed three crimes against their ancient dynasty: they lived extravagantly, died prematurely, and left no issue. Immediately on Vincenzo's demise in 1627, France and Austria began fighting over his strategically placed territory. But others, including King Charles, had their eyes, not on the Gonzaga lands, but on the Gonzaga art treasures. And Nys had got there first.

As the stocky merchant struggled into his clothes in the cramped space, he thought sourly of the narrow victory he had achieved at Mantua. Three months of arguing with wily agents. Three months during which Nys had been pushed to the very limit of his resources. Then, when all had been agreed, the vendors had suddenly claimed an attack of conscience. They really could not disperse their heritage. It was an ancient trust. They should preserve the collection for future generations. Etc. Etc. Very clever, but they reckoned without Daniel Nys. He had seen through their stratagems and refused to raise his offer. So, twenty magnificent paintings by such masters as Correggio, Titian, Caravaggio and Mantegna were now crated up and on their way to England. But at what a cost: £15,000! It was a fortune for a hard-pressed king whose parliament complained of his extravagance and kept him short of funds. He shuddered to think of it. And he did not look forward to presenting Charles Stuart with his bill. Suppose his royal patron refused to pay! How fortunate that he had met Teresa. Tonight's expedition might save the situation.

'You're quite sure he will sell?' he asked the question for the third time.

Teresa pulled back the curtains and Nys saw the single span of the new Rialto bridge – still the only one across the Grand Canal – looming ahead, shadows cast by torches fluttering on its bright stonework. 'Don't worry, darling. Just trust me. As I told you, Contarini wants his eldest son to move back into the old palace.'

It was certainly true that the *palazzo antico* had been empty as long as Nys could remember, and he had been coming to Venice for almost twenty years. And certainly the fine old house was widely regarded as 'unlucky'. Gondoliers crossed themselves as they passed it, and told visitors dark stories about it, though no two accounts agreed. Daniel, good Protestant that he was, had always regarded such superstitious nonsense as proof of the gullibility of papists. Teresa's romantic tale was more elaborate than most, and Nys knew that it could well be a concoction of her own imagination. But it just might have some substance. And if it were true... The Dutchman knew he had to find out.

The *palazzo antico* was dark, shuttered and silent. Nys could not suppress a shiver as he gazed up at its doleful, even sinister exterior. The massive door was, however, ajar. Teresa took him by the right hand. As they passed from the dimly-lit landing stage to the pitch-black interior, Nys kept his left hand firmly on his sword hilt.

'There's no one here,' he said, alarmed. 'Is this a trick?'

'Sh! This way.' Teresa led him along a wide passageway to an internal courtyard where watery moonlight splashed over a patterned marble pavement and illuminated the open galleries above. Turning to the right, they were confronted by a door beneath which there was a sliver of light. Teresa tapped softly and a man's voice answered from within. The courtesan pushed on the elaborately panelled and inlaid oak, which swung noiselessly inwards. Nys freed himself from her fingers and transferred his right hand to the rapier's haft. He eased the blade back and forth in its sheath.

The *stanza* which they now entered was small but high-ceilinged. It was well lit by half a dozen lamps placed on the few pieces of furniture, and presented a dismal picture of neglect and decay. The walls were painted with allegorical scenes but their once-bright colours had faded and they were pockmarked by areas of fallen plaster. The three walnut tables were uncovered save by a layer of dust.

In the midst of this faded grandeur stood a man of medium height, who looked taller and more imposing because of the long-sleeved, floor-length gown of crimson camlet which marked its wearer as a member of the *savii*, the doge's inner council. Sebastiano Contarini was in his mid-forties, thin of face and dignified of bearing. In the Venetian fashion he placed his right hand over his heart and made a slight bow.

'Master Nys, I do apologise for this secretive and somewhat theatrical assignation, but there are good reasons for the utmost discretion.'

'*Senatore*, it is an honour to meet you, under any circumstances.' The merchant made his best courtly obeisance and Teresa dropped a deep curtsey, a considerable accomplishment in the six-inch-high *zoccoli* she wore on her feet.

Contarini waved his visitor to a tall-backed chair of antique design, and seated himself in its partner. The whore, whom the patrician ignored completely, was left to stand. 'I trust you are enjoying your stay in our beautiful city, Master Nys.'

For some minutes the two men observed formal pleasantries. Then Contarini said, 'I must not keep you in these uncomfortable surroundings, Master Nys. You have come to see the Raphael. It is here.'

He led the merchant across the room. On a table beside the door an object draped in a black cloth leaned against the wall. Without any ceremonial, the patrician removed the veil.

Nys gave an involuntary gasp as the master's radiant colours blazed forth in the lamplight. He was transfixed by the elegance of the composition, the mingled intimacy and awe of the figures, and the painting's pervading sense of serenity. 'Beautiful! Quite beautiful!' was all he could find to say.

'Yes, isn't it? I have never seen a better example of his work.'

'But why—?'

'Why do I wish to part with it? Because, it seems, the Contarinis can never enjoy it. For generations there has been a black legend in the family. My ancestors believed that the painting was accursed, that misfortune would befall us if ever it was hung in our palace.'

'But it is such a lovely, peaceful, holy thing. What can have given rise to this . . .?' He checked himself from adding the word 'superstition'.

The *savi* shrugged. 'After all these years who can say? Like any other family, we have had our share of tragedy and sorrow. Yet, for some reason any serious reversal was blamed on *The Bloody Triarchs*.'

'*The Bloody Triarchs*?'

'That's our nickname for the picture. The three men there were all great rulers and men of violence. One was Pope Julius II. I forget who the others were. It doesn't really matter. The Raphael was always locked away in a storeroom. It was left there when my great-grandfather built the *palazzo nuovo*. No one has lived here since.'

'That seems a pity. It is a fine, old house.'

The other man smiled. 'There are many Contarini houses in Venice. But, yes, it is a pity to see our ancestral home fall into this state. Now my son wishes to rehabilitate it.'

'He doesn't believe in the black legend?'

Contarini laughed. 'You know what young men are like. Unfortunately, his wife is less of a free spirit. She utterly refuses to set foot in this place until *The Triarchs* has gone.'

Nys looked puzzled. '*Senatore*, I quite see that you now wish to sell the painting, but why all the secrecy?'

'Family politics, my dear Master Nys.' He folded his arms inside the wide sleeves of his gown. 'Our motto is *quod habeo teneo* – What

I have I keep. Contarinis buy. They do not sell.' He gave a self-deprecating little laugh. 'Why else do we have seven palazzi in Venice and scores of villas on the mainland, all stuffed with treasures? My brothers and my aged mother would be outraged at the thought of the Raphael being sold. Of course, not one of them would give it house room. The only answer is to dispose of it in great secrecy. Perhaps they will think it has been stolen. Whatever they think, I can disclaim all knowledge of its disappearance.' He turned a shrewd gaze on his guest. 'But the hour is late and I must not bore you with my problems. Are you interested in the painting?'

Of course Nys was interested. He examined the canvas carefully. Equally carefully he broached the subject of price. As he had hoped, the vendor was more concerned to be rid of the Raphael than to gain its full market value. Contarini named a modest sum. Nys, as a matter of course, offered less. They quickly reached agreement at four hundred ducats. They made an arrangement to conclude the deal at the same place in twenty-four hours' time. Then the merchant and the intermediary took their leave.

As he returned along the Grand Canal in the courtesan's barge, Nys congratulated himself on his good fortune. Four hundred ducats! Three hundred pounds! For the most magnificent painting he had seen in many years, certainly superior to any of those he had bought from the Gonzagas. *The Bloody Triarchs* would raise the tone of the whole consignment, and make Charles the envy of his fellow monarchs.

'Now are you glad you trusted your little Teresa?' The whore cuddled close to him on the cushions.

'You're a good girl and I am very pleased.' He pressed his lips against her full, painted mouth.

She pulled a face. 'A kiss? Is that all I get?'

Nys was in one of his very rare generous moods. 'No, my dear, you shall have something more substantial. Tomorrow, we will go to the goldsmiths and see what we can find.'

Teresa seldom rose before midday, and then spent a couple of hours at her toilette. First she had to brush out her hair, apply various dyes and lotions, and spread it out over a brimless hat. Then she had to sit patiently on the roof of her house for the afternoon sun to dry it. Only then could her maid apply the frizzing tongs and twist the tresses into tight cones and curls, ready to be adorned with pearls and gold combs. Tending her cheeks, eyebrows, teeth, breasts and fingers took scarcely less time. Nor did selecting one of her score or so brocaded gowns, her necklaces and rings, and the high ruff designed to show off to best advantage her slender neck and uncovered bosom. It was thus late afternoon before she was ready for the rendezvous with her fat Dutch merchant.

He was waiting for her outside San Bartolomeo, the little church used by northern visitors to the city – those who were not drab heretics, like Nys. There he stood in his unadorned black and his wide-brimmed hat. God, how she despised him for his dullness and lack of fun. She was glad she would soon be rid of him.

'Darling!' she called, running up and throwing her arms round him. 'Have you been waiting long?' She giggled as, embarrassed, he untwined himself from her embrace.

Two Germans, emerging from the church in their fur-trimmed gowns, pointed and laughed at Nys's discomfort.

'That's enough of that,' he muttered crossly. 'Yes, I have been waiting. And I don't like standing around with all this money on me.' He patted the bulging purse hanging from his belt. 'Come along!'

They meandered through the Rialto. At every goldsmith's and jeweller's stall Teresa stopped, admiring this trinket, trying on that, asking the price of the other. Nys fretted, urging her to make her choice and have done with it. But she would not be hurried. She knew that the longer she dangled a rich client, the more likely he was to agree to a very expensive present – anything to get a decision made. By this means, at the end of two hours, she extracted from Daniel Nys an emerald pendant set with pearls, on a long gold chain.

Slowly they walked back to Teresa's house, pausing to laugh at the antics of the mountebanks and jugglers whose stands lined the piazzas, or to throw coins to the street musicians. When they reached her door, close by the campanile of San Paolo, Teresa held up a hand.

'Darling, I must tear myself away from you for a little while. I have an appointment with a prince of the Church. A girl has to think of her immortal soul sometime.' She laughed and opened the door. 'Come and see me after you've bought the picture.'

'But aren't you coming with me?'

'Not possible, darling. I'm sorry.' She pouted a transitory penitence. 'But I will send my gondolier for you. Michele will see you safely to the old Contarini palace, then bring you back here – to my arms.' She blew him a kiss, skipped inside and closed the door behind her.

Three hours later Nys was once more making the journey by water to the semi-derelict palazzo. He was nervous on several counts. He did not like being alone in a strange city at night. Venice was no safer than London or Amsterdam. Cutpurses lurked in the *calli* and beneath the bridges. No morning passed without at least one body being spotted in the canals. He was thankful to have Michele with him. The cheerful, robust rogue was more than a boatman. Teresa, like every courtesan, kept a household of *ruffiani* to protect her and her clients. Nys was acutely aware of the weight of the gold in his purse. The sooner he exchanged it for the painting, the happier he would be. Then there was his anxiety about the deal itself. Supposing Contarini had second thoughts. He must know that the Raphael was worth twice – three times – what Nys was paying. They had clasped hands on it; but, then, the man was a papist!

The merchant had no time for further speculation. With the slightest of bumps the gondola reached the steps of the palazzo. Michele moored it to one of the *pali* and helped his passenger ashore.

Nys looked up at the façade. It seemed as deserted as it had the previous night. Lights from the other side of the canal flicked faintly over the patterned brickwork. The only sound was the constant sucking of the water at the ancient walls. Side-by-side the two men climbed the steps.

They followed the same route as on the previous evening. At the portal of the small room where Contarini had met them, they paused. Nys knocked, then pushed open the door.

This time there were fewer lamps. But by their light Nys clearly saw three men. One was Contarini. Not this time in an official gown. He wore a rough leather jerkin. And he was holding a drawn sword – they all were. The door slammed behind him, and Nys turned. Michele had gone. He tugged at the iron handle. The door would not budge. He spun around again, hand flying to his sword hilt.

'I wouldn't do that.' Contarini leered at him – and Nys knew now that he was not Contarini.

'What do you want?' He tried to sound firm, self-assured but the words came out husky and trembling.

'That must be obvious – even to a Dutchman.'

The man's companions laughed.

He advanced, rapier held before him, until its point was at Nys's throat.

'So the whole thing was a trick!' In the midst of his fear the merchant felt fierce indignation.

'You *do* grasp facts quickly. Perhaps you're not as stupid as I thought. That being the case, you will realise that we intend to take your purse. We can take it from you alive or dead.'

Nys felt the blade, sharp against his windpipe. He swallowed hard. 'You're going to kill me anyway, aren't you?'

The man threw back his head and laughed. 'Oh yes, Master Nys, we are certainly going to kill you anyway.'

Tim stopped the car at the point where the drive suddenly emerged from a belt of trees and Farrans came into view for the first time. He always paused here, never tiring of the prospect. The old house sat calmly in its hollow, content to let the world pass it by. It had never had pretensions to grandeur. Built from local stone, Farrans, like most of the Cranvilles, had aspired only to a local rôle. It was not a large mansion. To the medieval hall, chapel, squat central tower and domestic offices the Elizabethans had added two parallel wings. An eighteenth-century squire had closed the square by building on a north range but, some fifty years later, a fire had mercifully destroyed his handiwork. Now the Court looked much as it would have done four hundred years ago.

Tim wound down the window for a clearer view. How much longer would Farrans be left to enjoy its proprietorial peace? Venetia would sell it, and what then? A hotel? A country club, with golfcourse, swimming-pool and sauna? It was ironic that he, who had only been to the house half a dozen times, should love the place so much, while Venetia, who had spent part of her childhood here, felt nothing for Farrans at all. He thought of the Victorian terraces and post-war tower blocks of Walthamstow where he had grown up – cheek-by-jowl living boxes with neither architectural merit nor humanity. He recalled the chorus of the old music-hall song:

With a pair of opera glasses
You could see to 'Ackney Marshes,
If it wasn't for the 'ouses in between.

Perhaps if Venetia's formative years had also been spent on the soul-stifling streets . . .

'Oh, what's the use?' Tim released the handbrake and allowed the sleek sports car to gather momentum down the slope.

He let himself in with the kitchen key Mrs Strang had given him. Resisting the temptation to wander lovingly from room to room, he climbed straight to the attic. There, he flicked on his torch and let the beam play over the dusty piles of accumulated junk. He had no idea what he was looking for, or what he hoped to find. Perhaps, if he could just reconstruct the crime in his mind, using all the information Venetia had given him and the evidence of the police photos, he could test his own – very unwelcome – theory and see if there were other tenable alternatives.

He walked to the far end of the room. It was not difficult to see where Grosmith's body had lain. The dust had been scuffed up in a wide circle. Kneeling at the centre of that circle he found a few tiny, dark stains on the broad oak planks.

And that was wrong. Tim had seen enough violent death to know how much a deep wound bleeds. He had seen the police pictures of Grosmith's battered head. There should be more blood. Much more blood. A man's skull had been subjected to repeated blows from a heavy, sharp-edged object. The resultant wounds would bleed profusely for several seconds. There would be pools of gore all over the place, not just a few spots of it. Venetia had been horrified by the sheer amount of blood. The fact that there was so little to be seen now supported her version of events. When Grosmith had fallen, he had been holding a picture. That picture had lain under his body. The blood from his broken head had gushed out on to the canvas. That canvas had subsequently been removed: between the time that Venetia discovered the body and the arrival of the police.

Tim turned his attention to the pictures. There was, of course, no sign of the small pile Grosmith had put to one side – presumably because they were of particular interest to him. They were not here now, nor were they shown in the police photographs. Ergo they, too, had been removed. The beam of light passed rapidly over the floor – then stopped. Tim knelt quickly, staring at another blob of congealed blood. 'Bingo! That'll give Gantry something to think about.'

Tim stood up and transferred his attention to the paintings that were still stacked against the end wall. Venetia clearly remembered seeing the dull glow of old gilded frames. Yet the remaining pictures now were turned *towards* the wall, presenting only their stretchers and dusty canvas to view. Perhaps that was not significant. The police might well have moved them. Still, it was worth bearing in mind.

He laid the torch on an old marble-topped washstand and turned the paintings round, scrutinising them one at a time. There were seven. Four were wooden Victorian portraits. One was an eighteenth-century primitive depicting a prize cow of most unlikely dimensions. The sixth was badly damaged and looked as though it had been used for bayonet practice. And the last was a pretty amateurish landscape. Tim thought: put this lot in a sale-room and they might fetch one hundred pounds for the frames. They were quite obviously the discards of previous owners of Farrans who had found better items with which to decorate their walls. But there had been *other* paintings here. Paintings of an altogether different category. Paintings like *The Triarchs*.

Forty-five minutes later Tim had decided that he had seen all there was to see, had let himself out, locked the kitchen door behind him, and driven the mile or so back to Court Farm. There was no answer when he rang the front door bell, so he wandered round to the back.

The wide yard was enclosed on three sides by large sheds and barns, most of them open and filled with new-looking farm machinery. In the far corner two men had their heads inside the engine of a large tractor. They were deeply engrossed in their work and did not see Tim as he strolled across the impeccably tidy yard. He gazed around at the well-swept tarmac, the fresh-painted woodwork, the strict geometry of the roofs, where not a tile was out of place. He reflected how the farming industry, or at least its wealthier end, had changed. He was about to call out, when a splash of colour caught his attention. On his right was a double garage, built into one end of the range of buildings. The doors were closed but it had no interior side wall. Next to it stood a combine harvester. Tim stopped and peered through the framework of the huge machine. In the gloom beyond stood a bright green Range Rover.

'What can we do for you, then?'

Tim turned to see a stocky man in a battered jacket and a cloth cap. Mid-fifties. Black, bushy eyebrows. He stood with feet apart, hands on hips. Suspicious. Unwelcoming.

Tim smiled. 'I was looking for Mr Strang. Mrs Strang lent me the key to the Court. I've come to return it. There was no answer to the door bell.'

The man relaxed and held out his hand. 'I'm Harry Strang. The wife's gone to visit her sister. She said you'd be back. Mr Lacy, isn't it?'

Tim shook hands with the farmer. 'That's right. I'm a friend of Miss Cranville.'

Strang frowned. 'I reckon she needs all the friends she can get at the moment. It's a bad business.'

'You don't believe she killed that man from Marlborough, do you?'

'No, of course not!' Strang looked indignant. 'I've known Miss Venetia since she was so high – her and her sister. Nice kids. The idea of her . . . Well, it's ridiculous.'

'I'm trying to help her. I wonder if you can spare me a few minutes.'

The faintest flicker of apprehension passed over Strang's face. It was quickly banished by a broad smile. 'Of course. Come on in. It's time for a cup of tea, anyway.'

Tim sat at the long table in the large flagged kitchen, while the farmer busied himself with kettle and teapot.

'You've always kept an eye on things at Farrans, have you?'

'The wife's looked after the cleaning down there for years, and I did odd jobs round the place for the old boy. Did you know him?'

'Uncle Ralph? Yes, I met him a few times. He must have been quite a handful when he fell ill.'

Strang put a mug of strong tea and a sugar-bowl in front of him. 'Alzheimer's disease, terrible thing. We had to get him into a home eventually. Miss Cranville agreed. There was no alternative.' He leaned against the dresser to drink his tea.

Tim nodded. 'I'm sure you did the right thing.'

'I don't reckon it made much difference to the old boy. He didn't know where he was, anyway. It was a mercy he didn't linger long.'

Tim sipped his tea. 'When the place was empty, did you ever have any problem with prowlers? Any signs of someone breaking in?'

He detected the slightest hesitation before the farmer replied nonchalantly, 'No. The wife or I popped down pretty well every day, just to keep an eye on things. You get some weird folks around these days: bikers, drug addicts, vandals. Specially when these midsummer pop festivals are on. But there was no trouble. Not so much as a broken window-pane.'

Tim frowned. 'Hm. That's very puzzling, isn't it?'

'What do you mean?'

'Well, if Venetia didn't kill Arthur Grosmith, someone else did. Someone who knew the layout of Farrans.' He looked straight at Strang. 'Have you any idea who that could have been?'

The eyebrows met in a V above Strang's nose as he responded in sudden anger. 'Of course not! I'd have told the police, wouldn't I? What are you suggesting?'

Tim had found out what he wanted. He smiled disarmingly. 'I'm so sorry if I upset you, Mr Strang. I wasn't suggesting anything. I simply want to help Miss Cranville, if I can. She's in a great deal of trouble.'

The other man relaxed. 'Sorry. I shouldn't have flown off the handle. Naturally I'll do anything to help.'

Tim finished his tea and stood up. 'Well, I mustn't keep you.' He laid a visiting card on the table. 'Look, if you think of anything that might throw some light on this business – anything at all – please give me a ring.' He moved to the door. Then turned. 'I gather there was a burglary at the Grosmith Gallery the other night. Do you think that's connected with the murder?'

Strang shrugged.

'I just wondered if you'd heard anything. Local gossip – that sort of thing? Strangers seen in the area? Cars driving round the lanes in the early morning? He smiled disarmingly and watched the man's reactions intently. 'Well, thanks for the tea. Don't bother to come out. I can find my way.' He left the door ajar behind him.

Tim took a good look round the yard. It was empty now and the large tractor had gone. He walked to the corner of the house, turned it, then stopped. He counted ten, then moved soundlessly back to the kitchen door. He peered through the opening. He could not see Strang but he could hear his voice. He was on the telephone, and he sounded very agitated.

'. . . Lacy, yes. He's been here asking questions . . . Of course I didn't, but I think he knows more than he's saying . . . Yes, of course I'm worried . . . Yes, Jane, but you never told me it was going to involve killing . . . OK, OK, I know. You can rely on me to keep my mouth shut. All I'm saying is that you've got to watch Lacy . . . Yes . . . Yes . . . All right. Goodbye.'

As the receiver clicked, Tim entered the room silently. Strang was in the corner with his back to him. He half turned. But too late. In one movement Tim had his right arm in a strangle grip under the farmer's chin and his left fist boring into the small of his back.

He whispered into Strang's ear. 'There's no way to get out of this hold. If you so much as cough you'll break your own neck.'

'What the hell?' The farmer struggled and instantly wished he hadn't. He screamed with pain.

'I'll ask the questions and you'll supply the answers.'

'I can't breathe . . . You're killing me.'

'Well killing is what we're going to talk about. Did *you* murder Grosmith?'

'No! No, I swear I didn't.' Something between a squeal and a gasp.

'Who's Jane?'

'I can't tell you!'

'She's that frightening, is she?'

'Not her. The others! They'd kill me! They'd do things to the wife.'

'That's nothing compared to what I'll do now.' Tim gave the man's head a jerk by way of emphasis. 'Let's take it a step at a time. I think I've worked out most of it. You tell me if I'm right or wrong?'

'OK.'

'Someone approached you a few months ago, and said they wanted to store things at Farrans. Just a few old pictures. They offered you money to help them and to keep your mouth shut. How am I doing?'

'You're right.'

'How much did they pay you?'

'A thousand a month. There didn't seem any harm in it. The place was empty. They said it was only for a little while.'

'So everything was OK, I guess, until Ralph Cranville died and his niece came back.'

'They promised to shift their stuff from the attic . . .'

'Only they left it too late. Venetia had brought in an expert. As soon as he had done his stuff, he'd realise that the paintings in that dusty attic were major works of art stolen from top galleries and private collections. You must have worked out by then that you were mixed up with a gang of major art thieves.'

'I told them I didn't want any more to do with it.'

'But they said "Help us get rid of Grosmith, or else"?'

'Miss Cranville mentioned that the dealer was coming on the Tuesday, and I simply passed on the information. I didn't know they'd kill the poor bastard . . . honestly, I didn't. You must believe me!'

'It doesn't matter a damn what I believe. It's the police you have to convince now.'

'No! I daren't! I can't! They'd get to me.'

Tim ignored him. 'It was all very neat. At one blow they could silence Grosmith, implicate Venetia in his murder, and take the paintings away. Only one thing went wrong. When they did a tally they found that one of their pictures was missing. So they made you and this Jane, whoever she is, go and break into the gallery last Thursday.'

'No! It wasn't me!'

'It was your Range Rover.'

'They borrowed it – Jane and one of the men from London. Some expert, they said. I just left the Rover out for them, with the keys in it.'

'That'll do for now.' Tim released his grip, but grabbed Strang's arm in a half-nelson. 'Lie down on the floor.'

The farmer sprawled on the flagstones. With one knee in the small of the man's back, Tim removed his own tie. He rolled Strang over and bound his wrists in front of him. 'Right. On your feet!'

'What are you going to do?'

'I'm taking you to Swindon, where you'll tell Inspector Gantry all you've told me.'

'No way!' Strang struggled to his feet. There was sweat on his brow and real terror in his eyes. 'You don't know what these people are capable of.'

'I can guess. But what I do know is that Venetia Cranville is facing a life sentence for a crime she didn't commit. And you were ready to see her rot in prison without moving a finger to help. So don't look to me for sympathy. Now move!' He propelled Strang towards the door. 'We'll take the Range Rover. It's material evidence.'

Tim hustled his prisoner into the passenger seat of the vehicle. As he opened the garage doors he saw, hanging beside them, a drum of baler twine. So, for good measure, he lashed Strang's ankles.

During the half-hour journey the farmer's panic grew. He pleaded. He swore. He offered money. He warned of the retribution which would follow any interference by Tim with the gang's plans. At last Tim pulled into a lay-by and made very explicit what he would do to Strang if he did not shut up. Strang shut up.

Tim drove into the private car park at the back of the police station and left the Range Rover in a space marked 'Ch. Const.'.

He hurried into the building through the back door and sought out Gantry's office, and walked in without knocking. The inspector, sitting in his shirt-sleeves, was speaking on the telephone. He glowered at the intruder, covered the mouthpiece and bellowed, 'Get out!'

Tim sat down.

Gantry mumbled apologies into the phone and returned the receiver to its rest. 'Now, just what—?'

'I've got a witness outside who can tell you exactly how and why Grosmith was murdered.'

Gantry looked unimpressed. 'I'm not very pleased with you, Mr Lacy. I asked for your co-operation, but instead you persuaded Miss Cranville to shut up like a clam.'

'Look, Inspector, I'm telling you all that's irrelevant now. If you'll take a statement from this witness . . .'

'And just who is this mystery witness that you've found?'

Tim jumped up. 'Look, you must come quickly. He might try to escape!'

Gantry stared up, wide-eyed. 'My God, Lacy, do you mean to tell me you've brought someone here under duress?'

'I believe it's called a citizen's arrest. So will you *come*?'

Gantry heaved himself out of his chair.

It was at that moment that they heard a loud, hollow explosion.

For a moment both men froze. Then Tim rushed from the office and ran at full-tilt down the corridor, Gantry hard on his heels.

Tim went straight to the Range Rover and wrenched open the passenger door.

He looked inside and groaned. 'Oh, no!'

Now the inspector was at his elbow, pushing him aside to get a better view.

'Good God, Lacy, what have you done?'

Daniel Nys was not the stuff of which heroes are made. He had neither the athleticism nor the mental agility to qualify as a man of action. But he was no coward. Confronted in the half-light by three assassins, something deep inside the corpulent Dutchman rose in revolt. It took him by surprise. And it certainly caught his assailants off guard.

With one wide, sweeping gesture he whisked his rapier from its scabbard and knocked the false Contarini's lightly-held sword from his hand. Then he made a sideways leap. While the gang leader was fumbling on the floor for his weapon, and shouting orders to his accomplices, Nys desperately wrenched one of the tables away from the wall and moved behind it. The lamp upon it fell to the floor. It smashed and went out.

The expanse of walnut was not a very effective barrier, but it would keep his attackers at a slight distance and would certainly protect him from the left-handed stiletto-thrust. It was a trick he had learned during his lessons with one of the best and most unorthodox fencing masters in London.

Now the other two thugs were upon him, prodding across the table with their swords. Nys parried their thrusts with wild sweeps of his own weapon. He caught one of the assailants with a slash across the right forearm. Yelping an oath, the man dropped his sword.

'Contarini' was now on his feet. He stood in the centre of the room, a smear of dust across one cheek, his face distorted with rage. 'Kill him! The bloody Dutch bastard!' Nys now wondered how he could ever have mistaken this piece of common gallows-fodder for a Venetian nobleman.

The two of them advanced again, from different sides this time. Desperately, Nys flailed his sword right and left.

'Move the table!' The order was shouted to the man who leaned against the wall, still nursing his wound. There was no response, and Nys noted with satisfaction the blood streaming from the thug's arm and his frenzied efforts to stem the flow by winding his sword-belt around it.

Nys paid for the momentary distraction with a sudden stab of pain as a rapier point struck his left shoulder and pierced it to the bone. Now the blows were coming faster and faster. The merchant knew that he could not fend them off indefinitely.

That was the moment at which the door crashed open and several men rushed in. Shouting. Brandishing swords. Nys assumed they must be more of the cutpurse gang. Then he saw 'Contarini' and his accomplice drop their weapons.

The newcomers were all dressed in blue and white livery. One of them approached Nys. '*Signore*, are you all right?'

Nys nodded. Words would not come.

His saviour smiled. 'You are safe now. Please come.' He held out a hand.

But before they could leave the room a tall figure appeared in the doorway. A figure dressed in a long crimson gown. A figure which bowed, hand on heart. A figure which said, '*Signore*, I am sorry this evil should have befallen you in my house. My name is Sebastiano Contarini.'

They opened the back door of the Range Rover to get to the body. The interior looked as though it had been painted red. There was blood everywhere. Harry Strang, still bound hand and foot, lay on the floor. A twelve-bore shotgun was clamped between his legs. Its business end was in his mouth. Not that there was much left of his mouth – or his head.

Tim backed away from the vehicle, and almost fell over a constable being sick against the wall.

The inspector was dashing to and fro, red-faced, furious, shouting orders unnecessarily loudly. He called for the doctor, the photographer, and men to remove the body. 'And then get that bloody vehicle out of the Chief Constable's parking space!'

He turned, enraged, on Tim. 'Mr Lacy, you've got a hell of a lot of explaining to do!'

In Gantry's office Tim went over the earlier events at Court Farm and the drive back to Swindon. The inspector was not at all mollified.

'You should have just reported your suspicions to us, and let us talk to Strang.'

'But you wouldn't have got anything out of him that way.'

'Well, we're not going to get much out of him now, that's for sure.'

'I'm sorry. I knew he was terrified of reprisals from his paymasters but I didn't realise he had a gun in the back of the Rover . . . that he could wriggle himself over the seat and shoot himself.'

'You realise the press are going to have a field day with this?' Gantry stood up and went over to the window. ' "Suicide at police headquarters. Councillors demand enquiry into CID interrogation methods." My God, you've dropped me in it, and no mistake.'

'I was only trying to get evidence to release Miss Cranville.'

'Release Miss Cranville?' Gantry spun round. 'You can forget that! You're going to be banged up in the next cell!'

'On what charge?' Tim spoke quietly.

'I'll think of something, don't you worry. You can't rampage round the countryside trussing up innocent citizens.'

'Strang was an accessory to murder.'

'We've only got your word for that, haven't we?' Gantry resumed his seat and glared across the desk.

Tim stared back and wondered how to deflect the policeman from his feeling of outrage and back to the real issues.

'Inspector, you're quite right. I took matters into my own hands. That was wrong. As a result I've caused you a lot of embarrassment and brought about the death of an important witness. But haven't I, in fact, only confirmed the doubts you already had? Look, let's go back to Grosmith's murder. Your forensic experts must have commented on the absence of blood up in the attic. There wasn't much blood on the floor because most of it fell on to a painting positioned under the body – a painting subsequently removed.'

'That doesn't prove Miss Cranville didn't do the killing.'

'Absolutely right, Inspector, but you know what a good defence counsel will do with the forensic evidence. May I also point out something else on the scene-of-crime photos? I'm sure you noticed it, too, but it does support her account.'

Gantry frowned but opened the file and took out the pictures. Tim sorted them and selected the one he wanted.

'Miss Cranville told me – as I imagine she mentioned in her state-ment – that Grosmith had put aside a little pile of pictures. She noticed that some were framed and some unframed, and that they were lying beside his body on the floor. Now look there . . . eighteen inches or so from Grosmith's head.' He pointed to a dark stain. 'That's one of the few spots of blood still remaining. Look at its shape. On this side it's an irregular blob but on the other there's quite a clear right-angle. As though it dripped down the edge of something covering the floor. Something like an unframed painting?'

Tim shook his head. 'All this ties in with what I learned from Strang. I could kick myself for not getting names and descriptions from him while I had the chance. But, at least Miss Cranville should be able to describe some of the criminals.'

'And also explain what she was doing in their company?' Gantry was calmer now, but far from convinced.

'That'll be to do with the missing painting.'

'What missing painting?'

'Didn't she tell you about it?'

'There's a great deal Miss Cranville hasn't told me.'

'When Grosmith visited Farrans Court the first time, he took away one picture for closer examination. That was obviously one of the stolen paintings. Of course, when the gang checked later, they realised it was missing. That must be why they broke into his gallery the other night. But presumably they didn't find it, so they tracked Miss Cranville down, assuming she knew something.'

'You've got all the answers, haven't you, Mr Lacy.' Gantry scowled.

'I wish I had. I wish I knew who was behind all this. Somewhere out there is an utterly ruthless individual who will kill without a second thought, and whose methods can drive a grown man to suicide. He has a big organisation, a great deal of power, and he's very, very dangerous. Inspector, you must track him down.'

Gantry sat for several seconds with his head in his hands. Then he looked up wearily. 'I want a full statement from you. I want *everything* on paper – everything you know about this case. When you've done that, hand it to my sergeant. Then you can go – and take Miss Cranville with you. I'm delivering her into your custody. You're both to stay where I can contact you. And within twenty-four hours – which should give the lady long enough to consult her lawyer – I want her back here to make *her* statement – without any inconvenient bits omitted.'

Tim said, 'I'll need to go and collect my car from the farm.'

Gantry nearly blew his top. 'I don't want you anywhere near that place! Give me the keys. One of my men will fetch it.'

He stood up and, taking his jacket from a hook on the door, ushered Tim out. 'The sergeant will show you where to go. Meanwhile, I have to tell a farmer's wife that she's just become a widow.'

CHAPTER 5

Venice was *en fête*. Her citizens never needed much excuse for celebration. Saints' days, religious festivals, anniversaries of famous battles, the election of the doge or some other major official, the receipt of good news from the war front, the return of ships from a particularly successful commercial venture – anything which might be regarded as a cause for general rejoicing might set the bells ringing in the campaniles and bring the populace out on to the streets. Everyone participated in such conspiracies of pleasure. The church provided processions and open-air masses. Patrician families set up wine-gushing fountains outside their doors, threw sumptuous banquets, and kept open house. The state laid on regattas, fireworks, bull fights and other spectacles. Business stopped. Merchants, diplomats, tourists, glassblowers, officials, leatherworkers, boatbuilders forsook their labour, no matter how urgent, to besport themselves in their finest clothes on the canals and the piazzas. Ascension Day, which in the year 1628 fell on 1 May, was one of the highest peaks in the annual mountain-range of festivities. As well as being a religious occasion, it was also the day on which the centuries-old ceremony of the Marriage of the Sea was performed.

Daniel Nys was astounded to find himself a guest of honour in the ducal party throughout the sumptuous entertainments of that day. His life had become a succession of very agreeable surprises ever since his alarming adventure of three nights before. Sebastiano Contarini held himself personally responsible for making amends to the Dutchman for the brutal assault he had suffered. He was committed to good

93

relations between Venice and England, where his brother, Alvise, was ambassador and, as he explained more than once, he regarded it as a point of honour that someone who had come to the city on royal business should leave with the highest possible opinion of Venetian hospitality. Accordingly Nys was lodged in the best guest-chamber at the Contarini palace. His host threw a banquet in his honour. He was granted an audience with the doge, who expressed his own regret at the merchant's unfortunate experience. The ruler of *La Serenissima* declared his hope that this mishap would not impair Venice's relations with the King of England, and he presented to Nys a magnificent stiletto with a jewel-encrusted pommel.

The events of Ascension Day began when servants discreetly and gently drew back the heavy hangings around Nys's bed, and the waking Dutchman became aware of the shifting patterns cast on the plastered ceiling by sunlight reflected through the casement from the canal. Rising, he discovered a magnificent suit of clothes laid out for him. When he had washed in rosewater, and then been helped into the scarlet hose, the matching doublet patterned with gold thread and the cloth-of-gold cape, his host arrived to escort him to breakfast and thence, by barge, along the Grand Canal to the Molo. The wide landing-stage was thronged with cheering crowds who greeted with vociferous enthusiasm the arrival of each festively-decked craft. Contarini's oarsmen brought their boat to within a few feet of the doge's huge gilded barge. Nys assumed that this was to ensure a place at the head of the procession. He was, therefore, astonished when Sebastiano conveyed him ashore and then on board the Bucintoro itself.

Soon the ducal party emerged from the palace. Nys took his place among the dignitaries and honoured guests who lined up to bow Doge Giovanni Corner aboard. The events of the next few hours would always remain a jumble of magnificent images and impressions in the Dutchman's memory. The cacophony of bells and cannon echoing over the water. The rhythmic movements of the liveried oarsmen. The waters of the lido thick with craft of every size and shape. The simple but moving ceremony as the doge stood in the barge's prow and flung his jewelled ring far out on the glittering surface of the water. The tumultuous reception back at the Molo. The sedate procession along an avenue of pikemen to the palazzo, while the people applauded and threw their caps in the air. The feast in the immense banqueting hall, where long tables were decorated with intricate concoctions – towers, dragons, statues, barges – made of sugar or pastry. In after-years, when he struggled to recall details of that day for his friends or grand-children, they eluded him, fusing together and blurring in a golden haze of memory. But one episode always stood out stark and clear.

In mid-afternoon the banquet was at its height. Totally relaxed by wine and convivial company, Nys was engaged in lively conversation with one nobleman on the relative merits of the Florentine and Vene-tian schools of painting, while flirting with the daughter of another who was seated opposite. He felt a tap on his shoulder.

Sebastiano Contarini bent forward to whisper in his ear. 'Master Nys, may I tear you away for a while? There is something I very much want to show you.'

They left the palace and crossed the *piazzetta*, Sebastiano's servants clearing a pathway through the crowds. They entered the arcade of the impressive new building marking the southern boundary of the Piazza San Marco, turned through a doorway and climbed to the first floor. A fat man in dark robes stood at the threshold of one of the apartments.

'*Senatore.*' He bowed.

'Lorenzo.' The patrician returned the greeting. 'Allow me to present Master Daniel Nys, our distinguished guest.' He turned to the Dutch-man. 'This is Procuratore Lorenzo Ziani, one of the finest legal brains in Venice.'

The tubby lawyer bowed again. 'You are most welcome, Master Nys. We hope, today, to give you a clear demonstration of Venetian justice.'

He ushered the visitors into a large chamber where several other guests were already assembled. For several minutes he fussed with other introductions, then he led Nys and Contarini to high-backed chairs arranged by one of the room's three tall windows. The casement was open and gave on to a narrow balcony overlooking St Mark's Square.

As Nys took his place, he looked out over a wide expanse filled with people wandering among the stalls of the traditional Ascension craft market. To his right the afternoon sun bounced dazzlingly from the gilding and mosaics of the basilica. Nys found the vast church, of which the Venetians were so proud, not at all to his own taste. To his Protestant eyes its domes, pinnacles and over-decorated surfaces were grotesque, a monument glorying in the accomplishments of man rather than his creator.

But today it was not the elaborate carvings, the scintillating mosaics or the huge bronze horses of the basilica's façade to which his hosts directed his attention. In a cleared space in front of the edifice, an immense wooden framework had been erected, some thirty feet high. The crosspiece at the top had four pulleys attached, from each of which a rope descended to the ground.

Ziani, standing behind Nys's chair, leaned forward. 'Have you ever seen the *strappado*?'

'No. What is that?'

'A most effective method of discovering information from enemies of the state, for punishing criminals, and generally encouraging loyalty to the Serene Republic. But watch! The show is about to commence.' He licked his thick lips in anticipation.

An expectant crowd had gathered around the execution area. Now they cheered as a file of soldiers emerged from the palace, escorting five prisoners. With a shock, Nys recognised the three assassins who had attacked him, also Michele, the gondolier and, last in the line, Teresa. They were all manacled and chained together. Heads bowed, they shuffled out into the sunlight and were brought to a halt before the jeering citizenry. Even from a distance Nys could see streaks of blood on the men's shirts and weals across the courtesan's back. The impatient crowd had to tolerate a pause in the proceedings while a priest muttered various incantations in front of the felons. Then the chains were removed and Teresa was led to one side. Nys watched, fascinated and appalled, as the men had their hands tightly bound behind their backs. Then each was attached by the hands to one of the four ropes. As the onlookers roared, the criminals were hoisted slowly to the top of the gallows, bodies arched forward and swaying to and fro, faces distorted with pain as their shoulder joints took the strain. The soldiers working the pulleys now tied the bottom ends of the ropes at the foot of the uprights. Each produced an iron ring and, with the aid of long ladders propped against the cross member, they attached these to the ropes about half-way up.

The excitement of the crowd was now mounting. As the executioners untied the ropes and once more took the weight of the dangling prisoners, the watchers took up a well-known chant: '*Dieci! Nove! Otto! Sette!*' Each number was shouted louder, until the roar reached a tumultuous climax: '*Due! Uno! MOLLATE!*'

The ropes were released. They rattled through the pulleys. The bodies plunged earthwards. Then, with a clang and a thud that sent reverberations through the whole structure, the iron rings struck the apertures. Ropes tautened. Puppet-like figures wrenched to a stop in mid-air. Flesh, bone and muscle tore. The men's screams cut through the howl of the watching mob.

Three times the *strappado* was repeated. On the last drop, one of the victims had an arm completely torn from his body. A wave of laughter passed through the crowd as the front ranks were spattered with his blood.

The criminals were cut down. They lay, semiconscious and limp, like discarded dolls who had lost most of their stuffing. They were not allowed to rest there, however. One by one, they were dragged by their legs across the flagstones to where a wooden block had been set up. There they were finally despatched by the headsman.

Only after she had been obliged to watch the fate of her accomplices was Teresa conveyed to the point of execution. Her hair hung in tangled skeins around her bare shoulders. Her half-naked body had been stripped of all its accustomed finery. She struggled in the grip of the two soldiers who half-dragged, half-carried her to the block. She gabbled hysterically and tried to clutch at the priest who read the last rites over her. Then she was forced to her knees and, calm at the end, laid her neck in the wood's shallow depression. By now the executioner's axe was blunt. It took three blows to sever her head.

'Well, that's that.' Contarini's tone was conversational. 'A very satisfactory end. I hope you feel suitably avenged, my friend.'

The merchant could only nod, his senses still numbed by what he had seen.

'They told us quite a lot under interrogation. It seems you were far from being the first to fall into their clutches. They have been using my ancestral home for their ghastly deeds for several months. It's a great relief to have that episode over.'

Nys managed a smile.

'Or, perhaps, not quite over. There's just one more thing to do.' The Venetian stood up and beckoned to a servant.

The man crossed the room, carrying something wrapped in blue velvet. While the man held it in front of Nys, Contarini removed the covering and revealed *The Triarchs*.

'This was the cause of all your troubles, Master Nys, as indeed it has always been the cause of trouble and grief to my family. They say this lovely painting is unlucky to the Contarinis. Now I feel sure its evil has, at last, been exorcised. Please take it. And may it, from now on, bring you only good fortune.'

WHERE IS MURDER MYSTERY HEIRESS?

Massive security surrounded Marlborough Town Hall yesterday for the inquest on local farmer Harry Strang. A large crowd gathered, hoping to catch a glimpse of Venetia Cranville, the 27-year-old artist at the centre of a double-death mystery. But she failed to appear. Jetsetting Venetia vanished after her surprise release from custody on 23 October. At the time the police stated that there was insufficient evidence to bring charges against her.

It is more than three weeks since Marlborough art dealer Arthur Grosmith was battered to death at Farrans Court, the stately home recently inherited by Ms Cranville. Five days later, Harry Strang, the caretaker of the blonde artist's Wiltshire mansion, was found shot dead outside Wessex police headquarters.

The Coroner's Court – which was strictly off-limits to the press – decided that Strang took his own life. Evidence was given by Inspector George Gantry for the Wessex constabulary. The vivacious Venetia's ex-boyfriend, 35-year-old London business-man Tim Lacy, was also there. After the proceedings he disappeared at high speed in his expensive classic Porsche. Strictly no comment!

The people of Little Farrans are not best pleased with the behaviour of their new squiress. 'The family has lived at the Court for hundreds of years,' said Meg Tundy, who keeps the village shop and post office. 'They've always been a part of our life here.

But this one – she only pops down a couple of times a year with her arty friends. She hasn't even been to see Harry Strang's widow. It's a disgrace!'

The police seem no nearer to unravelling the mystery of this double tragedy. Meanwhile, Giles ffrench-Digges, managing director of Baron's, the Bond Street art gallery, confirmed that he was anxious to contact the elusive painter with a view to staging an exhibition of her work. It seems he is not the only art dealer anxious to cash in on public interest in Venetia Cranville. It's an ill wind . . .!

'When's it going to end?' Venetia dropped the tabloid on the floor beside the bed and fell back on the pillows.

Bobbed dark hair and the thick-framed glasses, with which she had replaced her contact lenses, had transformed her appearance quite dramatically.

'They'll get tired of it before long.' Tim stood by the window, gazing morosely out on the rain-swept hotel forecourt. 'They're just frustrated because, despite all the money laid out on private investigators, they can't find you.'

'That's what you said last weekend.' She lay scowling up at the ceiling. 'I can't take this kind of life much longer.'

Tim spoke without turning. 'An interviewer once asked Bob Hope how he felt about growing old. Hope replied, "Well, it sure beats the hell out of the alternative." '

'Well, I think I'd rather take my chance than stay cooped up here. It's all right for you: you do most of your business by phone and you can go swanning off to see your clients in Edinburgh, Amsterdam or Timbuktu. What about my painting? I can't do anything decent cooped up here in this . . . prison.' She waved an arm around the conventional bedroom with its standard dressing-table unit, refrigerator, TV and glazed print of Lake Windermere.

Tim had chosen this large hotel south of Manchester for its very anonymity. It was busy; people came and went all the time. It was also close to the airport, which meant that he could continue his professional activities with the minimum dislocation.

'Look, Venetia, we've been through all this before. Even Gantry agreed it would be best for you to lie low for a time. If the press can find you, the crooks can find you. And I don't need to tell you what they'd do to you.'

'So why don't we just let them have the stupid picture? Then we can go back to living our own lives. I'll be out of your hair and we can stop skulking like fugitives.'

He turned and looked down at her. She lay curled up on the bed like a sulking twelve-year-old, demanding, needing comfort and reassurance. And he felt very much like a frustrated parent. Half of him wanted to take Venetia in his arms, stroke her hair, and murmur consolation. The other half wanted to shake her out of her total self-absorption and make her come to terms with the harsh realities of the adult world.

He propped himself against the dressing-table. 'There's rather more at stake here than our personal convenience.'

Venetia pouted. 'You're just sore because they broke your home up.'

'Oh yes. I'm as sore as hell about that. So would you be. I also have an aversion to murderers. These people have caused two violent deaths. They weren't the first and they won't be the last. You're certainly not safe as long as these people are at large. Their greed is insatiable. They take whatever they want, by force when necessary. They don't only deprive private collectors of their treasures. They steal from galleries. They cheat the public. They impoverish us all. They make inroads into our heritage.' Tim's voice rose as his anger mounted. 'It's sheer, cynical cultural rape. They don't give a damn for beauty, talent, genius. All that matters is the price tag. I want these bastards behind bars!'

'And that's why you've turned yourself into a one-man army, is it?'

'I've just been putting out a few feelers, that's all. I happen to have business connections in the police and the art world, as you know. I've been trying to get some clue about who's responsible for what you've been through.'

'Oh, Tim, come off it!' Anger flamed in her cheeks. 'I'm not a complete idiot. You shut me up here out of the way, and then disappear for days on end. You take the keys to Farrans. You don't want the police to know anything about the Raphael. You assure me that every-thing's going to be all right. You obviously know a hell of a lot about

100

these criminals, but you don't tell me anything.'

He scowled his impatience. 'You're letting your imagination run away with you. I borrowed the Farrans keys so that some of my men could fit security alarms. It should have been done years ago. You may not care much about the place, but I guess you don't want to issue an open invitation to burglars to help themselves. And that's all there is to it. That and a few low-key enquiries.'

Venetia jumped up and stood facing him. There were tears of frustration in her eyes. 'Liar!' She shouted the word. 'You're hiding things from me. You always have. That's why we never made a go of it before. I know you too well, Tim. You've got some devious plan. You've never got the SAS out of your system. Now you're off on some private *Boys' Own Paper* adventure. Taking on the bad guys singlehanded.'

'Venetia . . .' He put his hands on her shoulders.

'No!' She shook herself free and sat down again on the bed. 'I *won't* be a pawn in your secretive little games. Unless you tell me what's going on, I'm going to walk out of here and start getting my own life together and take my chance with . . .' She looked up in exasperation. 'You see? I don't even know who these criminals are!'

Tim thought hard. How much could he tell her? She might panic and do something silly. Having Venetia back in circulation would ruin everything. She would then be in great danger and she would upset all his plans. Carefully he strung together a few selected facts, half-truths and downright lies.

'I don't know exactly who these people are but it's easy enough to narrow the field to three or four criminal syndicates. I spend a lot of my time trying to protect art collections from them. They are highly professional, international, specialist thieves, first-division criminals. Let me describe just a few of their exploits. In March 1990 two men dressed as American policemen walked into the leading art gallery in Boston in the middle of the night. They overpowered the security guards, neutralised the alarm system, and calmly walked out with two hundred million pounds' worth of Rembrandts, Vermeers, Degas, Manets and other specifically chosen items. A few weeks earlier a gang broke into Dropmore House in Buckinghamshire, held the caretaker at gunpoint, and blasted open the strongroom which had been specially installed to protect one of the finest collections of antique gold and silver in private hands. One of the officers on the case described the crime as "a well-planned, military-style operation". In September of the same year thieves got away with some of the best portraits by Gainsborough and Reynolds from Lincoln's Inn. They carefully avoided copies and inferior pictures. Early in 1991 four Picassos went missing from the Gallery of Modern European Art in Prague Castle. Major art theft is an epidemic of the Nineties. In Italy alone police have over 128,000 unrecovered artefacts on their books. Top-quality pieces are disappearing from Peking to Pittsburgh, from Copenhagen to Cape Town. Their theft is organised by a handful of experts who know where to find the best items, and who to sell them to.'

'Yes, but who *do* they sell them to?' From force of habit Venetia brushed a non-existent wisp of hair from her eyes. 'If a stolen painting or sculpture is famous, whoever buys it can never display it in his sitting-room.'

'That's where we get to the really sinister part of the story. If art theft has become second only in value to drug-running as a criminal activity, you can bet your bottom dollar that some very, very unsavoury people are involved. Until a few years ago it was a relatively simple business. An international black market providing masterpieces to rich, unscrupulous connoisseurs for their private enjoyment. I've seen a couple of these collections – one in Switzerland, one in South Africa. An incredible experience. You'd be staggered by what these wealthy magpies have salted away. Then the big corporations, oil barons and trade unions came into the market. They had long-term investment funds available. Through brokers on the fringes of the criminal under-world they could acquire important pieces relatively cheaply and shut them up in bank vaults.'

'But they could never resell them.'

'Oh, there are ways. Some countries have very relaxed laws about stolen property. If you claim to have bought something in good faith, you can't be forced to give it up. But, as I say, things have now taken a much more sordid turn.'

'Go on.' She was now sitting against the headboard, hugging her legs, chin on knees, fascinated despite herself.

'Let's get some tea first, shall we? I'm parched.' He phoned through

102

to room service and placed an order. Then he went across to the one armchair, removed a pile of Venetia's underwear and sat down. 'Where was I?'

'Sordid.'

'Fine art has now become a form of currency among the world's top criminals. The biggest problem for the successful drug baron or arms dealer is how to launder his proceeds. Governments have clamped down heavily on the movement of suspect funds. You can't just nip along to the bank and pop the odd million into your current account. The criminals have tried literally thousands of ways to clean up dirty money: gambling saloons, offshore funds, buying gold and jewellery, cover businesses from used-car salerooms to pizza parlours. Bit by bit the police get wise to them and close them down. So the crooks are left with bundles of banknotes rotting in cellars and lock-up garages, frantically looking for legitimate outlets.'

'Nice problem.'

'Yes, but a problem nevertheless. So, enter the "smurfing" expert.'

' "Smurfing"?'

'Strictly speaking it's the name of one kind of laundering operation, but it's come to be applied to a number of very clever, very inventive specialists who look after big financial transactions for the major crime syndicates.'

Venetia frowned. 'What's all this got to do with old masters?'

'Well, consider our friend *The Triarchs*. Let's say it's worth twenty million at auction. On the undercover market, after allowing for operating expenses, the thieves could probably get half that. So that three-by-four piece of canvas, which could be rolled up and carried in the bottom of a suitcase, is, in effect, a ten-million-pound note.'

'So the smurfer sells it to a Mafia boss?'

'Yes, or a Japanese Yakuza chief, or the head of a Turkish heroin syndicate, or a sleazy accountant in his luxury Riviera villa doing business for Abu Nidal, PKK or some other bunch of terrorists. It'll all be fronted by a "legitimate" fine-art gallery. The Raphael would probably go through the books as half a dozen works by lesser painters.'

'But what would the buyer do with it?'

'What he would do with a ten-million-pound note. Put it in

the bank. Use it to pay for the next consignment of cocaine or Kalashnikovs. Swap it in Athens or Istanbul for a load of smuggled antiquities which can be fed into the legitimate art market. There are lots of possibilities.'

There was a knock at the door. A white-coated waiter came in with a loaded tray. Tim busied himself with tea, milk, toast and jam.

Venetia accepted a cup of China tea with a squeeze of lemon, and sat on the edge of the bed to drink it. 'These smurfers are presumably only interested in the best.'

'Of course. It takes just as much organisation and manpower to steal a thousand-pound item as it does something worth a million. These men are experts. They know exactly what they want and where to find it.' He spread strawberry jam thickly on a triangle of toast and bit into it with relish.

'You'd be amazed just how well organised these people are. They've got plenty of money, so they can buy the latest technology. And they can corrupt the police. How do you suppose they traced you so quickly to my flat?'

'I've wondered a lot about that.'

'They had my car licence number. They must have passed it to some copper in their pay, and got him to check it on the police computer. The rest was easy.'

Venetia stared, wide-eyed. 'It's frightening.'

'That's right. You make sure you stay frightened. That's a very healthy response. These crooks are way ahead of the game. It takes far more resources than most police forces have, to bring them to book.'

Tim opened the briefcase on the floor beside him and took out a spectacles case. He removed the contents. 'What do you think these are?'

'They look like sunglasses.'

'Yes, sunglasses on a cord to hang round the neck. The sort of thing lots of tourists wear when they're going round museums and stately homes.' He slipped the cord over his head. 'Now, you see how part of the string is concealed under my coat collar. Imagine a wire attached to that and running to a small, battery-operated pack in my hip pocket. I don the shades, like so. Now, if there was an infra-red security beam anywhere in this room, I could see it.' He removed the glasses. 'This is the kind of toy today's thieves use when they're casing likely premises.'

Venetia poured herself more Lapsang Souchong.

'But I still don't understand what those pictures were doing at Farrans.'

Tim gulped down a mouthful of sweet Indian tea. 'I can only guess at the answer. The best I can come up with is something like this: our particular smurfer was getting together a consignment. They're usually shipped to the Continent in container lorries, so he needed storage space for a few months. But not just any storage space; the conditions have to be right for keeping old masters – dry and cool. For some reason he couldn't use his own premises. Perhaps the police were beginning to show an interest in his activities. He heard about Farrans and realised that it would be ideal for his purpose. It was empty because the owner was in a nursing home. It was deep in the country. It had a weather-proof attic that no one had been near in years. And it had a caretaker who could be bribed to hand over the key from time to time and ask no questions.'

'Poor Harry. I can't think of him as being dishonest.'

'I don't think he was, basically. He was offered money for jam. After he'd taken it, it was too late. He got dragged in deeper and deeper, till eventually he was an accessory to murder. At the end he simply couldn't think straight. He was terrified of the criminals, frightened of the police, and at root deeply ashamed. That's why . . .'

'It was horrible.' Venetia closed her eyes and shuddered. '*You're* used to violent death. You can shrug it off. But I feel—'

Tim responded sharply. 'You never get used to violent death! Not if you're anything like a normal human being. I feel terrible about Harry Strang.'

'But the way you treated him . . .'

'If I was going to get him to come clean, I had to make him more scared of me than he was of the crooks.'

'Well you certainly succeeded.' She walked across to the mirror and grimaced at her reflection. 'God, I look a mess. I can't think why I let you talk me into doing this.' She pushed a comb through the dark fringe that changed the shape of her face.

Tim sighed. 'You know perfectly well. Every newspaper in the country had published that old publicity picture showing you with languorous fair locks.'

Venetia gazed with distaste at the sensible blouse and skirt Tim had persuaded her to buy. 'You enjoy manipulating people, don't you?'

Tim struggled with his temper. 'Who manipulated me into this whole business?'

'I asked for your help, and you told me to go to hell. It was only when you found out about the painting that you became interested. Everything you've done has been to keep your hands on *The Bloody Triarchs*. My God, if ever a picture was well named... You're obsessed with it. You rushed down to Marlborough to find it. You hid it somewhere only *you* know. You wouldn't let me tell the police about it.'

'It was your idea to keep it secret from the police.'

'No, I mean later. After Harry's death. When I had to make a "complete" statement for Gantry.'

Tim jumped up, shouting now. 'Certainly I want to keep the Raphael out of the crooks' hands. It belongs to the world, not some drug-pushing billionaire who's going to use it to further his corrupt business! As long as it's in a safe place, and I'm the only person who can get at it, we just might manage that.'

He took hold of Venetia by the shoulders, spun her round and forced her to look at him. 'Somehow I'm going to keep you alive, and keep the painting – for you. At the end of the day it'll be yours to do what you want with. If I were in your position I'd sell it to one of the national collections, and use the money to save Farrans. But the decision will be yours.'

She struggled to free herself from his grip, but his hands held her too tightly. 'I don't want the damned thing. I can paint my own pictures to make money. Right now I've got a marvellous opportunity to sell them. A West End exhibition! It's incredible! If I let this chance slip I may never get another. I can't just sit around in this godawful hotel, hoping the police will track down the killers. If they're as slick and professional as you say, it could take Gantry and Co years to put a stop to them.'

On that Tim could only agree, but he did not say so. 'I know it's frustrating for you. But, look, will you give it just one more week? You were right: I *do* have just a couple of cards up my sleeve, and that's where they must stay until I'm ready to play them. Tomorrow I'm seeing someone who, I think, can help to bring this business to a pretty swift conclusion.' He stared at her hard. 'Look, today's Friday. Promise me you'll stay put for seven more days. Will you do that? Stay in this dreary place just till next weekend?'

After some seconds he extracted a grudging nod.

Tim inwardly sighed with relief. He had to keep Venetia out of harm's way because he was about to embark on something very dangerous. What he had not told her was that he was now almost certain of the identity of the man behind the art thefts and several murders, and that he was about to lure that man into the open.

Daniel Nys did not stay long in London. It was far from being a comfortable place for men known to be in favour at court. In the fifteen months that he had been away, the situation had deteriorated alarmingly. In the markets, rumours were more plentiful than merchandise. Outside Nys's own door in West Cheap a balladmonger raucously hawked lampoons that fell little short of treason. Gangs of apprentices swaggered round the narrow lanes shouting slogans against the king and his favourite, George Villiers, Duke of Buckingham.

> 'Let Charles and George do what they can,
> The duke shall die like Doctor Lambe.'

It was the most blatant defiance imaginable. Scarcely two months before, John Lambe, whose only offence was that he was Buckingham's astrologer, had been savagely battered to death by a mob in Old Jewry, a mere stone's throw from Nys's house. The murderers had got off scot-free; no one was prepared to inform against them. Charles had vented his spite on the lord mayor, levying a swingeing fine of six thousand pounds on him and the corporation. A few days later the king had haughtily dismissed parliament, and then left the capital for the New Forest.

Nys wasted little time in following. London in August was hot and fever-ridden at the best of times; now the passions of its populace were dry enough to burst into sudden flame. But the merchant had even more pressing reasons for hurrying to court. He had laid out thousands of his own money in pictures for the king. He wanted his account settled. Only three days after completing his long and tiring journey back to England, he loaded a waggon and, accompanied by stout, well-armed servants, set out to make his dusty, winding way into Hampshire.

His journey ended at Wickham, where he was lucky to find a lodging at the inn, and his men had to make shift in the stables. King Charles was staying three miles off, the guest of Sir Daniel Norton at Southwick, and every hostelry in a wide radius was packed with hangers-on. Nys's quarters were cramped. The food was poor quality and expensive because Norton's agents had systematically bought up all the best provisions in the area for feeding the royal entourage. The one thing that was plentiful at the sign of the Mitre was gossip.

'The king'll never get his ships to sea. One of the captains in Portsmouth told me only yesterday that half the crews have deserted.' A small man in the sombre habit of a lawyer, confided the news mournfully across the supper table as he picked fastidiously at his food.

'It's no wonder. They remember too well what happened to the poor sods who went to La Rochelle last year. Eight thousand of 'em. Only three thousand came back, and half of those had to be carried ashore.' His neighbour, a thin-faced horse-trader, scowled.

The law man smiled across the table at Nys. 'They say Buckingham's getting frantic in London because the victuallers haven't delivered all the navy's supplies. You've just come from the city, friend. What's the word there?'

The merchant was circumspect. 'I understand the duke has now left, and perhaps has already arrived at court.'

'Arrived last night.' A young man in bedraggled finery, who had seated himself at the head of the table, shook the crumbs from his lace cuffs. 'I had that from one of the queen's ladies. Nor was that all I had.' He smirked at the others, waiting for the laughter which was not forthcoming.

The lawyer pushed away his pewter plate with a grimace. 'Then let's hope "King George" has decided to abandon this ridiculous La Rochelle expedition. The country can't afford these expensive gestures of support to the Huguenots.'

'I disagree.' The courtier sat back in his wainscot chair, toying with his thin beard. 'It's time we taught the French king a lesson.'

The horse-trader grunted. 'And who's to fee this tutelage? Poor fools like me and this honest merchant, who must pay heavy duty on the goods we import.'

The young buck flashed a dagger and embedded it in the board. 'Are you saying the king has no right to levy taxes? That's close to treason, and by God . . .'

'Keep your bragging for the court doxies!' The thin-faced man spared him scarcely a glance. 'The king may do as he wills with his own. If he wants to send a third fruitless expedition to La Rochelle, let *him* pay for it instead of taking money out of our pockets. If he really cared about the French Protestants he'd spend less money on personal luxuries. Buying horses is one thing; the court has to travel. But do you know how much he spends on entertainments? And clothes for the queen? And gifts for his bugger, Buckingham? As for pictures: he pours out thousands every year. Has men travelling all over Europe to find paintings for his precious gallery.' He took a long draught of ale, wiped his sleeve across his mouth and stared quizzically at Nys. 'But tell us, friend, what brings you here?'

When Nys rode over to Southwick the next morning he was admitted to the great hall of Norton's house. A score or more other suitors lounged about in the vast, raftered chamber. There were ambassadors, sheriffs from distant parts of the realm, ships' captains, liveried couriers, bishops, men of business, men of property, penniless hopefuls – all waiting for a chance to pour their petitions, grievances or appeals into the ear of the king or favourite. They were destined to wait for hours, or days, or to depart unheard. But when the stocky Cheapside merchant presented his credentials, the information was conveyed immediately by an officious royal servant to the inner recesses of the household. The man returned almost immediately, to inform Nys that his majesty was impatient to see the paintings. A room would be placed at the Dutchman's disposal, and he was to arrange his wares there. The king would view them as soon as he returned from hunting in the afternoon.

The next few hours were hectic. Nys cantered back to the Mitre inn. Within minutes he had his waggon harnessed, and two of his men on the driving seat. But Dickon, his young groom, was nowhere to be found. Nys spent forty precious minutes scouring the premises before tracking down the lad in an adjacent haybarn and literally prising him from the embrace of the innkeeper's daughter. As if that delay were not enough, the girl's father arrived just as the discovery was made, and began laying about both of the young people with a length of chain which happened to be lying handy. It took the combined efforts of Nys and two stable boys to get the enraged innkeeper under control, and then the merchant was obliged to listen to a furious diatribe about Londoners who came down to the country corrupting honest folk.

By the time Nys and his valuable cargo were back at Southwick, the sun was already past its zenith. Then he could not find out where he was to display the paintings. Each servant and court official he asked shrugged and intimated that pictures were not his department. At last he came across Lady Norton having a heated exchange with her steward about the supply of wine for the royal table. Urgently interposing his request for information, the merchant caught part of the raking gunfire the lady had been directing at her servant. In God's name, why was he pestering her? Couldn't he see she was driven to distraction by her responsibility to her sovereign – a task compounded a thousandfold by being surrounded by idiots? Must she do everything herself? Paintings? Yes, his majesty had said something about paint-ings. Oh, well, she supposed the long gallery would do as well as anywhere. But he must be careful of the tapestries. If there was as much as a single snagged thread . . . Nys withdrew hastily to super-vise the unloading of the waggon.

With time running out, he had to divide his attention between watching his heavy-handed employees as they bumped the precious canvases off the cart, fussing over them as they carried the pictures up the broad oak staircase, and displaying the paintings along either side of the gallery. Time and again he had his grumbling servants move the items around so that a glowing Titian did not overpower a more sensitive Mantegna, or a brooding Caravaggio suppress the exuberance of a neighbouring Veronese. Only about the positioning of the Raphael did he entertain no doubt as he rushed to and fro in his shirtsleeves arranging the collection. The exquisite 'Adoration of the Magi' (or, as Contarini had called it, *The Triarchs*) he placed alone, on a simple oak table, against the gallery's far end wall. Nys was still hovering indecisively over the juxtaposition of three of the

110

larger items when Dickon, who had been told to guard the staircase, rushed in to say that the king was coming.

Charles entered arm in arm with his favourite, the two men deep in conversation. Neither gave the merchant a glance as he made a deep obeisance. They walked slowly the length of the gallery.

'All I say is that we should *use* parliament, not ignore it. Flatter these self-important shopkeepers and rural clods. Let them think that they are important, and they will do anything you ask.'

It was the first time Nys had seen Buckingham at close quarters. Now he watched the tall man, past his first youth but still handsome, to see if what gossips said was true that 'George plays the king, while Charles plays at being king'. Certainly, the favourite seemed the more intent of the two. Brow furrowed, head slightly bent forward. The smaller man responded in short sentences – probably because of his notorious stutter – and his attention was already distracted by the pictures.

'It is for s-s-s-subjects to flatter kings; not kings s-s-s-subjects.'

'If we are to raise enough money for the La Rochelle campaign we must cajole, make promises. Of course, we don't need to *keep* our promises.'

'I do not n-n-need p-p-p-parliament. They must learn that I s-s-summon them out of kindness. I c-c-can do without them.'

The two men passed out of earshot. Watching, Nys observed that Buckingham soon lost the king's attention. Charles was already pausing to examine the canvases minutely, pointing out aspects of the works to his companion.

'M-m-master Nys!' The summons came from the far end of the room.

The merchant almost ran in obedience to his royal customer. The king was standing back to appraise a large allegorical painting.

'This Veronese . . .'

'Majesty?'

'Not much, I think, is by the m-m-master's own hand.'

Not for the first time, Nys marvelled at Charles' obvious expertise. 'Your Majesty's eye is as keen as ever.' It was not flattery. 'The painting has, indeed, been finished in the studio. But all the important areas – the figures, faces, hands, the flesh tones . . .'

'Yes, yes, obviously.' Charles nodded impatiently. 'And the m-m-model; the s-same woman as my picture of War and P-p-peace at Westminster.'

He moved on to the next painting, giving it his full attention and making several perceptive comments. He and Nys were soon engrossed in an analysis of Caravaggio's chiaroscuro technique.

'This is magnificent!' Buckingham, viewing by himself, had stopped before *The Triarchs*.

Charles turned to look at the Raphael. 'Steenie, we'll make a c-c-connoisseur of you yet. I think you have p-picked out the finest in the c-c-c-collection. This is Raphael at his b-b-best.'

Nys hurried to agree. 'An early work of his most mature period. Probably his first painting of Pope Julius.'

'Tell us about it, master merchant.' Buckingham spoke without taking his eyes from the deceptively simple composition which seemed to exude tranquillity.

Nys gave a censored version of the story of *The Triarchs*, and of his own adventures in securing it. He was careful not to mention that the painting had come to him as a gift.

Charles lingered the whole afternoon in the long gallery, with favourite and merchant in attendance. He was delighted with all Nys's acquisitions and when the question of price came, he did not for a moment demur. At last he stood in the doorway, making a reluctant exit.

'Master Nys, you have s-s-served us excellently, as always. Have the p-p-paintings delivered to Whitehall. Steenie, you are c-c-captivated by the Raphael. It is t-truly exquisite. And it is yours. For your b-b-b-birthday next week.'

The duke was effusive in his gratitude and Nys watched the two friends descend the staircase, once more arm in arm.

Two days later John Felton, an aggrieved army officer, stabbed Buckingham to death in Portsmouth high street.

CHAPTER 6

The phone rang in the back room of a shop at the wrong end of Fulham Road. Jane Prentice stubbed out her cigarette, dropped the copy of the *Antiques Trade Gazette*, in which she had been checking forthcoming provincial sales, and squeezed past a stack of old frames to reach the desk.

'Prentice Gallery,' she announced in a flat, bored tone.

'Hello, Jane.'

The thin, nasal voice with the heavy accent struck her like an electric shock.

'Niki!' She forced herself to sound pleased. 'Where are you?'

'I'm still in Athens.'

That was a relief.

'Jane, I expected to have a report from you by now.'

'Funny you should say that, Niki. I was just about to give you a ring.' The middle-aged woman glanced at her reflection in the cracked mirror, and nervously prodded at her blotched mascara.

'Good. Then you have some progress to report?'

'Well, we're certainly narrowing the field. We've checked all the woman's contacts we can find, both here and in Italy.'

'But you still haven't located her?'

There was no way to conceal the facts but she certainly wasn't going to take all the blame. 'F.D.'s supposed to be finding the woman. I've had Lacy's flat staked out round the clock, but he hasn't been near it. His car's still in the garage. All his office will say is that he's away on business.'

113

'My God, what a bunch of incompetents!'

'Niki, that's not fair. The boys did a first-class job at Andover Hall, and you yourself said that lifting that Rembrandt from the Glasgow gallery was very professional.'

'And then you nearly lost the whole consignment by letting an interfering dealer into Farrans Court. If I hadn't taken care of that matter myself—'

'But, Niki—'

'I'm tired of clearing up your messes!' Jane held the receiver away from her ear as the Greek shouted his anger. 'I'm sending my own people over again to look after things.'

'Niki, just give us a couple more days.'

'We don't have a couple more days. The shipment is due out on the twenty-seventh. Everything is arranged. Thanos will be with you tonight. Wait for him. Tell him everything you know. Then you'd better pray that he finds the Raphael. If my consignment is short, Thanos has his instructions.'

The line went dead.

'Bingo!' Seated in a nondescript Ford Escort a few streets away, Tim smiled as he removed the headphones. He was inclined to agree with Niki Karakis. Jane and her cronies *were* incompetent. Burglary and GBH just about encompassed their entire repertoire. When it came to any crime requiring intelligence, he could run rings round the lot of them.

Given the names Jane and Bernie Stevens, and knowing that there were only three major international art-theft syndicates currently operating in Europe, it had actually been quite easy to track down the British end of the network. Enquiries through friends in the police and the art world resulted in converging streams of information. They had brought him to the Prentice Gallery. After that it was only a question of a little electronic gadgetry and a great deal of patience. For five days he had recorded all the crooked dealer's phone conversations on tape, and played them over in the evenings. It was a bit of luck that the vital call had come through now, when he was here to check the equipment.

He grinned broadly. 'Lacy, you're a genius. You were absolutely right. It *is* Niki Karakis, and he *is* impatient.'

There had been an element of inspired guesswork in his calculations. The Greek cartel had *seemed* the most likely and it was *probable* that they were running out of time. Now, both these hunches had been proved right. Now, he could bait the traps; and not a moment too soon. He checked his watch. It was time to leave for his meeting at the Savoy.

Fifty minutes later Tim entered the hotel suite. On the way he had called to collect the painting now lodged for safety in his bank. Jean-Marc Laportaire greeted him affably, a slightly raised eyebrow the only interest he displayed in the bulky brown-paper parcel. He had already ordered coffee, and for some minutes the two men sat in deep armchairs exchanging pleasantries.

Tim set down his empty cup and declined a refill. 'Jean-Marc, I'm very grateful to you for rearranging your schedule at such short notice, but I can assure you you won't regret it.' He was brimming with confidence. There was no way any top dealer could resist *The Triarchs*.

The elegant Frenchman uncrossed his legs and automatically rearranged the trouser crease. 'The tone of your phone-call was both urgent and mysterious. I assume therefore that this matter, whatever it is, is of great importance.'

'I want you to handle the sale – the very discreet sale – of a painting.'

'That depends, my friend. You know that I deal only in items of top quality.'

'I shan't disappoint you on that score.'

The Frenchman's relaxed smile betrayed no curiosity as Tim propped the parcel on a gilt console table and began to untie the string. Beneath the brown paper was a layer of soft material. When Tim had folded this back from the surface of the canvas he stood to one side, with the air of a magician reaching the climax of his best trick.

Laportaire made no move, but an intake of breath and a sudden widening of the eyes indicated his excitement. 'I did wonder . . . because of our last conversation . . . but I dismissed the thought as being highly improbable . . .'

He fell silent and remained absolutely motionless. For a full two minutes he surveyed *The Triarchs* from a distance, brow lined in total concentration, head occasionally nodding or shaking. Tim was aware of the distant hum of traffic in the Strand. At last the dealer went across to the picture and scrutinised its surface minutely. Then he picked it up and examined the back of the canvas. He replaced it against the wall, moved to the centre of the room, and stood gazing at it for several more seconds.

'Well?' Tim's patience collapsed under the strain.

The Frenchman replied slowly, deliberately. 'Always one must rid one's mind of what one *wishes* to see. Only that way can one arrive at a true critical judgement.'

'There's no doubt about its genuineness, is there?'

Laportaire would not be hurried. 'It was relined about a hundred years ago. The paint surface carries the signs of age: the pigment has flaked in one or two places and the craquelure,' he pointed to the minute cobweb of fissures which covered the picture, 'looks right for the period. The colours and the way some of them have darkened – as here in the greens and browns of the distant hills and trees – are exactly what one would expect in a sixteenth-century work.'

'So?'

Jean-Marc held up a hand. 'It is perfectly possible to fake all these things. Only when one has resolved each of them in the mind can one permit oneself to contemplate the more obvious elements: composition, style, "movement" and that indefinable feel of authenticity. And only at that stage may one allow the emotions to engage themselves. Does the painting set every fibre of one's soul tingling?'

This time Tim did not interrupt. At length Jean-Marc turned to him with an expression of the utmost seriousness. 'I would place this painting among the top ten Renaissance masterpieces in the world.'

Tim sank into a chair to conceal his deep sigh of relief. Everything, the whole elaborate plan, depended on Laportaire's co-operation. 'Then you will take care of the sale?'

The dealer resumed his seat and poured himself more coffee. 'Now that is what I believe you call a horse of a different colour. If I am to associate my name with this picture I must satisfy myself about its authenticity and provenance.'

'But you said it was genuine.'

'I am sure it is. But I could not offer it as such without having all the tests done: microscopy, X-rays, paint analysis. I must safeguard my reputation.'

'Yes, of course.' Tim nodded, but inwardly he was beginning to panic. There was no time for such verification. Karakis wanted news of the picture by the twenty-seventh: six days away. Venetia would refuse to stay hidden much longer. Tim had to move, and move immediately.

Laportaire continued, 'It is also essential for me to know where the painting came from. A work of this importance will create worldwide attention. Every major gallery and dozens of private collectors will want it. Inevitably there will be questions of export licences, perhaps even diplomatic exchanges. The press, of course, will pounce on the story. So, there must be no suggestion of anything louche, suspicious.'

Tim thought fast. The conversation was not going as he had hoped. Instead of jumping at the chance to handle the sale, the Frenchman was standing back. 'I didn't have in mind anything as ... public as that. As I said, it is important that the painting is disposed of discreetly.'

Laportaire frowned. 'Now that really does sound louche. A painting as significant and valuable as this to be sold in secret? My friend, if I did not know you better, I would suspect you of being involved in something shady. If you want me to help, you must tell me how *The Triarchs* came into your possession.'

Tim sighed, accepting the inevitable. 'The painting was stolen by Niki Karakis.'

'*Merde!*' The name penetrated Laportaire's patrician detachment. '*Cet excrément de la terre!*'

'Exactly. Where he got it, I don't know. Doubtless from someone who came by it equally dishonestly. Anyway, having acquired *The Triarchs*, the villainous Greek was careless enough to lose it. I can assure you, Jean-Marc, that it came into my possession quite by chance.'

'Karakis will not let matters rest there.'

'That's precisely what I am counting on. I thought if you could let it be quietly known that you have been asked to sell *The Triarchs*, Karakis would have to come into the open. You could tell him where to find it.'

'He is dangerous – and highly intelligent.'

'That's why I would have preferred you not to know that I am baiting a trap.'

'A trap?'

'Once Karakis sets foot in England, I'll make sure he doesn't leave it for a very long time. I've got evidence that will tie him to murder and several counts of grand larceny.'

'He will not come himself. He has many hardened criminals on the payroll.'

'They won't do him any good this time. The house where the painting will be is more secure than the Tower of London. I've had a team of men working on it for ten days. I defy any burglar to get in. And if he did, he wouldn't get out!' Tim thought of the three ex-army men currently fulfilling a dual function at Farrans, and handpicked for their combination of brawn and brain. As well as installing the most sophisticated surveillance and warning equipment, they were also very capable of handling any unauthorised visitors. 'Lacy Security' was nothing if not flexible in its approach to customers' problems, and it was the unconventional range of services offered which had enabled Tim's company to rise swiftly to the top in an overcrowded market. He was utterly confident that his arrangements at Farrans would prove more than a match for any criminal. 'If Karakis wants to get *The Triarchs* back – and I think he wants that very badly – he's going to have to come and trade for it.'

Laportaire straightened his tie – a nervous gesture. He shook his head thoughtfully. 'To close down the Athens operation . . . You would be doing the world a great service. But—'

'I can only do it with your help, Jean-Marc. Karakis must believe that I'm as crooked as he is and that I'm going to sell a stolen Raphael to the highest bidder. I could arrange an anonymous tip-off but he'd smell a rat. If he hears that a highly respectable art dealer is handling the business, I think he'll be caught off guard.'

It was several seconds before the Frenchman replied. 'A couple of years ago there was an explosion at the Galerie Serafine in Montmartre. Everything was destroyed: premises, stock, pictures taken in for restoration. The insurers refused to pay. My old friend, Victor Guyot, was ruined. The shock of it killed him. Some of us got together a fund for his widow. Now she is, thank God, well provided for. It was she who told me, several months after the atrocity, what poor Victor had been too frightened to tell the police. Apparently, a few days before the bombing, Karakis had asked him to sell three little Post-Impressionist pieces. Victor was suspicious. He turned Karakis down.'

Tim took the point. 'I realise I'm asking you to take a risk but I promise to keep your personal involvement to a minimum.'

'What exactly would you want me to do?'

'Inform some of your wealthier clients that a highly important Raphael has come on to the market, and that an English seller wishes to dispose of it very confidentially. I'll give you a phone number to pass on to anyone who asks to view the painting.'

'Phone numbers can be traced.'

Tim laughed. 'It will be the number of my mobile phone. Karakis will have no way of locating me, and no way of getting at the painting without making arrangements with me. Once I've lured him to Farrans Court – that's where I'll arrange the rendezvous – the rest will be up to the police.'

Laportaire stood up and took half a dozen slow paces towards the painting. He gazed at the young woman totally absorbed in her child, at the infant returning his mother's tender smile, at the magi standing or kneeling as intermediaries between the viewer and the private world of peaceful devotion. How could this be the motive force for violence, murder and human greed?

'I'll do what I can.'

Charles Stuart knelt at his prayer-desk, gazing up at Raphael's sublime portrayal of the Virgin and Christ child, before whom all kings, popes and emperors could only humble themselves in worship. Yet he could not, even at this moment, fasten his mind on holy thoughts. His eyes wandered to the empty wall beside *The Triarchs*. There had hung the portrait of George Villiers. Scarcely a day had passed during the last twenty years when the king had not thought of his friend, often with tears. How different things would have been if Buckingham had lived. *He* would have known how to handle parliament and preachers who showed no respect for their divinely-appointed sovereign, and jumped-up country squires who brought civil war upon the nation. But Buckingham was dead, his assassination the first in the long succession of tragedies which had befallen king and people, and culminated in civil war.

Buckingham was dead and his portrait stripped from the walls of Charles's bedchamber in Whitehall Palace. So were all the paintings, here and in the other royal residences; stolen and dispersed by the realm's new masters. More than one thousand seven hundred of the finest works of art ever created – brought together painstakingly over a lifetime, the best collection in the whole world, the envy of foreign monarchs; destined as a royal heritage for all future generations – now scattered or snapped up cheaply by gloating dealers to grace the halls of Charles's continental rivals or, worse still, the provincial hovels of his verminous enemies. Only *The Triarchs* was left. It survived because Charles carried it everywhere with him and because Sir Thomas Durville, in charge of the king's drastically reduced household, had preserved it from grasping hands. Dear Thomas, his devotion deserved far greater reward than it was now in his master's hands to give. Well, he would at least have the Raphael to remember his king by. Charles brought his eyes back to the serene gaze of the Virgin and resumed his prayers.

Minutes later there was a knock at the door. The king crossed himself, rose and received Archbishop Juxon with complete composure. Flanked by an armed escort, the two men left the bedchamber, passed through a series of bare rooms, and entered the banqueting hall, its ceiling vibrant with the celebration of divine monarchy painted by Rubens to Charles's commission. A window at the far end had been removed. Through this the little group passed on to the specially-erected platform. There, the soldiers, the executioner and a silent crowd waited in the bitterly cold January air.

Jean-Marc struck gold sooner than Tim dared hope. On Tuesday morning the Frenchman called to say that he had just had Karakis on the line.

'He used a different name, of course, but I am sure it was him, so you should be hearing from the villainous little man at any time. Incidentally I have also received two very serious enquiries, one from Switzerland and one from Amsterdam. I stalled them, of course, but when the painting is available for sale I shall have no difficulty placing it for you. I must return to Paris this evening. You will keep me informed, won't you?'

'Yes, of course, Jean-Marc, and many, many thanks for all your help. As soon as I've nailed this bastard, Karakis, I'll certainly be in touch to talk turkey about the Raphael. I promise that when it's put on the market, no one but you will handle it.'

'Thank you, my friend. I shall look forward eagerly to that. Well, *bon courage avec le petit grec*, and please be careful, eh?'

Tim smiled at the older man's almost paternal concern as he switched off the handset and returned it to his attaché case. Then he completed the dictation of his daily batch of letters, put the tape into an envelope, and addressed it to his secretary. He had persuaded Sally to work from home, giving office redecoration as his excuse. She probably did not believe him, and she must certainly have thought it odd that he had the post office redirect all his mail to her, and only spoke to her on his mobile phone. But she was too good at her job to comment, and at least he knew that she was safe.

He gazed round the small, unimaginatively furnished flat with distaste. It was one of hundreds of similar drab living units in the back streets of Kensington, once fashionable but now run-down and easily obtainable on short rental. Just as much as Venetia, he was getting fed up with this disruption to his normal life. Like her he wanted the whole wretched business over quickly. Should he call her, to let her know that things were progressing well? His hand hovered over the open attaché case. Then he thought better of it. She would only ask questions, demand to know what was going on. And there was nothing he could tell her. Perhaps tomorrow.

The phone buzzed like a disturbed mosquito.

'Mr Lacy? My name is Cristopoulos. I have been given your name by Monsieur Laportaire of Paris.'

Tim recognised the voice instantly. His response was casual.

'I presume you're interested in my Raphael?'

'I have a modest but very high-quality collection to which I am always interested in adding. What can you tell me about your painting?'

Tim thought of the ruthless murderer on the other end of the satellite beam, and enjoyed seeing him come cautiously within his grasp. It was like playing with a kitten – albeit a very dangerous one. Having dangled the ball of wool before it, he now tweaked it away. 'I'm sure you will have received an excellent report from Monsieur Laportaire. It is, indisputably, one of the artist's finest works. That is why I am obliged to dispose of it privately. I don't want a lot of hassle over export permits. I expect to sell within a few days.'

'You sound very sure.'

'I've already been approached by some of the more obvious people in the field.'

'When would it be possible for my representative to see it?'

'I only deal with principals.'

That stung Karakis. He muttered something in Greek. Then added, 'Mr Lacy, I'm a very busy man. I can't drop everything at a moment's notice to come to England.'

'With respect, Mr Cristopoulos, any really serious collector would do just that. This is the chance of a lifetime. The painting is well authenticated, and I am prepared to submit it to whatever tests a prospective buyer may require. On that understanding I already have three customers coming to see it in the next few days.'

Tim held his breath, waiting for the kitten to pounce.

Karakis took his time. 'You have the painting in London?' he asked at last.

'No, it's in the country.'

'How will I find the place?'

'If you're genuinely interested, I'll fax you the details.'

He could almost hear Karakis purr with satisfaction. 'If you send me the directions straight away, I will come tomorrow evening.'

'That will be perfectly satisfactory, Mr Cristopoulos. Shall we say about eight o'clock?'

The brief conversation ended when Karakis carefully gave his fax number. Tim immediately sent to Athens the typed directions to Farrans Court which he had prepared.

Then he made another phone-call. It was even shorter.

'George, everything quiet so far? . . . Good . . . Well, I reckon you can expect company tonight.'

Venetia gave Tim four days. On Tuesday, when she had received not so much as a hurried phone-call since his last brief visit, she decided to take her life back into her own hands. It was the tasteless Chinese meal that was the final straw – that and the rain. She had gone for lunch to one of the three restaurants within walking distance, in the conviction that eating alone in a mediocre café was marginally preferable to eating alone, yet again, at the hotel. She had been wrong. The spring rolls seemed to be wrapped in soggy wallpaper, and the prawns should have carried a government health warning. She had emerged, unsatisfied, into a drab street upon which a disconsolate sky was weeping profusely. Too depressed to run or seek shelter, she just let the rain soak right through her clothes as she squelched back to the hotel.

She peeled off the loathed garments and, draped only in a towel, sat down on the bed and put a call through to directory enquiries. She dialled the number provided by the BT computer.

'Baron's of Bond Street.' A woman's voice, cultured and aloof.

'Oh, good afternoon . . . I wondered whether I might have a word with Mr . . .' Venetia checked the name she had circled in the newspaper. 'Mr ffrench-Digges.'

'Mr ffrench-Digges is with clients at the moment.' The voice managed to imply that a multi-million deal was in progress, and that the proprietor of Baron's really could not be bothered with trivialities. 'If you would like to leave your name and telephone number . . .' The suggestion was left floating in the air that Mr ffrench-Digges might just condescend to return the call – if he had nothing better to do.

Venetia supplied the information, put the receiver down, and began to run a bath. Minutes later she was just about to step into the steaming water when the phone rang.

'Miss Cranville? Miss Venetia Cranville?' a man intoned reedily.

'Yes.'

'Giles ffrench-Digges here. I'm so sorry I was tied up when you rang. And I'm so very glad you did ring,' he added hurriedly.

'I noticed . . . in the newspapers.'

'Yes, yes, of course. Well I am very *interested* in arranging an exhibition and most *grateful* to you for getting in touch.' Venetia noticed that he overstressed most of his adjectives. 'The thing is, I've admired your work ever since I saw some *first-class* examples which Edward Gore showed me a couple of years ago . . .'

Eddie had taken some of her pictures from time to time, and

displayed them in his Hampstead shop.

'Then, when I saw your name in the press, connected with that most *distressing* incident . . . well, it sort of triggered my memory. I say, could we possibly meet? Whereabouts are you?'

Venetia hesitated, inhibited by Tim's elaborate security arrangements. 'Well, I'm in Manchester, but I could easily get down to London.'

'I quite understand your predicament, Miss Cranville. The *ever intrusive* media, eh? Well, look, why don't I pop up and see you. Tomorrow? Lunch?'

'That seems to be putting you to an awful lot—'

'No trouble at all, Miss Cranville. I am *most* anxious to meet. I'm sure we can arrange an *extremely* successful show – if we plan it carefully. I really am enormously *excited* at the prospect. If you can find your way to the Grand Hotel, I'll meet you there about twelve-thirty. How does that sound?'

Venetia was overwhelmed. Could this be her big break? Was a West End dealer really falling over backwards to display her work? If so, she could add a nought to all her prices, perhaps even attract some expensive commissions.

'That sounds marvellous, Mr ffrench-Digges.'

'Oh, please. That's such a mouthful. My friends call me F.D.'

At three-twenty-three a.m. and seventeen seconds an electric bell rang in what had once been one of the extensive range of domestic offices at Farrans Court. None of its previous owners would have recognised the use to which the old scullery was now being put. Newly-fitted shelves along one wall supported a dozen television screens and several other pieces of electronic gadgetry. The large deal table supported a map of the house and grounds, wired to a small grey box. It was the box which now emitted the high-pitched trill.

George Martin, a thick-set man in his early forties, wearing a navy-blue tracksuit, straightened himself in the down-at-heel armchair beside the table. He put down the paperback he had been reading. He flicked a switch on the box beside him, and it fell silent. But one of the tiny lights which formed concentric circles on the ground plan of Farrans continued flashing.

Martin eased himself out of the chair, crossed the room, and shook the recumbent figure on a camp bed in the corner by the door. 'Upsa-daisy, Pete. We've got customers.'

Peter Cole, younger than his companion by some five years, though the bald head and drooping moustache made him look older, was instantly awake. He threw off the blanket and came over to the table. He, too, wore the dark two-piece working outfit Tim Lacy supplied to his employees. He looked down at the flashing light. 'North-east corner,' he observed dispassionately.

Martin nodded. 'They probably came over where the wall's broken down along the Shalbourne road.' He was holding a walky-talky and prodding the call button rapidly. 'Come on, Jerry, you bastard!' He scowled. 'Bloody Jerry, asleep on the job again! If I have to go up there in person . . .'

The machine in his hand responded. 'Yeah?' A bored voice.

'What took you so long?'

'It's all right for you. It's bloody freezing up here on the tower.'

'Well, wake your ideas up. We're in business. Intruders have just entered the grounds about seven o'clock from your position. Get your glasses on that band of trees, I'll let you know as soon as they emerge.'

Three minutes later a new light flashed on the map, indicating that another sensor in Farrans's minefield of buried detectors had been set off.

Martin spoke into the walky-talky again. 'OK, Jerry, they're out of the trees now and heading towards the house, more or less in a line with the north corner of the stables.'

'Hang on a jiff. Let's have a look-see.' High on the squat tower which rose directly above the entrance porch of the house, Jerry O'Conor cupped gloved hands around his night-scanner and propped himself against the low, crenellated wall. He directed his image-intensifying binoculars over the sprawl of the house below him to the sweep of gently-rising parkland beyond the outbuildings. To the naked eye, landscape and sky were a wall of blackness relieved only by the myriad pinpricks of the stars, but Jerry's night-vision equipment brought him a world of detail in grey tones. He soon spotted the moving figures.

'Got 'em, George. Two men in dark clothes and Balaclavas. They're coming along, very casually, beside the overgrown carriage drive.'

'What are they carrying?'

'One's got a bag over his shoulder. No obvious sign of weapons.'

'Right! Sounds as though they're pretty cocksure. Keep your eyes on 'em. Let me know if they change their line of approach.'

Within a minute O'Conor reported that the interlopers had passed out of his vision in the lee of the square stable-block. Almost instantly the two men in the scullery picked up an image on one of the TV screens. A torch beam moving across the yard. Another camera then followed the intruders' progress from the stables to the rear terrace of the main house. George called Jerry again. 'OK, you can come down now and join in the fun.'

O'Conor had just entered the room when a buzzer and a flashing green light indicated that the main back door of Farrans was being forced. Martin grinned at his companions, and nodded. He slipped on a pair of dark leather gloves, flexed his fingers, and felt the strips of metal sewn into the lining. O'Conor weighed a short truncheon in his hand; its thong looped securely round his wrist. Cole, who had once been a regimental light-heavyweight champion, was satisfied with those weapons with which nature had endowed him. He dowsed the light and the three defenders of Farrans moved silently out into the kitchen.

They went over to the far door. Martin and O'Conor stepped swiftly across the screens passage and into the great hall, via a massive oak portal which opened on well-oiled hinges. Cole remained beside the part-open kitchen door. In the silence of the old house's lofty chambers the three men waited.

Not for long. The intruders entered the passage from a door at the far end, making no attempt at silence.

'It's this way.' A London voice was brimful of confidence. 'Nah,' in answer to a muffled query. 'These are only servants' quarters, kitchens and the like. Won't be anything there.'

The speaker led the way. His torch found the door to the great hall. 'Through here,' he announced, pushing it wide and playing the beam of light over ancient panelling and weapons arranged in patterns high on the wall. The two would-be burglars stepped into the long, echoing chamber.

What happened next was noisy, chaotic and brief. George and Jerry waded into the intruders, who were taken completely off their guard. One tried to dodge back into the passage, and walked straight into Pete Cole's right cross. Within a couple of minutes the two burglars were expertly trussed and lying on the cold kitchen flagstones, their Balaclavas removed.

'Who have we got here, then?' The Irishman prodded one of the recumbent forms with his truncheon. 'Tell us your name, rank and number, sonny.'

'Eff off!' Bernie Stevens' defiant glare was partially spoiled by a rapidly closing right eye.

'What about your mate, then?' O'Conor prodded the lithe, dark stranger with his foot.

The man muttered something in a language his captors did not understand.

Jerry laughed. 'Oh, no-speaka-da-Engleesh, eh?'

'OK, leave it.' George moved towards the door. 'I'm going to report to the major. Jerry, you slip out to the road and make sure they haven't got any back-up waiting there.'

'Why me?' The Irishman was heavily indignant. 'Mother of God, I've been stuck up on that tower the last two hours. It's someone else's turn in the cold.'

George grinned. 'That's what comes of being the junior member of the outfit. Off you go!'

O'Conor called Martin a sadistic bastard, but left the room quickly.

Back in the operations centre, George picked up the radio phone to give his boss an account of the night's events. Tim Lacy answered immediately, and listened attentively to the ex-marine sergeant's admirably concise report.

'Excellent, George, excellent! And you're sure they're carrying no ID?'

'Searched 'em thoroughly, sir. Not so much as a bus ticket. The Englishman was carrying only a Smith and Wesson .38 and the dago had a very nasty flick-knife. Of course, we could get any info you want out of 'em.'

'Tempting, George. But better leave interrogation to the police. I'll be down there first thing in the morning with the local constabulary. Meanwhile—'

'Hang on a minute, sir. I've got Jerry coming through on the walky-talky.'

George picked up the handset and had a brief conversation with the Irishman. Not a pleasant conversation. Martin roundly cursed his underling and expressed his doubt over several generations of his ancestry.

'What's up, George?' Tim asked when his *chef d'équipe* came back on the line.

Martin was fuming. 'That stupid bastard O'Conor's let one of 'em get away. They had a car waiting on the road. Mercedes. Instead of approaching it cautiously he just "assumed" it was empty and went bowling up, bold as brass. Of course, the driver saw him, panicked, and roared off into the distance.'

Tim chuckled. 'Don't be too hard on Jerry, George. It could have turned out very well. The sooner their boss man hears that his plans have gone down the pan, the better. Keep a watch out for any return visit and I'll be with you around nine-thirty.'

When Gantry arrived at Wessex police HQ, Tim was already waiting in the outer office. The inspector was not pleased to see him.

'And to what, sir, do we owe this pleasure?'

'Look, Inspector, I realise I'm not exactly *persona grata* around here . . .'

'I'm glad we've managed to make that clear.'

'But I've got a lead on the case, and I knew you'd want me to pass the information on to you straight away.'

Gantry turned his eyes upward in a silent appeal for divine succour. 'You'd better come through.' He led the way to his sanctum.

He sank heavily into his chair. 'Well, I suppose I should at least be thankful that you haven't been making any more of your citizen's arrests.'

Tim took the seat opposite. 'Funny you should say that, Inspector.'

Gantry groaned. 'Oh no! Tell me it isn't true.'

Tim decided to press on with the facts. 'In the early hours of this morning there was a break-in at Farrans Court. Fortunately, some of my employees were there . . .'

'Purely by chance, of course.'

128

Tim ignored the sarcasm. 'They overpowered two of the criminals, both of whom were armed and dangerous. They're now awaiting your pleasure at Farrans.'

For some moments Gantry stared silently at his visitor. Then he sighed deeply. 'All this happened several hours ago, you say, and yet only now has it been reported to the police. It didn't occur to you to let us in on your private war as soon as possible, so that we could get a proper investigation under way?'

'Since we have the culprits—'

'Mr Lacy, I'm tired of having cowboys galloping all over rural England as though it was the Wild West frontier. Now,' he struggled for self-control, 'if you have any more information, I would be extremely obliged if you would give it to me – all of it – and then go away and leave everything else to those of us who are paid to do this sort of thing. Contrary, perhaps, to your opinion, we do happen to know something about our job.'

Tim smiled. 'Gladly, Inspector. That's precisely why I'm here. Right, point number one . . . er, you might want to make a few notes, Inspector.'

Gantry muttered something under his breath but pulled a pad and a biro across the desk.

'Point number one, there are two criminals currently in custody at Farrans Court. Point two, I think you will discover that one of them is Bernie Stevens, and the other a Greek alien. Point three, they are both in the employ of one Niki Karakis.'

Gantry looked up, sharply. 'Karakis. That name rings a bell.'

'He's one of the world's top dealers in stolen art. The Met's art and antiques squad or the Interpol bureau at Scotland Yard can give you a complete dossier on his suspected activities.'

'I don't need a lecture on internal police communications, Mr Lacy.'

'All I was trying to say was that the police of several countries have wanted to get their hands on Karakis for a long time. But he's too clever. They've never been able to make anything stick.' Tim leaned forward across the desk and put all the force he could muster behind his next words. 'I can deliver Niki Karakis to you tonight, with enough evidence to tie him to the Grosmith murder. More than that: you could pull in all the members of his British network and close the case on several major thefts over the last few years.'

Gantry swivelled his chair round and stared out of the window for several seconds. Then he turned back to the desk, picked up the phone and said, 'Dawson, get in here.'

A detective sergeant entered.

'Dawson, take a car and a couple of men and go over to Farrans Court. Collect two break-in suspects. Also bring back anyone else you find at the house – I presume they have their own transport – and take statements from them. Have forensic send a team over as well, to get evidence of forced entry.'

When the sergeant had left, Gantry pushed the writing pad across the desk. 'Right, now I want a *full* statement from you.'

Tim took three sheets of folded typescript from an inside pocket. 'I've already done that, Inspector. I thought it might save time.'

Gantry read slowly Tim's account of how he had tracked down the Greek and tricked him into believing that an unspecified missing picture from Karakis's hoard was still at Farrans. Tim watched anxiously, knowing that his determination to omit all reference to *The Triarchs* left obvious holes in his narrative.

The inspector did not miss the weak point.

'I don't see how you managed to convince Karakis that you'd got his vanished masterpiece.'

'Sheer bluff!' Tim hurried on. 'Anyway, it seems to have worked. He wouldn't have sent his minions last night if he didn't believe my story.'

'Hm! So you're expecting him to show up at eight o'clock.'

'That's right. And he's sure to have some of his heavies with him.'

'You think I should get my men to draw firearms.'

'You've seen what his underlings are capable of, and the power he exerts over people. That sort of animal is most dangerous when he's unsure of himself. If I were you, I'd want to lay on a large, well-armed reception committee.'

'Easy enough for you to say that. Do you know what's involved: getting authority, diverting officers from other duties, bringing men in on overtime, obtaining permission to draw firearms? And to cap it all, it's the wife's birthday. We were going out for dinner. First time in months. Mr Lacy, you'd just better be right about this. You've caused me a hell of a lot of embarrassment already. If anything goes wrong this evening ... Oh, get out. I'll see you at Farrans Court about six-thirty. That should give us enough time to set everything up.'

King Charles I's possessions were all forfeit to Parliament. Indeed, his art collection – the finest ever amassed by an English monarch and, arguably, the finest private collection of all time – had been confiscated and dispersed by the king's enemies long before his death. However, the Raphael was numbered among the pitifully small group of objects – mostly minor items of jewellery and clothing – which the royal prisoner was permitted to bequeath to the handful of servants who attended him right to the end.

In those sad last days Sir Thomas Durville's office of Master of the Household had amounted to little more than getting the king's laundry done, ensuring that his meals did not fall below an acceptable standard, and losing small sums at cards or chess so that Charles could order a few little luxuries. His reward was *The Triarchs* and a few trinkets – a shirt, a lace collar, a pair of gloves – that he ever afterwards kept as mementos or relics in a casket beside his bed.

Durville, a weary forty-eight at the time of the king's execution, was allowed to retire to his estates in Derbyshire, where he lived quietly during the Commonwealth. Throughout those difficult years he seldom left his beloved Calton Durville in the quiet valley of the Dove, far from the rantings and antics of the new rulers of a topsyturvy England. Not that he could afford anything more than a subdued rural existence. Like all leading Royalists, Durville was subjected to a heavy fine by the triumphant Republicans. His lands were mortgaged to the uttermost. His staff was cut to a minimum. It became his constant worry that he would have nothing but debts to leave to his son, Harry. So, grey, prematurely aged and feeling that he had already lived too long, Sir Thomas passed his time poring over account books to ensure that rents and dues were promptly paid, repairing his own walls and felling his own timber to save the cost of hired labour, and praying daily for the soul of his late king.

Every morning he spent the first waking hour on his knees in the small chapel close to his house, part of the original monastic buildings mercifully spared when the old abbey had been torn down by Thomas's grandfather to provide the stone for his fine new house. It was here that *The Triarchs* had pride of place. It hung on the east wall, above where the altar (broken up by local religious zealots) had once stood. Before it Thomas knelt daily, as his master had done, solaced by its tranquillity, its quiet assurance that the ordinary world of terrestrial hills and valleys, of mothers and children, of kings and politics, is unobtrusively yet unquestionably permeated by the divine. In a land where, until recently, neighbour had taken arms against neighbour, brother against brother, son against father, that was profoundly reassuring. Scarcely a day passed when Thomas did not find something new in the picture, something which vibrated in sympathy with his own thoughts, or drew echoing melodies from memory. Sometimes the Virgin reminded him of Elizabeth, dead since the birth of their second surviving child, John. On other occasions the serious yet smiling infant led him to pray for studious Harry, working as a lawyer in London and pledged to redeem his inheritance. Try as he might, Thomas could find nothing reminiscent of the infant John in the serene Christ child. His younger son had fought with conspicuous bravery in the recent wars, and had subsequently escaped to France, where he lived at the court of the exiled heir to the throne, whom Royalists already called Charles II. John was wild, exuberant and enthusiastic. He never lacked for friends and never had a penny in his purse. Thomas worried about his younger son. Yet it was John, rather than responsible, plodding Harry, who suddenly and dramatically prospered.

On 25 May 1660 bonfires and church bells ecstatically announced the return of the monarchy. John Durville was among the retinue of Charles II which came ashore at Dover and basked in the cheers of a populace in festive mood all the way along the road to London. A week later he arrived home.

It was an afternoon of watery half-sunshine when the young man clattered into the courtyard, jumped from the saddle and flung the reins to an astonished servant who had rushed out of the house.

'Where's my father?' John threw off his travelling cloak to reveal a costume heavy with braiding and expensive embroidery.

'He's in the garden, sir. May I say, sir, what a pleasure—' But the 29-year-old courtier was already striding away round the side of the house.

He came upon the old man in the middle of the lawn, deep in

earnest conversation with an estate worker leaning on his scythe. He ran across the grass, calling his father's name. Sir Thomas turned and embraced his son, with tears of surprise and joy in his eyes.

Minutes later they were seated in the parlour, with goblets of the best Canary wine the cellars of Calton Durville could provide, the father pouring out questions and scarcely giving John time to answer. 'We've been starved of news, son. You never wrote.'

'I was afraid it might be dangerous for you to receive letters from the court. There were all manner of rumours in France about Cromwell's men taking revenge on the families of people close to the king.'

'Well you're safe home now. Though I fear it is not much of a home. The cursed Roundheads have stripped us almost bare.'

John smiled broadly. 'But that is all behind us. You have yet to hear my best news.' He leaned forward in the cane-back chair. 'I have grown very close to the king these last years.'

'You have served him well. He should be grateful.'

'Perhaps. He is also very conscious of your faithfulness to his father. And he wanted to show his love for our house. Well, you know Lord Keston?'

Thomas recalled that he had on a few occasions met the earl, who had commanded large estates in the North before going into exile with the young Charles Stuart.

'The old man is enormously rich.'

'His lands have been forfeit.'

'But they will all be restored now. Anyway, his wife is French and her property is across the water. So he had plenty of cash and could afford a handsome dowry for his only child, Henrietta. The girl is sixteen now, and of course there was lots of competition for her, but who do you suppose his majesty persuaded old Keston to marry her off to?'

'John, that is splendid news.'

The young man beamed at his father's pleasure. 'We were wed a month since. Eleven thousand pounds and a jointure of one thousand five hundred by the year.'

'And the girl – she will be a good wife?'

'You shall meet her tomorrow, Father. She could come no nearer than Ashbourne. The road is too bad for our carriage.'

'Carriage?'

'Ay, Father, a fine new carriage and four splendid horses, as befits the daughter of an earl.'

Sir Thomas Durville smiled at his son's happiness and enthusiasm – and could not say why he felt a sense of foreboding.

Tim spent the rest of Wednesday at Farrans. He went round the house and the grounds, personally checking all the security equipment. When George and the others returned from giving their statements, he went over the arrangements for the Karakis visit. In the midst of a busy day he made time to call Venetia, and was put out to discover that she was not in her room.

Gantry arrived with three carloads of policemen soon after 6.15. Under Tim's direction the vehicles were concealed in the coachhouse. With the inspector beside him, he led the way across the courtyard to the back entrance of Farrans.

'The chances of Karakis coming alone are absolutely zero. My guess is that he'll have the place surrounded by his own men.'

Gantry nodded. 'For once we're in agreement. I've been doing a bit of research on our friend. Very nasty piece of work. The Athens police are drooling at the possibility of seeing him behind bars. They couldn't have been more co-operative.'

'They'll be looking forward to interrogating Karakis and his confederates themselves. This evening's work will be quite a feather in your cap, Inspector.'

'Huh! I'm not counting my chickens yet, Mr Lacy.' Gantry decided he had let the mask of formality and disapproval slip too far. 'Still,' he conceded, 'it seems you were right about Karakis coming over here. Our Greek colleagues report that he left Athens suddenly this morning on his private jet. The pilot filed a flight plan for Stansted, and he touched down there just before eleven-thirty. According to airport police, Karakis was collected by car and drove off, presumably towards London.'

'Excellent. Did you get anything out of those two thugs we caught last night?'

'No, they're pros. Not a squeak till they've seen their lawyer.'

'That'll change when you bring in Karakis. It'll be every man for himself then.' Tim opened a door and ushered the policeman into a long, flagged rear corridor lit by naked bulbs.

Gantry shivered. 'What a bloody great barn of a place this is. I hope you've got a decent fire going somewhere.'

'There's half a tree blazing merrily in the great hall, and also some soup, sandwiches and whisky for you and your men. But first, Inspector, I think you'll want to see our little nerve centre.'

He led the way through the maze of old pantries, store-rooms, laundries and still-rooms to the ex-scullery where George Martin and Jerry O'Conor sat at one end of the table, playing pontoon.

'Good God!' Gantry's gaze took in the racks of electronic equipment. 'Looks like a bloody military command post.'

'We like to think so, sir.' Ex-sergeant Martin rose from the table.

For the next quarter of an hour Tim explained how the external surveillance system worked, and suggested how Gantry might best dispose his forces.

'We'll know exactly where Karakis's men are.' Tim pointed to the map. 'So, as soon as he's safely inside the building, we can go and mop up the opposition.'

The inspector nodded grudgingly. 'Looks all right on paper,' he admitted. He turned to a uniformed sergeant. 'Got the picture, Jenkins?' He issued his orders, then turned back to Tim. 'Now, Mr Lacy, I think you said something about a decent fire and some whisky.'

In the hall all the comfortable chairs Tim could find had been arranged in a wide semicircle around the huge fireplace, which radiated heat from a stack of large blazing logs. As the task force ate and drank appreciatively, he pointed out the tactical possibilities to Gantry.

'I thought, Inspector, you could, perhaps, have someone up there in the gallery – armed, just in case Karakis tries anything – and a couple of men waiting in the screens passage, ready to come in as soon as you've made the arrest. When that's done we can communicate with the officers outside, and round up any other visitors.'

Gantry shook his head. 'I think I'll feel happier with a couple of my men in the hall here, behind some of those dirty great bits of furniture. Karakis is sure to have at least one of his heavies with him – and probably more in his car.'

'With your permission, Inspector, my chaps should be able to take care of the car.'

They spent several more minutes sorting out the finer details. Tim was conscious of feeling very proprietorial about Farrans. He could imagine himself as some Civil War Cranville preparing to defend the grand old house against a Roundhead attack. The inspector, for his part, took up his rôle with far less enthusiasm. His doubts about the whole operation were obvious, and more than once he referred to a disgruntled Mrs Gantry sitting at home, deprived of her birthday treat.

At 7.30 all the men were dispersed to their various stations. Jerry cleared away the evidence of the meal. Then Tim and Gantry sat by the fire, waiting and checking their watches every few minutes.

They were still waiting at 8.00. And at 8.10. At 8.15 Gantry said, 'He's not going to show.' Tim called Martin on the walky-talky.

'Any sign of life outside, George?'

'Quiet as the grave, Major.'

Tim shook his head at Gantry and the two men continued to sit in depressed silence.

At 8.23 there was a buzz on Tim's mobile phone. With a start he grabbed it up from the floor beside him.

'Mr Lacy?' It was Karakis.

'Yes. What . . .?'

'I'm afraid there's been a change of plan. There will be no need for us to discuss a purchase price on the Raphael. You're going to give it to me.'

'What makes you think . . .?'

'One moment, please, and all will become clear.'

There were a few cracks and rustles at the other end of the line. Then Tim heard a different voice. A woman's. Venetia's.

'Tim? Oh, Tim!' The register was high-pitched, taut, very frightened. 'Tim, for God's sake do whatever they ask. They're terrifying people.'

Karakis came back on the line. 'I don't think I need elaborate. We'll talk again tomorrow. Be available on this number at 11.00 a.m. precisely. Miss Cranville's life and Raphael's masterpiece are both in your hands. Be very, very careful with them, Mr Lacy.'

PART II

PROFIT AND LOSS

'. . . all those who attain to great riches and great power have done so either by fraud or by force: and those things which they have usurped, either by deceit or violence, they make honest under the false title of "profit", in order to conceal the ugliness of their acquisition.'

Niccolò Machiavelli:
The History of Florence

CHAPTER 7

'I take it that was our Greek friend? Smelled a rat, has he?' Everything about Gantry's manner shouted 'I told you so'.

Stunned, Tim stared into the fire, still clutching the phone. 'Yes . . . he smelled a rat.'

Suddenly the policeman was all energetic action. 'We might still be able to nab him. Give me that thing!' He stepped across and took the instrument from Tim's hands.

He checked a number in his notebook and punched it in. 'Stansted? Airport Police, please.' There was a long pause. 'Come on! Come on!' At last there was a response. Gantry explained succinctly what he wanted, and rang off.

He spent the next few minutes reassembling his men. He had nothing to say to Tim, and for that Tim was glad. Most of the police had left, and the two men were once again alone in the great hall when the return call came. Gantry listened silently to the brief message, said, 'Thank you, sergeant,' and handed the phone back to Tim.

'Karakis's plane took off ten minutes ago.' He turned towards the door.

Tim faced the other man. He struggled for words. 'Inspector, I'm sorry . . . I thought . . .'

'Yes, sir. Perhaps that's the problem. In future leave the thinking to those of us who are paid to do it.' He turned abruptly and went through the entrance porch to his waiting car. Tim followed.

Gantry climbed into the back seat. He glared at Tim. 'Well, Mr Lacy, that was all very interesting. But, as they say in the theatre,

139

"Don't call us. We'll call you." ' He slammed the door and the car crunched off down the drive.

Twenty minutes later Tim was on the road, heading back towards London. He opened the window a crack to let in frosty air. He had to think clearly. Take stock. Dispel the swirling emotions clouding his brain.

Lucky Gantry didn't ask what Karakis actually said. I was so shocked I might have told him. Then he'd have told me we mustn't give in to kidnappers. Perhaps that's right. Perhaps I should call the Greek's bluff. Gain time. Track down where they're holding Venetia. The Prentice Gallery? Even if she's not there, Ms Prentice probably knows where they are holding her. A little bit of pressure in that quarter . . .

He remembered Karakis's words: 'Miss Cranville's life and Raphael's masterpiece are both in your hands.' Could he afford to gamble with either of them? Karakis wants *The Triarchs*, and he wants it very quickly. He won't harm Venetia as long as there's any chance of getting the painting . . . or will he? He's a powerful man, and all powerful men suffer, to a greater or lesser degree, from megalomania. No telling what Karakis will do if he's thwarted. Anyway, Venetia must have gone through hell already . . . Of course, it's her own fault. Why the hell couldn't she do as she was told: stay put, stay safe, and not louse up my plans? Still, I suppose I can't prolong her ordeal. What then? Just hand the painting over? Let Karakis make his millions out of it? Let it play its part in financing drugs and guns? Stand by and do nothing to hamper the appalling spread of narcoterrorism? Allow one of the world's greatest works of art to disappear without trace for another generation? All that has to be worth more than the life of one human being. Venetia said that the painting mattered more to me than she did. Well why not? *The Triarchs* is something immeasurably wonderful, and it's in my power to save it. Karakis and his organisation are unspeakably vile, and I can throw some grit in their works. All that stands in the way is one life. One dim woman who got herself kidnapped. Stupid cow!'

Tim was suddenly aware of the hire car's screeching engine. He glanced at the speedo's needle edging towards 100 mph and eased off the accelerator. He thought of men who had died for lesser causes. Friends. Brave soldiers who didn't think twice about putting their lives on the line for queen and country. And what about Venetia herself? She had not hesitated to snuff out an unborn human being. Why? Simply because its continued existence would have been inconvenient. Wasn't there some poetic justice about her life being forfeit for a greater cause?

All along the M4 and the Great West Road, Tim Lacy blundered through the labyrinth of his own mind. A fruitless exercise. There was never any real doubt what he must do. Yet he fought against it. He even turned off at the Hammersmith flyover and cut through towards Chelsea. He parked close to the Fulham Road and walked to the Prentice Gallery. The premises were in darkness, front and back. He climbed into a yard behind the shop. Not a sign of life anywhere. It would have been easy to force an entry, have a good scout round, see what he could discover. He did none of those things. He accepted the inevitable, went back to the Kensington flat, spent a sleepless night. Waited for the call from Karakis.

Henry Bennet, Earl of Arlington, was enormously proud of his new mansion in Suffolk. Not that it was, strictly speaking, new; Euston Hall had been bought from the Rookwoods soon after the Restoration. Yet its enlargement and its refurbishment in the fashionable French style had transformed it out of all recognition. The state rooms and the grand staircase were vibrant with the frescoes executed by Antonio Verrio, who had come straight to Euston from his extensive works at Windsor Castle. No expense had been spared on decorating and furnishing the lofty chambers. The house was the centre of its own little kingdom. Enclosed within a nine-mile wall was a landscaped park over which roamed a thousand head of deer. It featured a spectacular lake and a canal formed by diverting the local river. There was an orangery – the very latest idea from France – and little cupolas and arbours where Bennet and his guests might rest or be served refreshments by liveried servants. There were pleasure gardens with shaded walks and shrubs brought back from the orient and, closer to the elegant mansion itself, formal gardens where fountains sent their quivering jets arching over lilied pools. It all added up to a fitting statement about Lord Chamberlain Arlington, one of the richest and most powerful men in England.

Portly, pompous and self-seeking, Arlington was nobody's friend.

Courtiers often made fun of him for the little black patch he wore over his nose to draw constant attention to the scratch he had received in a minor Civil War skirmish. He was hated by some as a covert Catholic, despised by others as a pimp who kept Charles II supplied with bedfellows, and universally execrated as a man of humble origins who had wormed his way into the king's affections and was now one of the framers of state policy. Yet everyone who hoped for royal favour paid court to Lord Arlington, and were only too pleased to receive his patronage. That was why John Durville and his wife were at Euston in October 1671.

John, now forty and beginning to run to fat, had been created Baron Durville of Calton soon after the deaths, within a few months of each other, of his father and brother five years before. Since then his popularity at court had waned. Not so Henrietta's. Now a voluptuous twenty-seven and one of the undisputed beauties of the day, her amorous adventures were notorious. She made no effort to conceal them from her husband, nor did she hide her ambition to become one of the king's mistresses. She had grown into a black-haired termagant. 'The law permits you to do as you will with my estate,' she once screamed at John in one of their frequent rows, 'but I shall do as I please with my body.' In fact, the reality was not the bargain that Henrietta claimed.

Because of her taste in jewels, clothes and carriages, her insistence on running one large establishment in Hertfordshire and another in London, and her determination to maintain a 'proper' position in society, John had been brought to the brink of bankruptcy. What was left of the Keston estates was mortgaged three or four times over. Only John's own Durville inheritance, painstakingly freed from debt by his father and brother, remained unencumbered. There had been several occasions when Henrietta had demanded that he raise money against his Derbyshire lands to finance her latest extravagance. Why did he not sell them off and have done with them, she had wanted to know. They were only unproductive hill farms, and as for the manor house, well, she had never come across a more damp and poky little place. After her visit in 1660 she had consistently refused to set foot in Calton Durville again.

It was partly affection for his childhood home, partly loyalty to the

Dales families who had served his ancestors for generations, and partly the need to keep something between himself and total ruin, which determined John on retaining his property in the Dove valley. But with every passing month it became increasingly difficult to keep his creditors' hands off Calton Durville. There were only two possible ways of recouping the family fortunes. One was to hope for royal generosity in return for any services John and Henrietta might be able to perform. The other was gambling. Their stay at Euston Hall provided opportunities for exploiting both these sources of ready cash. The king had come into East Anglia to race his horses at Newmarket. Members of the court, many of whom were lodged at Euston, were there for their own intricate contests, games and petty intrigues. All of Arlington's two hundred guests vied for royal attention on the several occasions when the king rode over from Newmarket to dine or spend the night. In the intervals there was always gossip to pass the time.

Shrieks of female laughter splintered the air.

'But ladies, I assure you it is true. King Louis was absolutely furious.' The Comte de Goncourt was at his scandalmongering best as he regaled a small circle of ladies with the latest – embellished – news from Paris. His slender figure was shown to excellent advantage by the lilac breeches and purple surcoat, heavily embroidered with gold. The luxuriant, full wig softened his thin, cynical features.

It was a warm, languid afternoon such as only an English Indian summer can produce. The ladies sat along the stone edge of one of the pools, dipping their hands in the water, listening to Alphonse de Goncourt's outrageous stories and asking questions to show off their command of French. The young aristocrat held the stage like a professional, careful to flatter each member of his audience in turn with a smile or conspiratorial glance. Yet his real interest was in Lady Henrietta. It took him another half hour to detach her from her companions for a stroll along high-hedged avenues and across artificial glades where scarcely a fallen leaf had been permitted to mar the close-mown precincts.

Henrietta listened with amusement as the well-practised seducer turned the conversation by imperceptible degrees to the subject of passion. Suddenly she stood still. They had reached a wider arbour where stone benches were set in a semicircle.

'Please sit down, Monsieur le Comte.' She lowered herself on to one of the seats. 'No, over there, if you please' – this as de Goncourt tried to take his place beside her. Henrietta had been watching the young nobleman for some days and had concluded that he might make a useful ally. He was at Euston in the entourage of the French Ambassador, Charles Colbert, Marquis de Croissy. Few men were better placed to understand the secret diplomacy of the courts of Charles II and Louis XIV, which was the *real* diplomacy of Europe.

'You must not think of me as an easy conquest, Monsieur le Comte. You may win me; you may not. Who knows?' She favoured him with the wide-eyed smile most men found irresistible. 'But the game will be long and the rules are of my devising.'

De Goncourt opened his mouth to reply but Lady Durville held up a hand.

'What can you tell me about Louise de Kéroualle?' She named the Duchess of Orléans's young maid of honour, who was the principal subject of court gossip.

The Frenchman shrugged. 'She has a certain charm,' he offered cautiously.

Henrietta frowned her annoyance. 'She is exceedingly beautiful, and is being dangled before his majesty by Colbert and Arlington. Is that not so?'

'The king has expressed a desire to be better acquainted. He is tired, I think, of Lady Castlemaine.'

'Your master and the French party at court have been up to their stratagems for months. Everyone knows that! But what is behind it? Is this pretty little jade to be Old Rowley's next plaything, or is it designed to install her as *maîtresse en titre*?'

Casual bedfellows of the king could expect jewellery, houses, places at court for close relatives, cash payments amounting to a few thousands. But the king's official mistress could command titles, estates, monopolies and sources of wealth almost without limit.

'I think politics and pretty faces go together for this king. So it is said in Paris, and I think it is true. More importantly, Louis thinks it is true. If Mademoiselle de Kéroualle performs well enough in bed for Old Rowley, as you call him, to keep her on, it will help to confirm his loyalty to French interests.'

'And will she?'

'Milady?'

Henrietta frowned impatiently. 'Do not be obtuse, Monsieur le Comte! Will she perform well in bed?'

The exquisite little Frenchman shrugged. 'She is young – twenty-one or two, I think – vigorous and, it is said, not without experience.'

Lady Durville sat thoughtfully for several moments, smoothing the folds of her lime-silk gown. Then she abruptly changed the subject. 'You have brought some of your best horses to Newmarket, I believe.'

De Goncourt became suddenly animated at the mention of his second great passion. 'My two best stallions are here, Faucon and Triomphe. They are unbeatable on firm ground.'

'You have not raced them yet.' Henrietta raised an eyebrow. 'Some would say that your boasts are rather hollow.'

'Who says such things?' He laughed to cover his anger. 'The truth is no one dares challenge my horses or put up a worthwhile wager.'

Henrietta looked thoughtful. 'Oh, I am sure we can find your champions some worthwhile adversaries, Monsieur le Comte.' She stood suddenly. 'And now you may escort me back to the house.'

As they retraced their steps, the nobleman prattled away with inconsequential tittle-tattle of the great and the powerful. Henrietta heard scarcely a word. She was preoccupied with her own plans.

The telephone rang at 2.23 in the morning. Jean-Marc, always a light sleeper, was awake instantly. He lifted the receiver from its cradle on the bedside table.

'Monsieur Laportaire?'

'Yes.'

'Police here, monsieur. Sorry to trouble you. I believe you're the proprietor of Galerie Laportaire in the rue de Faubourg St Honoré?'

'That's correct.' Jean-Marc heard his heart beating fast in the silent bedroom. 'What's the matter?'

'We're investigating a break-in, monsieur. We've apprehended someone leaving the premises. We'd like you to come down and check that everything's all right.'

'Yes, of course. I'll come straight away.'

Five minutes later, the slim art dealer, managing to look elegant even in trousers and sweater, with his hair hastily brushed, was unlocking his garage. He took the Renault 5 Turbo which he always used in town. From his house in a quiet quarter near the Parc de Bagatelle he drove quickly to the Porte de Madrid and entered the route Mahatma Gandhi to cross the northern section of the Bois de Boulogne. The road and the surrounding parkland were deserted as he hurried towards the Museum of National Arts and the Carrefour des Sablons, thinking only of the problems which might be facing him at the gallery.

Suddenly another car came up behind, headlights blazing. Jean-Marc flicked the driving mirror to cut the blinding glare. The other driver seemed determined to pass. Without slackening speed, Jean-Marc kept well to the right. The other vehicle, a large white car, drew alongside. Laportaire's eyes were fixed on the road ahead. He did not see the open rear window and the muzzle of the submachine-gun.

Automatic fire flailed the Renault. Glass splintered. The driver's head flew apart. The car swerved off the road, engine racing. It bounced off a metal barrier, then a park seat. It smashed full-tilt into a wide tree trunk, and erupted into flames.

The call Tim Lacy received at precisely eleven o'clock the next morning was very brief. Karakis said, 'Phone your friend, Monsieur Laportaire. I'll get back to you in exactly half an hour.'

There was no reply from the gallery in the eighth *arrondissement*, so Tim tried Jean-Marc's home number. He heard the story from a near-hysterical housekeeper who gabbled in rapid, almost incoherent French. He understood enough to be almost physically sick.

'That wasn't necessary!' he shouted when the Greek phoned back.

'It has, I hope, made perfectly clear that no one fools around with me. You will realise that I am not bluffing when I say that Miss Cranville's life will be forfeit unless you follow to the letter the instructions you will be given. My representatives will contact you in a few minutes.' The line went dead.

Anger, guilt, fear – these and other emotions passed over Tim in waves as he paced around the cheap flat. There was no way he was prepared to be responsible for another violent death. Perhaps he would have to give up *The Triarchs*. But, by God, if he did, Karakis and his hirelings would pay dear for it!

The buzzing of the telephone broke into his dreams of vengeance.

'Mr Lacy, listen carefully.' Tim did not recognise the nondescript man's voice. 'The Craft Alliance Insurance building in Whittier Row, off Lombard Street, has an underground car park. Come there, with the picture, at seven o'clock this evening . . .'

'No!'

'Mr Lacy, you will do as you're told, or Miss Cranville . . .'

'I'm quite prepared to trade the painting but if you think I'm putting my life and Miss Cranville's at risk by meeting trigger-happy thugs in a deserted, underground car park you're crazy. Go away and come back with a better idea!'

Tim clicked the phone off and felt a bit better. What he had done was risky, but it was in line with a basic rule of military tactics: 'Whenever possible, keep the enemy guessing.' Anyway, he had made a gesture, and he definitely felt better for it.

When the crooks called next, they put a frantic Venetia on the line.

'Tim, for God's sake do what they say! You don't know what these people are like . . . They've already . . .' She broke down in tears. 'Oh, Tim, just get me out of here!'

Tim thought, that's exactly what I'm trying to do. He said, 'It'll soon be over, Venetia.' But she had already gone.

The man's voice returned. 'We're not playing games, Lacy. We want that painting today.'

'Fine. Meet me in the open where we can all see what's going on and we can get this business over as soon as you like.' He suggested a venue which provoked a spluttered protest at the other end of the line.

It took another two phone-calls to sort out the details. Tim guessed that the local heavies had needed to refer back to Athens before changing the plan. The fact that the plan *had* been changed meant that Karakis was not as sure of himself as he wanted Tim to believe.

As soon as the arrangements were complete, he called George Martin at Farrans on the radio phone.

'I want the three of you up here straight away, with small arms.'

'Expecting a spot of bother, Major?' Martin sounded pleased at the prospect.

'I hope not but I'm taking no chances.'

Henrietta began putting her plan into operation that night, as she and John prepared for bed in their commodious chamber. As soon as her hair had been brushed out she dismissed her maid.

'Were there many on the heath this afternoon?'

John arranged his wig carefully on the stand and scratched his close-cropped head. 'Not as many as yesterday, when the king's horses were running, but we had good sport. I won a hundred guineas off Mountjoy when William Percy's Troubadour beat Lord Graham's grey gelding.'

'And lost it all again this evening, I'll warrant.'

He scowled, not wanting another argument.

Before he could reply, his wife turned with a disarming smile. 'You have not raced Fleet yet?'

John dropped fully-clothed on to the solid four-poster bed. His head throbbed from Lord Arlington's excellent wine, of which he had drunk too freely all evening at the card table. 'No one who has seen him will take up the challenge. They all know what a prodigy my black devil is. At exercise this morning Charles Trevelyan on Touchstone tried us over an even mile. We came home half a furlong clear.'

Henrietta climbed on to the bed from the other side and knelt, looking down at her husband. 'If I could make a match for you, would it be worth a big wager?'

John rolled his head from side to side, then wished he had not. 'I'd back Fleet against any horse in the kingdom, but with what? Everyone knows I have precious little to stake my champion with.'

'You could put up your Derbyshire estate.'

John glowered, his cheeks red and hot. 'Not that tale again, madam! You know—'

'Listen, John. Listen.' She laid a hand on his mouth. 'There is a man here so vain that he cannot believe anyone else can best him at anything. In his eyes there is no finer horseman than himself, and no finer horses than the two stallions he has brought to Newmarket.'

'Who is this popinjay?'

'De Goncourt, one of Colbert's party.'

John laughed. 'Oh aye. I have seen that strutting peacock and heard his strident call.'

'Are his horses good?'

'Who knows? He is frightened to try them. He boasts what fine beasts they are, but when anyone offers a challenge he makes the stakes so high that no one can accept.'

She lay down beside him and rested a cool hand against his brow. 'You and Fleet could beat him, could you not?'

'I am sure of it.'

'Then what a marvellous opportunity. Call his bluff and you can win thousands on one race.'

He frowned. 'You're scheming something.'

'Only how to restore our fortunes.'

He wanted to think clearly but the wine, the soft bed and the nearness of a woman who, for all her faults, still excited his passion, sapped his will. He put out an arm to draw Henrietta closer. She was soft and smelled of rosewater. 'I will think about it tomorrow.'

Henrietta rolled away from him. 'Oh! Is this the decisive cavalier who led the breakout of the royal cavalry at the siege of Worcester?' She pulled up the chemise which had fallen open, and covered her breasts again. 'The best things only come to a man who knows his own mind.'

John propped himself on one elbow and gazed down at his wife. A sardonic smile hovered round her lips. Her dark eyes mocked him. Her hair spread out over the pillow like strands of black silk. 'Very well, little witch. Tell me what sorcery you are conjuring up now.'

Henrietta's plan – the details of which she only partially confided in her husband – was two-pronged. If one part worked, she and John would receive a much-needed cash prize. But if she could bring off the other aspect of her grand design, everything she had ever dreamed of would be within her grasp. No day passed in which Lady Durville's mind did not dwell enviously on the most powerful person at court. Barbara Villiers, Countess of Castlemaine, with her flashing blue eyes and auburn hair, had been *maîtresse en titre* for ten years. Her influence over the king and her impact on policy had first amused, then become the despair of ministers and diplomats. Even the most powerful politicians had come to realise that winning Charles to their viewpoint entailed 'persuading' Lady Castlemaine to speak on their behalf. She had made reputations and broken others. But – and this interested Henrietta Durville far more – she had become inordinately rich in the process. Old Rowley had showered lands and titles on her, her bastard children and her husband. She was driven about London in a carriage drawn by no less than eight splendid greys. A few months before, when Henrietta had encountered her at the theatre, she had been stunned by the jewels the favourite wore, and a merchant friend had estimated their value at more than forty thousand pounds. On another occasion Henrietta had watched Lady Castlemaine lose twenty thousand pounds at cards in a single night – and leave the table laughing.

But in the game of passion Barbara Villiers' luck was running out. The king spent more nights in the company of other lovers, as, indeed, did the countess. Society speculated on just how long the favourite could maintain her position. Every beautiful newcomer to the royal circle, such as Louise de Kéroualle, was carefully scrutinised. And the more ambitious of the younger court ladies, sensing a unique opportunity, flaunted themselves before the king whenever they could. With such thoughts and speculations uppermost in her mind, Henrietta Durville sought out Alphonse de Goncourt.

'Your servant, milady.' The Frenchman, clad now in a riding jacket of midnight-blue velvet, swept off his plumed hat and inclined his head while his bay mare pawed the ground. A large party had set out on horseback to explore Arlington's park, and were resting at the top of a rise from which Euston Hall could be seen to best effect.

'Good morning, Monsieur le Comte.' Henrietta smiled brightly as though his appearance at her side was both a delight and a surprise. 'Should you not be on Newmarket Heath, exercising your champions?'

'What is the point, when none of your English gallants will dare to pit themselves against me?'

'Ah, now, as to that I have heard a different story.'

'Milady?'

Henrietta stared at him frankly with a suggestion of mocking reproof. 'It is rumoured that you are the one who fears a contest and that is why you name high stakes.'

De Goncourt coloured with sudden anger. 'Who dares . . .'

Henrietta laughed. 'Who? Why, Monsieur le Comte, almost all the racing gentlemen.'

The party moved off and Lady Durville allowed the Frenchman to fall in beside her. She continued to taunt him. 'And, of course, what the gentlemen say the ladies are inclined to believe also. Perhaps it is true that the Comte de Goncourt promises more than he can deliver.'

With a quick gesture she prodded him in the groin with her crop. Then, as he swore under his breath, she urged her gelding into a trot and turned him on to a narrow track beneath massive, golden-headed elms.

She reined in where the path ended in a thicket-encircled glade. De Goncourt came close and grasped her bridle. 'You cannot believe these slanders. Tell me you know they are untrue.'

'That is for you to prove; not for me to say.' She eyed him shrewdly for several seconds, seeing him clearly for the mean, monied braggart that he was. 'However, I could perhaps help you.'

'In what way?'

'Suppose I were to persuade my husband to a match between one of your horses and his stallion.'

'Fleet?' The Frenchman looked apprehensive. 'He is, I am told, well named.'

'He has been a fine racer but I think he is past his best, and he is not happy on hard ground such as we have here in England this autumn. That is why John has not raced him yet. He is hoping for rain.'

De Goncourt frowned. 'And why are you telling me all this, milady?'

Henrietta replied slowly, watching closely for his reaction. 'Because it occurs to me that we may be able to help each other.'

'How so?'

'My husband has some wretched lands in Derbyshire. They are a financial millstone but he refuses to sell them. I thought you might persuade him to pledge them at Newmarket,' she smiled her sweetest smile, 'and then make over the pledge to me – secretly, of course.'

De Goncourt laughed, a sudden girlish giggle of a laugh. 'And have nothing to show for my victory?'

Henrietta joined in his laughter. 'Oh, I would not have you go empty-handed from your triumph. You would have scotched these evil rumours and proved your prowess as a rider. And then, I am sure I could find other ways to reward your generosity.' She pulled on the rein to stop her horse cropping grass, and turned his head back towards the path.

Within twenty-four hours it was all arranged: a match between Fleet and Triomphe for a purse of two thousand guineas, to be run the following afternoon. The Frenchman put up cash and his adversary handed the stakeholder a document giving first charge against his Derbyshire estates. As the hour of the race approached, Henrietta Durville complimented herself on her cleverness and reviewed the possible outcomes, either of which would see her emerge as the victor. Two thousand guineas would go a fair way towards resolving John's debts. But if John lost, she would be able to force the sale of Calton Durville – and perhaps gain much more. She rehearsed over and over in her mind the scene in which, clad in her most becoming gown, she obtained a private audience with the king and threw herself, weeping, on his mercy to implore aid for her ruined husband.

Trafalgar Square eased itself into a wet November evening. The frantic swirl of daytime traffic had slowed to a sedate, spasmodic circulation. The last office-quitting pedestrians had departed for home. The first theatregoers had not yet begun to make their way towards St Martin's Lane. The as yet unlit Christmas tree loomed like a black obelisk over the empty piazza. The fountains were still and empty. The floodlit figure of Nelson hovered in the gloom high above like Banquo's ghost come to the feast on the wrong day.

Tim and his three companions arrived early for the meeting. Clutching the canvas wrapped in brown paper, Lacy led the way across the north-east corner of the square, over the road to one of two flights of steps leading to the impressive, pillared portico of the National Gallery. It took only a few seconds to force the lock of the iron gates, slip inside and pull them to again. He stationed Jerry and Pete at the top of the steps. Then, with George beside him gripping a pistol in the pocket of his bomber jacket, he gazed out into the street, waiting. The two men did not talk. There was nothing to say.

Just before seven a dark Mercedes estate car slowed to a halt in the street below. George pointed it out but Tim had already seen it. Four figures emerged: three men and a woman. They walked up the steps. Venetia's arms were held securely by two flanking guardians. The third man, presumably carrying a gun, walked behind her. As they reached Pete, he stepped aside and followed them to the centre of the terrace. Then he took up his position with Tim and George. The two groups stood facing each other.

The third man now stepped forward. 'I must examine the picture.'

152

'As soon as your goons let go of Miss Cranville.'

Venetia sagged as her captors released their grip.

Tim walked quickly across. 'Are you all right?'

She could only nod by way of reply.

Tim went to put an arm round her, but was pushed roughly back by one of the crooks.

Meanwhile, the third man had torn away the wrappings of *The Triarchs* and was on his knees scrutinising it with the aid of a torch. George and Pete watched carefully, ready to react to any wrong move.

Tim turned impatiently. 'For God's sake, hurry up! It's perfectly genuine. Do you think I've had time to make a copy?'

But the man would not be rushed. It was some seconds before he stood up and nodded to his companions. One of them picked up the picture. The three men backed towards the steps then ran down to the pavement. The driver already had the hatchback open. Tim watched with a feeling of deep loss as *The Triarchs* was carefully laid in the back of the car. Then doors slammed and the Mercedes slid away from the kerb, turned left in front of St Martin in the Fields and disappeared from view.

Without words, Tim helped Venetia down to the street and hailed a cab. As the vehicle circuited the square and gathered speed down Whitehall, he looked back at the famous façade of the National Gallery. He thought of all the magnificent works of art slumbering securely in its dark interior, and of the masterpiece worthy to hang alongside them and now on its way back into the sewers of organised crime.

As soon as they reached the apartment to which Tim had now thankfully returned, Venetia went straight to the bathroom. She spent a long time in the tub, trying to wash away her ordeal. When, at last, she emerged, Tim settled her in a chair before the gas fire and poured her a large Irish whiskey. She sipped it wordlessly. She had said nothing all the way back in the taxi. Tim watched her – huddled, shivering, withdrawn – and did not know how to handle the situation. She needed to pour out her bitterness, anger and humiliation, but what would unlock it?

'Is there someone, a girl friend, I can call?'

She shook her head.

'Are you hungry? Would you like anything to eat?'

No answer.

He went over. Knelt in front of her. Took both of her hands, cradling the glass, in his own. 'Tell me about it, Venetia. They haven't drugged you or anything, have they?'

She stared at him vacantly for several moments.

Then, 'Bastard!' she shrieked at the top of her voice, and flung the rest of the whiskey in his face.

The weather did not prevent a large, expectant crowd from gathering on the heath. It had rained all night and most of the morning, and was still drizzling as the time appointed for the Durville–de Goncourt race drew near. There were several other contests for courtiers and townsfolk to watch, but it was the one between the French and English lords that most had come to see. National pride was at stake, and thousands were laid out in wagers.

'Will the rain affect Fleet's chances?' Henrietta asked as she and John made the journey by coach from Euston Hall.

John smiled, veiling his tensions with nonchalance. 'No, it will take a lot more than this to change the going. It has been dry for so long that the ground can soak up a great deal of water. It will make the course slippery on the turns but I had Fleet reshod this morning with spiked shoes for better grip.'

'Was de Goncourt there?'

Her husband laughed heartily at that. 'The little Frenchman has been at Newmarket since yesterday.'

'Exercising?'

'He has spent most of his time rushing round all the stables and owners, finding out everything he can about Fleet. He has been talking to everyone, even grooms and farriers. "How does milord Durville ride?" "Is the black horse a strong finisher?" "How will he like the wet conditions?" I think our little *comte* is a very worried man.'

'He will hate to lose face – or money. I hear that he even tried to lay a wager against himself, through intermediaries. When word of it leaked out he cried "slander" and threatened to fight a duel with anyone who dared repeat the story.'

'I can believe it. He is desperate. He has even asked me to change the course.'

'What do you mean?'

'He has obviously decided that Fleet will show Triomphe his heels on any straight run, so he suggested we run a track with as many bends and turns as possible – a sort of figure of eight.'

'You refused, of course.'

'Why should I? The more schemes monsieur le frog tries, the more foolish he will look when he is beaten.'

Suddenly anxious, Henrietta took her husband's hand in her own. 'Be careful, John. This man is more devious than I thought.'

'Have no fear, little witch. I know all the tricks of unsporting horsemen – barging, whipping, blocking and the like. I shall keep so far ahead of de Goncourt that he will have no chance to try anything.'

When they arrived at Newmarket Heath, John left to prepare for the race. Henrietta joined a group of friends watching from Lord Somerton's carriage, which was drawn up right alongside the platform erected for the royal party.

Henrietta found an excuse to leave her companions and pass in front of the stage. She dropped a deep curtsey as she did so. The king was in conversation with Lord Arlington and Ambassador Colbert, and she felt sure he had not noticed her. But she had gone only a few paces when she heard her name called.

'We are looking forward to Lord Durville showing his mettle.' King Charles smiled down at her. 'Would you like to watch the race from here, milady?'

The king, himself, gave Henrietta his hand as she climbed the steps to the rostrum. She exchanged civilities with the members of the royal party, including Mlle de Kéroualle. The French woman flashed a smile that was part welcome and part appraisal. As she did so, she deliberately toyed with a diamond and sapphire pendant which hung above the low bodice of her dress, and which could only have come from one source. At that moment there was a ragged chorus of cheers from the crowd. Taking one lady on each arm, the King of England turned to watch the sport.

The two horses approached the start, a white painted line on the turf. Fleet pranced lightly, smoothly, with the grace of a dancer. Triomphe, a rangy chestnut, skittered nervously, de Goncourt yanking at the bit to bring him under control.

'Who is more nervous,' Charles turned to Colbert, 'your champion or his mount?' There was a ripple of dutiful laughter and Henrietta took the opportunity to squeeze the royal arm more tightly.

A roar from the crowd signalled that the race judge had dropped his kerchief. The two horses started clockwise round the first loop of the eight. Fleet took the bend wide and Triomphe came inside him to steal an early lead. Down the long straight which followed, the English horse made up the ground, passed his rival, and was a good length clear as he entered the next, left-hand turn. Again Fleet drifted out and allowed Triomphe almost to draw level.

The crowd's roar was deafening as the two horses entered the next straight – the other crosspiece of the eight – neck and neck. Once again Fleet showed his speed and stamina. Despite whipping his mount hard, de Goncourt could not avoid dropping a couple of lengths before the last, right-hand bend.

Henrietta jumped up and down in her excitement, willing John to win. Nothing to gain now from a French victory. Everything was working out better than she could have dared hope. Charles's hand was now gripping hers. He had loosed his hold of the French girl's arm.

She saw John fight with the black stallion round the last bend. Fleet wanted to take it wide again, but John was determined to bring him as close as possible to the stakes marking out the course.

The crowd cheered him towards the line.

But Fleet could not respond. He tried to take the line John wanted. His hooves slipped from under him. He crashed on to his right side. He rolled right over. Crushed his rider. As Triomphe sped past and the crowd gasped, Fleet stumbled to his feet and limped, frightened, away. John Durville lay twisted and motionless.

With something between a sigh and a scream, Henrietta fainted.

CHAPTER 8

Over the next couple of hours Venetia half-sobbed half-shouted her story in disjointed fragments, and made it quite clear whom she blamed for her distressing experiences.

'If you hadn't been so obsessed by that bloody picture, this wouldn't have happened. And it was all for nothing! Those unspeakable people have got the damned thing anyway. And I'm glad! If it means they leave me alone . . . My God, when I think of that creepy F.D. character . . .' She shivered and held her hands out to the fire.

'F.D.?'

'ffrench . . . something . . . ffrench-Digges, the poncy art dealer who came up to take me to lunch.'

F.D. Tim remembered the conversation he had overheard between Karakis and Jane Prentice, and made the final connection on the circuit board.

'Smarmy little man!' Venetia grimaced. 'I suppose he must have put something in the wine or the coffee. My God, I felt ill afterwards. I can't remember a thing until I was in the back of a car and it was night and I was all tied up and that foreign slob told me to talk to you on the phone. Then someone stuck a needle in my arm . . .' Her voice trailed into silence.

'I'll get you some tea.'

Minutes later she sat, still hunched forward, sipping the hot, sweet liquid.

Tim floundered to find some appropriate words. 'Look, Venetia, I'm desperately sorry about all this. You're quite right; it is my fault. As soon as you've finished that we'll get you to bed.'

'Bed!' The monosyllable stretched into an anguished wail. Venetia shuddered violently, slopping tea over the carpet.

Tim eased the mug from her fingers.

'Tim, hold me!' She flung her arms round him. Kneeling beside the chair, he felt the deep sobs shaking her whole body.

Between the spasms she whispered the rest of her ordeal. 'When I came round again I was tied to a bed . . . naked . . . I was so cold . . . They'd put a blanket over me, but . . .'

He stroked her hair. 'Don't say any more. Not now.'

'I want to, Tim. Must get the poison out of the wound . . . There were these two foreign bastards – Greeks, I think. Small, vicious little men. One of them wore earrings . . . They stood around smirking at me. Making disgusting jokes in their own language . . . so brave with a naked woman all trussed up . . . Then they pulled the blanket off . . . Oh, Tim, it was *horrible* . . . I wanted to die, just to die.'

'Don't go on, Venetia. I can imagine—'

'When the woman came in – Jane, the woman I saw before – she tried to stop them. They just hit her around . . . Said they'd screw her, too, if she made any trouble.'

Tim tried to steer her away from this part of her story. 'Was F.D. there, then?'

'Who? Oh, the snivelling little dealer. No, I never saw him again.'

'Who was in charge?'

'There were just the two Greeks. They seemed to get their orders by telephone from someone called . . . No, I can't remember.'

'Karakis?'

'Yes, it might have been. I think so.'

'So who was the other man? The one I negotiated with? The one who came with you in the car tonight?'

'He wasn't there all the time. He came and went. I think their boss – Kar . . .?'

'Karakis.'

'I think he brought him in because he's English and because he knows something about pictures.'

'You didn't get his name?'

She mumbled something into his collar.

'Sorry, I didn't get that.'

'His name was Dawson or Dawkins or something like that. I was too scared to pay much attention. Anyway, what does it matter?'

She suddenly pulled away from him. 'You're not thinking . . .? My God, you are, aren't you?' Incredulity turned rapidly to loathing. 'You're still planning to outwit them. You never give up. Other people get killed and raped and knocked about, but Tim Lacy, the caped crusader, the soldier of fortune, the one-man band against crime, goes blithely on. God, how I hate you!' She jumped up. 'I'm going to have another bath.'

The next day Tim took Venetia back to Umbria. She said she wanted to go home, and he knew that was the best thing for her. They took the first morning flight to Pisa, phoned Venetia's mother from the airport, then headed south on the autostrada. From Chiusi they drove up into the hills, and in late afternoon reached the Villa Vagnoli, which gazed over forested slopes to the glittering surface of Lago Trasimeno.

The square house stood among well-disciplined lawns edged with terracotta urns, which overflowed with blossom in summer but which now stood as stern sentinels. Espaliered fruit trees were crucified against the pillars of south-facing arcades, which flanked the gravel drive and concealed the building from sight until the last moment. The car came to rest in the circular space before the symmetrical façade of the house, whose shutters were open to catch the last of the sunlight. Villa Vagnoli had been built by a seventeenth-century cardinal as a summer retreat from Rome; a haven where he could escape the heat of the city and the moral restraint required, at least in theory, of the papal entourage. Local legends told of orgies and even satanic rituals, but it was difficult to square such stories with the prim, austere aspect the house now presented, with its three rows of windows intersected by applied pilasters and the alabaster columns of the Doric order which supported the balcony over the entrance.

Within seconds of the car engine being silenced, the heavy front door opened wide and Contessa Peruzzi hurried out to greet them. Venetia's mother had reverted to her maiden name after her husband's departure, and had never remarried. She was a trim, dark-haired, intelligent woman still on the right side of fifty, and Tim, though he had only met her a couple of times, instinctively liked and respected her. He had often reflected that heredity had dealt Venetia a poor hand. A more liberal allocation of Peruzzi genes would have balanced Cranville fecklessness and impracticality.

After warm embraces and kisses, they went into the house and up to Isabella's private *salone* on the first floor, where a welcoming fire burned in the wide grate. They drank a glass of exquisite Brunello di Montalcino, opened by Isabella Peruzzi in honour of her guests, and talked family news for half an hour. Then the Contessa turned to her daughter.

'Venetia, you are tired after your journey. Go and rest.'

'But, Mother—'

'Run along. You look quite dreadful. And I want to talk to Timothy.' Isabella's was an ancient family, and about some things she was very traditional. One quirk was her aversion to all nicknames and shortened forms, which to her smacked of undue familiarity.

As the door closed, she refilled Tim's glass, then sat – on the edge of an upright chair – facing him.

'Well, young man, what is going on? She really does look dreadful. And what brings you here? I thought that you and Venetia . . .'

'We're not together again, Isabella. I'm here purely as a friend.'

'Pity.' She extracted a cigarette from a silver box on the table beside her and waited until Tim jumped up and lit it for her. 'Ah well,' she observed through an exhalation of smoke, 'I always thought you were too good for her.'

Tim gasped. 'You never told me that.'

'It isn't the sort of thing a mother says to a potential son-in-law. She needs a man. Not *any* man. Someone solid and dependable, who knows his own mind. She's very talented, as you realise, but she will never make a career for herself as an independent artist. She's like a climbing rose; she needs someone to cling to if she is to blossom properly. And I'm certainly not going to have her hanging round here, growing into a middle-aged spinster looking after her decrepit mother.'

Tim laughed. 'Isabella, you'll never be decrepit.'

She did not smile. 'Timothy, this is serious. Is there no chance of you and Venetia . . .?'

He shook his head. 'I don't think so. There was a time when I was very keen on the "till death us do part" scenario. I was really thrilled about the baby. I thought it would change her mind about a permanent relationship. When she had the abortion, I was absolutely shattered. It was like a kick in the teeth.'

'Stupid girl!' The Contessa stubbed out her cigarette impatiently. 'I think it is time I had a really good talk with her.'

'I should go easy on her at the moment. She's been through a lot recently.'

'Tell me about it.'

Tim wondered just how much of the story he should reveal. He had pondered the problem several times during the journey, and was still no nearer an answer. He was saved from an immediate decision by a tap at the door. A deferential little woman entered, went round the room switching on table lamps, closed the shutters, drew the floor-length velvet curtains, and silently withdrew. Tim, meanwhile, sipped the full-bodied wine and appraised his hostess over the rim of the glass. She was shrewd, tough and unflappable. Any woman who, deserted in her mid-twenties, could bring up two daughters, run an estate and preserve a meaningful independent life for herself, had to be. As the door closed again Tim knew that he would tell her everything.

John Durville was dead, his back broken in three places.

Everyone was very kind to Henrietta. Lord Arlington personally arranged the funeral and insisted that she stay on at Euston until she felt able to travel home. He had her moved to another room so that she did not have to sleep in the same bed that she and her husband had shared.

For a couple of days she remained in a stunned and bewildered haze. Then she began trying to piece events together and make some sense of them.

'Charles, what went wrong? I just can't understand what happened.' She was reclining on a daybed and talking with Charles Trevelyan, John's closest friend, who stood by the casement overlooking the sodden gardens.

Trevelyan, thin and tall, with brown sympathetic eyes, shook his head sadly. 'Henrietta, I fear it was his own fault. Probably in the rush of preparing for the race, he overlooked the vital detail.'

'*What* detail, Charles? No one will tell me exactly how it happened.'

He looked genuinely surprised. 'I'm sorry . . . I thought you knew it was the horseshoes.'

'Horseshoes!'

'The shoes Fleet was wearing were old and very worn. On that wet surface they gave the poor beast no grip at all.'

Henrietta sat up. 'But, Charles, he *did* change the shoes. He told me so. He had Fleet fitted with spiked shoes.'

Trevelyan came over and sat beside her. He took her hand and spoke softly. 'I'm sure John intended to. He must have overlooked it.'

Henrietta gripped his hand with both of hers. '*No*, Charles. He definitely said that the farrier had changed Fleet's shoes that very morning.' She stared imploringly at him. 'And stop looking at me as though I'm a befuddled, distraught widow. I *know* what John said, and I *know* he would not have been so stupid as to race without making complete preparations.'

'It's certainly not like him . . .'

'Charles, do me a great favour, please.'

'Of course.'

'Go over to Newmarket. You know the farrier John used?'

'Yes, I use him myself.'

'Find him and ask him. Will you do that?'

'If it will give you peace of mind, I'll ride over this afternoon.'

When Trevelyan had gone, Henrietta spent a long time thinking hard. It was a relief to take her mind off John and their relationship which, for all its storms, had had a goodly portion of love in it. But if the end result was a temporary lifting of the clouds of grief and guilt, they only gave way to dull, grey suspicion. At last she summoned her maid and gave her a message asking the Comte de Goncourt to call upon her.

The girl was back within half an hour with the news that monsieur le comte had already left.

When Charles returned from Newmarket shortly before sunset, Henrietta had spent several hours trying to tamp down the panic beginning to surge up within her.

'Well, what did he say?' she demanded, before the door had closed behind him.

Charles threw his plumed hat on to the bed and dropped into a cane-backed chair. 'I couldn't find the man.'

'What do you mean?'

'He seems to have left town suddenly. I asked around. The story is that he had come into a large sum of money, bought a fast horse and . . . disappeared.'

'De Goncourt!' Henrietta muttered the name through clenched teeth.

'I'm sorry, I didn't quite—'

'Is it not strange that the farrier who fitted the shoes that caused John to lose the race *and* the man who won the race should both have vanished?'

'Well, de Goncourt hasn't vanished.' Trevelyan spoke bitterly. 'Everyone knows where he has gone.'

'Everyone except me.'

Charles slumped in the chair. Awkward. Miserable. 'I didn't want to tell you . . . Not just yet. We all thought – after what happened to John – that the Frenchman should have cancelled the wager. It was the sporting thing to do. Well, the fact is that he refused. And, of course, he's within his rights to do so. So I'm afraid, Henrietta, that de Goncourt has gone to Derbyshire to enforce the sale of John's lands.'

For several moments Henrietta Durville sat silent and motionless, hands clasped lightly in her lap. When at last she spoke, it was in little more than a whisper. 'Then I am ruined. When de Goncourt has taken his share, all the other creditors will fasten their teeth on the carcase. There will be nothing left.'

Trevelyan crossed the room and knelt beside her. 'That is nonsense, Henrietta. We'll help you. You know that.'

'Thank you, Charles. You are very kind. But I think, perhaps, I should see his majesty, straight away, and throw myself on his mercy.'

Trevelyan shook his head. 'Did you not know? The court left for Westminster this morning.'

Although Isabella pressed him to stay for a few days, Tim left the villa the next morning. Venetia's recovery could not begin until she had severed the last connection with the appalling events of the past few weeks. And Tim was that connection. Isabella, of course, saw the sense of this and did not press the invitation. Nor did she reproach Tim for putting her daughter in such danger.

The nearest she came to it was when she said, 'Well, Timothy, you've left me with one hell of a job, haven't you?'

Tim did not return to London immediately. He, too, had some hard thinking to do. He needed a place of peace and quiet to do it. He made the short drive to Perugia, the region's capital, booked into a hotel, set out on foot for the old town, and wandered the steep streets and narrow alleyways crammed within its thirteenth-century walls. Tim Lacy was not one of those who sought soul-space in wide land-scapes and open tracts of country. For him reality was vertical, not horizontal. It was a straight line linking the present with the past, giving it meaning and therefore enabling it to be at peace with itself. Out-of-season Perugia soothed him because it helped him to make historical connections. Winter sunlight splashed across the warm brick-work of buildings that had stood here since the Renaissance. Washing hung on poles from upper-storey balconies, as it had done from time out of mind. The black-frocked elderly women who talked in disapproving groups, the children who chased one another round the Maggiore Fountain in the Piazza Quattro Novembre, the men in drab jackets who argued continuously in open-doored bars – all were descendants of the merchants, vineyard workers, noblemen and liveried servants who had walked these streets in the heyday of the city state, half a millennium ago.

But there was another reason for seeking out Perugia, among all the beautiful old towns of Umbria and Tuscany. Tim climbed the Corso Vannucci and entered the Collegio del Cambio, the chamber of commerce, built by the merchant fathers of the state in the fifteenth century. He entered the Sala dell'Udienza, annually thronged by thou-sands of tourists but quiet on this December morning. Today Tim had the frescoes almost to himself.

In 1496 Perugia's wealthy élite commissioned their local master, Pietro di Cristoforo Vannucci (known to posterity as Perugino) to decorate the walls and ceiling of their audience chamber. The great artist, then considered to be on a par with his contemporary Leonardo, duly arrived with his band of pupils and set to work painting a series of biblical and allegorical scenes filling every space with colour and sinuous figures. Tim stood in the centre of the room. He gazed up at the arcaded panels and the geometrical segments reaching up into the barrel vault. Perugino had, apparently, tried hard to lift the minds of the money men to a more elevated plane with his depiction of the birth and transfiguration of Christ and the figures personifying the virtues.

Had it worked? Had any of the self-confident oligarchs who had sat on benches round these walls, resting their backs against the carved and inlaid oak – men made rich from trading in wine, oil, majolica, horses or hides – had any of them drawn spiritual nourishment from these masterpieces? Or were the results of Perugino's imagination just so many square yards of paint, bought as cheaply as possible and then displayed to citizens and visitors to enhance the patrons' prestige? Had any of them grasped the immense privilege they had been granted? On their walls a young artist had left his mark, one who was destined to be far greater than Perugino. Among the master's pupils was a teenager, recently arrived from Urbino in the Marches, called Raffaello Santi.

Tim stared up at the figures of Fortitude and Solomon, widely accepted as the young apprentice's own work, and at Daniel considered by many to be Raphael's self-portrait. In his mind Tim addressed the boyish, wistfully serene face. If you only knew the trouble you've caused. Not only now – all down the ages. Men and women fighting, stealing, killing, grabbing, cheating – just to say they own a genuine Raphael. You were wasting your time trying to help us meditate on higher things. Taking on human corruption was too big a job. But I guess you knew that. Your own times were just as violent as mine. All those petty principalities and dukedoms constantly warring with each other and the internal feuding which made Shakespeare's Montagus and Capulets look like the best of chums. What was it one of your cynical contemporaries wrote about Perugia? 'It is distinguished by men of infamous habits and iniquitous conduct.' Perhaps you were there when four members of the leading family were assassinated at a wedding, and the cathedral had to be washed out with wine to purify it.

He emerged into the sunlight and made his way by tortuous back streets to the church of San Severo. It was an undistinguished building, lifted from obscurity by a Raphael fresco in its tiny chapel. He sat facing the relaxed figures of Christ and a group of saints watching the mortal scene from a cloudy heaven, and tried to think.

How far back did one have to go to find the true cause of tragic events? Two men were dead, and Venetia had been through hell. Was that his fault for trying to rescue *The Triarchs*? Was it Karakis's fault for stealing it? Was it the fault of previous owners whose mania for possession had prevented the masterpiece ending up in a secure, public collection? Was it Pope Julius who, all those centuries before, had somehow cursed the painting by having a holy subject depicted for an unholy purpose? Or was it Raphael, himself, tempted by money and fame, who had created a diabolical monster with an angelic visage, destined to rampage through the years and earn its nickname '*The Bloody Triarchs*'?

Tim prided himself on being neither religious nor superstitious. Material objects did not carry curses from generation to generation. Stories about 'unlucky' paintings were just that – stories. Except that this one was too close to home. An old friend and a stranger had been brutally murdered, and a woman he had once loved had been bestially assaulted as a direct result of his intervention in that story. If one discounted the supernatural agencies, who was left to shoulder the blame? It was a question he preferred not to answer. He was a man of principle: a man for whom ends never justified means. Had he not left the SAS because he could no longer convince himself that a trained killer doing a job for his country was absolved from the responsibility for his actions?

Repent, then? Without realising that he had moved, Tim found himself on his knees, his head in his hands. But did not repentance involve restitution? If so, what could he possibly do now for Jean-Marc, or poor Harry Strang, or even for Venetia? 'Nothing. Absolutely nothing.' He muttered the words at the stone floor. What then? Go home and slip comfortably back into a successful business life? Carry on as the lone vigilante Venetia, probably rightly, despised? Single-handedly bring Karakis to book where all the police forces of Europe had failed? Ridiculous! He gazed up at Raphael's Christ. 'Well, then? You're supposed to be the one with all the answers.'

Exorcise!

Tim fell back against the chair and knocked it over. The word came into his mind suddenly, clearly and unexpectedly. For several seconds it filled his thinking to the exclusion of all other sensations. He saw, felt, heard, smelled nothing else. The word was the only reality.

The moment, the vision, the experience, whatever it was, passed. Shaken, Tim jumped to his feet and hurried from the church.

He continued his planned mini-tour: medieval Gubbio with its spectacular views over a wide valley; Orvieto for Signorelli's Last Judgement frescoes in the cathedral; quietly sophisticated Spoleto – and so to Rome for his flight back. By the time he reached home he felt refreshed and relaxed. But something had changed deep down inside. There was a determination and a conviction. Somehow, Tim knew, the curse of *The Triarchs* would be lifted, once and for all.

It came as a complete surprise to him when that process began in Japan.

De Goncourt strutted from room to room at Calton Durville, followed by his clerk, carefully taking notes, and two servants. The tenant farmer, to whom the land was leased, followed at a surly distance. The house, closed up since Sir Thomas's death, was dank and every surface was thick with dust.

'Lady Durville was right,' the Frenchman muttered. 'The place is a hovel.'

He tugged open drawers and cupboards. He poked around in their interiors. He peered closely at tapestries. He prodded bed coverings. He pulled books from the library shelves. He had his men prise open coffers if the keys were not immediately available. Whenever he encountered something of value or use, his scribe noted it. By the time they had been through the house from attic to kitchen, the list was not very long.

'Ye gods, is this what I risked my reputation for?' He crossed the courtyard to inspect the stables and barns. What he discovered in their dilapidated and chaotic interiors did not improve his temper.

'You there!' He summoned the farmer. 'What is the value of land by the acre here?'

The man did his best to explain, but the barriers of language and dialect meant that de Goncourt was not greatly enlightened. He turned to his clerk. 'You and Pierre, see these things transported to London. I'll sort them out and decide if there's anything worth taking back to France.'

He called for his horse and sprang into the saddle. 'See what price you can get for the land and buildings, but consult me before any contract is drawn up. Jean!' This to the other servant. 'What are you hanging about for? Mount up and let us get back to civilisation.'

He walked his horse round to the front of the house, followed by the rest of his little entourage. 'Jacques!' He called to the clerk. 'You have money for lodging and waggons. Report to me at the embassy as soon as you return.'

He was about to put spurs to his gelding when something attracted his attention. 'What are those ruins over there?'

'An old abbey, Monsieur le Comte.' Jacques, having an antiquarian turn of mind, had stolen a few minutes earlier in the day to wander among the fallen pillars and overgrown flagstones.

'We will have a look.' De Goncourt cantered his horse across the field and dismounted where the great west end of the abbey church had once stood.

After some minutes of aimless wandering he came to the chapel. He tried the door but, though the iron ring turned in his hand, the heavy oak did not move. He put his weight against it with no result. He ordered his servants to try. Together they applied their shoulders. The door yielded a couple of inches, then stuck fast. Jean and Pierre redoubled their efforts.

'No matter. It was just curiosity.' De Goncourt walked back to his horse. He had one foot in the stirrup when there was a loud echoing thud behind him. He turned to see his men sprawling on the ground, and the chapel open for his inspection.

The interior was depressing. Though in better condition than the ruins which surrounded it, the chapel had now lost part of its roof. It was a pile of tiles which had fouled the door. Someone had filled the windows with clear glass and these were still intact, but the light filtering through the grimy panes fell on a desolate, empty space. No altar, no statues, no crucifix – just neglect, godlessness. De Goncourt shivered and involuntarily crossed himself.

He was turning to leave when something caught his eye. Something in the shadow at the base of the east wall. He walked the few paces to the altar space and lifted *The Triarchs* from where it had fallen, face down, on the dusty flagstones.

The frame was cracked, and in fact it fell apart as he set the painting down on an empty plinth against the right-hand wall. He took out a kerchief and wiped over the paint surface. He stood back to take a good look at his discovery. As he did so, curiosity turned to astonishment, astonishment to wonder, and wonder to awe. He was transported back to his childhood. To the Benedictine monastery where he had received part of his education. The monks had had many fine religious paintings. One especially, a *pietà*, had moved him profoundly every time he looked at it. The pain, the anguish and yet the serenity of the group mourning the dead Christ had spoken directly to his soul. Now he found himself feeling that same spiritual intensity. Almost it drove him to his knees. Then he recollected the others, mere servants, watching him, and the mood passed.

Still he stared at the painting – and knew it for a masterpiece. He felt sudden pity for the Durvilles. What uncultured clods these English are, he thought, and how stupid. If the owners of this place had possessed any spiritual sensitivity they would have known what a priceless treasure they possessed. Its sale would have gone a long way towards solving their problems – at least until Lady Durville ran up another mountain of debt. Poor Henrietta Durville: vain, foolish, gullible woman.

He picked up the Raphael and handed it almost reverently to his clerk. 'Have this wrapped up very carefully. I shall take it with me. Oh, and I have changed my mind about the estate. I shall be magnanimous. When we have removed these few trifles, the pledge is to be cancelled and the property returned to Lady Durville. See to that, will you, Jacques?'

The letter was headed: 'For the personal attention of Mr T J Lacy.' It was a model of economy.

Dear Mr Lacy,
    Your company has been recommended to me as one capable of carrying out security installations in circumstances requiring total discretion.

I should be glad of an opportunity to discuss such an installation here.

Yours sincerely,

I. Tonashi

President Tonashi Electrical Industries

Half a dozen letters and faxes later, Tim found himself checking into Tokyo's Akasaka Prince Hotel on a late afternoon in mid-June. During the last six and a half months, the Karakis affair had seldom been far from his thoughts. He had even opened a file on the Greek crook. Into it went not only everything he knew about Karakis and his associates, but also Interpol stolen art notices (obtained from a friend at Scotland Yard), press cuttings on European art thefts, snippets of information picked up in the trade – anything that might enable him to work out the pattern of the man's nefarious activities. Yet, inevitably, the pressing concerns of work and the numbing effects of office routine relentlessly edged such thoughts into a dusty corner of his brain. And now this important Japanese commission had come up. Tonashi had refused to be more specific about what he wanted, beyond saying that it was a big job and that Mr Lacy would have to see it for himself. Since the industrialist had offered a free trip to Tokyo, Tim had seen no reason not to humour him.

The secretive tycoon certainly did him proud. Tim was met at the airport and conveyed to the city centre in an air-conditioned Cadillac. At the hotel, an awestruck reception clerk bowed slightly as he handed over – it might almost have been on a velvet cushion – the key to Mr Tonashi's suite. As the uniformed bell boy withdrew deferentially, Tim surveyed the apartment. The decor was ultra-modern but not too harsh for comfort. The view from the thirtieth-floor window was spectacular. There were freshly-cut flowers in every room and a huge basket of fruit on the breakfast table. But it was the 'office' which provided the largest surprises. This teak and leather chamber sported a sizable desk complete with a word-processor. On a side table there was a fax machine. But it was the item in the middle of the desk that most intrigued him. It was a bottle of excellent Armagnac. Tim picked it up and ran his eye appreciatively over the label. Someone has done his homework very thoroughly, he thought.

There was an envelope beside the bottle. The contents provided another example of Tonashi's terse, uncommunicative style.

Dear Mr Lacy,
    Welcome to Tokyo. I hope you will have an enjoyable stay.
    Enclosed please find an itinerary for your visit. Should you have any questions, please do not hesitate to contact my personal secretary, Miss Younger.
    Yours sincerely,
        I. Tonashi

So the Jap had an English secretary. Perhaps that was the explanation for the frigid precision of his business letters. Impatiently Tim scanned the programme which had been arranged for him. It included two days of sightseeing, interspersed by dinner on the following evening with Mr Tonashi. The third day had been designated for 'business discussions'. Tim grabbed up the phone, called the number typed at the top of Tonashi Electrical Industries' embossed notepaper, and asked for Miss Younger.

'This is Catherine Younger. How may I help you?' Not English. American.

'My name is Tim Lacy.'

'Mr Lacy, how are you? Was the flight OK?'

'The flight was fine . . .'

'And everything is all right at the hotel?'

'Everything's very . . . luxurious. It's just that . . .'

'Yes, Mr Lacy?'

'Well, I don't wish to appear ungrateful. I'm sure you've been to a great deal of trouble, but I'm used to planning my own programme. I was hoping to get down to business with Mr Tonashi as soon as possible.'

A slight pause. Then, 'Have you been to Japan before, Mr Lacy?'

'No, I—'

'Aha.'

'And just what does "Aha" mean?'

'Well, things tend to happen rather differently here. There are formalities, proprieties that have to be observed.'

'When in Tokyo . . .?'

'Precisely. I assure you Mr Tonashi has made these arrangements so that you will find your stay enjoyable as well as profitable. Now, is there anything you need?'

'You're not Japanese, are you?'

A light laugh. 'No, of course not.'

'Then you're not personally bound by all this formality and protocol. Will you have dinner with me this evening?'

'Ah, I see, Mr Lacy. You want some female company. Well, of course, I can arrange—'

'I'm sure you can set me up with a call girl or a geisha. All part of the Tonashi service, no doubt. What I had in mind was a little intelligent conversation with someone who can help a stranger in town to find his bearings.'

'I see.' A slightly embarrassed silence, then, 'I'll call you back, Mr Lacy.'

Ten minutes later Catherine Younger accepted his invitation.

'Did you have to get the boss's permission for this?'

They were sitting at a table in the Akasaka Prince's elegant circular dining-room. The hum of conversation in the well-patronised establishment was penetrated now and again by the Gershwin medley produced from a white baby grand in the centre of the room by a pianist wearing a tail-coat colour co-ordinated with the instrument. Catherine Younger had turned out to be a slightly freckled natural blonde in her late twenties, who wore little make-up and surveyed the world with a cynical smile. Over aperitifs they had covered the basic ground. Tim had learned that Catherine came from Maine, was a graduate in Japanese language and literature, and had worked as a translator and interpreter at the UN in New York before Tonashi made her an offer she could not refuse. The Tokyo-based computer king was expanding his business in the USA and needed a PA who understood America and the Americans.

'I can't date Mr Tonashi's clients with impunity, Tim.' She raised an eyebrow.

'And did he approve?'

'He said he was happy if it helped you to relax and enjoy yourself.'

172

'He's certainly gone to a lot of trouble over my welfare. Including having me watched.'

'Watched?' She laughed, and Tim again noted with approval the light, contralto trill.

'You see that young man in the coffee-coloured suit, three tables away. He was in the reception area when I arrived, in the bar when I met you, and I'm pretty sure he was at the airport earlier.'

Catherine shook her head. 'Just another guest in the hotel. Anyway, you've only been here a few hours. I'll bet all Japanese still look alike to you.'

'There can't be many Japanese men who have the end of the little finger of their left hand missing.'

'What!' She glanced round sharply, taking a fresh interest. The man was wearing a green silk shirt open at the neck to display a thick gold chain. He turned his wrist over to check the time and Catherine saw the shortened digit.

She frowned. '*Boryokudan*!'

'Is that his name?'

She gave a half smile. 'It's a word meaning "the violent ones". It's what the police call them. They prefer the name *yakuza*.'

'Now *that* I do know something about.'

'I suppose you've heard it called the Japanese Mafia. That's a misnomer. It's something rooted deep in the feudal past. Absolutely unique.'

She was warming to her subject when the waiter arrived with their steaks. Tim had ordered filet because he was not yet ready for the local cuisine, and Catherine had decided to join him 'for a change'.

'And do they all have their little fingers cut off?' Tim took a draught of the Longhorne Creek heavy red wine before cutting into his meat.

'No, they do it to themselves. Usually it's an act of bravado to prove loyalty to their *oyabun* – a sort of father figure. Sometimes it's *yubis-ume*, a penance imposed for some misdemeanour.'

'You sound as though you admire these customs.'

Again the cynical smile. 'I think they're a load of adolescent crap designed to lend nobility to a range of vile activities: extortion, drug-pushing, fraud, prostitution. But, then, you men always have to band together in ritualistic societies, don't you? Develop your own

173

mythologies to create an aura of romance and give your activities a spurious glamour. Freemasonry, church, IRA, army – they're all just glorified street gangs, don't you agree?' Her frank stare challenged him to argument.

Tim shrugged, refusing to be drawn. 'Some of us are loners,' he observed. 'Anyway, that's getting us away from the important point of why I'm being followed by one of these *boro* . . .'

'*Boryokudan*. We don't know for sure that you are.'

'Well we can soon find out. Would you care to join me in a little experiment? Is there somewhere in walking distance where we can go for a drink after dinner?'

'Sure, lots of places.'

'OK, let's do that and see if we have a tail.'

They finished their meal in leisurely fashion. Then they strolled three blocks of Tokyo's brash, humid nightscape. The pavements were crowded. The garish neon lights blazed the city's affluence. Slow-moving traffic soiled the air with pungent fumes. Catherine led the way down a side street, and found a bar fractionally quieter than its neighbours, which meant that, instead of American pop music blaring from banshee loudspeakers, a Japanese game show host screeched his enthusiasm from a TV set in a corner of the room. They had just elbowed their way to the counter when, looking back towards the door, Tim saw the man in the coffee-coloured suit come in.

CHAPTER 9

When Alphonse Edouard, Comte de Goncourt died on 12 August 1718, full of years but sadly deficient of a direct male heir, there were few expressions of sincere regret. Throughout his life, and especially in later years, he had been widely known as a miser who beat his servants, exploited his tenants, cheated his neighbours in order to extend his own estates, and regarded his family with paranoid suspicion, convinced that they were all plotting to get their hands on his money. Those most closely involved had little concern for the late count and his eternal welfare, but they were passionately interested in his estate.

There were three people who were especially delighted to hear of de Goncourt's passing. Each was anxious to know about the disposition of the old man's worldly wealth and each had a particular interest in his most valuable and celebrated possession, *The Triarchs*. Though few people had ever seen the Raphael, its fame had spread far and wide among cognoscenti, and there had been more than one popular lampoon depicting *Alphonse l'avare* counting his piles of *louis d'or* while Raphael's Madonna gazed disapprovingly down from her canvas.

The first hopeful beneficiary was the 33-year-old Henri de Goncourt, Alphonse's only nephew and the inheritor of his title. He was at an orgy when the news of his uncle's demise reached him.

It was three years since the reign of Louis XIV, the Sun King, had set, not in a blaze of golden glory but in the dismal *crépuscule* of a country exhausted by war, a treasury all but empty, and a court dominated by priests and religious old women. When the aged king, who had reigned longer than most people could remember, at last died, it was inevitable that France should react with relief, and bound enthusiastically into a new age of gaiety and licence. Philippe, Duc d'Orléans, regent during the minority of Louis XV, seemed the very embodiment of the new spirit. He was a man of culture and taste who freely patronised the theatre and built up superb collections of paintings, jewels and objets d'art. He read avidly. He had his own laboratory where he spent hours in chemical experiments – some said concocting poisons. And he was a sexual libertine. In the sumptuous Palais Royal, Philippe concluded affairs of state promptly at five o'clock every afternoon. The rest of the day was devoted entirely to pleasures as unrestrained and inventive as the regent and his cronies could devise. It was among those cronies that Henri de Goncourt was seated, flushed with wine, on the evening of 12 August, when a messenger brought the news from Loiret.

The long table had been cleared of the remains of the *petit souper*, and the light from crystal chandeliers fell upon bare, glistening flesh. Six young women – actresses and tradesmen's daughters rather than whores – paraded sinuously up and down the boards between two lines of courtiers. The men prodded, poked and fondled the 'exhibits', and noted their detailed opinions about the charms on display on slips of paper provided for the purpose. Afterwards they would grade the girls in order of merit, then draw lots among themselves to see in which order they would test the women's sexual performance. At the end of the entertainment, which would be well into the next morning, the 'queen of the night' would be solemnly crowned and she and her companions handsomely rewarded.

'What the devil do you want?' Henri reluctantly allowed his hand to slide off the thigh of the brunette kneeling before him as he took the letter proffered by a liveried footman. He broke the seal and struggled to make out the spidery writing. It was not easy. His head was far from clear, the din of his colleagues beating the table and cheering was deafening, the lights flickered, and he had only one good eye to read with. Eventually he managed to decipher the simple message. He clutched his wig off to cool his head, and went over the words again. 'At last! At last!' He threw the wig in the air and lifted his head in a laugh of triumph and joy.

He lumbered to his feet and made his way round the table. The Regent of France lolled in his chair, a sardonic smile on his fleshy features, and ran his hands over the contours of a lithe girl, no more than sixteen, stretched out before him. 'Ah, Henri, come and feel this – firm and yet supple. Virtual perfection, don't you think?'

Unable to conceal his excitement, the courtier whose face appeared permanently twisted by the old duelling scar which ran diagonally across one cheek from his sightless eye, held out the letter. 'Your Highness, it has happened! My dear uncle has done the only decent thing he's ever done in his mean life. He's died!'

'My dear Henri, I'm delighted!' Orléans slapped the girl on the stomach by way of dismissal. 'This is splendid news!' He banged the table and, after several seconds, managed to bring his rowdy friends to silence. 'My lords, gentlemen, allow me to present Henri Charles, Comte de Goncourt.'

The announcement was greeted with a roar of approval. Everyone gathered round the new nobleman to shake his hand or thump him on the back. There were several enthusiastic toasts and the impromptu celebrations ended up with de Goncourt being carried round the room on the shoulders of several of his friends until they all collapsed in a laughing heap.

It was a little later that Orléans drew Henri on one side. 'When are you going down to Crétigny?'

'I haven't thought yet, Your Highness.' De Goncourt drew a hand across his sweating brow. 'I suppose I ought to leave tomorrow.'

'Better not to delay that long.' The regent smiled but there was a calculating firmness in his voice.

'You mean . . .?'

'Order your carriage and leave straight away.'

'Your Highness, do you really think . . .?' Henri felt in no fit state to embark on the jolting six-hour journey.

'I am anxious that you should secure your inheritance. Your dear aunt is a very religious lady.' He grimaced. 'And, as you know, religious people are of all the least to be trusted.' He laughed lightly.

Henri giggled his appreciation of the witticism. 'Well, if Your Highness really—'

'I do. I do. And don't forget that you and I have an agreement.'

Enlightenment pierced the clouds of de Goncourt's fuddled brain. 'Ah, the Raphael.'

'Precisely, the Raphael, for which I have promised you twenty-five thousand francs. Acquiring the celebrated *Triarchs* is very important to me. I should hate to be thwarted by an old woman just when it was within my grasp.'

'Of course, Your Highness. I'll leave at once.

Philippe put an arm round his shoulder and walked with him to the door. There he paused. 'But what am I thinking of? We must give you something for your journey.'

He turned to face the company. The men were sitting in a group at one end of the table, comparing notes and arguing over their verdicts. The women, temporarily ignored, stood at a side table, helping themselves to sweetmeats.

Orléans waved a hand towards them. 'Take your pick,' he said magnanimously.

The Abbé de St Raymond was just about to mount his horse for a day's hunting when a breathless figure came hurrying through the gate in the wall separating the conventual buildings from the secluded splendour of the abbot's dwellings.

'Monsieur l'Abbé! Monsieur l'Abbé! Wait!'

Ronsard de Grossville frowned as he handed the reins back to his groom. He hated his routine being disturbed. He turned, impatiently tapping his boot with his whip, as the black-habited monk covered the last few yards of gravelled drive, lifting his skirts above his thin ankles.

'Well, what is it, Father Peter?'

The elderly religious came to a halt before the young man who was, by the law of France and the law of the Church, his superior, and respectfully averted his eyes. 'Monsieur l'Abbé . . .' he gasped, holding a hand over his heaving chest.

'Calm yourself, Father. Whatever the crisis you come to report, it will wait until you have recovered your breath. Is the abbey on fire?' He smirked at the leader of St Raymond's dwindling band of holy men. 'I see no smoke.'

'Oh no, indeed, Monsieur l'Abbé. No indeed.' The little monk looked quite shocked. 'It is the Comte de Goncourt.'

De Grossville looked up sharply. 'De Goncourt?'

'Yes, Monsieur l'Abbé. Brother Anselm had the news from the kitchen boy, and he was told by the baker. I was sure you would want to hear straight away.'

'Hear what? Get to the point, you garrulous old fool!' He gripped the whip tightly with both hands.

'Yes, yes, of course, Monsieur l'Abbé. It seems that the Comte de Goncourt has been taken to his maker. The Lord have mercy on his soul.'

De Grossville automatically crossed himself, but his face showed no concern for his neighbour's eternal repose. 'De Goncourt dead? You're quite sure? When?'

'Well, I haven't checked the report, but it seems that the poor man collapsed yesterday afternoon.'

'Yesterday afternoon! And I only get to hear about it now?'

'News reaches the cloisters slowly, Monsieur l'Abbé.'

'Rubbish! You're the worst bunch of gossips in the whole valley. Well, you did the right thing in telling me. Now, get back to your prayers.'

'Yes, Monsieur l'Abbé. Will you be joining us for mass?'

'Maybe, maybe.' De Grossville dismissed the monk with a wave of the hand. As commendatory abbot and secular figurehead of the community, he rarely attended mass or any of the other services. He had, as he often observed, more important things to think about – keeping up the three-hundred-year-old monastery buildings, ensuring that the farms were run productively and tithes promptly paid, entertaining important visitors, and making the abbot's house a worthy place to receive them. He stared across the gleaming white façade with its neat rows of long windows to where scaffolding clung to the half-built walls of the east wing. Seven months since the workmen had left, vowing not to lay another stone until their arrears were paid in full. Seven months of humiliation and vain appeals to wealthy neighbours, and scraping together every last sou to meet his daily household expenses.

Well, thank God, that was all over. At last he would be able to pay his way again thanks to *l'avare* at long last having the good grace to die. De Goncourt had bequeathed his famous Raphael to the monastery where, apparently, he had spent several happy years as a child. Repeatedly de Grossville had assured him that it would be given pride of place in the abbey church. In fact, it would serve a far more useful purpose. Instead of being hung where only a few monks could see it, it would be sold. The proceeds would ensure the abbey's continuance in good repair for years to come – and, of course, the completion of a suitable residence for the abbot.

He turned to the groom. 'Put Zephyr away and saddle me the bay instead.'

The man, a well-meaning halfwit, shook his head with a puzzled frown. 'Monsieur l'Abbé is not going hunting?'

'M. l'Abbé does not go hunting on the bay mare, does he? M. l'Abbé is going to Crétigny, to pay his respects to the Comtesse de Goncourt.' He smiled and added under his breath, 'and to prevent the insane old bitch doing something stupid.'

When Marguerite de Goncourt heard the news she went straight away to pray for the soul of her husband and to praise God for her own deliverance. When, after an hour, she rose from her knees in the chapel at Château Beauregard, she found a deferential servant waiting to tell her that supper was ready. She dismissed him and went out to walk in the formal gardens, to watch the sun set over the Beuvron valley, and to think. What did food matter when there were important plans to be made?

She loved solitude. Over fifty years ago she had begged her father to let her take the veil. It was, she had decided at seventeen, the only kind of life that would be as happy as the childhood here at beautiful Beauregard. She walked the well-kept paths between the immaculate box hedges, clutching a rosary in her thin fingers and remembering the blissful days with her brother Paul: the summer picnics in the Forêt de Russy and the boating trips on the river; racing up and down the long gallery in winter, or making up stories about the stern-featured men and women whose faces stared down from the 363 portraits round its walls. It should have gone on for ever. But then Paul had inherited the title and moved to Paris to be near the court and his new business interests, and the family had married little Marguerite off to the Viscomte de Cordelay. What did she want with marriage, or with men and their lusts and their horrid, groping hands. How she had prayed for deliverance – and God had answered her prayers. After seven years of childless marriage he had smitten Cordelay with a fatal fever. And she had come back to her lovely home in the Loire valley. But not for long. Ten months! That was all she had been allowed – ten months. Then the unimaginable. Paul, her own beloved Paul, arranged to marry her off to the unspeakable de Goncourt. It had taken many years for her to understand how God could do this to her. But at last it had all become clear. She was the agent of his wrath. Her husband was an evil man. Nothing interested him but worldly riches and a son to pass them on to. Well, she had not been able to prevent him accumulating wealth, but she had denied him his other desire. And she had done everything else possible to make his life a misery, until five years ago, when worn out by decades of bickering, he had banished her from Crétigny-sur-Loire and she had returned to the peace of Beauregard. Once more, in her old age, she had been able to enjoy peaceful seclusion. Only one prayer remained to be answered. And today it had been granted. De Goncourt, at last, had gone. Gone undoubtedly to hell, despite her prayers. And all his wealth, his gold, his treasures were left behind. Now, they could be put to good use. But first she had to lay her hands on them. More importantly, she had to keep other hands off them. Lecherous hands like those of one-eyed Henri. Profane hands such as those of the man who called himself the Abbé de Saint Raymond. She would have to make an early start in the morning for Crétigny.

Marguerite de Goncourt hugged her shawl around her to keep out the evening chill. Slowly she made her way indoors and summoned the coachman.

'This is getting beyond a joke.' Tim glared in the direction of the man who had just entered the bar. 'Can you see another way out of this place?'

Catherine surveyed the room and pointed to a door in the far corner.

'Come on, then.' Tim grabbed her hand and ploughed a furrow through the protesting crowd.

At the door he turned to make sure that their pursuer was still in attendance. Then he pushed it open and tugged Catherine through.

They emerged into an ill-lit alleyway strewn with garbage.

'OK, keep well out of the way.' Tim gave the order in a low voice, as he flattened himself against the wall.

Catherine stared at him, horrified. 'Tim, what on earth do you think . . .?'

The door opened. The man in the coffee-coloured suit rushed out. Looked up and down the alley. Saw Catherine, standing paces away. Realised, too late, that something was wrong. His right hand moved across inside his jacket.

Before it made contact with the gun, Tim had his neck in a grip that allowed the victim no movement. The man moved, screamed his pain, and then stood very very still.

'Catherine, get his gun!'

She made no move. 'Tim, what the hell do you think you're doing?'

'Trying to find out what he's up to.'

'Look, this is silly. You don't understand . . .'

'Precisely! Now, get his gun and ask him why he's following me around and who he works for.'

Slowly, Catherine stepped forward, felt inside the jacket and removed a small, squat pistol.

The next moment she had backed away and was pointing it at Tim. 'Let him go!' Her voice quivered with nervousness and fear.

Tim shook his head. 'Point number one, I can break this fellow's neck quicker than you can squeeze the trigger. Point number two, if you do squeeze that trigger nothing will happen because the safety-catch is still on.'

Catherine threw the weapon away and it fell with a metallic clatter among a pile of discarded cans.

'Good. Now ask him what all this is about.'

'Tim, listen to me—'

'Ask him!'

Catherine loosed off a stream of faltering Japanese. The man answered with a series of curt sentences.

'Well?' Tim looked at her impatiently.

'He says he was ordered to keep an eye on you. Strangers in Tokyo can get into difficulties if they're not careful.'

'And just who is it who's so solicitous for my welfare. Your boss?'

'It's not Mr Tonashi. I'm quite sure of that.'

'Who, then?'

'He won't say. It's more than his life is worth.'

'Ask him again.'

Catherine shrugged and put the question.

Tim felt the man stiffen. He made no sound.

'Tim, for God's sake, let him go. You won't get any more out of him, no matter what you do.'

With a sudden movement, Tim changed his grip and pushed. The man was propelled across the narrow space, hit the opposite wall and slithered limply to the ground.

'OK. Come on!' Tim led the way back through the bar, along the sidestreet to the main thoroughfare. Neither of them spoke until they were sitting in a taxi.

By then Catherine was ready to blaze her anger. 'Well done, Mr Lacy. You have just made yourself a very nasty enemy.'

'Don't exaggerate. All that's happened is that an amateurish young thug has learned that not every British tourist is fair game.'

'All that's happened is that you have made him lose face – and in front of a woman. For a Japanese, and particularly for a member of the *Gamakuchi-gumi*, that is unpardonable.'

'What's this Gamakuchi thing? I thought you said our friend was a *boryokudan*.'

'There are several yakuza societies. *Gamakuchi-gumi* is the biggest and most powerful.'

'And how do you know that guy was a member? I didn't see a badge, and there wasn't time for a secret handshake.'

Catherine shook her head angrily. 'It doesn't matter. What matters is that you've jumped into the trough with both feet and achieved absolutely nothing. You may have shaken that guy off, but the people who sent him know where to find you.'

'Well, we can soon change that: I'll move. Would you be kind enough to ask the driver to take us to another hotel – somewhere a bit less ostentatious.'

'What about your things?'

'Would it be asking too much of you to arrange for them to be sent to your office? I'll pick them up tomorrow.'

183

'But tomorrow your itinerary—'

'Forget the sightseeing. I want to meet your boss. He brought me out here supposedly to discuss a security problem. Well, I would feel a lot happier to be face to face with the evasive Mr Tonashi a.s.a.p. Now, either he fits me into his schedule tomorrow or I book myself on the first London flight.'

Catherine wound down the window and let in a gust of warm, wet air. 'Do you realise how difficult you're making things for me? Mr Tonashi and I planned your programme very carefully. He was concerned that you should enjoy your stay to the full. In this country, hospitality is a point of honour.' She paused. 'And to refuse it is an insult.'

'OK, Catherine, point taken. I don't mean any disrespect. If he wants to give me the full VIP treatment, that's fine by me. All I want is a slight rearrangement of the schedule. That's not asking too much, is it?'

She made no answer. Instead, she gave the driver some instructions. Then she sank back on the seat. 'I've told him to drive us straight to my place. Someone's got to keep an eye on you.' She glared at him. 'And don't get any ideas.'

Twenty minutes later, as Tim appraised the contents of Catherine's high-level apartment in what was obviously a fashionable quarter of the city, he thought that Tonashi Electrical Industries must pay very well. The decor was spartan yet feminine and of excellent quality, the few items of furniture and embellishment conforming to a regime of straight lines and pale colours.

'I see you're into supporting local artists.' Tim indicated the contemporary Japanese watercolours and drawings round the walls.

'Yes. I sometimes think it's a bit strange that Mr Tonashi avidly collects Western paintings which don't grab me at all, and I'm very excited by the new wave of Japanese artists which he can't stand,' Catherine called from the kitchen where she was preoccupied making tea.

It was the first Tim had heard about Tonashi as a connoisseur, and he wondered whether Catherine had let this information slip out unintentionally. He followed up, deliberately casual. 'I'm greatly looking forward to seeing the celebrated Tonashi collection. That's one reason why I'm impatient to meet him.'

She emerged carrying a tray with a steaming dish and porcelain bowls for the tea. 'You're very privileged. Not many people get to see the gallery.'

'Is it the security of his collection that he wants to see me about?'

'You'll have to discuss that with him.' She set the tray down on a low table, and arranged herself elegantly in an armchair.

Tim smiled. 'I'm glad to see that your love of things oriental doesn't extend to wearing kimonos and expecting your guests to kneel on cushions.'

She laughed, and he was glad at this sign that she was thawing.

He said, 'I'm sorry about what happened earlier. Maybe it was a stupid thing to do.'

Catherine handed him a bowl of green tea. 'You can't bear not being in control of any situation, can you? Anything you don't understand is automatically threatening.'

'I suppose you're right. Perhaps you'd better help me to understand. Tell me some more about the character who was following us, and the outfit he works for. You knew him, didn't you?'

She began cautiously. 'I've seen him. He's one of Kodomo's henchmen.'

'And Kodomo . . .?'

'Masyoshi Kodomo is the oyabun, the godfather, of the *Gamakuchi-gumi*. That means he controls around twelve thousand society members running every kind of racket from prostitution and gambling to kidnapping and narcotics.'

Tim shook his head. 'But what I don't understand—'

'Is how a nice girl like me, etc, etc?'

'Well, yes.'

'I work for one of the country's biggest businessmen. In Japan big business, politics and *boryokudan* are all intertwined.'

'That sounds like a pretty sick society.'

'Don't jump to conclusions before you've heard the whole story. Western-style democracy here is only a modern graft on to a feudal stock that's thousands of years old. Hierarchy and authority are ingrained into the people's way of thinking. Most Japanese still believe the emperor is divine. Society depends on a very precise interplay of relationships – that's one fact. Another is the warrior code. After 1945 we took away Japan's military capability, closed the door on her imperial pretensions. All that achieved was turning her militaristic tradition inwards. The *boryokudan* societies claim descent from the ancient warrior caste of the samurai, and there's a lot of truth in such claims. That's why young men cut their fingers off and have their bodies tattooed all over. That's why the societies have elaborate religious initiation rituals. That's why the oyabuns fight each other just like the warlords of old. It's all a matter of total commitment to something ancient and splendid and powerful.'

'It sounds as though you approve of them.'

'I think they're crap, but I know nothing's going to change the way things are.'

'You don't believe in the political process?'

'Politics are polarised here. There's no such thing as a cosy, reasoned liberalism. The only people who challenge the status quo are the communists, and they want to overthrow the entire social order. That's why there's an unspoken alliance between right-wing politics, big business, the machinery of law and order – and the yakuzas. As they see it, it's a choice between sticking together or seeing Japan throw away all it's gained since the war in an orgy of red revolution.'

'So your boss and this Kodomo character are, literally, as thick as thieves?'

Catherine yawned. 'Are things here all that different from the West, when it comes down to it? Tonashi needs a new factory; the contract goes to one of Kodomo's construction companies. Tonashi has a problem with shop-floor agitators; Kodomo provides the muscle to sort it out. So? These things don't happen in Chicago or Birmingham?' She stood up. 'Well, I've about had it for today. Come on, I'll give you your bed.'

She opened a cupboard, took out a futon, and unrolled it on the floor behind the sofa. Tim looked dubiously at the unyielding pallet.

Catherine laughed. 'You've never tried a futon?' She handed him a bundle of bedding. 'It's very comfortable. You'll sleep like a baby.'

It was, and he did.

When he woke, after 9.00 the next morning, the flat was empty and there was a note in the kitchen. 'Hang around. I'll call you as soon as I have spoken with Mr Tonashi.'

The phone rang just over an hour later.

'Hi! I told you you'd sleep well.'

'Thanks. You were right. Have you had a word with the little yellow chief?'

The perfect personal secretary giggled in spite of herself. She quickly recovered. 'Mr Tonashi has to be in Kyoto this afternoon, but he could fit in a brief preliminary meeting with you at midday.'

'Fine.'

'Mr Tonashi has a sauna every day at the Celebrity Club. It's in the Rappongi quarter, not far from my apartment. I'll send a car for you at ten to twelve.'

'Thanks. Will you be coming?'

'Down, boy!' She laughed and rang off.

Tim's escort turned out to be a tubby, middle-aged Japanese with a smattering of English. Glancing casually at the man's hands during the brief car journey, Tim was relieved to note that all his fingers were intact. The Celebrity Club was a large, exclusive establishment set in its own small, Japanese-style park of lawns and lakes overspread by cedars, and offering its wealthy clientele every diversion from luxurious restaurants and a casino to a gymnasium, sauna and both indoor and outdoor swimming pools.

Tim's companion, who introduced himself as Doshida, led the way to the Scandinavian-style wooden complex adjacent to the main building, which was labelled 'Exercise Wing' in Japanese and English. They changed, draped themselves in towels, and handed their clothes to smiling kimono-clad girls. Bowing and beaming, Doshida motioned him towards the steam room.

'Mr Tonashi?' Tim enquired.

'Soon,' came the confident reply.

They took their places on wooden benches around a surprisingly large square chamber. At first Tim could see little through the clouds of steam which entered intermittently through a grill in the centre of the floor. Gradually he made out the forms of half a dozen other occupants. Save for a swarthy man, sitting directly opposite, who might have been Syrian or Turk, they were all Japanese. None of them spoke or moved. It was too hot for any unnecessary effort.

Long minutes passed. Customers came and went. Tim felt the sweat flowing from his pores. Twice he pointed to his watch and drew from Doshida a cheerful 'Soon!'

Tim noticed that the Levantine also seemed impatient. Several times he spoke quietly but urgently to his companion. Suddenly he stood up, shouting angrily. 'Tell Mr Tonashi I couldn't wait any longer!' He strode, alone, towards the exit.

Tim looked round, aware of four pairs of eyes fixed upon him through the clouds of steam. Aware, suddenly, that something was very wrong. Aware, above all, that the man whose voice he had instantly recognised was Niki Karakis.

Henri de Goncourt would have arrived first at Crétigny-sur-Loire if one of the carriage wheels had not shattered on the road south of Etampes. By the time one of the servants had unhitched a horse, ridden back into town with the broken item, roused a wheelwright, had the repairs done, ridden back and, with the help of men from a nearby farm, got the carriage roadworthy again, the sun was well up. It was past eleven when the horses took the long avenue of limes at a canter, swept through the iron gates and came to a halt in a swirl of dust before the château.

Hung over, tired and dishevelled, the new Comte de Goncourt descended and walked towards the house to claim his inheritance. He walked straight into an argument.

As he strode proprietorially up the steps he noticed that the façade of the château, set between its matching round towers, presented a prospect of neglect. Most of the windows were shuttered. Veins of ivy stood out against the cream-coloured stone. A brace of wood pigeons waddled away along the terrace, indignant at the unexpected intrusion. The main door stood open, and no servant was at hand to greet him. It was clear, however, that the house was not totally deserted. The sound of voices came from the direction of the salon – loud, angry voices.

Entering the room, which would have been comfortable but for the musty smell and the disorder of chairs, tables and commodes littered with books, papers, bottles and discarded clothing, de Goncourt observed his aunt perched erect on a wide fauteuil in front of the high windows. The other occupant, a tall young man in thigh boots and a leather jerkin, strutted around as he spoke.

'Madame, all I ask is your permission to search for what is the rightful property of the abbey.'

Marguerite's voice was as sombre and lacking in lustre as the black gown she habitually wore. 'And, I repeat, you'd be wasting your time. Anything of value is concealed, and what isn't concealed has been made off with by the servants. Anyway, I am no longer mistress of this house. Here is the new count. You must ask him.'

Henri crossed the room and made a brief obeisance. He forced a smile. 'My dear Aunt. I am sorry to hear of your loss. Of course, I came as soon—'

'As soon as you could tear yourself away from the Paris whores.' Marguerite cackled. 'Well you needn't have hurried. This threadbare inheritance certainly isn't worth the effort.' She waved a hand round the room's chaos.

Henri decided to humour the old woman. Her behaviour was as eccentric, in its own way, as that of her late, parsimonious husband. 'Come now, Aunt.' The smile remained fixed. 'What's all this "threadbare" business? Everyone knows the Comte de Goncourt was as rich as Croesus.'

The stranger came towards him. 'Madame la Comtesse insists that there is nothing of value in the house. Her husband, it seems, trusted no one. He fell into the habit of hiding his money, plate and small treasures, no one knows where.'

The courtier surveyed him haughtily. 'And whom, sir, have I the pleasure of addressing?'

'Ronsard de Grossville, at your service, Monsieur le Comte . . .'

'He calls himself the Abbé de St Raymond.' Marguerite snorted her contempt. 'Abbé! Huh! He wouldn't recognise a holy thought if it jumped out from behind a bush and said "Boo!" '

De Goncourt ignored the taunt. 'And what brings Monsieur l'Abbé to Crétigny?'

De Grossville decided to ingratiate himself with the new master of these impressive lands. 'Monsieur le Comte, it is a small matter to trouble you with at such a time as this. You will have many important affairs to attend to. However, it is important for the abbey. The late comte made a bequest to the brothers: a thank offering for their prayers.'

De Goncourt prowled the room, examining the dust-covered bottles.

He felt an urgent need for wine. 'And just what is this little "offering"?' He sniffed at the neck of one squat container and winced at the stale, vinegary smell.

'A small painting, Monsieur le Comte. A religious work depicting Our Lady and the Holy Christ Child.'

Somewhere deep inside the courtier's throbbing head the words connected up with another image. 'Who was the painter of this pious object?'

De Grossville was deliberately vague. 'Some Italian, I believe. I know little of such matters.'

'Could it have been some Italian by the name of Raphael?'

'Now that you mention it, Monsieur le Comte, that name does sound familiar.'

'Bravo!' Marguerite clapped her bony hands together. She was greatly enjoying the charade being played out before her. '*The Triarchs*! That's what he wants! Crétigny's most proud possession! Don't be deceived by all this talk about the brothers. They won't get a sniff of the painting. He only wants—'

De Grossville turned on her, trying hard not to show his anger. 'Madame, I really must ask—'

She waved a hand at him. 'Help me up. I've something to show you.'

The abbé gave her his arm. Once on her feet, she made her way surprisingly nimbly across the room, leaning only slightly on an ebony cane. She led the two men across the château's marble-flagged hallway to a doorway on the far side.

'This was my late husband's chapel.' She preceded them into a chamber which was almost a mirror image of the one they had just left. It, too, was untidily strewn with miscellaneous objects. Marguerite waved her stick around the chaos. 'This is where he worshipped his god – money. And there is his altar.' She indicated the large walnut table with ormolu mounts, in the centre of the room. 'That is where he sat to receive his rents. There he lent money at usurious rates of interest. There he cheated debtors out of their lands and their homes. I have seen many leave this room in tears. I have seen them stride out screaming vengeance. People in the village will tell you that Monsieur le Comte kept nightly tryst in this room with the devil.'

Henri gazed around at the oppressive clutter and could readily understand why such superstitions were believed. He shivered. 'Uncle never let me in here.'

'He let very few people in, lest they should see where he put his money. And where did he put it, eh?' Her wrinkled grin challenged them to answer the question.

The abbé shrugged and pointed to the iron coffers and wooden chests around the walls.

Marguerite laughed. 'No! Look for yourselves. I found all the keys earlier, and opened them.'

When the two men pulled back the lids they discovered piles of ledgers, bundles of scrolls and sealed documents. There was not a single canvas purse or gold louis.

'Where did it go then, all that money? For certain it never left this room. And where is all the family silver? And the jewels that were part of my dowry? And *The Triarchs*?'

De Grossville turned to the wall opposite the large, stone fireplace. 'It used to hang there. Monsieur le Comte brought me in here once to show me what he was leaving to the abbey.'

Marguerite gazed triumphantly at the empty space. 'Well, it's not there now. And it wasn't there five years ago, when I was last in this room.'

The abbé gazed around urgently, as though he expected to see *The Triarchs* behind a pile of logs in the hearth, or partially covered by the litter of books and papers on the floor. 'Then where . . .?'

'Hidden!' The old woman's peals of laughter taunted her hearers. 'Now, do you see? The old skinflint was so fearful for his treasures that he put them all in some secret place where no one else could ever find them.' She waggled her stick at her nephew. 'A threadbare inheritance, indeed, eh, young Henri? Nothing here for you to spend on fripperies and fancies with the Duc d'Orléans and all your other atheistical friends.'

De Goncourt smiled and shrugged. 'My dear Aunt, the problem is not a difficult one. If the late comte hid things, then they must be in this room somewhere: a cupboard behind the panelling, a space under the floorboards. In all likelihood, one of the servants—'

'Servants?' Marguerite was enjoying herself hugely now. 'There were only three who would stay here in the last few years. Only three who could put up with his tantrums and didn't mind having to pester him for their wages. And they're gone. Gone before the old fool was cold in his bed. Gone with whatever nick-nacks they could lay their hands on. You'll not find them if you scour the whole Loire valley with a troop of horse.'

Henri struggled with his temper. 'Then I must search alone. But at this moment I am parched and famished after my journey. Is there nothing left in the larder or the cellar to set before hungry travellers?'

Marguerite sent her own attendants into the village for provisions, and some bottles of wine were found in the château. With these the two men and Alys, Henri's buxom travelling companion, made a simple dinner, while the old comte's widow went to find the local priest and make arrangements for the funeral.

After the meal Henri suggested politely to Monsieur l'Abbé that there was no need for him to neglect any longer his doubtless pressing duties at St Raymond. But Monsieur l'Abbé was in no hurry to leave. He was here, he insisted, on monastery business. The late comte had been kind enough to remember the brothers in his will. He was anxious to locate the will and prove the abbey's title to *The Triarchs*. Henri insisted that the Raphael was an important de Goncourt heirloom which must not go out of the family. He was sure that his uncle would not have made any such bequest. De Grossville suggested that the best way to settle the matter would be to find the will. It was finally agreed that the visitor might remain at the château for the afternoon, or at least until old Alphonse's testamentary intentions could be established.

The two men spent a couple of hours in the study, searching in every drawer, chest and cupboard they could find. They discovered sheaves of bills, inventories, deeds, agreements and indentures. They came across account books and rent rolls in plenty. But there was no sign of a last will and testament.

At last they faced each other across the wide, document-strewn table. The young abbé voiced the thought in both their minds. 'Perhaps there is some truth in the comtesse's story of secret chambers.'

Selfconsciously at first, and then with growing zeal, they tapped the wainscot, inspected the furniture for hidden cavities, pulled aside the rugs and tried to prise up the floorboards.

While this frenzied treasure hunt was going on, Marguerite de

Goncourt was busy with her own arrangements. By mid-afternoon her late husband had been coffined and moved to the church, and she was free to concentrate on the living. She had arrived at Crétigny with her maid, a coachman and a groom. She augmented this workforce with the men who had come with Henri from Paris. She even pressed the pouting Alys into service. The kitchen was tidied, the stove relit, and the dining table set for a substantial meal whose preparation the old woman carefully organised. The wine she took care of personally. Some of the bottles in Crétigny's cellar were of excellent quality. She selected a dozen and brought them, two at a time, up the broad stone steps which led from the cobwebby, rat-scurrying *cave*. In a deserted scullery she drew the corks, emptied a tiny amount of wine from each bottle, and then refilled it with a measured dose from a flask she kept in a purse hanging at her waist. Then she conveyed the bottles to the dining-room and set them on a side table.

Supper, which was served soon after six o'clock, began in a very tense atmosphere. The two men were tired and frustrated after their fruitless search. Alys was annoyed at being translated from the luxury of the Palais Royal to a decrepit old house where a decrepit old woman treated her like a servant. It was Marguerite who infused life into the party. She asked de Grossville about the planned extensions to his residence and the difficulties of attracting young men to the religious life. She questioned Henri about the regent and his government. Were the rumours true about an incestuous relationship between Orléans and his own daughter, the Duchesse de Berry? What did his wife think of this, and how many lovers had *she* taken? De Goncourt was soon in his element, regaling the company with scandalous stories about France's leading citizens and half revealing secrets of state. He helped himself liberally from the bottles which Marguerite was careful to keep circulating. She restricted herself to one glass of wine, diluted with water. By the time the candles and lamps had been lit, everyone was in a very good mood. The strange circumstances of this impromptu meal in the house of death created a surprising camaraderie.

At last the party broke up. Young Ronsard ordered his horse and set off home through the twilit woods and pastures along the valley. Before he had travelled a couple of miles, his head was drooping and his body lolled limply in the saddle. Try as he might, he could not keep his eyes open. He slumped forward, his head resting on the bay's soft mane. He might have reached St Raymond quite safely: the mare trod the roads and tracks sure-footedly, following the unerring instinct which drew her to her own warm, dry stable. All would have been well had it not been for the owl which leaped suddenly from the hedgerow on a quiet forest path between Bouteille and Sully. Startled by the heavy fluttering only a few feet from her nose, the mare reared and then bolted. De Grossville was thrown and fell heavily among stones at the roadside.

It was shortly after dawn that he was found, blood congealed along a bad gash on the side of his head. He was taken back to the abbey on a haycart. There he remained unconscious for almost two days. However, aided by the infirmarian's herbs, ceaseless nursing, and the prayers of the community, Ronsard de Grossville was brought slowly back to health of body. But something had happened in his brain; something from which it never recovered. His speech was slurred. His memory at best was patchy. He became, at twenty-nine, a shuffling, staring old man. It was widely believed that the Abbé de St Raymond had met with the devil.

Henri de Goncourt staggered heavily up to his chamber, relying for support upon his pretty companion. Despite the presence of Alys's delectable body in the same bed, he was asleep as soon as he pulled the coarse sheet over him. The girl, too, rapidly slipped into unconsciousness. Her drug-aided slumber was deep and restful. But Henri had ingested much more of the narcotic. It coursed his body, numbing his limbs and organs, until, shortly before midnight, it reached his heart.

The bright light from a sun already high in the sky slanted through the casement and touched Alys's eyelids. Slowly, reluctantly she emerged into wakefulness. She sat up yawning. It took her several seconds to remember where she was, and why. Then she stretched out a hand to rouse the recumbent figure beside her.

She stifled the scream by stuffing a bundle of sheets into her mouth. She leaped from the bed. For several minutes she stood trembling with fear in a corner of the room. Slowly she forced herself to think. When a girl spent the night with a wealthy nobleman – and a friend of the regent, at that – and that nobleman was found dead the next morning, she could expect very little mercy. She would be accused of witchcraft or poisoning. No one would listen to her pleas of innocence. With heart racing, Alys dressed carefully. She took all the money she could find in Henri's clothes. Then she crept out of the room, down the turret staircase, and out of the château by a side door. She went across the overgrown parkland for over a mile before reaching a road. She turned to the left and stumbled along its rutted surface, not knowing where it led.

Marguerite waited an hour after the others had retired. They would certainly be sleeping soundly by now, she calculated, and the servants were out of the way at the other end of the house. She had plenty of time to go into Alphonse's treasure store and take everything that was rightfully hers. Carrying only a candle she descended to the ground floor and entered the study. Given time, even fat, stupid Henri would discover his uncle's hiding place. She had come upon it years before, when her husband had been ill several days with a fever. It was a clever place of concealment and he had constructed it with his own hands, first walling off part of the cellar, then creating an entrance during several of those long days when the door of his sanctum was firmly locked.

She made her way through the piles of rubbish to the large stone fireplace. Of course it had been many years . . . Could she remember? The opening was high enough for her to stand up in. She set down the candle. She moved the pile of unlit logs to give herself more room. The large iron fireback seemed to be securely fixed to the wall, but somewhere along the right-hand edge . . . Yes, here it was. Her fingers found the catch and unfastened it. She pulled, and the metal plate swung outward on concealed hinges. Behind was an aperture where four large blocks of stone had been removed.

Marguerite took up the candle, whose flame fluttered in the chimney's up-draught. She stepped carefully through the hole. She checked that the bolt on the inside of the fireback was working, then closed it, just in case any servant should come snooping around. She was standing on a wide ledge. In front of her she could see the top of a wooden ladder whose other end rested on what had been the cellar floor, ten feet below.

This was the difficult part. She had known it would be. Not since those childhood escapades with Paul in the hayloft at Beauregard had she climbed up or down a ladder. But she had not laid her plans with such care to be defeated now. She gathered her skirts around her. Then slowly, carefully, she eased her stiff legs on to one of the round, wooden rungs. Taking her time, firmly gripping the ladder with one hand and the candle-holder with the other, she descended. At last she felt the stone floor beneath her. At last she had reached the miser's hoard. She turned, holding the candle aloft. And another pair of eyes met hers.

She almost dropped the light. Her already pounding heart raced. Then she realised that she was looking at a painting – *The Triarchs*. It was propped up on a large, iron-bound chest. It was the eyes of the figure on the right, the bearded man staring straight out of the canvas, that she had seen.

Marguerite found a resting place for the candle and looked around. It was a small room; little more, in fact, than a large cupboard. As well as the chest there were half a dozen wooden boxes piled on top of each other. She lifted down the painting and tried to raise the lid of the coffer. It was locked, and there was no sign of a key. She tried the smaller containers and had more luck. Most of them were full of gold and silver coins. And one held her jewellery. She lifted out a pendant of emeralds and pearls. She took up and joyfully remembered the necklaces, rings and intricate, filigree clasps. Well, Henri should certainly not have these.

She found that by climbing three rungs up the ladder she could lift the jewel casket on to the ledge above. She did so. How much of the money should she remove? Now that it was *all* hers for the taking, it seemed a pity to leave any of it. But she had to be realistic. The boxes were too heavy to carry full. She decided to half empty two of the coffers. Even then she had difficulty manoeuvring them, and the ladder creaked ominously as she lifted them.

She was tired now. The effort and the excitement were taking their toll. She dabbed a kerchief on her cheeks and forehead. It was getting warm in here. Warm and stuffy. Alphonse's secret chamber was well sealed, and there was little draught. She sat on the iron-bound chest and rested for a while. What she had taken, she told herself, was fair and just. The jewels were rightfully hers and the gold was a small recompense for years of misery. There was only one thing more to rescue. She picked up *The Triarchs* and gazed at it in the flickering light. She wanted to cry with the purity of it. Here was womanhood, holy motherhood, respected, honoured by men. How different from the reality! She thought of Henri, flabby and dissolute. Henri who could not even come down for his uncle's funeral without bringing a doxie with him. Henri, carousing night after night with the Duc d'Orléans whose behaviour scandalised the whole nation. Unthinkable that he should have *The Triarchs*. Scarcely less awful was the prospect of it going to that arrogant popinjay, de Grossville, a man who inherited an abbey as one might inherit an orchard or a baker's shop, and was intent on exploiting it for all it was worth. No, she would keep Raphael's masterpiece. She alone could venerate it properly. She alone was free from the taint of money and vice.

Marguerite de Goncourt took the painting carefully in both hands, and once more set off up the ladder. It was awkward and heavier than she had thought, and her ankles and calves were throbbing. She rested for a moment, the picture between herself and the frame of the ladder. That was the moment at which the rung on which she was standing broke. She fell heavily backwards against the chest. One foot was caught between two rungs. The leg twisted. Simultaneously she heard the bone crack and felt the sudden thrust of pain. A flailing arm sent the candle crashing to the floor. It guttered out and total blackness claimed all.

Impossible to doubt that the old Château de Crétigny was haunted; it was a well-known fact. Everyone within a hundred-mile radius would tell you so. The ghost of an aged miser stalked its empty chambers, guarding his hidden treasure. If you pressed one of the locals for more details, they would tell you how, before the old man was even in his coffin, four people had come to the house – two ladies and two gentlemen. One of the men – heir to the estate – had been found dead in bed with a look of unspeakable terror on his face. The other had been discovered miles away, wandering the countryside, quite beside his wits. And the ladies? Disappeared! Gone to be the devil's brides. Never a trace of them was ever seen again. And since that day no mortal man had set foot inside the château.

Tim jumped to his feet. 'What the hell's going on!'

Doshida stood up and tapped him deferentially on the arm. He indicated the exit through which Karakis had just passed. 'Please.'

'Like hell I will!'

Tim made for the other door. Before he could reach it one of the towelled men had placed himself in front of it. From beneath his skimpy covering he produced an automatic pistol.

Tim turned. Doshida stood a few paces away. He waved towards the exit. 'Please.' He smiled and bowed.

Cautiously Tim pushed the door and went through. He walked on the balls of his feet, ready to leap to one side or the other. Three doors led off to the right. Doshida indicated one of them. Inside was a small pool of very cold water. Doshida removed his towel and plunged in. Since the man with the gun stood by the door, Tim had no choice but to complete the sauna experience. He dived into the water and came up gasping with shock.

When he and Doshida had dried themselves, they went back to the changing room, collected their clothes and got dressed. They appeared to have lost their armed guard.

'You feel good, now?' The rotund Japanese smiled.

Tim had to admit that he did feel remarkably good. Angry, apprehensive and puzzled certainly, but also vibrant, tingling and alert. He said, 'And now do I get to see Mr Tonashi?'

'This way, please.'

Doshida took him to a remarkably luxurious suite of offices on the first floor of the main building. He motioned Tim to a deep armchair, knocked deferentially on a door and, in response to a summons, entered. Seconds later he reappeared and beckoned.

There were four men inside the room. The one seated behind the desk in a high-backed swivel chair was old, wrinkled and wore very thick glasses. Two men stood behind him. One was the man in the coffee-coloured suit – except that now he was wearing less flamboyant grey. Tim was gratified to see the large plaster across his forehead. The fourth member of the reception committee was Doshida.

Tim advanced, hand outstretched. 'Mr Tonashi, is this how you treat all your business associates?'

Doshida, switching now to perfect English, shook his head. 'Mr Lacy, I have the honour to present Mr Masyoshi Kodomo.'

CHAPTER 10

Tim Lacy sat in the proffered chair and warily accepted a goblet of Armagnac. He held the glass up. 'You obviously know a great deal about me, Mr Kodomo, even down to my taste in liquor. That puts you at a very great advantage. All I know about you is that you're probably Japan's top criminal boss.'

Doshida translated.

The yakuza chief nodded with the faintest hint of a smile. The reply, delivered through his portly henchman, was serious and businesslike. 'Mr Lacy, I regret the element of compulsion which some of my associates were obliged to employ but, if I may say so, you seem an impulsive young man.'

'I don't like being followed and threatened with guns. What's more, I don't see the point of it all. Didn't it occur to you to arrange an appointment by conventional means – a phone-call or a letter? Perhaps kidnapping is just second nature to you.'

When the taunt was translated, Kodomo's bodyguards suddenly stiffened and scowled. Tim guessed that they had never heard anyone address their leader with anything less than a respect bordering on reverence. He decided to press home his advantage. 'And another thing: why all this charade about arranging a security system for Mr Tonashi?'

Kodomo was unruffled. 'There were very good reasons for secrecy, Mr Lacy. And, in any case, would you have travelled halfway round the world to meet *me*?'

Tim sipped his brandy. 'Well, now that I am here, perhaps we can get down to brass tacks.'

Doshida was puzzled by the colloquialism. 'Brass ticks?'

Tim laughed. 'Brass tacks – business.'

'Ah.' The translator frowned thoughtfully, and filed the expression away in his memory bank before converting the suggestion into Japanese.

Kodomo passed a large black-and-white photograph across the desk. 'You are, of course, familiar with this.'

Tim nodded cautiously as he gazed at a very professional print of *The Triarchs*.

'And this man?' Kodomo pushed towards him a picture showing Karakis walking along a Tokyo street.

Tim decided to give nothing away. 'Wasn't he in the sauna this morning?'

'And you have never seen him before that?'

'No.'

Kodomo seemed very relieved. 'Good. He did not recognise you either. We had to establish that fact. That is why we contrived to bring you face to face today. It wasn't easy to arrange.'

'OK. You've brought two complete strangers face to face. What now?'

'Not complete strangers, Mr Lacy. That man's name is Karakis: a Greek dealer in stolen works of art and antiquities. You are, I believe, very familiar with his activities.'

'There's no point in denying it.'

'You have suffered much at the hands of this Karakis?'

Tim nodded.

'You would welcome an opportunity to settle scores?'

'I would like to see Karakis where he belongs – behind bars. For a very long time.'

Kodomo smiled broadly, revealing a row of gold fillings. 'Good. If we combine our resources you will be able to realise that dream.'

Tim took refuge behind his brandy goblet while he thought fast. Was this really the opportunity he had been waiting for to destroy Karakis and all his works? The very thought of it set his nerve ends tingling. But to get tangled up with one of the world's top ten criminal organisations? This Kodomo character, for all his grandfatherly benignity, probably had a lot more blood on his hands than the

Greek did. He stared candidly at his host. 'Just what has Karakis done to upset you?'

'I can't tell you that until I know that we have a deal.'

'Then let me guess. Karakis comes here to sell you *The Triarchs*. You like the painting, but you don't like his price. You want me to help you get the Raphael and turn the Greek over to the police at the same time.' It was not very good but it was the best Tim could do on the spur of the moment. Anything to draw more information out of Kodomo.

It worked. The old man laughed again, his colleagues dutifully joining in the mirth. 'The matter is not that simple, Mr Lacy. I will explain. Here in Japan we have many wealthy collectors and also very lenient laws about the ownership of works of art with dubious provenance. Here, if you buy a stolen object in good faith and own it for two years, no one else can ever lay claim to it. This means that Japan acts as a magnet to men who deal in "hot" works of art – men like Karakis. Hundreds of items from famous collections and galleries are now in this country. Under Japanese law their original owners have no redress. Of course, the buyers don't advertise their whereabouts, but in the art world these things are known. The whole trade is becoming embarrassing for our government and our diplomatic corps.'

Tim shrugged. 'Cultural rape has been going on for centuries.'

'Ah, yes. The Elgin Marbles and all that. Certainly no country is free of blame. But we have reached the point where there is so much pressure on our government that they may be forced to bring Japanese law in line with the laws of other countries. That could prove very embarrassing for several of our leading citizens.'

'I'll bet!'

'Including my good friend Ichiro Tonashi. He has built up a fine representative collection of European painting.'

'Of which not every item is of unsullied provenance?'

Kodomo nodded. 'Now Karakis wants to dump some of his latest acquisitions on Ichiro.'

'Including *The Triarchs*?'

'Yes. When such a deal became known internationally, it could prove to be the final spring thaw that swells the river.'

Tim puzzled over the literal translation, then grasped the point. 'Ah yes, the last straw. But, surely, all Mr Tonashi has to do is say "No, thank you"?'

Kodomo surveyed him shrewdly. 'Mr Lacy, I have shown you several of my cards. I must know if you are in the game before I go any further.'

There was a long pause before Tim replied, choosing his words carefully. 'I will do anything legal to bring Karakis to justice but I assume that you are not expecting me to make you a *gift* of my services as a gesture of Anglo-Japanese goodwill?'

The old man laughed. 'Far from it, Mr Lacy. What I propose is five hundred thousand pounds paid on your acceptance of my commission, and a similar sum upon its successful completion – paid, of course, wherever in the world you wish.'

Tim did his best to remain impassive. For a million quid there had to be a hell of a lot more in this than met the eye. Slowly, expressionlessly, he nodded.

'Good.' Kodomo gestured to one of his men, who set before him a tray with a satsuma flask and two matching bowls. Kodomo poured saki and handed one porcelain dish to Tim. 'We drink to our partnership.'

Both men gulped down the spirit and Kodomo continued, briskly now. 'The police will not catch Karakis without help. We intend to provide that help – indirectly. If it is known to the people who really matter in Washington, London, Paris and Rome that certain anonymous Japanese interests have helped to close down one of the top fine art syndicates and recover several important stolen artefacts, our international standing will be much enhanced and the voices clamouring for reform will be silenced.'

Tim shook his head. Something did not ring true. 'You could write *finis* to Karakis's career tomorrow. All you have to do is put out a contract on him.'

Kodomo scowled. 'That's not a very practical solution.' He hurried on. 'Let me outline my proposal.'

'Just a minute, Mr Kodomo. I don't buy this patriotic altruism. You're not going into all these elaborate and costly games just so that the Japanese government can save face. What's in it for you?'

Kodomo muttered something under his breath. Then he treated Tim to another gold-rimmed smile. 'You are very shrewd, Mr Lacy. That is good in a business partner.' He paused, arranging his thoughts carefully. 'Karakis has his supporters in Japan – contacts, intermediaries.'

Tim was a jump ahead. 'A rival gang?'

'The *Ichimaku-gami*: another, smaller yakuza society.'

'And you're sore at them for getting to Tonashi, who is strictly your property.'

'Mitsuru Osawa, the oyabun of *Ichimaku-gami*, is a very ambitious young man. He has little regard for the agreed boundaries between our societies.'

'I'm sure you know how to deal with upstart rivals, Mr Kodomo.'

The old man nodded sagely. 'Better to clip the bird's wings than wound him in flight. I am a man of peace. Even the police will tell you that.' He chuckled. 'They send me good wishes on my birthday. They know that only I can keep the more unruly ones in check. If I eliminate Karakis, Osawa will be obliged to revenge his colleague's death. Within days we shall have gang war on the streets of every city in Japan. Does that answer all your questions, Mr Lacy?'

'It'll do for now.'

'Good. I will outline my plan, then. After that Mr Doshida will give you lunch and show you round my club. I hope you will feel free to enjoy all the facilities here, as my guest.'

In March 1793 the château at Crétigny-sur-Loire was razed to the ground. The French Revolution was entering its bloodiest phase: the Terror. Louis XVI had been executed two months before on the Place de la Concorde, and become merely the most exalted of the 2,690 victims claimed by the Parisian guillotine in less than a year and a half of unleashed fanaticism and hatred. In the provinces there were many even worse acts of barbarity. At Nantes, for example, 'enemies of the people' – men, women and children – were bound hand and foot, crammed into old boats, towed out into the Loire estuary, and capsized. It was, in fact, the peasant army returning from its campaign against royalist forces in the Vendée which sacked the de Goncourt château.

The Loire valley lands had, by a tortuous genealogical process, passed into the hands of a distant branch of the family who seldom visited the area and had never lived in the house. These cadet de Goncourts had been among the first to flee to England. The revolutionary Convention had declared their estates forfeit, along with those of all *émigrés*. That led to egalitarian chaos. Local officials had no idea how to turn central decrees into sensible arrangements on the ground. Hurried fences were erected and as swiftly torn down, as rival claimants divided up fields and pastures, commandeered barns and byres. The returning people's army, in the spring of 1793, took account of none of this. They spread out over the land, helping themselves to grain, livestock and whatever else took their fancy. Frustrated at finding nothing to loot at the château, they set fire to it, and then continued on their victorious way.

In 1807, by which time Napoleon Bonaparte had stamped a new order and discipline on France, Bénédict Legrange, an architect on the municipal staff at Orléans, bought the site of the château. He was a man who specialised in ruins, a human vulture attracted to the carcases of dead abbeys, mansions and churches. It was his custom to buy up cheaply buildings left derelict in the wake of revolution, and pick them clean of stone, lead, panelling, fireplaces, staircases – anything that he could sell to his many friends in the building trade. It was a lucrative sideline. But all who knew Bénédict Legrange were astounded at his sudden emergence as a man of wealth and property.

It was soon after he had cleared the site at Crétigny that he unexpectedly gave up his job, announced that he was going to build himself a new house, and proceeded to raise from the dusty rubble at Crétigny a mansion scarcely less splendid than the one which had preceded it. Legrange seemed to have money to burn. His house was spacious. He had his extensive gardens laid out in the latest fashion. He boasted the finest carriages and carriage-horses in the whole region. Everyone speculated about where the architect's money had come from, and inevitably one of the rumours was that he had discovered the legendary miser's hoard. But no one ever knew for certain, and the enigmatic Legrange never said.

As for *The Triarchs*, the painting's next public appearance was in London; to be precise in Beneti's Rooms, Pall Mall on 19 October 1818. Signor Beneti's catalogue read:

Lot 43, The Property of a French Gentleman.

RAFFAELLO SANTI, known as Raphael,
ADORATION OF THE MAGI
Signor Beneti is privileged to offer to his Distinguished
Clientele one of the finest examples of
Renaissance Art to be seen on the London Market
for several years

Pietrangelo Beneti was one of the new breed of art dealers-cum-auctioneers sired by the opportunism of war. For a quarter of a century, plundering armies had marched back and forth across the Continent. Collections had been dispersed as victorious soldiery broke into castles and palaces. Others had been disposed of by fleeing aristocrats in need of ready cash. Some had come on to the market simply because their owners had been ruined. Thousands upon thousands of paintings, ancient sculptures, items of plate and porcelain, pieces of jewellery, rugs, tapestries and examples of the finest furniture were readily available. And there was no shortage of nouveau-riche industrialists, financiers and entrepreneurs ready to buy up the objects that had graced the homes of the old aristocracy, as they set about turning themselves into the new aristocracy.

Beneti had come to England to follow his father's trade of carver and gilder. It had not taken him many years to realise that, while creativity is poorly paid, selling the results of other men's genius is highly profitable. In the intervals of the fighting, he toured war-dislocated Europe, buying items of beauty at knock-down prices and persuading reluctant owners to allow him to sell their family treasures on commission. He brought the trophies of his continental campaigns back to London, already established as the art centre of the world. Within two decades his sale-rooms in Pall Mall had become one of the major attractions of the cognoscenti.

Certainly, on that moist autumn afternoon in 1818, the elegant first-floor Grand Salon was gratifyingly full as the portly Signor Beneti mounted his rostrum and gazed round at his clientele. The double doors at the far end, giving directly on to the impressive staircase, had been thrown wide and through the portal came lords and ladies, ambassadors and foreign dignitaries, the 'new' men from the City and their selfconscious wives. They received their glasses of wine from the liveried footmen, and disported themselves in groups on the

207

powder-blue and gilt fauteuils and sofas clustered around the room. Beneti recognised at a glance the court set: men and women who were, or aspired to be, friends of the Prince Regent. He smiled at the little knots of intellectuals who wandered from picture to picture earnestly discussing the merits of masterpieces few of them could afford to buy. He noted with particular pleasure the tall figure with the gaunt features who moved slowly but purposefully around the room. So, the Duke himself was here – and with little Mr Bestwick who advised him on all the furnishings for Apsley House, which a grateful nation had bestowed upon him after his victory at Waterloo. Beneti congratulated himself. There was every reason to believe that prices would be high and competition keen.

He was not disappointed. The bidding was enthusiastic as the leaders of London society and their continental counterparts vied with one another to show just how wealthy and cultured they were. With deferéntial good humour, Signor Beneti steered the distinguished company through the earlier lots. It was when he announced Item 43 that the gentle breeze of conversation rose to a sudden gust of expectancy. Every eye was fastened on the radiant masterpiece now held aloft for their admiration. *The Triarchs*, re-framed, and minor damage expertly repaired, looked as fresh as on the day when it was rescued from the artist's blazing studio.

The auctioneer allowed a long pause before he steered his audience from veneration to acquisitiveness. 'My lords, excellencies, ladies and gentlemen, it is my privilege now to offer you the most superlative example of Italian Renaissance art to come on to the market in many years. It was rescued by my own modest efforts from several generations of obscurity. I will not insult this masterpiece by expatiating on its virtues in mere words. It is eloquence itself. The fortunate possessor of this painting will be the envy of all the connoisseurs of Europe. It would be a slight to start the bidding at anything less than four thousand guineas.'

The shade of Raphael had to endure a minor rebuff: the opening bid was two thousand five hundred guineas. But after that the price rose rapidly. So did the tension. Necks craned and heads turned to see who was competing. Ears were attuned to Beneti's litany.

'Four thousand two hundred guineas.' That was Bestwick.

'Four thousand three hundred.' Beau Beauchamp, a friend of the Prince Regent, propped against the doorpost, languidly signalled his bid.

'Four thousand four hundred.' Bestwick again.

These two took the price past five thousand guineas. Then Bestwick faltered. After a whispered conversation with Wellington, he shook his head. The Duke turned and walked abruptly from the room, his agent bustling in his wake. All eyes turned to the smirking Beauchamp, and one or two friends went up to congratulate him.

It remained only for Beneti to wind up the formalities. 'Five thousand one hundred guineas, then, my lords, excellencies, ladies and gentlemen. Have you finished at five thousand one hundred?'

Silence.

'I am selling, then, at five thousand one hundred guineas.'

'Six thousand!' The words, pronounced with a foreign accent, came from somewhere in the centre of the room.

They provoked a buzz of excitement, and Beneti had to raise his voice to make himself heard. It made little difference. All opposition had been stunned into silence. Within seconds the Raphael had been knocked down to a portly, middle-aged gentleman whose brown and grey costume was of a formal cut. He gave his name as 'von Nisa'.

The smell of incense drifted across the precincts as Tim and Catherine left the bustle of the city street and walked through the temple gateway.

'You may not be into the tourist routine, Tim, but I wanted you to see Sengakuji. It may help you understand the Japanese character.' Catherine looked even more cool and composed than usual in a dress of ice-blue silk.

He surveyed the shade-blotched area of grass, raked sand and tidy paths surrounding the small temple, and searched for something complimentary to say. 'It's delightfully quiet.'

'Very few foreign visitors come here. Yet it's the home of one of Japan's greatest legends.' Catherine led the way into a small enclosure beside the temple. It was a graveyard. All the stones were of venerable age. Yet flowers and bundles of joss sticks were strewn liberally over the memorials, and the pungent smell of incense was now almost oppressive. A dozen or so men and women wandered quietly among the graves, some adding their own offerings. Catherine gestured towards the rows of simple stones. 'Behold the Forty-Seven Ronin.'

They walked slowly around the melancholy cemetery and Catherine told its story. 'Thanks to the Tokugawa shoguns, the seventeenth century was largely a time of peace. That was good news for everyone except the warrior caste.'

'The samurai?'

'Well done, that boy. Go to the top of the class.' She treated Tim to a cynical smile. 'Some of the leading thinkers were saying, "Who needs these idle bums who throw their weight around and live off the fat of the land and don't earn their keep?" There was a strong move, as I guess we'd say now, to cut the defence budget.'

'Things don't change much. The soldier's still a hero in wartime and a politician's plaything when there's no fighting to be done.'

'Well, no bureaucrat likes to have army generals breathing down his neck. As for the samurai, they were, on the whole, a pretty basic bunch of psychopaths. Unthinking thugs who'd elevated combat into a science and violence into a creed. But they weren't all dim. Some of their leaders decided to hit back on the philosophical plane. The result was *Bushidō*.'

'I've heard of that, too. It was a sort of warrior code. Do I get another brownie point for that?'

Her laugh was light and brief. '*Bushidō* went beyond its martial origins. It was nationalist and neo-Shintoist. What its originator, Yamaga Sokō, was saying was that Japan was the centre of the civilised world, and that the samurai were an élite who existed not only to defend but also to embody everything that was best in Japanese culture and ethical values.'

'It all sounds pretty esoteric to me.'

'Yes, it was – until the Forty-Seven Ronin brought it vividly to life and stamped it on the Japanese consciousness for all time.' She paused in the shade of a tree. The sun was nearing its highest point, and the day was hot. 'In 1701 – every schoolchild here knows the date and the details: just as any English kid can tell you about Drake playing bowls on Plymouth Hoe – one of the barons, Asano Takumi no Kami, was provoked by one of the shogun's noble attendants, Kina Yoshinaka, into drawing his sword in the court. This was an unpardonable offence

210

and Asano was ordered to commit suicide. Of course, he did so. But forty-seven of his retainers were determined to avenge his death. They laid siege to Kina's house in Edo, and killed the bumptious young upstart, which was probably no more than he deserved. But this act of revenge was in itself a crime, and so the *ronin* – that means "leaderless samurai" – were also ordered to disembowel themselves. They came here, where their master was buried, ceremonially committed suicide, and were interred in the same sacred ground as Lord Asano.'

Tim looked into Catherine's frank, unblinking eyes and noted that they were green bordering on hazel. 'You're pretty much into this oriental world view, aren't you?'

'I think there's a reverence here for some values we've lost sight of in the West.'

'Such as?'

'Loyalty, stability, family pride, respect for tradition, a sense of history.'

'Don't forget massive corruption, hatred of foreigners, and economic imperialism.'

'Oh, I'm not starry-eyed about the Japanese.' Suddenly she took his hand and stared intently at him with an expression devoid of cynical detachment. 'Look, what I'm trying to say is that if you don't make some attempt to understand them, you could find yourself in bad trouble. Don't be fooled by the business suits and the skyscrapers and the pizza parlours and the imported pornography. They're not imitation Westerners. I don't know what sort of a deal you've made with Kodomo but, whatever it is, he will demand absolute loyalty.'

'You mean I'm expected to fall on my sword if I fail?'

'Don't joke about it, Tim. In London, if you make a contract with someone and they let you down, what do you do?'

Tim shrugged. 'Take them to court – or just chalk it up to experience.'

'Don't suppose for a moment that Kodomo would adopt the same attitude. He brought you all the way out here to do something for him. Whatever it is, he'll expect you to deliver. If you get cold feet or fall down on the job, he won't be understanding or chalk it up to experience.'

211

Tim was lost for a reply, disconcerted by this sudden display of concern.

Catherine, too, seemed suddenly embarrassed by her change of front. She withdrew her hand with a quick, selfconscious movement and looked at her watch. 'I shall be in trouble if we fall behind schedule. My instructions are to give you lunch and get you back to the Tonashi building by 3.00. My boss wants us on the helicopter and ready to leave at 3.15 sharp.'

They started to walk back towards the entrance and the waiting limousine.

Tim broke the silence: 'Do you really not know what any of this is about?'

'No, Tim. I just make the arrangements.'

'Including having me abducted by Japan's biggest crime syndicate? You deliberately lied to me.'

For the first time Catherine's perfect PA poise was shaken. 'I'm sorry about that. I was told that Mr Kodomo wanted to meet you, and that I must arrange for you to be where his car could collect you. But I knew you wouldn't come to any harm – and you didn't. It was only a white lie – well, greyish perhaps.'

'I suppose that makes up for the scare I gave you the other evening. It seems we're both being used. Well, as one pawn to another, I think it's time I told you about the game we're involved in.'

'I really don't want—'

'Oh, but I insist. I'll give you all the details over lunch.'

They ate, inevitably, in Tokyo's most expensive restaurant, La Tour d'Argent, which for sumptuousness of decor and sheer 'Frenchness' overtops its Parisian counterpart. For Tim the lunch was not a success. It brought back memories of meals shared with Jean-Marc Laportaire, discussing art, artists and the latest scandals in the art world. Such reminiscences gave a harder edge to the story he unfolded for Catherine. He left few gaps in the narrative. He needed someone to confide in, and the blonde American was an excellent listener.

'So you see,' Tim came to the end of his monologue, 'although I hate getting involved with this Kodomo character, he's making it very much worth my while, and he's offering me the only way to wind this whole business up.'

'This "business" being revenge.' Catherine's quiet words carried a suggestion of reproach. 'Kodomo thought he had to buy you, but my guess is that you'd have signed up for free to get even with Karakis.'

That drove Tim on to the defensive. 'You were telling me earlier how much you admired those Forty-Seven Ronin.'

'Not admired – understood. Sorry if I sounded critical, but are you sure there's no other way?'

Tim toyed with his *caneton pressé*. 'Well, plan A was a disaster. I thought I could outsmart Karakis on my own, and I was tragically wrong. Gantry told me in no uncertain terms to leave these things to the experts, but the police of several countries have been trying to nail the bastard for years. He's always a jump ahead, and they're hopelessly crippled by procedures and red tape and judicial processes that well-paid lawyers can exploit. So, all things considered, the time seems to have come to send in the samurai.'

Catherine finished her sole in thoughtful silence. She laid down her knife and fork. 'How's Venetia coping?'

'I phone up from time to time and talk to her mother. Isabella managed to get her to see a shrink in Florence. He seems to be doing something for her. She's started painting again. That must be a good sign.'

'It'll take a long time. After all she's been through, she could go off men for good.'

'I get the impression that you're not all that struck on the other half of the human race, yourself.'

'OK, let's get this bit over – just so that we can avoid misunderstanding. I don't believe in casual sex. That doesn't make me a lesbian, or a female chauvinist or a fanatical women's libber. It doesn't even mean that I'm frigid.' She explored his face, looking for a reaction.

'Is this vow of celibacy lifelong?' He smiled.

Catherine did not. 'You simply can't accept this as a normal feminine attitude, can you?'

'It's not an attitude I've met very often, but I certainly respect it.'

She made no immediate response, and Tim thought the subject was closed. Then she went on, looking at her plate, not at him. 'My parents were strict Scottish Presbyterians – second-generation Americans. That meant no late-night dates, no boys in my room, keeping myself pure, and waiting for Mr Right to come along. Of course, I eventually kicked over the traces. It took a couple of heartbreaks to make me realise that perhaps my folks were right after all – that and the experiences of my friends. By the time I left college most of the girls I grew up with had been married and divorced or gone through several "permanent" relationships. It all seemed very messy. So I've settled for a fascinating career until I meet the man I want to make a home and children with.'

'I hope you recognise him when he comes.'

She shrugged, and laughed away her embarrassment. 'Now, what about you? It's your turn to bare your soul.'

Tim told her about his affair with Venetia.

'I'm sorry. I shouldn't have probed. I guess it still hurts.'

'That's OK. But, yes, it does still hurt.'

Catherine sat back and watched him finish his duck. 'What will you do when this is over? Business as usual or a spending spree with Kodomo's money?'

'Well, I must admit, since yesterday I've been tossing around an absolutely crazy idea.'

'Has it got something to do with Farrans Court?'

Tim was taken aback. 'You're a very perceptive lady, Miss Younger.'

'It was the way you spoke about the house. It's obviously very special to you. Tell me your dream.'

'It's wildly impractical. It could never happen.'

'Tell me anyway.'

Tim spent the next ten minutes putting into words for the first time a plan which he suddenly realised had been maturing deep in his unconscious for months, and now existed in surprising detail. 'I said it was a crazy idea,' he ended sheepishly.

Catherine's green eyes smiled understanding and encouragement. 'I think it's a great idea. When this business is over, I insist that you show me Farrans.'

'It's a deal.'

She shook her fair hair. 'Right now, I guess we ought to talk about the next forty-eight hours.'

'It seems that I really am going to meet the elusive Mr Tonashi.'

'That's right. And you'll love his house in the mountains. It over-

214

looks Lake Chuzenji. It's beautiful up there – all forests, rivers and waterfalls.'

'And that's where the famous art gallery is?'

'That's right. The culture bunker.'

'Why do you call it that?'

'You'll see.'

'And Karakis is due there tomorrow afternoon?'

'Yes, although I have been told to expect a Mr Cristopoulos.'

'One of our Greek friend's many aliases.'

'He's not the only one concealing his identity, is he?'

'You've been told?'

'Oh yes. I have strict instructions that you are to be introduced as Dr Charles Timothy, a lecturer in art history at Aberdeen University.'

'Mr Kodomo has worked out the script for our little farce in great detail.'

'Don't you mean the dramatis personae? It's one thing to put the characters on stage. Quite another to make sure they get their lines right. What happens if the performance goes wrong?'

'That's something I don't care to think about. Anyway, the important thing is to make sure you keep out of it. Remember, you know nothing except what your boss has told you. Whatever passes between us, you're not involved.'

'Don't worry. I intend to die an old maid – or an old something. It's you I'm concerned about. Being mixed up with Kodomo *and* Karakis is bad news. You're between the devil and the deep blue sea.'

That was something Tim did not need to be told.

'Herr Jacob Seligman and Frau Seligman.'

A stunned silence fell across the crowded ballroom as the little banker and his slightly-overdressed wife were announced in the major-domo's ringing tones. Had the emperor himself appeared stark naked in the doorway, it could scarcely have caused a greater shock to the assembled leaders of Viennese society.

Georg von Nisa, resplendent in the pendant and purple sash of the Order of Leopold, greeted his new guests courteously and introduced them to his elegant Hungarian-born wife. Then, as more than two hundred interrupted conversations were taken up again, Jacob and

Adelheid Seligman moved stiffly into the cavernous chamber where the light from chandeliers was flung in all directions by tiaras, necklaces and the gold braid of uniforms, as the dancers swirled and intertwined in a quadrille. No face turned towards them in greeting as unflinchingly they walked the social gauntlet, but they felt the eyes staring from beneath lowered lids as they passed.

The Seligmans were guilty of three offences: they were new, they were rich and they were Jewish. The élite of the Austrian Empire might be prepared to forgive them their wealth. Given time and strict adherence to the rules, they might be able to atone for not having a long and noble lineage. But being born descendants of Abraham was an unforgivable social gaffe.

Traditionally, the place for Jews was the ghetto. That was where most of eastern Europe's Israelites lived, trading with each other in their overcrowded streets by day; locked in to prevent them contaminating their Christian neighbours by night. If some managed to crawl out of their stinking squalor, they found the walls of respectable society too steep to scale. They were denied citizenship. They bore the burden of extra taxation. They had no political rights. And they could not own land.

The trouble with the Seligmans was not that they were making an absurd bid to be accepted by the hereditary ruling class of Europe, but that they aspired to dominate it. In 1790 old Joseph Seligman and his four sons had been obscure Hamburg merchants and moneylenders. Twenty-five war-shattered years later, they were – quite simply – one of the richest families in the world. They had invested heavily in government stocks. They had provided the funds which had paid for the armies that had defeated Napoleon. They had made loans to kings and princes eager to reclaim their thrones. While other bankers had struggled to overcome wartime dislocations, the Seligmans had stolen a march on them. And they seemed as intent on exploiting peacetime conditions as they had been on profiting from war. In the years after 1815 there were broken national economies to be reconstructed and exciting new industries to be financed. Seligmans, through their offices in Hamburg, Paris, London and Vienna, intended to be in the economic forefront of the new age. Von Nisa and his friends had other ideas.

Half an hour later, seven of those friends were gathered with their host in his study. They represented between them most of the leading financial institutions of the Austro-Hungarian Empire and there was only one issue on their minds. Von Nisa stood with his back to the fire, facing a hostile semicircle of accusers.

'Why bring the little yid here?'

'It makes it look as though he's accepted in society.'

'It's very embarrassing for our wives, Georg.'

'How can we keep these Seligmans out of business if you're seen to be receiving them?'

'Can't you see that this is exactly what the odious little man wants – to wear down our opposition until he's become one of us?'

Von Nisa held up his hand. 'Gentlemen, gentlemen. Your indignation does you credit but, if I may say so, it blinds you to some very important facts. Please, take a glass of this excellent Hochheimer and be seated.'

The bankers helped themselves from a silver tray on the wide desk. When they were all settled, their stocky host, who remained on his feet, explained his strategy.

'Gentlemen, our houses have financed the needs of government, agriculture and commerce in the empire for generations, and there can be no doubt that we can continue our traditional rôle for generations to come – without the intervention of new and untried institutions.'

There was a murmur of agreement.

'The late wars imposed a great strain upon the banking system of Europe, and there is no point in denying that if houses such as the Seligmans had not come to our aid . . . well, the conflict with Napoleon might have had a different outcome.'

'But the war is over . . .' Baron von Druck of Schillers und Druck interposed.

'Precisely, Otto, the war is over and we . . . Austria has no more need of the Seligmans and their ilk.'

'That's putting it mildly, Georg.' Carl Herschel was the youngest present – a soldier who had fought with conspicuous bravery in the recent conflict and had lost an arm at Leipzig. 'We didn't drive out the French in order to hand our country over to the Jews. We all know that's what they want – financial control first, then subsequently political power.'

'Quite right, Carl. We face an insidious enemy potentially more dangerous than Bonaparte. That being so, the sooner we make young Jacob Seligman realise that we will not tolerate his presence in Vienna, the better it will be for all concerned. Now, we could use our influence to exclude him from business until he is forced to accept the inevitable. That might take a long time. I have another plan, however, which is why I invited the Seligmans here this evening.'

Von Nisa allowed himself a dramatic pause. Slowly his gaze passed over the gratifyingly attentive faces of his little audience. Then he delivered his bombshell. 'My little stratagem centres on the new state loan.'

'New loan!'

'What do you mean?'

'I've heard nothing . . .'

'What's all this . . .?'

'Gentlemen!' Von Nisa raised his voice above the babble. 'I have had this information in strict secrecy from the finance minister himself. In two weeks he will be floating a second loan.' He paused again, for maximum effect. 'Twenty million thalers.'

He relished the exclamations of astonishment and lively interest. 'I don't need to remind you how well we and our clients have fared from the 1816 loan. The stock is already showing a profit of twenty-six and a half per cent at today's price. Now, as we all know, Seligmans also profited from that flotation. Think how agreeable it would be, gentlemen, if the Jews were to be excluded completely from the new issue.'

Carefully, Georg von Nisa laid out his proposals.

Half an hour later, the Seligmans were sitting by themselves in a corner of the ballroom, mournfully watching the dancers. Adelheid's beauty was of a dark, wistful variety which seemed slightly at odds with the brash brilliance of the clustered diamonds at her throat and the silk flounces bedecking her slim body.

'Oh, Jacob, it is as I said. We've been invited in order to be shunned and humiliated. Can't we go home?'

Her husband shook his head. 'That would give them what they want.' He took her gloved hand in his own. 'Patience, my sweet. Patience will win us everything.' He smiled. 'It's supposed to be a mark of our race. It's certainly a virtue the Gentiles don't understand.

But then they haven't had seventeen hundred years to practise it. After all this time I think we can wait a little longer, don't you?'

Adelheid managed a half-smile. 'It's all very well for you. You have the bank. You meet people and they have to talk to you, even if they despise you, because they want money. But no one calls on me, and I'm not invited to call on anyone.'

'Herr Seligman.' A tall man with one arm stood before him, bowing formally. 'May I steal your charming wife from you for a few minutes?'

Jacob stood up and introduced Carl Herschel to Adelheid. Blushing slightly, she allowed the young man to lead her on to the dance floor.

Before Jacob could resume his seat he was accosted by Otto von Druck.

'Herr Seligman, how delightful to see you here.' The forced smile reached to the edge of the old man's bushy side-whiskers. 'We so seldom meet socially.'

Jacob refrained from commenting that this was scarcely his fault. He made a polite, noncommittal reply.

'As a matter of fact, I'm very glad to have bumped into you. There's a little matter I'd like to broach – confidentially. Shall we?' Von Druck indicated the sofa, and the two men sat. 'It's about a major client of mine. He's a large landowner – estates in Bohemia, Styria, Transylvania.' The old man lowered his voice, until it was difficult to hear him above the orchestra and the hum of conversation. 'Now, this client has discovered coal on his property near Prague. He needs considerable capital to start mining. We are lending a substantial sum but I should be happy to have a partner prepared to advance, say, fifteen thousand at six per cent.'

Jacob stroked his short, dark beard. 'Well now, Baron, that could be interesting.'

'Good, good. Perhaps you'd like to call in at my office tomorrow, and I can go into details.' Again the wide smile.

Jacob's face betrayed no emotion. 'Or perhaps, Baron, you could call at *my* office.'

Von Druck choked back his anger. 'Of course, Herr Seligman. Until tomorrow, then.' He rose abruptly, offered a stiff bow and walked away.

Jacob was still musing on this unexpected turn of events when

Herschel returned Adelheid to him at the end of the waltz. Moments later the couple were confronted by their host and hostess.

'My dear Seligman. Frau Seligman.' Von Nisa beamed. 'I do hope you are enjoying yourselves. My wife was just saying that we see so little of you.'

Caroline von Nisa nodded. 'Dear Frau Seligman, you really must not hide yourself. I have an idea.' She seated herself on the sofa beside Adelheid. 'The Princess Amelia holds her salon every Monday afternoon. Do say you'll accompany me next week.'

'Now, talking of salons has reminded me, my dear, that there was something I wanted to show Herr Seligman. May we detach ourselves from you ladies for a little while?'

Von Nisa took his guest by the arm and guided him, through a series of withdrawing rooms, to the library. 'Now, Seligman, they tell me you have quite a collection of paintings in your house in Hamburg, and that you're a real connoisseur in these things.'

'It is pleasant to surround oneself with beautiful things.'

'Indeed it is. Indeed it is, Seligman. What's the use of having money if you don't buy the best of everything, eh? Well, I've been buying one or two things lately, and I'd value your opinion.'

Jacob glanced around the room. There were half a dozen paintings on the walls. They were hung in the spaces between the heavy bookcases, with virtually no regard for careful arrangement or visual impact. Two of them were difficult to see at all, because the light from the lamps was reflected from the paint surface. Jacob tried not to wince his disapproval. 'My own modest collection is of seventeenth-century Dutch and Flemish masters. I know a little about that . . .'

'Then you must look at my Rembrandt.' Von Nisa indicated the head and shoulders portrait of an elderly merchant wearing a stiff, white ruff. 'There, what do you say to that?'

Jacob said, 'Remarkable. Quite remarkable.' He thought: a student copy – and a damned bad one at that.

'I found it in Paris. It was a bargain at two and a half thousand thalers. I think you will be impressed also by my Salomon van Ruisdael.' He waved a hand at the large canvas over the fireplace.

'Jacob.'

'I beg your pardon?'

'Jacob. It must be Jacob van Ruisdael, Salomon's nephew . . . And an incomparably better painter,' he added hastily. He stared up appreciatively at the expansive landscape, with its glitter of sunlight on the river and its heroically massed clouds poised to unleash a rainstorm on the flat meadows and crouched houses.

'Cost me over two thousand but I think it was worth it.' Von Nisa continued the tour of his oddly assorted collection, to each of which he attached a verbal price tag.

At last he came to rest beside a shallow alcove. He fetched a lamp so that his guest could see *The Triarchs* more clearly. 'This one I call my Waterloo. You see, Seligman, I succeeded where Bonaparte failed. I defeated Wellington.' Von Nisa gave a long and much-embellished account of the Raphael's sale, in which he appeared as a champion engaged with the Iron Duke in a battle of will and purse.

Jacob was not listening. He was stunned. The limpid gentleness of Raphael's composition was suddenly the only reality. He saw, heard and felt nothing else. His senses were focused on the sunlit world where three men paid homage to a young woman and her child. He wanted to cry for its sheer perfection.

Then the scene faded as his host lowered the lamp on to a side table. '. . . six thousand English guineas! But I'd made up my mind. I'd have paid twice that if necessary. Such a *holy* painting, don't you think?'

With a shock Jacob realised what he had been admiring so unreservedly. He moved hastily away from the picture. 'You realise, I know nothing at all about Christian art.'

'Ah, no, of course not. Don't suppose my Raphael means anything at all to you. Pity. I've been told it's a very good painting.' He paused. Then, drawing his guest to a chair beside the fire, he said, 'While I've got you alone, Seligman, there is just one little business matter I wanted to mention.'

In the small hours of the following morning Jacob Seligman lay awake beside his quietly slumbering spouse. His mind ran over, and over again, the extraordinary events of the evening. Could it really be that the leading citizens of Vienna, Europe's most anti-Semitic capital, had suddenly opened their hearts to him and Adelheid? His wife had returned home flushed and excited by what appeared to be her sudden acceptance into society. As for Jacob himself, he had been offered no less than four pieces of lucrative business by men who had hitherto found it difficult to be civil to him. Were Vienna's money men bowing to the inevitable or were they, in some obscure way, scheming against him? Time after time he posed the question. But, as he slipped into unconsciousness, it was not bankers or ballrooms but another image which rose clearly and radiantly in his mind. Five immaculately counterpoised figures in an Italian landscape.

Six working days later, Jacob had reached a decision. 'The ramparts are breached,' he wrote in his weekly report to his elder brother, Mayer, in Paris. 'We are admitted into the Gentile stronghold. Since von Nisa's ball signalling our acceptance, Vienna's haughty financial leaders have been queueing up to do business. Even Eisenach, who up till now would have put a pistol to his head sooner than go "cap in hand" to "those accursed Jews", has asked us for a loan. I have been obliged to call on our parent house for an extra million in specie. Soon, I think, we shall be doing as much business here as you in Paris, or Anselm in London. Everyone here has been working very hard. I have made it a policy not to turn away any reasonable request, lest the door, so widely opened, should be suddenly slammed in our faces. However, I think this now unlikely . . .'

A week later, the announcement of the new government loan took Jacob completely by surprise. Worse was to come. When he presented himself at von Nisa's, the bank handling the issue, he was stiffly informed by a clerk that the stock had been completely subscribed within the first hour of business by the city's leading banks and their clients. The following day's issue of *Allgemeine Zeitung*, the leading German-language outlet for anti-Semitic sentiment, informed its readership:

JEWS OUSTED FROM AUSTRIAN STATE LOAN

A new issue of twenty million thalers of government stock was made today. We are informed that it was completely taken up by the major banks in Vienna, acting for themselves and clients.

Only one house was excluded from the issue. J. Seligman and Sons of Hamburg, Paris, London and Vienna appear to have received no advance information of the flotation. According to an unimpeachable source, Herr Jacob Seligman, who heads the Viennese branch of this Jewish bank, is angry at being prevented from taking up a share of the loan. It seems that his rivals have used Herr Seligman's ample resources against him. They and their major shareholders have recently taken out large loans with Seligmans at favourable interest rates. These funds have gone into the purchase of the new stock, and Seligmans are much embarrassed by this stratagem.

Ichiro Tonashi, when Tim at last got to meet him, proved to be a grey-haired, bespectacled sixty-year-old who listened more than he spoke. Although his English was well above average, he was hardly more communicative in the flesh than he was on paper. His greeting was formal when Catherine and Tim emerged from the helicopter on to the lawn beside his luxurious mountain retreat an hour from the centre of Tokyo. They entered the house, exchanging their shoes for delicate cloth slippers. Tonashi offered his guests tea in a room whose screen wall had been drawn back to offer one of those few views that can honestly be called breathtaking. Beyond the enclosed Japanese garden, with its stream arched by wooden bridges and overhung with willows, the ground dropped sheer to the emerald expanse of Lake Chuzenji, and then rose as steeply, through forested slopes, to the crest of Mount Nantai. The industrialist confined himself to pleasantries, and left Catherine to point out items of interest in the landscape. Tim realised how much Tonashi relied on his American PA. She was his go-between, not so much bridging the language gap between the Orient and the Occident, as interpreting the Western mind to him and him to the Western mind. He listened intently to Catherine's explanations and the Englishman's reactions. Tim, forewarned by his companion, refrained from asking, at this first encounter, the questions that were hammering on the bars of his mind, clamouring for release.

Later at dinner, which was served, western-style, on an oval glass-topped table, he made one or two conversational lunges but they were effectively parried by his unsmiling host. By now his frustration with pointless small talk had reached bursting point. He laid down his knife and fork noisily. 'Look here, Mr Tonashi . . .'

The businessman nodded, impassive.

At that moment Tim felt the impact of a pointed toe on his right shin.

Catherine gracefully swallow-dived into the pool of painful silence. 'Mr Tonashi would appreciate the honour of showing you his art collection immediately after dinner. He suggests that you might find that an excellent opportunity to discuss business privately.' Her imploring half-smile half-frown said, 'For God's sake, Tim, let him play it his way.'

After the meal and the agonisingly lengthy formality of coffee and brandy, Tonashi rose and offered a slight bow. 'And now, if you would care to see my few modest examples of European painting . . .'

The two men left the house and walked along a gravel path lit by a colonnade of electric lamps. The track ended before a sheer wall of rock into which massive teak double doors had been set. Tonashi operated the lock by pressing his palm against a hand-print scanner beside the portal. He motioned Tim to precede him, and as he crossed the threshold a hundred lights lit automatically.

'Good grief!' Tim was stunned by the sight which met him.

The gallery had been carved out of the rock to form a Gothic grotto. The rough surfaces were white-painted and pierced by niches and arbours each individually lit and each displaying its own masterpiece. Some of the paintings were displayed around the side walls. Others were set into square columns of virgin rock which had been left as punctuation marks in the elegant architectural statement.

Tim voiced his genuine admiration. 'Mr Tonashi, this is magnificent!'

The grey head bowed again. 'I am glad it pleases you.'

'And very clever from a security point of view. Just the one entrance, I presume, to which only a few people have access.'

'No system is perfect, as you know, Dr Timothy – I must get used to calling you by that name – but this seems fairly effective.'

'And the fact that it's burrowed into the mountain means, I suppose, that you can add to it whenever you want.'

Tonashi nodded. 'It is also easier to maintain the right temperature and humidity.'

They advanced into the cavern. With the minimum of words and with a reserve that masked his obvious pride, the owner introduced each item in turn. He explained that the collection was arranged chronologically, and that it was his objective to possess one item from each of the major European schools, from the pre-Renaissance to the post-Impressionist eras.

Tim wandered, as though in a trance, from exhibit to exhibit. He stood dazzled by a glowing quattrocento Sienese triptych whose saints and angels were assembled in a gilded paradise and absorbed by their adoration of the Virgin. He closely examined a rumbustious picture depicting peasants dancing outside an inn, and knew it instinctively as a genuine Teniers and not one of the many copies of the great Fleming's work. The eighteenth century was represented by Gainsborough, Canaletto and Watteau among many others. For the Romantic period Ingres was there, and Corot and an early Turner. Millais stood for the Pre-Raphaelite Brotherhood, with a hugely sumptuous 'Samson and Delilah'. And the historical sequence ended in a riot of radiant Degas, Cézannes and Seurats. It was a chaotic, whimsical selection but there was no doubting the quality of any of the works displayed in this cave of treasures. Tim was able to identify positively one painting – a small Velasquez – as an item that had gone missing from a private collection in Switzerland some five or so years before. And there were a couple of others that he could be fairly certain had not reached their present location through legitimate channels. He wondered how few genuine art lovers or students were ever admitted to this secret vault where some of the world's finest masterpieces were doomed to almost unrelieved darkness. He thought of *The Triarchs* perhaps destined to end up here, once more hidden from public view. Not if I can help it, he vowed.

'Come and have another brandy.' Tonashi motioned towards an arched entrance in the side wall of the gallery, which led to an annexe furnished with Persian rugs, leather armchairs and cubes of polished rock which served as low tables. He poured spirit from a crystal decanter and handed Tim the glass. Lacy relaxed into the soft, supple hide, swirled the liquid in his goblet and breathed in the aroma of well-aged Armagnac.

He gazed at his host over the rim. 'How do you know so much about me?'

'Masyoshi Kodomo has excellent contacts.' The Japanese delicately sipped mineral water.

'Has Mr Kodomo helped you to assemble your magnificent collection?'

'I, too, have many excellent contacts.' Tonashi's face came its closest to a smile. 'There are several experts who advise me, and buy for me in Europe and America. But, yes, Masyoshi has enabled me to make some significant additions to the gallery.'

'But not Mr Osawa?'

Tonashi frowned. 'Mitsuru Osawa is a young savage. He's unstable – a psychopath. His followers are a volatile rabble. They get their ideas from the West. Drugs, violence, easy money, killing for the sake of killing – that's their code. No sense of loyalty or tradition.'

'And he's also getting too big for his boots. Muscling in on Kodomo's territory. That's what all this is really about, isn't it? That's why you've brought me here?'

Tonashi appeared not to be listening. 'Ours is a structured society, Dr Timothy. An ordered society. There has always been a balance, and the yakuzas have helped maintain that balance. But now? Street crime is on the increase. There are motor bike gangs everywhere. Drug trafficking is up twenty per cent on last year. We have had to open new remand centres for young offenders – children!'

Tim wanted to say something about not fighting fire with fire, but he knew that would not do any good. He also knew this was not the time. There were more pressing topics to discuss.

'What exactly is going to happen tomorrow?'

But now that Tonashi had elected to speak, there was no stopping him. He would explain things his own way.

'There is an English saying about birds of a feather flying together. Osawa has not enough power in Japan – yet. So, to achieve his ambitions, he is making alliances with *gaijin* – foreigners, ruthless and unprincipled like himself. Cocaine barons from South America. Taiwanese and Hong Kong triads. And—'

'Karakis?'

'And the man who wishes us to know him as Cristopoulos.'

At last the fog was lifting. The landscape emerging was not the simple one described by Kodomo. This had nothing to do with Japanese laws about the recovery of stolen art. And Osawa was not just a troublesome upstart. Kodomo feared him; perhaps feared even more what he stood for – change, new ideas, the internationalising of crime. Osawa was the target, not Karakis. The Greek was to be destroyed, certainly. But destroyed in such a way that Osawa would be discredited. Perhaps so completely discredited that his *gaijin* associates would, themselves, turn upon him. The realisation of what he was involved in brought the sweat out on Tim's brow. It was not so much a question of being between the devil and the deep blue sea as being in a whole seething cauldron full of devils, all bent on destroying each other. His chances of escaping from the pot were slim. If he let his mask slip for a moment, if he gave any of these demons the slightest cause for suspicion, then exit one bit player. The combatants would go on fighting over his trampled body, and not even notice it. No wonder Kodomo had been so generous. It was a good gamble: if the plan worked and his rival was brought down, that would be worth much more than a million. If it did not work, he would not have to pay up anyway.

Tonashi's voice penetrated these nightmare thoughts: '. . . selected these three.'

Tim took another gulp of his brandy. 'Sorry, I didn't quite catch that.'

'Are you feeling quite well, Dr Timothy?' His host seemed genuinely concerned. 'More Armagnac, perhaps?'

Tim held up his glass. 'I'm fine, thanks. I was just fascinated by the Dürer.' He indicated a woodcut of 'The Four Horsemen of the Apocalypse', terrifying in its conception and clarity, which bore Dürer's monogram and the date 1495. 'It must be an early treatment of a subject he came back to later. Sorry, what was it you were saying?'

Tonashi handed him a large buff envelope and resumed his seat. 'Cristopoulos sent me his dossier, and I selected these three items as ones which might possibly interest me. They would fill obvious gaps in my own collection, as Cristopoulos will not fail to notice when he comes tomorrow.'

Tim extracted the prints. As well as *The Triarchs*, there was a fifteenth-century Flemish 'Annunciation' and a Lucas Cranach 'Resurrection', which he had seen three years before in a West End gallery. 'Nothing but the best for Mr Cristopoulos. Is he bringing these tomorrow?'

'No, he is far too cautious for that. He only allows the originals to be inspected on his own territory. Tomorrow is just a preliminary meeting. The plan is that I should go to Greece to conclude the deal. That, of course, is where you come in.'

'I am to go in your place as your "expert". Do you think he'll swallow that?'

Tonashi nodded. 'He will have no choice if he wishes to make a sale. I will tell him that I always rely on my advisers to authenticate works that I contemplate buying. As it happens, that is perfectly true.'

'The only snag in this plan is that I'm not an expert. Karakis . . . Cristopoulos may be a crook, but he's also an art dealer. He's been in the business for years. I'm just an amateur.'

Tonashi took the objection seriously. 'But you have made a study of Renaissance painting. If we keep the conversation in that area, I am sure you will be completely convincing.' He picked up a file from the table beside him. 'There are two Italian paintings in my collection which I propose introducing to Mr Cristopoulos as acquisitions you have made for me. There are full details here. If you study them you will be able to speak about them with absolute authority. Should you wish to refresh your memory on any other aspect of the art of the period, my library is entirely at your disposal.' He waved a hand at the well-stacked bookshelves which filled the wall behind him.

Tim sank back in the chair, eyes closed. 'We're skating on very thin ice.' Another thought struck him and he stared at the other man. 'Supposing Cristopoulos checks to see if there really is a Dr Charles Timothy of Aberdeen University?'

'He will discover that Dr Timothy has been on the staff for eight years . . .'

'He could ask to speak to him on the phone!'

'. . . and that he is currently taking a sabbatical.'

'Where is he?'

'Touring Japan, with the aid of a grant from the Tonashi Foundation, to prepare a monograph about European influences on indigenous art.'

228

Tim could not help laughing. 'You think of everything, don't you?'

Tonashi nodded, still serious. 'Attention to detail is a national characteristic, Dr Timothy.'

Tim got little sleep. He sat up late, studying the dossier, lay on his futon for three hours worrying about everything that could go wrong, and finally went for a walk in the starlit garden. Immediately after breakfast he went to the gallery and spent the morning with his host's books and pictures, till his brain was stuffed to bursting with facts.

Lunch was a quiet meal. Tonashi had reverted to his usual taciturnity. Tim had too much on his mind. Catherine responded to the prevailing mood.

It was just after three o'clock that the helicopter arrived. Tim was sitting in his room, draped in the loose silken *yukata* provided by his host, when the chopper whirred over the house and settled on to the lawn.

Twenty minutes later Catherine knocked at his door and came in.

'I've been sent to fetch you. Tea? How do you feel?'

Tim stood up. 'A cross between the condemned prisoner and the fatted calf.' He stood before the mirror and pushed a brush through his hair.

Catherine came and stood beside him. She gazed at his reflection. 'You really do look the part – quite studious.'

'Do the jangled nerves show?'

'Not a bit.'

As he turned to face her, she obeyed a sudden impulse and kissed him on the lips: a hesitant, unlingering kiss which was yet more than sisterly. She laughed to cover her own embarrassment. 'Remember, champ, I'm in your corner.'

In the salon the three men rose as Tim and Catherine entered. Tonashi made the introductions and Tim found himself for the first time face to face with Niki Karakis.

PART III

ENDS AND MEANS

'He who is violent in order to spoil things is to be reprehended, not he who is violent to repair them.'

Niccolò Machiavelli:
The Discourses

CHAPTER 11

The Seligmans planned their revenge with the patient determination for which their race was renowned. Within days of the announcement of the Austrian state loan, the heads of the four houses assembled in Hamburg and agreed their strategy.

Von Nisa and his friends enjoyed their triumph to the full. As the months passed, a delicious sauce was added to the sweet meat of their success: the value of their Austrian stock rose steadily. All over Europe people were clamouring for a share of what rapidly came to be seen as the most attractive peacetime government issue ever offered. Britain and France might be more advanced industrially, and certainly had untapped colonial resources, but any loan secured against the immense reserves of the Habsburg empire had to be a sound investment. By March 1819 the stock, which had originally traded at 1.75 thalers, stood at 11.0. Every day several parcels changed hands on the main exchanges of London, Paris, Vienna and Berlin. There was no shortage of purchasers, nor of speculators eager to buy and sell on a rising market. Several of von Nisa's banking colleagues had taken the opportunity to make a short-term profit.

But Georg himself, whose house was still the major shareholder, was not tempted. There were no storm clouds on the political horizon. The dynasty was secure. Commerce and industry, some of it government-backed, were increasing. There was every reason to sit tight. As the wealth of the von Nisa bank increased, so did its prestige. New customers clamoured to do business, the more so since Seligmans had been all but ousted from the Viennese banking fraternity. Von Nisa's was expanding. Its premises in Rotenturmstrasse were already impressive; now the bank had acquired the neighbouring block on the corner of Stephensplatz, in the shadow of the cathedral.

It was in this new extension, amidst the dust and the builders' rubble, that his chief clerk found the head of the house on a wet morning in late March. He waited respectfully until his employer had finished giving instructions to the contractor.

At last von Nisa turned to him. 'Yes, Karl, what is it?'

'I thought you would want to know straight away, sir. Second Government Loan stock opened a point lower this morning.'

The banker shrugged. 'I've said for some time that it can't go on rising indefinitely. I expect it to level off at about 10.0. Nothing to worry about, Karl.'

'No, sir.'

Faced by his boss's confidence, Karl hesitated to disturb him again with the news coming in from the bourse. But an hour later he had to pluck up courage to knock at the proprietor's heavy mahogany door.

Von Nisa was engrossed in conversation with a client as the clerk entered. He glanced up angrily at the intrusion. 'Karl, you know better than to interrupt when I am with Baron von Steglitz.'

'A thousand apologies, sir, but if I might just have a brief word in private.'

'Certainly not! Nothing can be more important than my business with the Herr Baron.'

'But, sir . . .'

'Damn your impertinence, Karl! Get out! I'll deal with you later.'

For the next forty minutes the clerk hovered unhappily outside the door on which the owner's name was painted in heavy gold letters. Occasionally he looked into the banking hall. Already it was more crowded than usual. Every few minutes members of staff came up to him bringing the latest news from the exchange, or presenting the cards of customers clamouring to see the head of the bank.

As the minutes ticked by, indecision rapidly turned to panic. Half a dozen times Karl's hand rose to knock on the sacred mahogany. Half a dozen times it halted.

At last the door opened.

Von Nisa shook hands with his visitor. He noticed Karl. 'You there, see the Herr Baron out.'

'But, sir—'

'And then report to me!' Von Nisa closed the door behind him.

Two minutes later Karl was standing before the wide desk while his employer checked through columns of figures in a ledger. He knew from experience that von Nisa would deliberately keep him waiting, and would be furious if he spoke first.

The banker turned a thick page and began on the next rows of numbers. Karl could stand it no longer. Staring at the carpet, clenching his fists tightly at his side and speaking as calmly as he could, he said, 'Sir, I came to tell you that Second Government Loan stock had fallen to 7.50. Since then it has dropped a further two points.'

'What!' It was part roar, part screech, like the reaction of a wounded animal.

Eyes fixed on the red and blue pattern beneath his feet, not daring to look up, Karl continued.

'There are several customers here demanding that you sell the stock you are holding for them . . . And one or two who have called to close their accounts.'

He heard the creak as von Nisa stood suddenly and pushed his chair back from the desk. Trembling, he waited for instructions.

'Well, don't just stand there! Order my carriage! I'm going down to the exchange to sort this madness out.'

There was pandemonium on the wide, marbled floor of the exchange. The stands of the dealers were surrounded by crowds of sellers waving slips of paper. At the sight of von Nisa some detached themselves and rushed across to him. The banker brushed them aside. Seeing a dejected von Druck slumped against one of the pillars, he strode across the intervening space.

'Otto, what the hell's going on? I've only just heard.'

Von Druck scarcely looked up. 'It's obvious, isn't it? The market's collapsed. First it was government stock. Now it's everything. Look at them: panicking like chickens who've seen a fox! Sell! Sell! Sell! You wouldn't believe the rumours I've heard here this morning. A government scandal's been unmasked! The emperor's about to abdicate! Austria's going to war with France, or Prussia – or someone!'

'But how? Why? What started it all?'

'Late yesterday afternoon Seligman dumped all his government stock at one go – two million thalers' worth.'

'Seligman! But he hasn't—'

'Oh yes, he has – or had. He's been quietly buying up any Austrian stock he could lay hands on. He and his family. That's why the price has been going through the roof.'

'But two million . . . that doesn't explain all this.'

'You really don't see it, do you.' Von Druck sneered contemptuously. 'You thought your plan was so clever that it couldn't fail. You thought you could put the Jews out of business. What a blunder. Whoever goes bankrupt today, it won't be Seligmans.'

'But I still don't understand . . .'

'When the couriers got in this morning from Berlin and Paris, do you know what they reported? Massive selling of Austrian government stock late yesterday afternoon. You can bet the story will be the same when news arrives from London. It's all been planned for months. All over Europe, brokers, bankers and merchants have been buying up every parcel of Second Loan stock that became available. We thought it was all because of confidence in our government. My God, what fools we've been! It was the Seligmans who were behind the boom. Most of the stock ended up in their hands. They waited till they'd got enough to control the market. Then, at a prearranged hour, they let it all go. They sold at anything between 8.0 and 11.0. Do you know what it's worth now, if you can find a buyer – 1.50 if you're lucky!'

Georg von Nisa stared at his old friend's pallid features. He gazed at the faces in the growing circle around him: faces of frightened men, broken men, angry men, men looking for a scapegoat. He backed up against the pillar, legs trembling, needing support. He tried to think clearly. There had to be an answer. Only one way to steady the market. Buy! Beat the damned Jews at their own game. Buy stock! Buy! Buy! Buy! He closed his eyes. Pressed his hands over his ears. Made some desperate calculations. With the tens of millions wiped off the value of his own share holding, his expenditure on the new building and other investments, and the inevitable loss of business, there was nothing to spend on acquiring more stock. Bluff, that was all he could do. Bluff and hope to turn the market tide.

'Find my dealer! Find Schmidt!' Georg shouted the words to no one in particular. 'Tell him von Nisa is buying!'

'Von Nisa is buying!' The news ran through the exchange like a tidal wave of hope.

At the end of a day of frenzied dealing, von Nisa left the exchange, climbed into his carriage and slumped on to the leather seat. He had acquired another two and a half million shares. The value of each stood at just over three thalers. It was not enough. He was finished. He stared out at the empty, rain-sodden cobbles drifting past the window. 'Broken by a bloody Jew!'

He reached up to the panel above his head. He slid it to one side. He took out the loaded pistol that was kept there for security purposes.

Jacob Seligman did not go to the sale of the von Nisa house and contents some six weeks later. It would have been insensitive to do so. But he had another reason for not being seen among the Viennese élite squabbling over the dead banker's furniture, porcelain, silver and carpets. There was only one item that interested him. Something he had to have. Something that, as a Jew, he ought not to covet. Something whose acquisition Rabbi Hirsch and the leaders of the synagogue would certainly not approve. So, it was through an agent, anonymously, that Jacob Seligman bought *The Triarchs*.

The three men shook hands and Tim took careful stock of Karakis. The Greek was in his fifties, clean-shaven, immaculately and expensively dressed. There was no trace of grey in his wiry, black hair, but Tim suspected that cosmetics probably accounted for that. There was something distinctly effeminate about the man and the way he moved. Effeminate but not weak. Karakis was certainly not slim. The cut of his suit concealed quite a paunch, but his slow, balanced, almost balletic steps and his economy of gesture gave a suggestion of gracefulness and controlled energy. His eyes were attentive to every detail passing before them. The mind behind them was, obviously, sharply concentrated. Tim thought of a hawk resting lazily on warm air currents, seemingly detached from the world below and uninterested in its affairs – until some small animal, moving carelessly from cover, discovered the folly of being taken in by such languid motion.

237

'Dr Timothy, I'm surprised we haven't met before.' Karakis's smile was cautious. 'We obviously have so many interests in common.'

Tim returned the frank gaze. 'Aberdeen is a bit off the beaten track. Are you based in Athens?'

'I have a gallery there but my business takes me all over the world, of course.'

There was nothing remotely feminine about the other man. Mitsuru Osawa was tall by Japanese standards, thin and very muscular. Tim guessed that he was aged about twenty-eight. His whole bearing spoke arrogance and aggression.

As on the previous afternoon, teatime conversation was rigidly kept to small talk. Tim could sense that Karakis was as impatient as he had been with the inexorability of Japanese etiquette.

'It is an honour to have the opportunity to contribute to your collection, Mr Tonashi. Naturally, I am dying to see it.'

Their host nodded solemnly. 'After dinner this evening—'

'Oh, surely, you are not going to keep me so long in suspense. Could we not go to the gallery straight away?'

'Unfortunately, Mr Cristopoulos, I have business to attend to this afternoon.'

'But could not your charming assistant be our guide?' He smiled at Catherine appraisingly – not for the first time, Tim noticed.

The Greek's libidinous glances had not been lost on Catherine. 'I know very little about the collection. Mr Tonashi is the expert.'

'But I thought Dr Timothy was the expert. I'm sure he would be able to answer any questions. Isn't that so, Dr Timothy?'

'I can't imagine *you* having to ask *me* anything about fine art, Mr Cristopoulos.' Tim was equally adept at verbal fencing. Yet he, too, was anxious to cut short the agony of waiting. He was as ready as he ever would be to have his academic art historian's disguise put to the test. 'However, I would be delighted to accompany you around the gallery, with Mr Tonashi's permission.'

He saw Catherine's frown and quick, slight shake of her head. But Tonashi acceded to the Greek's insistence, and agreed to allow his assistant to lead the gallery tour.

As they all left the house twenty minutes later, she drew Tim to one side. Concealed by a bank of shrubs from the others walking on

down the path, she gripped his arm. 'Tim, this is not a good idea.'
Her tone was quiet, tense, urgent.

'Bit late to pull back now.'

'These men are—'

'Evil? Ruthless? Psychotic? Too true.'

'Back off, Tim! It's not too late. I'll square it with Tonashi. If
Karakis or Osawa even suspect they're being tricked . . .'

He squeezed her hand. 'Thanks for being concerned but I'm a big
boy, now. And the good guys always win in the last reel.' He doubted
whether his bravado reassured her. It certainly did not convince him.
He was dreading the next hour or so. Everything – probably including
his life – depended on his giving a convincing performance to someone
for whom caution was a natural animal instinct.

'Anyway, the risk is irrelevant. Karakis has some debts to pay – and
I'm the broker's man.' He forced a smile. 'Come on, into the fray –
and, whatever happens, make sure you stay out of the line of fire.'

They caught up with the others. Catherine used her handprint to
open the door. They all entered, exchanged their shoes for slippers,
and began their exploration of the subterranean treasure-house.

'I don't like dealing with intermediaries.' Osawa spoke with a
pronounced east-coast American drawl.

Tim wanted to tell the egotistical slob that he didn't give a damn
what he liked and didn't like. He contented himself with 'Mr Tonashi
only relies on me for authentication. He handles all financial transactions personally.'

'So what, precisely, are your instructions, Dr Timothy? Your
employer is not exactly a mine of information.' Karakis was inspecting
a painting of St Jerome by Annibale Carracci and spoke casually,
without diverting his gaze.

'Since you are not prepared to bring the items here for inspection,
I am to view them on your premises. I assume you keep your stock
in Athens?'

Karakis appeared not to hear the question. 'You are to check for
authenticity?'

'Authenticity, condition, and suitability for this collection.'

'That is a heavy responsibility. Are you sure you are up to it?'

'Dr Timothy is a leading Renaissance scholar.' Catherine decided she should enter the skirmish. 'He has helped Mr Tonashi in a number of negotiations.'

Karakis gave her a smile revealing teeth that were the pride of the technician who maintained them. 'Oh, I am quite conversant with Dr Timothy's reputation.' He turned to Tim. 'I was most impressed by your recent article in *Apollo* on the fake Fordheim Mantegna.' The Greek moved at a nonchalant pace along the gallery.

Tim was about to follow silently. But there was an aspect of the man's casual air that checked him. Something was wrong. In his mind he rummaged through the file on Dr Charles Timothy that Tonashi had given him to study. Quiet seconds passed. In the nick of time he spotted the verbal trap.

'Masaccio.'

'I beg your pardon?'

'Masaccio. My article was on the fake Fordheim Masaccio. You said Mantegna.'

'Did I?' Karakis feigned astonishment. 'How stupid of me. I suppose it was their common fascination with perspective that linked the two names in my mind.'

'Yet the similarities are more real than apparent. Where Mantegna is theatrical, Masaccio is dramatic.'

Osawa intervened. 'Which are the pictures you bought for Mr Tonashi?'

'I *advised* Mr Tonashi to acquire this Van der Goes.' He indicated a depiction of the martyrdom of St Stephen. 'And a Giorgione school painting of an allegorical subject, further along on the right.'

'Ah, yes, I remember the Venetian painting.' Karakis moved down the gallery and stood back to admire a scene depicting armed horsemen set in a sylvan landscape. 'Sotheby's, New York, about two years ago, wasn't it? So Tonashi was the mystery buyer. There was much discussion at the time about whether it might be a genuine Giorgione. What is your feeling, Dr Timothy?'

Tim gazed, enraptured, into the painting's blue-green depths, where sunlight glowed on marble columns and glinted from armour, and tried to remember his script.

'Well, of course, one must always err on the side of caution in attributions, especially with an artist like Giorgione. When only half a dozen recognised works exist, one would hesitate before claiming that one had discovered another.'

'But?'

'But there's such a feeling of space and light here that it's hard to believe it's the work of a mere follower. Giorgione was the only member of the Venetian cinquecento who had a real feel for landscape. None of his contemporaries were able to break away from the importance of the human actors in the scene. But here one feels – or so it seems to me – ' Tim slipped in what he hoped sounded like a diffident scholar's qualification, 'that the brooding, storm-threatening sky and these trees bending in the wind are the central characters in the drama.' He glanced at Karakis to see what impression his pseudo-erudition was making. The Greek mask remained impassive.

As the tour continued the strain of maintaining the pretence of profound artistic knowledge kept Tim's heart racing and the adrenalin pumping.

Catherine, who engaged Osawa in conversation in his own language, managed to conceal her tension, but Tim knew from her occasional anxious glances that she was longing for the charade to be over.

At last the group emerged into the sunlight. Catherine suggested that the visitors might like an opportunity to refresh themselves before dinner, but Karakis was in no hurry to break up the party. For almost an hour the quartet wandered in the grounds, the Greek interspersing innocuous questions about the scenery with sudden probes about the Tonashi collection and Dr Timothy's connection with it.

Eventually, Catherine excused herself and disappeared in the direction of the house. Karakis and Osawa followed soon after.

Tim lingered in the deepening shade of a large maple. A bank of shrubs screened the house behind. In front spread the amphitheatre of lake, forest and mountain. As he sank on to the lawn, it was as though he had his own private balcony seat from which to view the drama of nature. Not that he was in a reflective frame of mind. His whole being was fizzing and alert.

'How did it go?' Catherine emerged from behind the massed foliage at his back. 'I watched for the others to leave, and then came straight back.' She dropped on to the grass beside him. 'Do you think Karakis bought it?'

Tim smiled, grateful for her company. 'I don't know. I really don't know. He's incredibly astute. Never takes anything or anyone at face value. I guess that's the only way to survive in the criminal underworld.'

Catherine shuddered. 'He gives me the creeps! I don't understand how you can bear to discuss art with him so calmly – knowing what you know about him.'

'It's *because* of what I know about him. Karakis isn't a man, he has no human feelings, so I don't react to him as a person. He's a thing, a killer disease, a cancer. All that matters is finding the best way to cut it out. If someone doesn't do it, he'll go on killing, maiming and destroying.'

Neither of them spoke for some time, then Catherine said, 'Please take care. Especially when he gets you to Athens – in his spider's web.'

Tim stood up. 'I'm not underestimating the risk, but at least I have one advantage. I know exactly what's going on, and Karakis doesn't.'

He helped Catherine to her feet. And at that moment Niki Karakis appeared from behind the shrubbery – smiling.

> 19 Kirchnerstrasse
> Vienna
> 23 May 1897

My dear Nathan,

I received your disturbing letter on Friday and it made me quite ill. I had to retire to my bed so I could not reply immediately and, of course, yesterday was the Sabbath.

What terrible news! I am writing to Ruben by the same post to forbid this marriage. I expect you to support me in this. Your brother will listen to you, and you must make him see what a terrible thing it would be for the family and the business if he were to persist with his absurd notion of marrying a Gentile.

You tell me that this Louisa Davenant is sweet-natured and intelligent, that she is the daughter of an English peer and, therefore, an excellent 'catch'. I have nothing against the girl, and no doubt she is as charming as you say. But were she the daughter of Queen Victoria herself, such a match would be quite unthinkable. For the head of Seligmans, Vienna, to marry an English Roman Catholic, and in a Christian church! Even as I write the words I can feel my heart racing, and that is very bad for someone of my age and delicate health. Does Ruben want to kill his poor, old grandfather? Perhaps this is heaven's judgement on me. I have been too indulgent with both of you since your father died. I should never have allowed Ruben to take this long holiday in England. He is a very impressionable boy.

Well, Nathan, you must reason with him. Be firm. Make him see that such an alliance is shameful. It would split the family. It is an affront to our religion and our people. Our luck, our success and our fortune depend, as they always have, on our keeping the faith of our forefathers. Once one member of the family breaks this contract, others will feel free to do the same. All your young cousins, nephews and nieces will want to rush off and marry into Christian nobility. Our ancestors made Seligmans Europe's biggest bank next to Rothschilds. They did not do that so that a later generation could dissipate the fortune among Christians. That is what would happen if Ruben's children were brought up as Catholics. That I could never allow. We would all disown him sooner than see that happen.

I feel another attack coming on. I must close this letter. I know you will help Ruben to come to his senses.

Your affectionate grandfather
    Salomon Seligman
P.S. I need hardly add that your poor mother is utterly distraught.

Nathan crumpled the letter and threw it across the drawing-room. 'Interfering old bigot!'

The tall twenty-three-year-old with the black, curly hair and luxuriant moustache removed the long, scarlet-lined evening cloak and let it fall to the floor. He dropped into a deep leather armchair, took out a cigar and lit it with elaborate care.

'Damn the old fool!'

Nathan had returned to his cousin's house in Piccadilly a few minutes earlier in the best of spirits. He had hugely enjoyed an evening at the theatre, followed by supper at Romano's. Before him, after he had slept away what was left of the night, lay the pleasurable prospect of a few days at Epsom, where he had horses running in both the Derby and the Oaks. The letter awaiting him on a silver salver in the hall had completely dispersed his good humour. He drew heavily on the long Hupmann, and exhaled the smoke with a sigh. What on earth was he going to do about grandfather and Ruben?

As the nineteenth century drew to a close, the Seligmans and other prominent Jewish families were facing a whole new set of problems. A hundred years before, they had struggled painfully out of the ghetto, resisting the pressures of a society that wanted to push them back into it. They had been a people without rights: non-citizens, or at best partial citizens, with no voice in national or local affairs, and heavily taxed for the privilege of being permitted to live alongside their Gentile neighbours. Now, everything had changed. Well, perhaps not quite everything. There would always be a stigma attached to being Jewish. But the Seligmans and their co-religionists had won legal equality almost everywhere in Europe. Three of Nathan's cousins were parliamentarians, daily meeting in Berlin, Paris and London to discuss the affairs of their respective states. They were major landowners. Nathan, himself, had a magnificent house in Vienna's most prestigious suburb, two country estates, and a summer retreat high above Lake Constance.

Socially they had outplayed the traditional arbiters of fashion at their own game. It was the Seligmans and their friends who gave the most lavish balls, the most entertaining houseparties, the most sumptuous dinners, who raced or hunted with the finest horseflesh, who championed the latest expensive crazes – steam yachting, skiing and, now, motoring. They had achieved what many Jews had always wanted: assimilation. And now they found themselves in danger of losing their identity. Some had married Gentiles. Some had converted to Christianity.

But not the Seligmans. They were among the leaders of world Jewry. They founded Jewish hospitals, schools and orphanages. They campaigned on behalf of their persecuted brothers in Russia. They helped finance city tenements for the Jewish families who constantly streamed westward, fleeing from tsarist oppression. They symbolised the triumph of the Chosen People – rich, successful, superior and distinct.

244

The underpinning of their position was of course the bank (or rather the banks, for the houses in Hamburg, Vienna, Paris and London maintained distinct identities although they worked closely together and were corporately invincible).

The bank – that great golden millstone. Nathan pictured the familiar, monolithic building which occupied almost one complete side of Renngasse. He pictured it and he hated it. Hated its cold marble, frigid mahogany and hard brass. Hated its scores of scrupulous clerks and their high desks and their big black ledgers. Hated the intricate, whirring, relentless money-making machine to which his family was tied. The machine which had killed his father. The machine which would crush Ruben unless someone intervened to prevent it.

Nathan crossed to the mahogany cooler beside the sideboard. He uncorked the bottle of champagne the butler always left for him when he was out late. Then he retrieved Salomon's letter, smoothed it out and re-read it in the flickering gaslight. It was all very well for grandfather to make his demands about the family and the business. *He* had been brought up to the bank, introduced to it before he was out of adolescence by *his* father, the Great Jacob, the founder of Seligmans, Vienna. So he had inherited a flair for finance; it was his life.

But Salomon had not passed on that skill to his only son, Mayer. Nathan tried hard to remember his father. He saw a quiet man with a pallid, thin face, a face which seldom smiled, a man who frequently visited the nursery and always had the most captivating stories to tell of exotic heroes and fabulous creatures and breathtaking adventures in distant lands. Nathan could not recall having ever seen his father without a book in his hand. Even at meal times there was usually a small volume beside his plate, its tooled leather reverently caressed by Mayer's long fingers. Then suddenly father had disappeared from his life, and mother had shut herself in her room for weeks, red-eyed and inconsolable. And no one would tell the children why. Nathan had entered adolescence with a black demon of fear and mystery ever present to torment him.

Though he half guessed the truth, it was years before Nathan confirmed his awful suspicions. Mayer Seligman had hanged himself in his office. 'Overwork' was the official family story, but Nathan had known, with a thirteen-year-old's unshakeable conviction, that the bank had killed his father. He had vowed that it would not kill him, too.

No one had been able to break that resolve. At twenty-one Nathan had automatically inherited a sizable quota of Seligman shares, and he had not hesitated to enjoy his wealth and independence. He could afford to spend lavishly. Even if he seriously depleted his own capital – a difficult enough feat – much more would be coming his way when his seventy-four-year-old grandfather died.

Salomon had been forced to abandon the preoccupations of his old age – his art collection and his gout – in order to return to the bridge of the Austrian bank. But he insisted on maintaining the fiction that he was there only in an advisory capacity, to guide the new chairman, his sole remaining direct male heir. For Nathan's freedom had been bought at the expense of his younger brother's bondage. Maintain the succession – it was an inviolable law, a solemn creed that there had to be in every generation a member of the family to preside over the marble halls of Renngasse. Since Nathan had refused that rôle, Ruben had been forced to assume it.

Nathan's conscience troubled him over Ruben. His twenty-year-old brother was quiet, studious, pliant. There was much of their father in Ruben; he was the clever one. Nathan had been the despair of their private tutor, but Ruben had constantly won Professor Schlayer's approval. It was ironic, then, that Nathan had been allowed to go to Cambridge, where he had devoted two very happy years almost entirely to hunting, racing and drinking, while Ruben had been forced on to the Renngasse treadmill, learning from the age of sixteen how each department of the bank worked, and always under the predatory eye of Grandfather Salomon.

Nathan refilled his glass and made his way thoughtfully up the wide staircase to his rooms on the first floor. He flung himself down on the canopied bed and rang for his valet. He thought about his life. It really was remarkably pleasant: travel, good company, his beloved horses – Lionheart's Derby chances were really very good this year – but, above all, freedom. And all thanks to a younger brother who uncomplainingly occupied that accursed swivel-chair in the senior partner's room in the dreary offices of Seligmans, Vienna.

There was a tap at the door and Nathan's Italian valet sidled deferentially into the room.

'Ah, Giorgio.' Nathan stood up and removed his tail coat. 'Have you had a good evening?'

'I packed our trunk for Epsom, sir, and then played cards with Mr Palfry.' He collected the items of clothing as his master discarded them.

Nathan chuckled. 'You should know better, Giorgio. All these English butlers cheat. I suppose you'll need another advance to cover your losses.' Then, suddenly serious, 'Has Mr Ruben retired?'

'Oh yes, sir, an hour or more ago. Miss Davenant's carriage came for her at eleven. After she'd gone, Mr Ruben read for a while in the library, then went to his room.'

'What do you think of Miss Davenant, Giorgio?' He watched in the mirror as the young man paused in his work and smiled.

'Ah, Miss Davenant. *Bellissima, elegante, spiritosa*, and at the same time very kind and gentle.'

'Do you think my brother should marry her?'

'Oh, *si*. They are a perfect couple. She makes him very happy.'

Nathan climbed into bed. He watched as Giorgio finished folding, brushing and putting away.

The valet moved to the door. 'What time are we departing for Epsom, sir?'

'Epsom.' Nathan pictured the lush green course, the crowds, the excitement. He thought of cheering Lionheart to victory. He sighed. 'I'm afraid you'll have to do some re-packing in the morning, Giorgio. We're going back to Vienna.'

Half an hour before dinner, Tim was summoned to Tonashi's private suite of rooms.

The Japanese bowed and motioned him to a chair. He seated himself behind a massive desk, which had the effect of making him look even smaller.

'Will you please listen to something?' He touched a button in a panel on the tidily arranged teak surface.

Tim heard a slight hiss from hidden loudspeakers, then the sound of a door opening. Voices, muffled at first, then coming closer and clearer.

'... *realise how important this deal is to me?*' That was Osawa.

'*Of course I do. That's why we don't want it to go wrong.*' Karakis's voice had moved into its nervous upper register.

247

'Nothing will go wrong as long as you keep your head. Relax and have some of this excellent vodka so thoughtfully provided for us.' There was a clinking of glasses and ice.

'You've got their rooms bugged.' Tim stared at his host.

Tonashi frowned and held a finger to his lips.

Karakis's disembodied voice sounded again. 'Mitsuru, I've been in this business a long time. I know when something isn't right.'

'Perhaps you have been in business too long, my friend. Fear comes more easily to old men.' The listeners could almost see Osawa's arrogant sneer.

The response was swift, loud, angry. 'And young men are inclined to take stupid risks! I've told you what I heard them saying . . .'

'What you think you heard them saying.'

'It's not just that. There's something not right about this Timothy character. I can't pin it down but . . .'

'How many times do I have to tell you, Niki. We checked him out thoroughly.' Osawa was losing his patience. 'Anyway, supposing our art expert is not all he seems, what can he possibly do when you've got him on your boat? He will be alone and unarmed. Surely your people can handle a simple accident at sea.'

'Listen, Mitsuru . . .'

'No, you listen, Niki. I want Tonashi and his commercial empire in my pocket. That is central to my plans. You and I have a deal. If you were to back out, that would make life very difficult for me. But for you . . . life would simply become non-existent.'

There was a click as Tonashi pressed another button. It was followed by several moments of silence.

Tim broke it. 'Do you eavesdrop on all your guests?'

Tonashi ignored the question. 'Do you want to cancel our contract? In view of what we have just heard, I must give you that option.'

Tim considered the question seriously. 'No, I guess not. It's my fault for not putting on a sufficiently convincing performance. But at least forewarned is forearmed. Do you know anything about this boat they were talking about?'

Tonashi shook his head. 'No. Perhaps we can get him to talk about it over dinner.'

Dinner was a tense affair. Everyone was on edge and determined not to show it. Several conversational avenues were explored – and turned out to be cul-de-sacs. They took coffee in the 'culture bunker'. It was there that the serious business talk took place. They discussed Tonashi's three selected pictures. Tim enthused about the contribution any of them would make to the collection; 'if they are genuine'. Prices were mentioned, and Tonashi demurred at the twelve million pounds asked for *The Triarchs*.

Karakis sat forward eagerly in his chair. 'We are talking about one of the world's most famous and intriguing paintings – not to mention one of the most beautiful.'

'But can it really be genuine?' Tim smiled. 'I confess I am agog to see it. But a painting lost for so many years? One must be sceptical.'

'I assure you, you won't be disappointed, Dr Timothy.' Karakis accented the last two words heavily. 'I expect to touch even Miss Younger's heart with my Raphael.'

There was an awkward silence.

Karakis looked round the circle of blank faces. 'I assume, of course, that your charming assistant will be joining us, Mr Tonashi. I am planning a short cruise around some of our Greek islands and Miss Younger would add beauty and elegance to our little gathering.'

Tim looked across at the Greek in alarm, recognising his stratagem immediately.

Catherine laughed. 'It sounds delightful, Mr Cristopoulos, but I'm afraid . . .'

Karakis held up an imperious hand. 'I will not hear of a refusal. It's not just for my sake that I ask. I feel sure our young art historian' – he smirked at Tim – 'would be desolate to be deprived of your company. I gather that you and he—'

Tim protested. 'Oh, I'm afraid you've got that one wrong. Miss Younger and I are no more than colleagues.'

Karakis shrugged. 'Even so, you would not want to deny her a holiday? Miss Younger, think of going aboard my schooner *Phidias* in the lovely little harbour at Poros, and then spending days drifting lazily over the blue Aegean, soaking up sunshine, lunching on deserted beaches skirted by groves of citrus and wild olive.'

Tonashi intervened. 'I wish I could spare her, Mr Cristopoulos. Unfortunately, her next few weeks are going to be very busy.'

The Greek looked searchingly at Tonashi, Tim and Catherine in turn. 'I get the impression there's a conspiracy afoot. Do you suggest Niki Cristopoulos and his friends are bad company for Miss Younger, or have you some other reason for wishing to keep her away? Personal relations with my clients are of the utmost importance to me, since in my profession business and pleasure are inextricably linked. Ichiro, I would love to have you yourself as my guest of honour aboard the *Phidias*. But if that cannot be, you must let me honour your lovely assistant in your place. She could discuss our negotiations with you by phone every day – every hour if need be. That way I could satisfy myself that you are completely happy about everything.'

Damn the man: he's too clever by half. While the ensuing silence stretched like already tense elastic, Tim grappled with the Catch 22 that Karakis had just presented. Refuse his invitation and the Greek's suspicions would certainly be confirmed. Accept and he would be handed a female hostage on a plate. No way, Tim thought. Not again, after Venetia's ordeal. He opened his mouth to back Mr Tonashi's decision.

But it was Catherine who spoke first. 'Well, now, Mr Cristopoulos, since you put it so eloquently, how can a girl refuse? Perhaps I could be spared for just a few days, Mr Tonashi?'

Tim had no opportunity that night to talk to Catherine. Soon after lobbing her grenade into the conversation, she retired. It was another hour before he could extricate himself, and when he knocked on her door there was no reply.

Back in his room he lay on his futon and pondered the stupidity of women. Catherine angered and disappointed him. She had seemed to be intelligent, detached, capable of sound, unemotional judgement – the sort of woman . . . Yet, here she was acting on impulse – just like Venetia. Thrusting herself into dangers she did not even begin to understand. Well, not if he could help it. He was damned if he would have someone else on his conscience. He *would* sort out the Karakis affair, but sort it out alone.

Well, perhaps not quite alone. He picked up the phone, spoke briefly to Sally in the London office, then got her to put him through to George Martin.

'George, I need you and the boys to pack your bags and meet me in Poros next week.'

'Anything you say, Major. Where's this Poros when it's at home?'

'It's a Greek island. You'll love it – sea, sand and ouzo. You fly to Athens and take the hydrofoil from Piraeus. Better book in somewhere discreet, and let Sally have the address so that I can contact you. You won't be able to travel with weapons, of course, but I'll arrange to get some to you.'

'Like that, is it, Major?'

'Yes, it's like that, George. We're after Niki Karakis again. On his own territory, this time.'

'Well, we've all got some scores to settle with that gentleman.'

George's cheerful, efficient, military confidence had a calming effect. Tim decided it was time he made another call to the Villa Vagnoli.

'Isabella, how are you? How's Venetia? I'd like a word with her.'

'She's getting over it all – slowly. But she's not here. She had to go to London for the auction.'

'What auction?'

'Farrans Court.'

'Shit!'

'Timothy?'

'Sorry, Isabella. I had no idea Venetia was selling the house so quickly.'

'Oh, yes. I asked her to get rid of it as soon as possible. It's part of her life that she has to exorcise. And the money will help her to make a fresh start.'

'When is the sale?'

'The day after tomorrow. The Sotheby's people went down three or four months ago to look over the furniture and stuff. They decided there was nothing of interest to justify a special contents sale, so advised us to auction the place lock, stock and barrel. Gerrison's of Jermyn Street are handling it.'

Tim made no response. Instead he was juggling dates and figures in his head.

251

'Timothy, are you there?'

'Yes. Sorry, I was thinking. Can you give me Gerrison's number, and the name of the person dealing with Farrans?'

Now it was the turn of the Contessa Peruzzi to fall silent. At last she said, 'Why do you want it?'

'I thought that I might try my luck . . .'

Isabella's reply was abrupt. 'Timothy, don't be absurd! Don't let yourself be carried away by totally impracticable romanticism. Even if you could afford to buy Farrans Court, the upkeep of it would cripple you – just as it crippled that muddle-headed idiot, Ralph Cranville. You've got more sense, I hope.'

'Isabella, please, just humour me. You're probably quite right and, in any case, there's no way I can get back to England in time for the sale. But I would like to know what's happening to the place.'

After a moment of frozen silence, Venetia's mother went to fetch the information. 'The agent's name is Giles Cantrell, a decidedly precious young man.'

Tim made a note of the name and number, and rang off.

Immediately he got through to Gerrison's, he realised why Isabella had not taken to Giles Cantrell. The supercilious, minor public school accent oozed condescension. No, it was quite impossible to accept a pre-sale offer at this late stage. There had, of course, been considerable interest, and he was confident of achieving a figure well in excess of a million pounds at auction. No, he couldn't possibly accept a telephone bid. Mr Lacy would appreciate that they had to check the bona-fides of all potential purchasers. If Mr Lacy would care to pop into the office tomorrow . . .

Tim cut through the silken chord of self-importance. 'It's a bit bloody difficult to pop in from Tokyo. Now, listen, these people will vouch for me.' He gave the names and numbers of a top merchant banker, a senior official at New Scotland Yard, and a major London art dealer. 'And I will fax you, overnight, a personal financial guarantee from one of the world's leading industrialists. Now, may I get to take part in your sale?'

The man's tone changed. Of course, he hadn't wished to imply . . . If the references were in order, as he was sure they would be, he would be happy to make the necessary arrangements. If Mr Lacy could tell him his top figure, he would be happy to bid on his behalf. Alternatively if Mr Lacy wished to participate personally, that could be arranged. The sale was taking place at Farrans Court itself, but he would have a line open to the London office. If Mr Lacy would call the London office on a special number, he would be kept informed of the progress of the auction and could register his own bids. If Mr Lacy would care to give him his fax number, he would send the appropriate documents through straight away.

Tim replaced the receiver and stretched out on the bed. Was it, as Isabella had suggested, just a foolish, romantic obsession? Or could his plans for Farrans really be made to work? And even if the finance sorted itself out, would he still be alive to mastermind the elaborate, ambitious project? He rose wearily to his feet. Only people who lost faith in themselves stopped making plans for the future.

He looked at his watch: ten minutes to one. Tonashi would still be up. The man was a workaholic, and seldom retired before 2.00 a.m. Tim walked into the bathroom, applied cold water to his face, brushed his hair, straightened his tie. Then he went to find his host. There were two highly urgent matters to discuss. The first was just why Tonashi should underwrite a young Englishman's million-pound-plus dream. The second was to find some way of extracting Catherine Younger from the serpents' pit she had blundered into.

CHAPTER 12

The small team from Gerrison's had arranged the six semicircular rows of folding chairs in such a way as to take up as much space as possible in the great hall at Farrans. Giles Cantrell had set up his desk on a platform in front of the empty fireplace. Now, as he faced the forty or so potential buyers, he wished he had not. He found himself squinting to read the punters' faces against the searchlight beam of coloured sunlight falling full on him through the tall windows filled with armorial glass. However, as he ruefully reminded himself, the show must go on.

'Good afternoon, ladies and gentlemen. On behalf of T. Gerrison and Son, may I welcome you to this lovely old house. Farrans Court is one of the finest historical buildings to come on to the market this year and, as you will have observed, the house and its small, easily manageable estate are in excellent condition. Before we begin the bidding, I must draw your attention to the conditions of sale . . .' The thin young man in the grey suit, striped shirt and discreet silk tie went into his routine introductory patter.

His secretary – the middle-aged, immaculately-coiffed and efficient Miss Scott – sat at a desk by the carved oak screen, holding a telephone to her ear. There had been several minutes of real panic as her nervous underling in the London office had made a hash of opening up lines to the three overseas bidders interested in Farrans. But Miss Scott's sharp exhortation to the hapless Fiona to 'pull herself together' had achieved the desired result, and now all was in readiness for the disposal of the Cranville ancestral home.

Cantrell opened the bidding at half a million. The price rose easily to eight hundred thousand pounds. Then progress became sluggish. The auctioneer coaxed another fifty thousand out of the representative of a leading hotel chain, but when that was topped by a phone bid from New York the man in the front row shook his head, stood up abruptly and left the room.

From that moment everyone's attention was divided between Miss Scott and Mr Cantrell. All interested parties in the hall had dropped out of the race. It was clear that Farrans would go to a foreign buyer. Like spectators at a Wimbledon final, heads turned first one way then the other as the auctioneer and his secretary lobbed figures back and forth.

'Nine hundred thousand pounds?' inquired Cantrell.

Miss Scott repeated the query into the mouthpiece, waited a few seconds then nodded. 'Nine hundred thousand pounds.'

'And fifty thousand?'

Again the sum was relayed by the miracle of modern technology to three separate points on the globe.

'Yes, nine hundred and fifty thousand pounds.'

'One million, then?'

A longer pause this time, before Miss Scott intimated that one of her overseas clients would pay the round million.

There was no sound in the cavernous hall except Cantrell's quiet, 'One million, one hundred thousand?'

'Yes, one million, one hundred thousand.'

'And two hundred thousand?'

Everyone heard the figure passed on crisply to London. They waited. Miss Scott shook her head.

Cantrell looked round at his mute audience. 'Selling, then, at one million, one hundred thousand pounds.' He banged his gavel. 'Sold . . . to?'

Miss Scott passed on the enquiry. 'A buyer in Tokyo,' she announced.

'Bloody Japs!' someone muttered, as the pent-up flood of conversation was released.

The flight from Tokyo to Athens was passed in almost unbroken, hostile silence. As soon as the Olympic Airways jumbo threw itself into the sky, Catherine pointedly immersed herself in a Japanese novel. Tim ostentatiously worked at business papers, read the in-flight journals from cover to cover, and watched the movie. During the brief Bangkok stopover they wandered separately around the transit lounge. They did make occasional forays into conversation, mostly over meals, but these were short and emotionally void. Catherine slept easily through the night. Tim just worried.

Their quarrel over the previous three days had gone the full distance, ineffectually refereed by Tonashi. And Catherine had won on points. That was why she was now huddled in the window seat with the maximum space between her and Tim. She had countered all his protests about the dangers of walking into Karakis's trap with the injured riposte that Tim should be grateful to her for salvaging his plan – not to mention the fee he was being paid for nailing the unspeakable Greek. Since neither Tim nor Tonashi had been able to come up with a way of cancelling Catherine's reservation aboard the *Phidias*, without arousing Karakis's suspicions, there was no answer to that. But the unassailable logic of his unwanted companion's argument had only made Tim angrier. Being responsible for Catherine, he had pointed out, was going to make a difficult job well nigh impossible, and he had not been able to restrain himself from illustrating his thesis with references to women who 'got in the way' and 'went to pieces in a crisis'. Catherine had thrown back at him charges of 'insufferable arrogance' and 'masculine superiority'. Hence the current arctic atmosphere.

The two travellers emerged from their emotional igloos for breakfast. It was as the plastic trays were being cleared away that Tim attempted an approach – brisk and businesslike.

'Come on, it's time to stop sulking and get down to—'

'Who's sulking?' Catherine had no intention of making this easy.

'We're both professionals. Let's try and behave like professionals. It's only a couple of hours to touchdown, and we have to work together.'

'Well, it would be a good start if you condescended to share your plan of campaign with me.' Catherine's hands were demurely clasped in her lap, and her eyes registered Job-like patience.

' "Plan of campaign" is far too grand a term.' Tim leaned towards

257

her, voice lowered, although no one else was within earshot in the first-class cabin. 'It's just a matter of keeping our eyes and ears open. Karakis is very clever inviting us on to his yacht. He doesn't intend to let us anywhere near his storehouse of stolen goodies.'

'But he will have the three pictures on board – the ones he wants Tonashi to buy?'

'Presumably. My guess is that he'll only let us see the paintings when we're well out to sea and there's no other vessel in sight.'

'So, all we have to do is tell the police as soon as we get back on dry land.'

Tim shook his head. 'Karakis will have thought of that. Remember, he doesn't altogether trust us. No, we have to make sure the Greek authorities intercept the yacht before Karakis can spirit his ill-gotten gains away.'

'How?'

'That's the sixty-four thousand dollar question, isn't it? I've got a small radio transmitter – one of your boss's little toys – set to a prearranged frequency. Some of my own men will be around, trying to stay in range without being picked up on the boat's radar. As soon as we're absolutely sure the incriminating evidence is aboard, I'll try to get a message to them.'

'In other words, we have to improvise.'

'That's right. And, every moment, Karakis and his cronies will be watching us like hawks. He leaves nothing to chance. Don't ever underestimate him. I made that mistake once. Never again.'

At Ellinikon airport they were met and conveyed by car to the marina at Piraeus. There two well-built 'matelots' in white T-shirts and blue shorts conveyed them and their luggage to a sleek power boat. The crew cast off and the craft streaked across the Gulf of Saronikos towards the distant mountains of the Peloponnese. Forty minutes later, one of the Greeks pointed ahead and said, 'Poros.' The boat entered the channel between the island and the mainland, and slowed to approach the harbour. Several large boats were moored by the quay, which was also the town's main street. Poros was busy in the late morning sunshine. A group of boys were fishing with a makeshift rod and line, the tourist shops were doing a vigorous trade; the pavement cafés were full; a dozen passengers disembarked from the water-

taxi which had brought them across from Galatos, on the mainland –
and George Martin was scanning the straits through binoculars.

Good old George – on the ball as usual, Tim thought. He raised a
hand, apparently pointing to where the hillside rose steeply behind the
town, and muttered something to Catherine which was drowned by
the roar of the engine. He hoped Martin had seen the signal. The burly
figure disappeared behind a flashy motor launch before he had time
to respond.

One of the crewmen waved an arm. '*Phidias*,' he indicated.

'We should have guessed it would be the biggest toy in the nursery.'
Catherine grimaced.

'She is a beauty, though.' Tim admired the vessel's slender lines
and glistening paintwork. *Phidias* was berthed apart from the other
vessels, and took up about as much space as three of them. She was
triple-masted, with sails neatly furled along the yards. The superstruc-
ture ran most of the length of the deck and obviously housed accommodation for several people. A crewman occupied himself, not very
strenuously, with a bucket and mop. Two well-proportioned young
women draped themselves decorously on the cabin housing.

Karakis was on the afterdeck to greet them, immaculate in cream
shirt and flannels and a spotted navy-blue choker. 'Welcome aboard
the *Phidias*!' He glowed with proprietorial pride. He kissed Catherine
on both cheeks, and shook Tim's hand enthusiastically. 'How wonderful to see you again, and you have arrived in such good time. The
Athenian traffic can be dreadful.'

He led the way through into the saloon. Bench seats in navy-
blue leather formed a horseshoe, cupping a circular, polished oak table
with a brass rail. An ice-bucket and glasses stood ready on its
gleaming surface, together with bowls of salad, grilled octopus and
fruit.

'Champagne to celebrate your arrival.' Karakis motioned them to
be seated. 'And a light lunch. Then I'm sure you will want to rest
while we get under way.'

Tim started. 'Under way? I was rather hoping to have a brief stroll
around Poros.'

The Greek shook his head and smiled, and Tim was sure he sensed
a look of triumph. 'Alas, Charles – I may call you Charles, mayn't I,

now that we're away from those terribly formal Japanese. My friends call me Niki – as you say in England, "Time and tide wait for no man." '

Gazing out through the companionway, Tim saw one of the crew hauling in the mooring rope.

Salomon's house, one among many large old buildings in the crowded streets around Vienna's Staatsoper, was a mausoleum – or so Nathan regarded it. Bought by Jacob Seligman 'the Great' seventy years before, it had been kept by his son exactly as Jacob had left it. Even on such a fine summer's morning the windows' heavy drapes seemed to stifle the sunlight. The long drawing-room was more like an emporium stacked with heavy, ornate furniture. As Nathan negotiated the obstacles of mahogany and rosewood encrusted with ormolu, he longed to fling wide the casements to let in fresh air and the friendly noises of the street. But from childhood he had been aware of his grandfather's strict ban on opening the house up to 'contagion'. So he prowled among the ghosts, the memories and the entombed past, fighting back claustrophobia until Salomon deigned to see him.

After forty minutes Nathan heard voices. The door to Salomon's private suite opened, and a group of black-coated and -hatted rabbis emerged. They crossed the room to another door, where a footman had appeared to show them out. Another servant appeared at the inner door to inform Nathan that his grandfather would now receive him.

As he sauntered through the next chamber to Salomon's inner sanctum Nathan gazed around at what was a museum and art gallery rolled into one: cabinets stuffed with miniatures, fine porcelain, carved crystal and *bijouterie;* mantelpieces laden with ornate vases, marble clocks and elegant bronzes; and every square inch of wall-space hung with paintings. He shivered at the sheer, naked acquisitiveness of it all. Only in these private chambers had Salomon allowed his own personality to express itself. But even here it was not one man's taste and vision that was on display. The head of the Austrian house had inherited his father's already impressive collections, and simply added to them. The result was one man's ideas superimposed on another's to produce a top-heavy, disorganised, unarranged conglomeration of rare and expensive artefacts.

'Come in, come in! Don't waste time!' The greeting was as gruff as Nathan had expected.

Salomon Seligman was propelled by a servant towards the door in his large wicker bathchair. He was a bulky figure with a neatly-trimmed white beard and a black velvet skullcap covering his bald head.

'When you're rich, everyone wants your time. Money isn't enough for 'em. They want your precious hours and minutes, too. And mine are running out. That lot,' an impatient flick of the hand indicated the recently departed delegation, 'getting up a fund to settle our Russian brothers in America. Terrible business, that. You *do* keep up with some of the news, I suppose.' He glared querulously as his grandson stooped to kiss his cheek. 'You do find some time for serious matters amid all your parties . . . and . . . gambling . . .' The sentence disintegrated into a fit of coughing.

'Yes, grandfather, of course I know about the atrocities in Russia. Our cousins tackled Tsar Nicholas about the situation when he was in London last year. The Rothschilds are organising cheap housing for the Jews pouring off every ship from the Continent. We've all contributed.'

'Well, I'm glad to see that your head isn't entirely filled with nonsense. Oh, *do* sit down. I can't bear people hovering over me. And *you* can go!' This to the servant.

As the man in the pale blue and white livery silently withdrew, Nathan looked around. The room was strange to him. He had been in here less than a dozen times over the years. Few members of the family were admitted to what they called, behind the old man's back, 'the holy of holies'. Salomon kept it for business and other religious pastimes. It was not very different in feel to the anteroom, except that the precious objects with which it was lavishly decorated had been more spaced out, with some sense of display. But the ornaments and the paintings in their heavy gilt frames meant little to Nathan. The only beauty he appreciated was the kind that went on two or four well-shaped legs.

The old man glared at his grandson. 'So, you received my letter?'

'Yes, I did.'

'Good, good. You've spoken to Ruben, then.'

Nathan clasped his hands over his silver-topped cane and stared straight before him. 'No, grandfather, I haven't.'

Salomon was taken aback. 'What do you mean . . .?'

'I mean I don't think it's any business of mine who my brother chooses to marry, and frankly I don't think it's any business of yours.'

The old man was stunned by this defiance, but only momentarily. 'No business of the head of the family to preserve our honour!'

'Honour has nothing to do with it, grandfather. It's no disgrace to marry a Gentile – not today. In England all the leading Jewish families have made alliances with the aristocracy – Rothschilds, Sassoons, Cohens . . .'

'The fact that other people deny the faith doesn't make it right to do so.'

Nathan jumped to his feet. 'Right? How can you talk about right? Is it right to use threats and religious cant to force Ruben to your will? You made him take over the bank. He didn't want to, but he didn't have the guts to stand up to you. For heaven's sake allow him the happiness of marrying the woman he loves.'

'He owes love to his family first!' Salomon did not raise his voice, but his tone was bleak, severe and unyielding.

'There you go again, taking words and twisting them into whatever shape suits your purpose. Honour! Love! All you love is money and the power that goes with it!' Nathan strode round the room brandishing his cane excitedly.

Salomon watched the slim, handsome young man and realised that the petulance of spoiled adolescence had hardened into adult determination. He knew immediately that victory could not be achieved through confrontation. He smiled. 'Nathan, you really are remarkably like your great-grandfather. He was a man who saw things clearly and knew what he wanted.'

Nathan was taken unawares by the change of tactics. Before he could respond, Salomon pressed home his advantage.

'Come, lad, we have a problem. How shall we solve it? You know I mean young Ruben no harm. But my responsibility is not just to him. It's to all that's gone before and more important, all that is yet to come: to his children – and yours, if you ever do the sensible thing and settle down. Pour yourself a glass of that excellent Madeira, then come and sit by me over here.'

Nathan picked up the heavy decanter. 'Will you, grandfather . . .?'
'No thank you, lad.' Salomon tapped his chest. 'I dare not.'

Nathan perched on the chaise longue, sipped the sweet wine, and
gazed at the old man warily over the rim. 'I don't see that there is a
problem. Louisa is absolutely devoted to Ruben. When you see them
together you'll realise how right she is for him. She's quite prepared
to come and live in Vienna. She'll be a great support for him. Without
her, I think the bank might well drive him insane.'

'But will she accept our faith?'

'Does it matter so much? We're almost in the twentieth century.
These religious barriers are not so immovable now.'

'Try telling that to the poor wretches crammed into Lord Rothschild's tenements. No, Nathan, religion does matter. How did we build
the Seligman fortune? How have we kept it? By being united. By
standing up to the forces of anti-Semitism. By not letting anyone take
away from us what we've worked so hard to build.'

'We've survived through good business sense. Nothing more.'

'No, Nathan. I've seen hundreds of enterprises rise and fall – banks,
railway companies, engineering concerns, textile manufactories. Built
up by able, dedicated men, and soundly financed. But nevertheless they
failed. Why? Some weren't tough enough to stand up to unscrupulous
competitors. Some were inherited by incompetent sons or sons-in-law.
Some simply lost the vision. They lacked that golden cord of unity
which has always kept the Seligman houses together. And religion is
the main strand in that cord.'

'Ruben is a good Jew.'

'Of course he is. But what of his son? Will he be a good Jew when
he takes over? Or a Christian? And how will he feel about the rest of
the family? Perhaps he will be closer to his mother's people. And
where will he bequeath his fortune?'

Nathan drained his glass and crossed the room to pour another. 'If
you drive a wedge between Ruben and Louisa, don't imagine that
you'll ever be able to persuade him to a more "suitable" match. You
may never have any grandsons at all – and then what will become of
the bank?'

Salomon sighed deeply. 'You've no idea of the weight of responsibility I carry.'

'That's where you're wrong. I know you think of me as a feckless young man whose only interest is pleasure. But I made a conscious decision not to shoulder the Seligman burden. I made it a long time ago. I made it on a December day when I was thirteen years old. The day I discovered that my father had been driven to suicide.'

Salomon slumped in his chair, silent. Suddenly he looked his age, seemed almost to shrivel within his clothes, so that Nathan regretted his brusqueness. Eventually the old man muttered, almost inaudibly, 'Your father was also my son. Not a day passes when I don't remember him, when I don't share his longing to be free of all this responsibility. So I escape here, to my beloved pictures. Only there's no escape. Not for me. Nor for Ruben.' His voice gained strength as he continued. 'Not even for you, however hard you try to distract yourself with horses and . . . young boys.' He looked up sharply.

Nathan gasped, stunned by the suddenness of the attack. The words sabre-slashed the elaborate veils he had drawn around his secret. Hacked down his confidence that no one, outside a very small, intimate circle, knew the truth that could ruin him. Assiduously he had kept this fact, above all, from his family. For fact it was – exotic, delicious, esoteric, vile, forbidden fact. Only a few days before, the gloating British press had been exulting in the degradation of Oscar Wilde, just released from jail, a broken, burnt-out wreck of a man condemned to hide away from the society before which he had once peacock-strutted. Nathan felt physically sick. He could only stare in open-mouthed disbelief and shame.

The old man's shrewd, bright eyes were fixed upon him. 'Yes, Nathan, we're all fallible. We all have passions that consume us. Ruben desires his Louisa above all things. You are possessed by your secret vice. And my obsession is to keep our family and the business together. And now, alas, these three cannot coexist. Which one must be sacrificed, Nathan?'

'You couldn't! You wouldn't!'

'Overmastering passions, Nathan. Mine every bit as unyielding as yours.'

Silence. The monotonous, metallic thudding of an ebonised long-case clock measuring rather than breaking the stillness.

Nathan contemplated the emotional cliff-face to which he was committed. Above him, narrow footholds marking a precarious, painful route to safety. Below him, the abyss.

Salomon was speaking again. 'I'm going to show you something I've never shown anyone – not even your father. It's my source of great solace. For me it's ultimate beauty. I contemplate it whenever I'm deeply troubled, and it never fails to bring me peace. It may help you now.'

He took a small key from his waistcoat pocket and held it out. 'Open that little door on the wall behind my desk.'

Nathan went over to what looked like a small cupboard set in the thickness of the wall. As he turned the key and drew back the door, he saw that it was not a cupboard at all; just the covering of another picture. He stood back – and saw a woman with her young child, flanked by three men in rich clothes.

'But it's . . .'

'Exquisite. The most wonderful, moving masterpiece in the whole history of art.'

'But it's a Christian painting!'

Salomon was unmoved by his grandson's surprised indignation. 'It's the absurd Christian legend about Jesus being recognised as King of the Jews and worshipped by earthly monarchs. But the story is unimportant. Look at . . .'

'Unimportant!' Nathan hurled the word back with all the force of confused, unleashed emotions. 'You damned old hypocrite! You pose to the world as an upright, orthodox Jew! You preach to me about the importance of our faith! You fly into a rage because Ruben wants to marry a Christian! And, all the time, you're skulking here, secretly venerating this . . . thing!'

Impelled by sudden fury, he snatched up a heavy glass inkpot from the desk and hurled it at *The Triarchs*. It gashed the top right corner and sprayed the canvas with black ink.

Nathan turned on the figure in the bathchair. 'That's what I think of your precious picture, and you, and your cantankerous threats, and your hypocrisy and cant!'

He blundered from the room, and never saw his grandfather again.

That was the moment when Seligmans, Vienna, ceased to exist.

Although Salomon kept the bank going until his death, twelve years later, it died, in effect, on that June morning in 1897. Ruben was banned from the business the following year, when he married Louisa. So, in 1909, it was sold, and the old man's two grandsons shared the not inconsiderable proceeds. Nathan took out English citizenship, bought an estate near Newmarket, and devoted his life to breeding racehorses (Salomon's vindictiveness fell short of exposing a member of his family as a bugger). Ruben remained true to the land of his birth and made a family home near Salzburg. He lost a son at Caporetto, on the Italian front, in 1917. And *The Triarchs*? Louisa Seligman was astonished when the old man, who had steadfastly refused to meet her, bequeathed his most treasured possession to her in his will.

Tim opened his suitcase carefully. On top of the neatly-folded clothes was a file cover. Without removing it, he opened it and looked closely at the half a dozen sheets of typescript clipped together. At the bottom of each there was an almost imperceptible hole made with a pin. Tim held the papers up in front of the porthole. Light should have passed through all the carefully aligned holes. It did not. In fact, the perforations were separated by as much as a centimetre. It confirmed what he had expected: the oh-so-cautious Niki Karakis was taking no chances whatsoever. The baggage had been searched while Tim and Catherine had been lunching with their host.

Had the searchers discovered anything? He felt beneath the pile of shirts and removed the compact cassette recorder. He slid it from its plastic sheath. As he did so, the tiny door at the back opened and two small batteries fell out. Tim smiled his relief. The machine was exactly as he had left it. No one had bothered to examine it. No one had discovered that it was one of Tonashi's gimmicks: a disguised short-range radio transmitter/receiver.

He turned his attention to the cabin. The accommodation was not spacious, but it more than made up for that in luxury. The bed, with its navy-blue covering, was transformed by a bank of deep cushions into a divan, which folded into the wall when not required. Drawer space was beneath the bed. There was a dressing-table/desk, an adequate wardrobe, and an adjacent shower/toilet. Tim went over every inch, looking for concealed microphones, cameras, sensors. He examined the smoke alarm. The room was clean.

He picked up the radio, set it to transmit, and called George. Nothing. He tried for five minutes. He turned to other frequencies to check the machine. He picked up various ships' messages in Greek. He hailed his assistant again. The channel was silent. He went over to the porthole. The rugged Peloponnese coastline was slipping past rapidly as *Phidias* moved seaward, under power. Poros was obviously out of radio range already.

He stretched his jet-lagged body on the divan. Ah well, so much for Plan A. Pity there was no Plan B. Catherine was right: taking on Karakis on his own turf was a dumb idea.

He was woken by a member of the crew gently shaking his shoulder and telling him that dinner would be served in half an hour.

When the party assembled before the meal, Tim and Catherine were introduced to the other two guests. Anna and Zoe were the blonde, bronzed Athenian bimbos who had been sunning themselves earlier. They had little English, seemingly less intelligence, and had presumably been brought along for the amusement of Karakis and his men; although Karakis was paying very close attention to Catherine. Tim subsequently calculated that there were six crew aboard – captain, cook, steward and three hands – whose quarters were in the forepart of the yacht. They were all well built, and there was no doubt that they were heavies. This was confirmed during dinner, when Catherine innocently asked their host, 'Did I see one of your men cleaning an automatic rifle earlier?'

Karakis shrugged. 'Very likely, my dear. With such a valuable cargo,' he patted her hand, 'we can't afford to take any chances.'

Tim noticed that the Greek continued to caress Catherine's fingers, and that she made no attempt to extricate herself. He said, 'Talking of valuable cargo, when can we see the pictures?'

Karakis feigned surprise. 'Oh, my dear Charles, you don't suppose I have them aboard, do you? This is one of the safest vessels afloat but such priceless objects . . . No, I have them stored in perfect conditions, ready for your inspection.'

'And when will that be?'

'Charles, Charles, what a glutton for work you are. I promised Catherine a romantic voyage among the Greek islands.' The hand grip tightened. 'And I intend to keep my promise. Do relax. There will be time enough for business. Do have a little more of this excellent lobster.'

The lobster was, indeed, excellent. So was the rest of the meal. Karakis presided attentively and entertainingly. Surrounded by pretty women, basking in luxury and protected by his armed thugs, the criminal was in his element. Tim watched the laughing face, flushed with wine, and longed to smash it. He wanted to shatter the Greek's self-confidence and security. But there seemed little chance of that. Karakis really was holding all the cards.

'Do you think he was telling the truth – about the paintings not being on board?' Catherine gazed down at the yacht's creamy wake bubbling along the black surface of the gulf before losing itself in the darkness. *Phidias*, under sail now, her engine silenced, seemed to be making good speed. It was late, gone midnight. Catherine and Tim were leaning against the stern rail and talking almost in whispers.

'It figures. He's paranoid about being spied on. He probably has his own shadow security checked. He's not going to run the slightest risk of us being tailed. If any police were to swoop down on us, this ship would be clean as a whistle. Anyway, we certainly can't go snooping around looking for smuggled art. That certainly would blow the gaffe. We'll just have to play the game by his rules – for the time being.'

'Whereabouts are your men?'

'I was hoping you wouldn't ask that.' He told her about not being able to make contact with George Martin.

'No chance of the seventh cavalry riding over the hill, then?'

'I'm sorry. You really shouldn't be involved in this.'

'Nuts! We've worked that mine to exhaustion. Anyway, what's to be sorry about?' She breathed in deeply the warm night air. 'I sure could get used to this life.' She gazed across to the lights on the mainland. 'Do you know where we are?'

'Judging by the delights our host was dangling before us over dinner, we're making for the Cyclades. Since we're sailing virtually due east, I'd guess that that headland over there,' he pointed out a dark mass to port, topped with lights, 'is the southern tip of Attica – Cape Sounion.'

Catherine gazed at the crag's black outline.

'Place me on Sunium's marbled steep,
Where nothing, save the waves and I,
May hear our mutual murmurs sweep;
There, swan-like, let me sing and die.'

'Very impressive.'

She laughed. 'Surely they taught you Byron in your English school.'

'Like hell they did!' he snapped the answer. 'East End kids weren't supposed to mess with genteel things like poetry. We did games to keep fit, maths because it was useful, metalwork and woodwork to fit us for practical jobs befitting our station. Poetry? Literature? Music? Art? Religion? What use were they? Unmanly, cissy things. That's why I left school with a hell of a lot of learning still to do. Poetry's one of the delights my plebeian brain still hasn't grasped!' He turned abruptly. 'It's getting cold. I'm going to bed. Goodnight!'

Catherine watched his retreating figure. 'Damn!' she muttered to the night.

'Why have we got to go? Grandma said we could stay all afternoon!' The eight-year-old stared through her tears at the other people gracefully gliding round the ice-rink, and made little attempt to unlace her skates.

'Caroline, do as you are told! And do hurry up! Elizabeth has changed already!' Miss Jenkins, outwardly as duty-bound and unyielding as her formal grey uniform, hid her annoyance and worry by brusquely chivvying her two young charges. 'Your grandmother has sent the car for us early and told us to hurry, so hurry we must.' Edith Jenkins did not like unheralded changes of plan. Children needed a routine. Sudden excitements and disappointments should be avoided at all costs. But there was more to her anxiety than the petulance of an English nanny put out and put upon by capricious employers.

With the help of Schultz, the chauffeur, she collected up the skates, rugs and other paraphernalia of the aborted outing, and shepherded the girls back to the large black car. As the Daimler made its way through the narrow streets of old Salzburg she stared out of the window, leaving Elizabeth to deal with her still sulking younger sister. She had been against this holiday from the outset. What with all the troubles in Germany, this was not the time to bring two impressionable English girls to the Continent. But the visit to the Austrian grandparents had been long promised, and her employer – always over-indulgent in Miss Jenkins's opinion – had not wanted to disappoint his daughters. He had actually laughed at her mild protest. 'A paper tiger' – that was what he had called Mr Hitler.

They crossed the river bridge, and Miss Jenkins gazed down into the swirling Salzach, already swollen with the first melted snow. Paper tiger he might be, but he had an uncomfortably loud roar. And the girls' grandparents, Mr and Mrs Ruben Seligman, were certainly worried by the dictator's antics in neighbouring Germany. She shivered, and drew the rug up further over her knees. She smiled reassuringly at her two dark-haired charges, and knew that she would not be happy until she had put the English Channel safely between them and whatever it was these excitable continentals were up to.

At the Schloss Eberhardt, ten kilometres south of Salzburg, Louisa Seligman, tall and very straight despite her sixty years, met them in the hall. She folded her arms around the girls who rushed up to her. 'Darlings, I'm so sorry about the skating. But what do you think? There's a special tea to make up for it. Anne-Marie has made your favourite strudel. It's all ready in the nursery. Run along, my darlings. I'll come in a few minutes.'

As the girls ran up the wide curving staircase, Louisa turned to the nanny. 'Miss Jenkins, please come to the study.'

Ruben Seligman was busy on the telephone as they entered. Louisa motioned Miss Jenkins to a leather sofa and then, somewhat to the latter's surprise, sat down beside her.

Ruben hung the earpiece on its hook and returned the telephone to the desk. He removed his pince-nez and rubbed his eyes wearily. He had a thin face, topped with luxuriant waves of grey-white hair. He looked across the desk with a slight, tired smile. 'Miss Jenkins, you are not to be alarmed and, above all, we must not alarm the girls. However, it is vital that you return to England without delay. My wife will accompany you.'

Louisa opened her mouth to protest, but Ruben held up a hand.

'No, my dear, there really is no more to be said. I have just booked a compartment on the 7.20 train to Zurich. I'm afraid it won't be very comfortable. There were no sleepers to be had, and I fear the train will be crowded with people leaving the country.'

Edith Jenkins nodded, calm and businesslike. 'What am I to tell the children? They will overhear other people talking. I don't want them to be frightened.'

'Tell them that we are all leaving Salzburg because grandma and grandpa are coming to stay with them for a little while. For the rest, I should say as little as possible. It's a sorry story, and they wouldn't understand anyway. German troops are reported to be massing on the frontier. Of course, our leaders tell us that Hitler would not dare invade, that France and Britain would refuse to stand idly by. But the government is only saying that to prevent panic. No one stopped the Germans marching into Czechoslovakia, and it's unlikely that Paris or London will come to our aid. The Germans will not come for several weeks, perhaps even months. Hitler will need to find a pretext for crossing the border. But when he does, he will be welcomed by the Austrian Nazis – simple fools who believe that *Anschluss*, or union with the German Reich, will magically solve all Austria's problems. It won't, of course. We shall have government by fanatics.' He shook his head. 'But, by then, *we* shall all be safely in England. As soon as I've tidied up as much as possible here, I'll follow you.' He caught his wife's anxious glance. 'It will be a matter of days, I assure you.' He forced a wide smile. 'Now, let's all have tea in the nursery, shall we?'

In later life Edith Jenkins always vividly remembered glancing at Herr Seligman's little silver desk calendar as she left the room. It read: 11 March 1938. On the morning of the twelfth, Adolf Hitler personally led his army into Austria.

The next three days had a surreal quality. Catherine felt like a little girl being taken round a fabulous toyshop by a convicted child abuser. *Phidias* meandered gently among the Cyclades – rugged islands whose granite peaks, sparse vegetation and limestone crags were perfectly reflected in the green-blue sea. Karakis proved an excellent guide to the historic sites of the archipelago. Lovingly he explained the layout of ancient Andros, whose ruins litter the cultivated terraces encircling the bay of Palaiopolis. He waxed lyrical about the legends of the holy island of Delos where, during the period of Athenian domination, no one was allowed to die or give birth for fear of defiling the place sacred to the worship of Apollo and Artemis. He strode enthusiastically up the steep, narrow streets of Astipalea, scattering anecdotes about the medieval Venetians who built the castle overlooking the harbour of Percyialo. When the complement of the *Phidias* were not dutifully following their leader around amphitheatres and the fallen columns of long-deserted temples, they swam in the glistening, waveless water, ate fish freshly grilled by the cook over improvised barbecues on empty beaches, and lazed on the yacht's sunbaked deck.

For Catherine, and even for Tim, the cruise would have been idyllic if they had not been constantly on their guard. Karakis made frequent advances to the American woman. When Tim told her not to play with fire, she replied that she was a big girl now, that she had no need of his moral guidance, that snubbing their host would be counterproductive, and that he might let some useful information slip in an intimate moment. The Greek also engaged Tim in long conversations about art, and the 'Aberdeen lecturer' had to strain his concentration to the utmost to keep up his pose. And, all the time, they had to prevent themselves forgetting two things: they were there to destroy Karakis, and he would not hesitate to destroy them.

It was at noon on the fourth day that *Phidias* came to anchor off a tiny island whose steep cliffs sloped towards its southern end, where a hook-shaped spit of land formed a natural harbour.

'Lunch on the beach, again, Niki?' Catherine, in a dark green bikini and a straw sunhat, perched against the afterdeck rail.

Karakis reclined in a deckchair, wearing shorts and a loose shirt covering his ample stomach. 'No, my dear. This is an exceedingly uninteresting island, and plagued with snakes, which is why no one lives there. I'm afraid the time has come for tedious business to intrude on our little holiday, but only briefly, I promise you. Now, where's young Charles?'

Catherine pointed. 'He's over there, with his nose in a book as usual.' She called out, 'Charles, can you come a moment?'

Tim was sitting with his back to the mainmast. Thankfully he laid aside *The Great Venetians: Studies in the Development of Renaissance*

Symbolism, dropped down to the deck, and came round to the boat's stern.

Catherine poured an orange-coloured fruit cocktail from a jug into a tall glass half filled with ice, and held it out to him. 'It seems we've reached the end of the rainbow. The crock of gold is about to appear.'

'Cleverly put, my dear.' Karakis rose and placed an arm round her shoulder. 'I was just about to explain that I have arranged for the paintings to be brought here for your inspection. It is a suitably peaceful and private spot.'

Tim gazed around the empty horizon, and nodded. No other islands. No ships or boats. He guessed they were well off the ferry and trade routes. They were alone somewhere to the north of Crete, in a marine no-man's-land where the Aegean meets the Mediterranean. 'Just how do the paintings get here?'

'They're being brought by helicopter.' Karakis smiled.

Congratulating himself on his security arrangements, Tim thought. And well he might. Tim was sick with frustration. With George and the others kicking their heels on Poros, a couple of hundred miles away, he was powerless. Karakis was free to bring the pictures from their hiding place by chopper, and take them back again. For Tim that meant failure. The whole elaborate, expensive charade set up with Kodomo and Tonashi had been a waste of time. He forced a smile. 'Excellent, Niki, excellent. I can't wait to see them.' Then he went back to his cabin to think.

Lying on the divan, he looked at the situation from every angle, like an oriental puzzle box which defied opening. Overpower the crew while the pictures were on board, and put out a call to the police? Out of the question. Get to the radio phone without being seen? Impossible – the equipment was in the wheelhouse, next to the saloon, and always manned. He turned the problem over and over, but there was no key, no concealed catch which would open the lid. There was nothing he could do to stop the bastard slipping through the net again. Quite apart from Tim's personal outrage about that, he had to face the fact that the Japanese would be even angrier. Kodomo was not the sort of man to be understanding about failure. As for Tonashi, he would certainly cancel his backing for the Farrans project. Tim stared up at the ceiling. At best, the future held financial ruin. At worst . . .

His thoughts were interrupted by the snarl of a helicopter engine.

It was only when a delegation of servants presented themselves in the study that Ruben Seligman was persuaded to leave Austria. It was two days since he had despatched Louisa and the girls, and twenty-four hours since his wife had telephoned to tell him of their safe arrival in Zurich. Ruben had spent the time in a frenzy of activity. He had drawn from the bank as much cash as he could without arousing suspicion. He had paid all the staff at Schloss Eberhardt three months' wages in advance. He had instructed most of them to go back to their family homes, and had made arrangements for their travel. With his secretary's help, he had boxed up all his private papers and had them deposited in a far corner of the attic.

Then he had turned his attention to the family treasures. Distractedly, he went from room to room, mentally cataloguing the porcelain, the silver, the bronzes, the paintings, furniture, rugs, tapestries and objets d'art. Every item spoke of generations of Seligman connoisseurship. Many of them had their own stories, quaint, humorous or tragic, which had been passed down in the family. There was no time to pack them all up and arrange for them to be stored safely. Some of the smaller pieces he gave to the men and women who had served long and faithfully in the house or on the estate. Then, painfully, he selected those which were particularly precious to him and Louisa. Working through the night with what remained of the male staff, he brought them into the library, where two maids wrapped them in cloths and pieces of curtain and packed them in chests and laundry baskets.

Ruben hovered over the operation, channelling his anger, indignation and anxiety into brisk efficiency. Presenting a calm, businesslike appearance to the fearful members of the household, some of whom were in tears.

'Maria, be sure to wrap all of those Meissen pieces very carefully. Teresa, you must dust the books thoroughly before they go into the crate.'

He gazed around at the scattered treasures. How invidious it was to choose which items were to be saved from the barbarians. His precious first editions – of course, they must be preserved. And the monogrammed Sèvres dinner service made for the Great Jacob. And the

274

Raphael Louise loved so much. And the bronze bust by Benvenuto Cellini which Ruben himself had recognised in a sale of undistinguished antiques in Rome. But what of the Flemish tapestries in the hall? There were none finer in the whole of Europe. Should he have them taken down? No, the girls had quite enough to do, and there simply was not enough time. With a shake of the head he went through to the study.

He sat at his desk and looked at the list he had compiled as soon as he heard of the German invasion. The next item was '*Horses*'. He must get them away into the country. '*Phone Carl.*' He ought to check that the family in Vienna was all right and reassure his son about his own safety. So much to do. And he was tired. And too old for all these upsets. He slumped forward across the desk, resting his head on his arms.

Half an hour later he was woken by a knock on the door. He looked up to see all his remaining six servants in the doorway. Schultz, the chauffeur and the longest standing member of staff, was the spokesman.

'With respect, sir, we all think you should leave now – straight away. It's not safe for you to stay any longer.'

Ruben removed his pince-nez and smiled weakly. 'That's very thoughtful of you all, but there's still a great deal to do.'

'Nothing that we can't take care of, sir. Thing is, *we're* safe. None of us have a good opinion of the Nazis, but they won't do anything to us. We're not important. But, if you'll forgive me referring to it, sir, you know what's been happening to the Jews in Germany. They say the Gestapo are even rounding them up and sending them off to labour camps.'

'Now, now, Schultz, you mustn't listen to rumour. I've heard those stories, of course, and I assure you that they are exaggerations.'

'Maybe so, sir, but you really mustn't fall into their hands. *Please*, sir, there's no time to lose. We've just heard that the Nazis have taken over the townhall and the police station. And someone's daubed slogans over the synagogue.'

Ruben wavered. 'Well, perhaps, when I've had time to sort a few more things out and pack . . .'

'Maria's already packed a bag for you, sir. And I've got the car at

275

the front door. If we leave now, I reckon we can get into Italy before the new government closes the frontier.'

Still Ruben hesitated.

Schultz came right up to the desk. '*Please*, sir. Your place, right now, is beside Mrs Seligman. We'll look after the schloss till this crisis is over and you can both come back home.'

Ruben rose. Slightly dazed he allowed himself to be hustled through the library and into the hall. He shook hands with the other servants. Then Schultz almost pushed him into the car, jumped into the driving seat, and drove the Daimler faster than it had ever been driven before, down the long drive.

They got as far as the main gate. Another vehicle was coming in between the tall stone pillars. A black Mercedes. It stopped as the Daimler skidded to a halt on the gravel. The man who emerged wore a heavy civilian overcoat and a swastika armband.

'Herr Seligman?' he enquired as Ruben wound down the window. His tone was courteous but unyieldingly authoritarian. 'My name is Taubmann. I have the honour to be the head of the local Gestapo. There are some matters we would like to discuss with you at our headquarters. One of my men will take you there.'

When he had seen the Daimler on its way, Taubmann returned to his own vehicle, climbed in beside the driver, and continued up to the house. He surveyed the baroque façade for a moment before getting out. He turned to his young assistant at the wheel. 'So, Hugo, let's go and see how these bloodsuckers live.'

Five minutes later he had informed the terrified servants that Schloss Eberhardt had been commandeered by the glorious German Reich, and despatched them all to pack their bags. Then he toured the house, pointing out to his colleague, Hugo von Zalen, its sumptuous furnishings and exquisite decor.

'It's at moments like this that you realise how right the Führer is. For centuries the Jews have been draining all the wealth of the German people in order that they can live in unbridled luxury.'

'Parasites!' the younger man observed.

'Yes, while they've been accumulating this stuff, Germany, Austria and all the countries of Europe have been sinking into poverty and degradation.' He led the way down the wide, marble staircase. 'Just look at these tapestries.' He pointed to the large allegorical panels whose muted greens and blues gave the lofty hall a feeling of cool yet intimate splendour. 'They must be worth thousands. How many mouths would they feed, eh?'

'What will happen to all this?'

'It must be inventoried, crated up and sent to Berlin. It will glorify the Reich, not these squalid little Hebrew vermin.' He threw open the library door. 'O-ho, what have we here? Look, Hugo. We obviously arrived in the nick of time. Herr Seligman was parcelling up his treasures, doubtless to send them out of the country.'

From an open laundry basket he picked up a pair of exquisite Höchst figurines: Harlequin and Columbine. 'German porcelain, Hugo. The finest quality. And about to be shipped abroad. We must save them from that. German art for Germans, eh?' He picked up some pieces of towelling, wrapped the gaily-coloured pieces carefully, and tucked them inside the open collar of his greatcoat.

His subordinate stared. 'You're going to take . . .'

Taubmann chuckled. 'Don't look so shocked, Hugo. We have saved a fortune in plundered art for the Fatherland, haven't we?'

The young man nodded.

'Then we have earned a small reward. Come, what takes your fancy?'

Hugo looked round, bemused, at the piles of precious objects.

'Then let me decide for you. How about a present for your father? Something to add to his great picture collection, perhaps? Otto von Zalen serves the Führer well. Our leader would not grudge him a token of the Reich's gratitude.'

Taubmann strode round the room, looking at the half a dozen paintings which were propped against the furniture. 'Ah, here we are. This is quite pretty. Take it and put it in the car.'

So *The Triarchs* went to the Bavarian castle of the iron-and-steel baron, Otto von Zalen. And Ruben Seligman, after being detained in various prisons, eventually arrived at Auschwitz. He died there in June 1942.

CHAPTER 13

The yacht's dinghy was sent across to the island, and returned with the helicopter pilot and the three pictures. Minutes later the paintings had been unwrapped and were propped against the cushions of the saloon's bench seats.

Tim stared at *The Triarchs*. He could not help himself. The other works were masterpieces: the Cranach dramatic and bursting with colour; the Flemish 'Annunciation' magical and mysterious. But the Raphael outclassed them in every way. It was marvellous to see it again. To know that it was still safe. That it had not been in some way tainted by Karakis and his minions. Tim gazed enraptured at the Virgin and her companions, as at much-loved friends who had emerged safely and unexpectedly from some ordeal.

He was aware of Karakis watching him closely. He went into his act, examining each of the paintings in turn, both back and front. At last he told Karakis that he would have to confer privately with Catherine.

Alone with her on the afterdeck, Tim shrugged his helplessness. 'We've blown it. No, *I've* blown it. There's no way we can nab him red-handed. I'm afraid your boss is going to be pretty sore with me.'

'Don't worry. Tonashi always knew he was asking you to take on something very difficult. What happens now?'

'Go through with the charade, I suppose.'

He led the way back into the saloon.

After all the build-up, the formalities were an anticlimax. Tim announced that he could recommend the purchase of the Raphael and

279

the Flemish painting at the prices already agreed. Catherine phoned Tonashi. The industrialist confirmed that he was happy with his expert's decision. Delivery and payment arrangements were made. And that was that. Ten minutes later, the pictures had been reloaded into the dinghy. As soon as it had returned from the island, Karakis gave the order to weigh anchor.

Tim hung gloomily over the stern rail and watched the helicopter rise into the sky, hang there for a moment, then head towards the mainland at maximum speed.

After a few minutes Catherine joined him. 'Cheer up. It could be worse.'

'The only worse thing that could happen is Karakis unmasking us.'

'Don't worry about that. Right now he's as happy as Larry. He's done a good deal. This morning he was rich; now he's stinking rich. Incidentally, I see what you mean about *The Triarchs*. It *is* beautiful.'

'Well, I hope Tonashi appreciates it. God, I hate to think of it buried away in that underground mausoleum of his!'

They stood in silence for several minutes, watching the island shrink until it was indistinguishable from the sea.

Suddenly they were aware of shouting from the deck behind them. They made their way forward to where most of the others were standing in the bows.

Catherine went up to Karakis and linked her arm through his. 'What's the excitement?'

The Greek pointed. Half a mile ahead a fishing boat lay wallowing in the water. Someone on its deck was waving frantically. 'Probably some stupid Cretans broken down too far from home.'

'Are you going to help them?'

'Of course, my dear. It's the rule of the sea.'

Phidias drew close to the stricken vessel, and her captain hailed it in Greek.

The answer came back in a very different language. 'Sorry, mate, don't understand your lingo. Does anyone there speak English?' George Martin stared across the water with grease marks on his face and shirt.

Tim could have swum across to the trawler and hugged the man. He forced himself to show no reaction at all.

Karakis answered. 'What seems to be the matter?'

'Engine's packed up on us. Have you got a mechanic aboard who could have a look at it?'

'Who are you? What are you doing in a Greek boat?' Karakis's suspicions rose quickly to the surface.

'My friends and I are on holiday. We bought this old tub off a bloke in Heraklion. He said it would take us all round the islands and back again. Lying bastard!'

Karakis seemed satisfied. 'We'll come alongside, and one of my men will look at your engine.'

Now Tim could see Jerry O'Conor and Pete Cole. None of the men on the other boat registered recognition as he showed himself at the deck rail. Pete took a line aboard, and one of the Greek deckhands crossed to the trawler. He went below with Jerry.

George smiled his appreciation. 'This is very kind of you, sir. We've been stuck here for hours. I was beginning to get worried.'

'Haven't you radioed for help?'

'We've put out three maydays but no one's showed up.'

'We didn't receive anything.'

George shrugged. 'Perhaps there's something wrong with our transmitter, too. I'd like to get my hands on that thieving Cretan slob.'

Karakis laughed. 'Never trust a Cretan, my friend.'

George joined in the laughter. 'Any chance of a decent wash and brush-up? We're all a bit of a mess.'

Karakis frowned. He muttered something to one of his crew. The man lifted his T-shirt to reveal a small pistol tucked into his waistband. 'You can come across one at a time.'

George scrambled aboard.

Karakis said, 'Charles, perhaps you could take your compatriot to your cabin to freshen up.'

'Certainly. This way, chum. Where are you from?'

When they reached the cabin, Tim left the door slightly open in case Karakis sent someone to check up on them. He stood in the doorway of the shower room and spoke very softly as George ran water in the hand-basin. 'George, how the hell did you find us?'

'Long story, Major. What's the score here? Do you need any help?'

'I'm afraid you're too late. There's nothing incriminating on board.'

'Sorry, sir.'

'Not your fault. It's a miracle you're here at all.' He thought hard, reassessing the changed situation.

'There is one thing you could do. It's a long shot, but we might get lucky.' He tore a sheet of paper from the pad on his bedside table and scribbled some numbers and letters on it. 'Go back to Crete as quick as you can. I assume there's not much wrong with your engine?'

'Blocked fuel lead. It won't take your chap long to find it.' George rubbed his face vigorously with a towel.

'Good. See if you can get the police to call their colleagues in Athens, and ask them to locate the helicopter with this licence number. Tell them it's carrying stolen goods. As I say, it's a slim chance, but it's our only hope of salvaging something from this fiasco.'

They returned to the deck. Jerry and Pete came across in turn. By the time they were cleaned up, the trawler's engine was running. Pete revved up. George waved from the bridge.

Jerry cast off the line. As the space between the two vessels widened, he called out, 'Very grateful. Thanks a million, Mr Karakis.'

There was a moment's silence. Then all hell broke loose. Karakis yelled, 'Stop!' and shouted orders in Greek to his men. The trawler streaked off at full speed. *Phidias*'s engine sprang to life. The yacht leaped in pursuit. Two crewmen spilled on deck, carrying submachine-guns. Once again Karakis called out, 'Stop, this instant.' The fishing boat kept on going. There was a crackle of gunfire, and spurts of water danced round the trawler's stern. Almost immediately she cut her engine.

Minutes later the three members of Lacy Security were lined up on the afterdeck of the yacht, hands tied behind them, SMGs pointed at their chests and a very angry Niki Karakis raging at them.

'Who the hell are you, and why are you spying on me?'

No answer.

Karakis nodded. One of his goons went up to George and swung the butt of his gun against the prisoner's jaw. Martin reeled, and blood trickled down his chin. He scowled his defiance at Karakis.

The Greek shrugged. 'That's only a beginning. However tough you think you are, you'll tell me what I want to know, I promise you.' He paused, looked thoughtful – smiled. 'But, of course, there's an easy and quicker way. Let's see what light our other guests can throw on this situation.'

Now Karakis sent for Tim and Catherine, who had been locked in their cabins before the three captives were brought aboard.

Tim came out bristling with indignation. 'Niki, what on earth's going on? Why are your people shooting off guns and shutting us in our rooms like naughty children?'

Karakis stared back, and Tim could see that, for the first time, he was unsure of himself. 'Do you know these men?'

'No, of course not. Just because they're English, it doesn't follow . . .'

'How about you, Catherine?'

'I've never seen them before in my life.'

Karakis walked slowly across the deck and back again. 'These men have been spying on me.'

Catherine's eyes opened wide. 'Why would anyone want to spy on you, Niki?'

The Greek glowered. 'There's been something wrong about this whole deal from the beginning. You two were up to something in Japan. I knew it, but I couldn't put my finger on it.'

Tim took a step forward. 'Don't be absurd.'

'Shut up! I've got a sixth sense that tells me when things aren't right.'

Catherine took a more oblique approach. 'Niki, can't we stop this now before it's gone too far. Mr Tonashi would be very—'

'You can button up, too! Tonashi's nothing to me. There are scores of Tonashis I can do business with. Someone's trying to foul up my whole operation, and I'm going to find out who.' He turned to one of his men. 'Search the trawler.' To another he said, 'And you search these three.'

It took very little time for the thug to go through the pockets of the three captives, and make a small pile of coins, keys and handkerchiefs on a low table. Karakis stared at it and extracted a small, folded piece of paper. He opened it up. Nodded. Smiled.

'And how does a piece of *Phidias* notepaper come to be in your possession?'

George Martin shrugged. 'I just took it to make a note of something.

283

I didn't realise stealing a sheet from one of your pads was a court-martial offence.'

'It isn't – but writing down the number of my helicopter is. Who gave you this information?'

George stared defiantly into space. One of the guards raised his gun to strike again.

Karakis stopped him. 'That's too time-consuming. I need to know quickly who these people are, and who they're working with. They might already have contacted their principals. Take the girl below and find out all she knows.'

The captain and the cook advanced towards Catherine. But she did not wait to be grabbed. With two agile steps she crossed the deck, vaulted the rail and dropped into the water.

Karakis screamed, 'Get her back!'

The man with the SMG ran to the rail and levelled his weapon. With a roar, Jerry O'Conor bent double, charged at the gunman, and head-butted him in the small of the back. The Greek hit the rail, overbalanced and fell overboard.

The next second there was pandemonium on *Phidias*. Tim went for Karakis, fists flying. His team, George, Pete and Jerry, laid into the opposition – as best they could with their arms tied. The two bimbos cowered in a corner and screamed. Shots were fired. Karakis shouted orders no one listened to.

But the rebellion was short-lived. The odds were too uneven. Within minutes Tim and his three associates lay face-down on the afterdeck, closely guarded by armed men, and Catherine was climbing back aboard, with blood streaming from a flesh wound in her shoulder. As she set foot on the deck, Karakis hit her full across the face.

'Now you'll tell us everything!'

Catherine recoiled from the blow. She stared at him with total contempt. 'You stupid slob!'

Karakis drew back his heavily-ringed hand to strike her again.

'Stop!' Tim looked up from the deck. 'That's not necessary. She knows nothing. Let her go to her cabin and dress that wound. Then I'll tell you all you want to know.'

Karakis stared down at him. 'Are you really trying to make a bargain? You've nothing to trade.'

Tim tried a bluff. 'Don't you care to know how soon the Greek police will be here?'

Karakis thought for a moment, then nodded to one of his men. 'Take her below and get a bandage on her. I don't want her bleeding all over the upholstery.'

When Catherine had disappeared, Tim was forced up into a sitting position in a corner of the deck.

Karakis wiped perspiration from his brow. 'OK, Dr Timothy. Everything – from the top.'

'My name is Lacy. You may have heard of me.'

The Greek's eyes widened in genuine surprise. 'The enterprising Mr Lacy? Well, that explains a lot. So all this is some personal vendetta?'

'No, indeed, Mr Karakis.' From this point Tim improvised; his story was part truth, part imaginative fiction. 'It's true I have very personal reasons for seeing you brought to justice. But so do lots of others. You'd probably be gratified to know how extensive Interpol's computer file on you is. This whole operation was set up jointly by the British, Greek, and Japanese police forces. It's a trap, and you walked right into it. My colleagues here have been shadowing *Phidias* for days, and have already radioed your position to Athens and Heraklion. This is the end of the road for you.'

'You're bluffing.'

Tim shrugged. 'Easy to find out. All we have to do is sit here and wait.'

'If what you say is true, you wouldn't be telling me.'

'Why not? You've nowhere to run. *Phidias* is a very distinctive craft, and it won't take the police long to find her. You'll never make it back to the mainland.'

'Why should I even want to evade the police? There's nothing to hide aboard *Phidias*.'

Tim laughed. 'Abduction? Attempted murder? That'll be enough for starters.' Desperately, he tried to look confident. He was playing verbal poker for five lives – hoping Karakis would not call his hand.

Karakis called his hand. 'And evidence for these supposed crimes, Mr Lacy? Who's going to be around to provide the evidence?' The Greek smirked. 'I observe from your silence that you take my point.'

Tim swallowed hard. 'Five more murders? You wouldn't be that insane!'

Karakis shook his head and laughed. 'No, just a tragic accident. Three foreigners inadvisedly hire a leaky fishing boat. They meet up unexpectedly with two friends holidaying with a respected Greek businessman. He tries to dissuade his guests from joining their compatriots for a visit to Crete. Alas, they reject his advice. No sooner have the two vessels parted company, than the trawler starts taking in water. The crew call for help, but their radio is as useless as their boat. Within minutes the sea has claimed five more victims – a tragic but not uncommon occurrence.'

Karakis snapped out an order, and his men shepherded the Englishmen below. Tim was locked in his cabin, and the three others were shut into another.

Tim heard *Phidias*'s engine start up. He looked out of the porthole and saw the other boat also get under way.

Just over an hour later, the hum of the motor ceased and he was ordered back on deck. Catherine and the others were brought out immediately afterwards. Karakis was standing beside a small pile of grubby-looking life-jackets.

'Absolutely criminal that a vessel should be taken to sea without the most basic safety equipment.'

Phidias's cook climbed aboard from the trawler, which was once more alongside. Karakis asked him something in Greek. The man nodded, and brandished the axe he was carrying.

Karakis motioned to his captives. 'Quickly!'

The men stumbled across the deck and jumped on to the other boat. Catherine followed last.

'Let her go. She's got nothing to do with this,' Tim yelled.

'Now that would be stupid, wouldn't it?' As Karakis handed Catherine down into the trawler, he pushed a penknife into her hands. 'I'm sure your friends would rather face death unbound – and I certainly wouldn't want any corpses found with their hands tied. Not that anyone's likely to find you soon. I can tell you from the radar that there isn't another craft within miles.' He waved. 'Goodbye, my friends. Have a nice day.'

Phidias cast off, engaged her engine, and made top speed towards the empty horizon.

On a spring afternoon in 1988, Al Benson – short, thickset, curly-haired and thirty-two – emerged from the terminal building at Los Angeles airport and made straight for the cab rank. 'Freemont Hospital,' he ordered as he sank on to the back seat. 'Quick as you can.' As a freelance he had to watch his expenses very carefully. If this was a wild-goose chase he wanted to get back in time for the last flight to New York, in order to save himself an overnight hotel bill.

The hospital was modern, faced in gleaming white stone, set among undulating lawns and tidy shrubberies. Expensive, Al thought, as he paid off the taxi. At the desk he asked for Dwight Morello. A crisply-laundered nurse consulted her computer screen, then directed him to a first-floor office. There he found the division sister, who took him to Morello's room but informed him that the patient was very weak and easily excitable. Visits were limited to half an hour, and she would be back in precisely thirty minutes.

Dwight Morello sat on the balcony in a reclining chair, everything but his face and arms concealed by blankets and pillows. The sunken features and parchment-like skin were enough to tell the visitor that this was a dying man. Morello looked at least twenty years older than sixty-eight. Benson knew that was his age because he had checked with army records. The sister introduced him, fussed briefly over the old man's coverings, and withdrew.

Benson seated himself and said a cheery 'Hallo, Mr Morello. Thank you for getting in touch with me.'

'You the newspaper guy?'

'That's right.'

'Any proof of identity?'

Benson snapped open his wallet and produced his *Congress* press pass.

The old man held the document close to his eyes to scrutinise it. 'Got to be careful. Don't want any cops or lawyers.' He seemed satisfied. 'I read your ad in the paper. What exactly is it you want?'

'I'm doing a series of articles about the billions of dollars' worth of works of art that went missing in Allied-occupied Germany and Austria after the Second World War. Tracing servicemen, like yourself, who actually handled these things. Trying to locate some of the artefacts.'

'Had any luck?'

'A bit.' Benson glanced quickly at his watch. Six of his thirty minutes had already gone. 'Your wife kindly wrote and suggested that you might have a story for me.'

'Rose wants me to make a full confession. Clear my conscience before I croak. She's a Catholic. Got a cigarette?'

'Are you allowed . . .?'

'Listen, mister, smoking's brought me to the edge of the great abyss. It's a bit late to kick the habit now.'

Benson produced a cigarette and lit it for the old man. Morello puffed at it, but did not inhale. Even so, the smoke brought on a thick cough and set Morello fumbling for a handkerchief to wipe his mouth.

Al pressed on with his questions. 'I gather you were in Bavaria in 1946. What can you tell me about the works of art you saw there?'

'I got stuff that'll blow your mind. Worth millions.'

' "Stuff"?'

'Gold, silver, porcelain, paintings, jewellery, medals . . .' The catalogue disintegrated in another fit of coughing.

'Are you telling me you have a hoard of stolen works of art?'

'Sure. Stolen by the Nazis. Then stolen by me.'

'Where is it?'

'Right here in LA.'

'Can I see it?'

'Fifty thousand dollars.'

'I beg your pardon.'

'It's going to cost you fifty grand to print my story and see my treasure trove.'

Benson groaned inwardly. He had been here before: talking with people who plucked astronomical figures out of the ether, who believed newspapers were gold-lined, who were convinced that their mundane revelations were worth record payments. 'Mr Morello, I don't have that kind of money.'

'Look, son.' The old man's voice was rising in pitch. As the nurse had warned, he was easily excited. 'The stuff I got is worth millions. Governments and private owners are clamouring to get their treasures back. When you publish, all these things will go back where they belong. My family won't get anything out of it – any more than I have. I could never come clean about what happened in '46. I could have sold my story, but they'd have put me on trial and sent me to prison. Bastards! Well, they can't do that now. But Rose and my son, Wayne, they deserve something. They put me in here and it's cost them every penny. I've got to make that up to them. Fifty thousand will put them straight. So that's my price. Take it or leave it.'

Benson thought of Sam Grice, the *New York Times* editor who had commissioned his series. Sam had very fixed ideas about paying money to criminals. Of course, there were the potential syndication rights. Benson had great hopes of selling the articles in Europe. But fifty thousand? There was no chance of him coming up with that. Anyway, the Morello story could not possibly be worth it.

The old man was talking again. 'I guess you want some proof.'

'Well, that would certainly—'

'Look in there.' He nodded towards the room behind him. 'Bottom of the closet you'll see a box. Bring it here.'

Al walked across the clinically-appointed private ward and slid back the closet door. It contained one set of clothes and a pair of down-at-heel brown brogues. Beside them was a shoe-box. He carried it back to the balcony.

'Look inside,' Morello ordered. 'But for God's sake don't wave it about.'

Al removed the lid. Whatever was inside was heavily wrapped in tissue paper. Carefully he removed the protective layers. The next moment . . .

'Good God!' Benson was dazzled by the sunlight reflected from gold and precious stones. He lifted the object from the box, being careful to keep it between himself and Morello's chair-bed. He gazed speechless at a goblet, or chalice, worked in gold, enamel and jewels. The base was a swirling coil of serpents – red, green and white. The stem was composed of two interwoven female figures reaching up to hold the bowl, which was in the shape of an open flower, each petal veined in dark green enamel. Spaced around the rim were eight smooth emeralds. Benson did not need to be an expert to recognise a priceless example of Italian sixteenth-century Mannerist craftsmanship.

The old man smiled, gratified by the journalist's response. 'There's plenty more where that came from.'

'Exactly where did you get it?'

'Fifty thousand dollars.' Morello closed his eyes. 'Up front.'

'But, I don't know . . .'

'Come back same time tomorrow – with the money. Then I'll tell you everything, and give you the key to my treasure chamber. Now you'd better put that thing away before our hawk-eyed sister gets back.'

Most of that evening Al Benson sat by himself in a downtown bar, turning the problem over and over in his mind. The first fizz of excitement passed, leaving him facing an insuperable obstacle. If Morello was genuine – and Benson did not really doubt that – then this *was* a big story. Forget the articles; a recovered World War II hoard, coming to light forty-two years after being stolen, was good for front pages worldwide, not to mention special articles for the quality journals. He knew a dozen editors who would back the story heavily. But none of them would put up fifty big ones within twenty-four hours on the basis of the information he had so far. And without the money he could not obtain the story. There was no way he could get heavy-handed with a sick old man. Lean on the wife, then? That would only give him a secondhand narrative. He needed the story of the Morello hoard from the horse's mouth. And the horse might drop dead at any moment.

He was up early the following morning. From his hotel room he put several calls through to offices in New York, Boston and London to see how much he could get in the way of advances. They amounted to nothing like fifty thousand dollars. After breakfast he went for a walk in Elysian Park, and worked out a plan of campaign. He would offer Morello a couple of grand – all he could afford – for a sight of the hoard. He would take some photographs, get back to New York with them and secure the backing the project needed. He could return within a few days and obtain the whole story. It was not a foolproof scheme, and there was the chance that Morello would not play ball. One thing was certain, though: he was not letting this one slip through his fingers.

When he got back to the hotel, there was a phone message waiting from Sam Grice. He called back from his room.

'Sam, hi. What can I do for you?'

'I've been thinking about that problem you mentioned earlier. I

290

think I know someone who might help. Have you ever met Carl
Phreminger?'

'The playboy and dilettante? Runs a string of west-coast fashion
boutiques and antique shops? Suspected of being part of the drug
scene?'

'That's right. He's a friend of mine. Don't believe everything you
read in the papers. He's right there in LA, and I think he might
help you.'

'How, exactly?'

'He's a speculator. Fingers in lots of pies. Fancies himself as a
connoisseur. Your story could intrigue him. Get him excited and he
might put up your fifty grand.'

'For a price.'

'Sure. He's a businessman. He'd demand a slice of the action. But
if you want a lot of money in a hurry . . .'

'OK, Sam. Thanks. How do I get hold of him?'

The editor dictated a phone number. 'I called Carl about an hour
ago. Said a very good friend of mine might have an interesting propo-
sition to put to him. I gave you a hell of a good testimonial.'

'This is very good of you, Sam. I won't forget it.'

'The hell you won't. I expect a New York exclusive on the story.
G'bye now. Let me know how it goes.'

Al put down the phone and thought: clever bastard, he gets someone
else to put up the money, and then scoops the story. He dialled the
local number.

When he had sidestepped a reluctant and protective secretary a
languid voice came on the line. 'Al Benson? Good to talk to you. Any
friend of Sam's . . . What can I do for you?'

Al gave Phreminger the outline of the story, without mentioning
any names.

'Hm. Sounds tempting.' Phreminger paused. 'How much do you
reckon to make from worldwide exclusive rights?'

'Hard to say exactly. Must be worth at least a quarter of a million.'

'Hm. How about I lend you the money until you sell your story,
and then take ten per cent of everything you earn from it, as my
commission?'

'Sounds OK to me.'

'Good. When are you due to see your informant?'
'Four o'clock this afternoon.'
'OK. Here's what we do then.'
They made their arrangements, and five minutes later Al Benson put the phone down. He was excited, scenting the story that would lift him into the top league. If he felt a little dubious about the too-good-to-be-true Phreminger, he suppressed the feeling.

Al was startled when he saw Dwight Morello that afternoon. The old man was in his bed this time, and was noticeably weaker than he had appeared a mere twenty-four hours before. The journalist had expected an argument when he offered a cheque for the fifty thousand dollars, and was ready to explain that he could not get hold of cash at such short notice. But the dying man seemed relieved and grateful. He was also anxious to get his story off his chest while there was still time. Al put his tape-recorder on the bedside cabinet and let the ex-soldier tell his tale in his own way.

'I had a lucky war. Fought right through France and Germany without a scratch. Lost lots of friends, but I was OK. I ended up in Bavaria, right on the Austrian border. They thought, at that time, that Hitler was going to make a last stand in the Alps around Obersalzburg. So the Seventh Army was sent in a crazy dash across southern Germany. But there was no fight left in the Krauts. That's where I was when the war ended. And that's where I stayed for the best part of a year.'

He stopped, struggling for breath. Al said, 'Take a break for a bit,' but Morello waved the suggestion away and took up the story again.

'It's a lovely place, Bavaria. Do you know it? I always said I'd take Rose back there one day. Never did. Never did. They set up a lot of rest camps in the area for Allied troops. I was helping to equip them. I'd got to lieutenant by then, and I was in charge of a transport detachment. We had to requisition furniture and stuff in the area, or fly it in from the States. We went round all the empty houses and castles. No one to stop us. So we picked up souvenirs. Mostly small bits and pieces – silver, porcelain. Stuff you could send home by post or on the empty transport planes going back.'
'That's how you made up your collection, was it?'
The old man's head moved slightly from side to side on the pillow.

'Just listen,' he muttered impatiently. 'I had a thing going with one of the local Fräuleins. Her name was Lisa. I never knew what became of her.' He had to stop for a fit of coughing. 'One night I was drinking at her place with her grandfather. We got pretty high. Suddenly the old guy says, "Do you want to know where the Hitler gang's loot is stashed?" You see, all round there the top Nazi brass had their Alpine chalets and schlosses. Hitler, Goering, Borman, that industrialist von Zalen – they all had luxury homes there. And most of them were flattened by Allied bombing. Later on the ruins were levelled and planted with trees, to wipe out even the memory of the Nazi bosses. Did you know that? Well, what this old man told me was that, before the raids, truckloads of loot were taken to a special hiding place – one of the old salt mines above the town.

'I thought it was the drink talking. Everyone had heard about the hoard discovered at Alt Aussee, so I guessed the old fool was just confused. But next evening, by golly, I had to think again. After dark he took me through the forest to the old salt working. I tell you, son, you can't begin to imagine what I saw. We shone our flashlights over statues, furniture, paintings, gold and silver ornaments, porcelain. All just dumped there, anyhow. The Nazis hadn't had time to pack properly. Some things were lying on the floor, broken. It was like Aladdin's cave.

'When I got over the shock, I said I'd have to report to my top brass, and to keep everything secret till I'd done so. I *did* report it. But not before I'd taken a truck up to the cave the next night and half filled it. I just helped myself to anything that took my fancy. I figured it was a just payment for everything I'd suffered since D-Day.'

'How did you get everything back here?'

'No problem. Like I said, there were transports going back and forth all the time. When I came home on leave, I rented an office on the edge of town and stashed the stuff in it. It's been there ever since.'

'You've never disposed of any of it.'

'Nope. Too scared. At first I had great plans to sell my treasure off, bit by bit. I reckoned I'd be a millionaire inside ten years. Then I realised you couldn't just walk into an antique shop with a long-lost Rembrandt or a rare Renaissance chalice, without people asking questions.' His voice was fading and Al had to adjust the controls on his tape-recorder to catch the last words.

'Thank you, Mr Morello. That's a great story. I'd better go now, and let you rest.'

Again the old man feebly shook his head. 'Open the drawer of the cabinet.'

Al did so.

'At the back there's an envelope.'

Al found a dog-eared rectangle of brown manilla under a couple of paperback thrillers.

'That's the address and the key. Make sure all the stuff gets back to the right people. It didn't do the Nazis any good, and it sure as hell hasn't helped me any.'

The old man closed his eyes and was asleep before Al Benson quietly left the room.

A couple of hours later he met Carl Phreminger in the bar of his hotel. The businessman was tall, moustached and fiftyish. His clothes were hand-tailored, exuberant and twenty-ish. He sipped a Manhattan and asked how the journalist had got on with his informant.

Al glanced anxiously at the relaxed, loose-limbed man sprawled in the chair opposite. 'First, have you got my cheque? I've paid out mine for fifty thousand. Without yours to back it, it'll bounce as high as the Empire State.'

Phreminger slowly took an envelope from his inside pocket and handed it over. 'You didn't think I was going to welch on the deal, did you? Now, just where is this fabled treasure?'

Al showed him the address. 'Do you know it?'

'No, but my chauffeur will find it.' He drained his drink. 'So, let's not waste any more time. I guess I'm as excited as you are to check out this story.'

Phreminger's Cadillac stopped, thirty-five minutes later, in front of a run-down office block in a run-down part of the city. Morello's premises were on the third floor. The door opened on to a room occupied only by thick, undisturbed dust. The inner office was piled with crates and boxes stencilled with numbers and 'Property of US Army' signs. Every container was securely fastened.

Benson voiced his sense of anticlimax. 'So near and yet so far.'

Phreminger smiled. 'There must be some tools in the car. Go and ask my chauffeur.'

Benson found himself obeying the order. He returned with a screw-driver and a heavy wheel brace. With these makeshift weapons he attacked one crate which stood on the floor, leaning against a pile of boxes. Slowly, painfully, the rusted nails yielded. Carefully, Al tore away the inner covering of tarred paper. A bearded face stared out at him. He stepped back, pulse racing. The two men gazed in stunned silence at a peaceful scene depicting the revelation of the infant Christ to the Gentiles.

After that, they attacked some of the other cases with feverish vigour, even Phreminger taking a turn with the tools. After an hour, every inch of floorspace was littered with precious objects: illuminated books, piles of Sèvres dinner plates, elaborate jewellery, more paintings, silver candelabra, and a miscellany of other objects which shared only one common feature – they were all of the highest quality.

At last, Al said, 'I guess we'd better call it a day.'

Phreminger agreed. 'Yeah, I have things to do, and a certain young lady who will be disappointed if I don't show up to do them. What's your next move?'

'I'll come back tomorrow and take some rough pictures, then file my story pdq. After that, I guess we'd better shift this lot to some secure premises where they can be professionally photo-graphed.'

'I can help you there. I have a private studio I use for the same purpose. What about the police?'

'When I've finished with everything, that'll be the time to turn it over to the authorities – not before.'

They returned the treasures to their various containers and loosely covered them. Then they left. Phreminger dropped Benson back at his hotel before returning to his Beverly Hills apartment. He went straight to his study, sat at his desk, flipped open a leather-bound address book, found the information he wanted, picked up the phone and punched in an overseas number. He had to wait a long time for a disgruntled response at the other end of the line.

'Hi, this is Carl Phreminger,' he announced. 'OK, so it's the middle of the night there. Calm down. You're going to thank me for waking you. Niki, have I got news for you.'

Two days later, when Al Benson returned to Morello's office to repack the hoard for removal to Phreminger's studio, all he found was a pile of broken boxes and torn paper.

The boat was already listing as Catherine hacked through the cords binding the men's wrists.

Tim gave orders briskly.

'Pete, check the radio. I expect it's smashed. If it is, take this and put out a mayday call on the emergency channel.' He produced Tonashi's little transmitter from his pocket. 'The rest of you find anything that'll float – empty cans, boxes, anything.'

George Martin rushed into the wheelhouse, and returned with some parcels wrapped in oilskin. 'Lucky Miss Younger's escapade distracted them from searching this tub properly. These were hidden at the bottom of the chart cupboard: the guns you fixed us up with. Might as well hang on to them.'

Catherine called from the stern well. 'There's an oil drum here. I think it's about a quarter full.'

Tim jumped down beside her. 'This could be useful.' He pulled it over and unscrewed the cap. Thick engine oil plopped out on to the sloping deck. 'Right, all of you! Smear this over yourselves. It'll give you some protection if we're stuck in the water a long time.'

Jerry peered into the engine hatch. 'She's filling up fast. We don't have much time.'

'OK, let's get all this stuff overboard.' Tim sealed up the oil drum. He and George heaved it into the water. 'Pete! Come on!'

Pete struggled out of the slanting wheelhouse doorway, talking into the radio as he came. 'Just checked our rough co-ordinates on the chart, Major.'

The boat was now creaking, groaning and leaning further over.

'Right, everyone jump! She's going to roll!'

They leaped into the sea, and swam hard for several seconds to distance themselves from the capsizing craft. When they looked round, the fishing boat had gone.

The next minutes were spent rounding up the assorted flotsam and bringing it together in a very loose raft. They were able to lash some items to the oil drum with bits of rope, to stop it rolling. Tim hoisted Catherine up on to it, and she was able to sit astride and get her breath back. The others lay, only half out of the water, sprawled over bits of wooden debris. George clung on to the weapons; Pete was holding the radio, wrapped in plastic sheeting, well out of the sea.

Catherine gazed round the horizon, blonde hair streaking round her face, her bronzed skin gleaming under its sheen of oil. 'Well, at least I saw something of Greece before I died.'

Tim stared up at her. 'I'm sorry . . .'

She glared back. 'Don't apologise. I came into this with my eyes open.'

'Anyway, miss, it's too early to throw in the towel.' George wedged his waterproof bundle between the rope and a large crate. 'If we can keep transmitting our SOS, someone's bound to hear sooner or later. How's that radio doing, Pete?'

'I think it's OK.' With his elbows resting on a plank, the bald-headed man unwrapped the small machine and spoke into it.

'Here, let me do that. It's easier up here.' Catherine took the radio from him and repeated the mayday call.

'Thanks, miss. About every five minutes should do it.'

The men rested awhile, then began working more methodically on their floating island. Gradually, they were able to create a more solid platform that would support two of them at a time, almost completely out of the water.

Tim sat on a lashed plank, his back resting against the oil drum, and gazed up at the sun. It was still well above the cloudless horizon. Given these conditions, they could survive a couple of days – perhaps a bit longer. Night would be the problem. Darkness would bring a steep drop in temperature. They would be tired, depressed, cold. Their will to survive would be sapped. Well, perhaps it would not come to that. Perhaps – just perhaps – some vessel would come within range of their transmitter.

'We have to get ourselves out of this, just to nail that Greek slob.' Catherine scowled.

Tim shook his head. 'I doubt we could do much about Karakis, anyway. I don't know much about Greek courts, but it would be his word, well supported by all his cronies, against the complaints of a few foreigners.'

'If he's got nothing to fear, why's he done this to us?'

Jerry provided the answer. 'Because he's a sadistic bastard. That kind doesn't need reasons.'

'And tomorrow he'll be safely back in Athens.' Catherine angrily shouted another distress message into the radio.

Conversation dwindled as the evening drew on. A stiffening breeze chilled their bodies and flicked wavelets against their makeshift raft. Every half hour the men changed places. Catherine maintained a desperate watch for potential rescuers. Twice she pointed excitedly to a dark speck among the waves, only to realise that the craft had been conjured up by her imagination. Now the sky was darkening and she was feeling almost unbearably cold.

Cautiously she stretched her stiff legs, and rubbed her arms to induce some friction heat. Suddenly she stopped, ears straining. Surely that was a sound above the slapping of water against the hollow drum. No. Wishful thinking.

But there it was again. She shook her head, refusing to raise her companions' hopes a third time. But she continued staring towards the eastern horizon, from which the intermittent noise seemed to come. Was that really something above the grey-blue of merging sea and sky?

Finally she reached over and tapped George on the shoulder. 'Is that something over there?'

Gingerly, Martin changed his cramped position, until he was leaning against the oil drum. 'Chopper!' he shouted suddenly, and began waving.

They all waved and – irrationally – shouted, as they watched the helicopter working to and fro, low over the sea – still a couple of miles away.

Jerry yelled his frustration. 'They'll never see us! It's too dark.'

'Here, give me that thing!' Tim grabbed the radio. 'Calling helicopter. Calling helicopter! We see you. We are due west of your position.' He repeated the message several times.

George muttered, 'Either they can't hear, or they can't understand English.'

Then they saw the aircraft turn and move slowly towards them.

Fifteen minutes later, they were all sitting, wrapped in blankets, in a Greek naval helicopter, heading for Heraklion. In faltering English one of the crew explained that an island trader had picked up their distress call, relayed it to the Cretan coastguard, who had passed it on to the navy base.

It was that base they reached in another half hour. Warm showers and fresh clothes had never felt so good. And food – chicken stew and cold lager – had never tasted better. The rescued 'mariners' sat around a table in the officers' mess, eating hungrily, feeling exhausted but amazingly light-headed. A senior officer, speaking very good English, explained that the police would now want to interview them. 'But that can wait till tomorrow. You can sleep here, tonight.' He seated himself astride a chair. 'Tell me, how did you get into such a mess?'

Tim hastily gave an edited version of their movements over the last few hours. He said nothing about their being deliberately scuttled; that would have taken *too* much explaining.

The officer looked puzzled. 'I still don't understand how you met up where you did. It's normally a very lonely stretch of water.'

'Our yacht just stopped for lunch off some uninhabited island,' Catherine explained.

'Antimos,' George added.

Tim looked up sharply. 'How did you know its name?'

'Well, that's how we knew where to look for you. In Poros we met this chap who used to work on *Phidias* – till our friend sacked him for heavy drinking. We asked if he knew where the yacht might be heading, and he said Antimos. He said the owner was always going out there by either yacht or chopper.'

Tim stared across the table, thinking hard.

The Greek officer had not picked up all Martin said. He now smiled at Catherine. 'You're wrong about Antimos being uninhabited. It's owned by some Athenian millionaire. There's an old monastery there, which he's done up. There's usually someone there, left in charge.'

'That's it!' Tim turned to the officer. 'Can I speak to your police now, or to someone who can get things done quickly. This is urgent!'

The Greek was bemused. 'No need to do anything now. Tomorrow will be OK.'

'Tomorrow *won't* be OK! I must speak to someone now!'

It took some more arguing – then a great deal of telephoning in slow, monosyllabic English. But at last Tim got a navy car to take him to the police HQ in Heraklion. Then more arguing. More explaining.

Eventually someone high-ranking came into the office from his home, and listened while Tim repeated his story. The officer spoke to his opposite number in Athens. He rang off.

'Well?' Tim demanded.

'He will phone back.'

The return call came in about midnight. Tim could not follow the rapid exchange of Greek. After fifteen minutes the policeman put the receiver down and looked at Tim expressionlessly. 'Very well. A police launch will leave the harbour at dawn. Now go back and sleep.'

The others were waiting up for him.

'What's going on, Major?' George wanted to know.

Catherine sat at the table, weary, head in hands. 'We've been trying to puzzle it out ever since you left. We think we've got to the bottom of it. But it'll be quicker if you tell us. Then we can all hit the sack.'

Tim sat down at the table. 'It suddenly struck me that the cautious Mr Karakis had overplayed his hand. He wanted us to think that he had taken us to an island that was unnamed and uninhabited – because of poisonous snakes! – and that the paintings were brought to the island by helicopter. Why did he want us to believe all that? Because none of it was true. Knowing how devious he is, I should have seen it before. He took such elaborate care to cover his tracks that I should have been able to stand back and see where those tracks were. But it didn't hit me until this evening, when we were told that the island has a name, Antimos; that it isn't uninhabited; and that Karakis regularly visits the place. There can only be one reason for all that. Antimos is his warehouse, his depot. That's where all the paintings are – or were.'

'What do you mean "were"?' Catherine yawned.

'Knowing our slimy Greek friend, what do you suppose he's doing right at this moment? He's had a nasty scare. Someone's come within an ace of blowing the lid off his operation. OK, he thinks he's got rid of us, but that's not good enough for him. Karakis is your original belt and braces man. A pound to a penny he's gone straight to Antimos. He'll get his chopper back there and he'll ship out all the incriminating evidence. So if anyone should turn up on the island, there'll be nothing to find. I've persuaded the police to send a launch out first thing in the morning. But I've got a horrible feeling they'll be too late.'

Catherine rose wearily to her feet. 'What time do we start in the morning?'

Tim had anticipated this moment. '*We* don't.' Before she could protest, he went over and took her gently by the shoulders. 'I've nearly got you killed once, and that's quite enough.'

'I came along of my own free will.'

'Yes, and I should have stopped you.'

'Are you trying to say that I loused things up for you?' She felt her body sagging, too tired to give much force to her words.

'Quite the contrary. You were absolutely marvellous out there.' He gazed steadily into her green eyes. 'Catherine, you're very special. That's why I want you here, safe and sound, when I get back.' He drew her to him and kissed her softly, not caring about the embarrassed silence of the others.

The launch was powerful, but it took nearly four hours to reach Antimos. Inspector Meniates, the officer Tim had spoken to the night before, had decided to lead the expedition himself, and he had brought six men with him, all armed. Meniates either did not notice or did not choose to enquire about the bags Tim and his colleagues were carrying.

More than once during the exhilarating voyage, Tim recalled the last time he had called out a police posse to arrest Niki Karakis. Supposing this trip, too, ended in humiliation and failure? Supposing the bird had already flown? Supposing he was wrong about the island, and there was nothing suspicious there at all? As often as the thoughts intruded, Tim brushed them aside.

It was almost eight o'clock when Antimos appeared on the eastern horizon. Tim braced himself against the side of the bucking boat and tried to focus binoculars on the small, rocky mass. Was *Phidias* there? It was several minutes before he could make out the three bare masts. The yacht was moored closer inshore.

He pointed her out to the inspector. 'What will you do?'

Meniates pointed out the boat's loudhailer. 'Challenge her.'

'They might make a fight of it.'

'Then we shall know how to react. But I have to ask, first, to be allowed aboard. It's the rule.'

Tim scanned the yacht and the shoreline as they drew nearer, looking for Karakis. There were men on deck and others hurrying back from the island in the dinghy, but he could not see the leader. He watched as the dinghy reached *Phidias* and her crew climbed aboard. Then he saw something else.

'She's weighing anchor!'

Meniates smiled. 'She can't outrun us.'

Tim thought: no, of course she can't. And Karakis knows that, so why . . .? He turned back to the inspector. 'Put some of us on the island first. Fast!'

The launch raced in towards the wide, curved beach, turned and throttled back hard as it reached the shallows. Tim, George, Pete, Jerry and two policemen leaped into the water.

A well-worn track led obliquely up the cliff, which was low at this end of the island. They took it at a run. They came over the top into a valley hidden from the sea. Tim made a gesture and they all dropped behind the cover of some rocks. Below, some two hundred yards away, was the helicopter standing on the flat valley floor. Its engine was already turning over. Fifty yards beyond stood the old monastery: a low, grey-stone, unprepossessing building.

And there was Karakis! He and one of the white-shirted henchmen were carrying paintings towards the chopper.

Tim turned to George. 'No time to lose. Take Jerry and the police along the ridge here. Keep out of sight, but stop that machine taking off! Pete, you come with me.'

The two men slithered twenty yards to the right. That was when their cover ran out.

Pete tapped Tim on the leg. 'Can we make a run for it next time they're both back inside the building?'

'No, the helicopter pilot would see us. We'll give George a couple more minutes to get in position. Then we'll have to go in the front door.'

They watched Karakis and his men make two more trips. Then Tim whispered, 'Cover me, Pete,' and stood up. He walked steadily down the slope. He called out. 'Karakis! It's all over!'

A bullet whined past his ear. As he dropped to the ground, Tim recognised the gunman as *Phidias*'s cook. He was firing from the hip as he dashed for the helicopter. There was an answering burst of fire from behind. Karakis, too, sprinted for the aircraft.

'You've nowhere left to run, Niki!'

As the Greek scrambled aboard, the engine revved and the rotor blades began to turn.

A burst of fire from the rim of the hill sent the dust spurting all round the chopper.

As Tim watched, Karakis jumped down again and ran towards the monastery.

'Come on, Pete!' Tim darted forward, bent double.

A cascade of shots from one of the monastery windows forced him flat on the ground again. Now, the building came under a fusillade from the ridge. Another dash brought Tim and Pete to the granite wall.

They paused for a moment, then edged their way round the side of the monastery. The air was heavy with a pungent smell: a row of aviation fuel drums along the wall had been punctured, and the octane was dribbling out. They splashed through it to reach the main doorway. Tim stood beside it and called again, 'Come out, Karakis! You can't escape!'

The answer was another volley of bullets from inside.

Tim turned to his companion. 'Pete, see if there's a back door.'

The bald man nodded and ran back along the wall.

'Give it up, Karakis. What's the point of prolonging the agony?'

This time the Greek answered. 'Why don't you come in and fetch me, Mr Lacy?'

'I can afford to wait.' Tim squinted inside. The roof was supported on pillars, like a church – which is probably what this part of the building was. One of the pillars might afford cover.

'Oh, do come in, Mr Lacy. Since you've travelled so far, you ought to see my collection. There are so many great masterpieces here, including *The Triarchs*, which has caused you so much trouble.'

Then Pete's voice from inside. 'I'm with you, Major!'

An exchange of gunshots echoed round the interior. Tim grabbed the opportunity, and rushed from the entrance to the nearest pillar. He looked around him in the gloom. Along each side wall stood a row of wooden racks. In these racks were stored dozens of paintings, some framed, some just unadorned canvases. A few pictures were propped against the pillars. Tim recognised a Gainsborough that had disappeared in London two years before.

'I'm impressed, Karakis.'

'So you should be, Mr Lacy.'

Tim tried to locate the voice, but there was too much of an echo. 'Pete, can you see him?'

'No, Major. He's moved since I came in.'

Karakis's laughter filled the building. 'There are lots of nooks and crannies here, Mr Lacy. And the fun of it is, I know them and you don't.'

Tim decided to try for another vantage point, so made a dash for the next pillar. He reached it, but not before a bullet nicked the back of his left leg.

'Please, try that again, Mr Lacy. This is rather like a shooting booth at the fairground.'

'Karakis, this is pointless. You can't . . .'

There was another shot, followed by a screamed oath from Pete and a metallic clatter.

Tim heard the Greek shout, 'Don't move, my friend!'

'What's going on?' Tim kept his back pressed to the stone column.

'I have winged your friend, Mr Lacy. He is now disarmed and covered by my pistol. You have five seconds to throw down your weapon and come over here. If not, I will kill your colleague.'

'Pete, is that true?'

'Afraid so, Major. He got round behind me, somehow. But don't worry about me. You just finish off the job we came here for.'

Karakis's answer was another shot.

'Bastard!' Pete bellowed in pain and anger.

'He's a sitting target, Mr Lacy. Shall I continue?'

Tim threw his gun on the flagstones. 'No, I'm coming over!'

He edged cautiously out into the open space. 'Where are you?'

'Head straight forward.'

Tim moved slowly, trying to locate the source of the echoing voice, completely at the mercy of a cornered psychopath. At the back of the building he saw Pete leaning against the wall. He had removed his belt and was trying to wind it one-handed round the upper part of his gashed and bleeding right arm.

Tim ran over to help him.

'No time for that! Come up here, both of you.'

Tim turned and stared up a flight of stone steps. Karakis sat at the top, covering them both with his gun.

He waggled the barrel. 'Come. Quickly!'

Ostentatiously, Lacy turned his back on the Greek and finished fastening the tourniquet.

Another crack. The bullet chipped the stone by Tim's right foot, then whistled away into the dim interior. 'I said, "Come here." '

Tim turned and glared at the crook crouched above. He stepped forward.

'No, the other one first,' Karakis ordered.

As the two men mounted the steps, the Greek withdrew into the room above. The prisoners emerged into a sizable chamber with large, north-facing windows, which Tim instantly recognised as a well-equipped restorer's studio. There were easels, benches, and shelves containing brushes, paints and solvents – even frame-making equipment.

'So this is the nerve centre of your international racket. I'm impressed.' Tim looked around with mingled admiration and anger. 'I'm also delighted to be closing it down.'

'A petty triumph, Mr Lacy.' But Karakis was struggling to regain his habitual calm. 'A few thousand pounds' worth of equipment, and a hundred or so recovered paintings. What do they matter? I shall escape, and my organisation remains intact.'

Tim laughed. 'Not even Houdini could escape from here. The whole place is surrounded by armed police.'

'But when I walk out with two hostages held at gunpoint, not one of them will dare open fire. We will then climb aboard the helicopter, and they will make no attempt to stop us leaving.'

'The police have helicopters, too.'

'By the time they can mobilise their forces I shall be safe among friends in Lebanon or Syria, or perhaps Italy. Who knows where Karakis will set up his new base? Now move! That other door leads to an outside staircase. We will descend it and make our way very slowly—'

The roar of the helicopter interrupted him.

'Sounds as though your friends have decided to make a run for it.'

'Idiots!' Karakis rushed across to a small window. 'Stop! You fools! Stop!'

But his futile words were drowned in the shrill whine of the rotor blade and the accompanying crackle of rifle fire.

Through the square of glass they saw the tail of the chopper rise into view. He shook his head. 'It's suicide. They'll never make it.'

The next instant there came a searing blast of light and a thunderous roar. The window shattered. All three men were thrown to the ground.

For several moments Tim was too shaken to move. Then he noticed Karakis's pistol had fallen within inches of his left foot. He sat up and grabbed the gun – pointed it at the Greek, who was kneeling amidst splinters of glass, wiping away the blood which trickled from a gash in his cheek. He was clearly dazed, swaying gently. Groaning like a sick child.

Tim stood unsteadily, and looked round, then he saw the other figure slumped against the wall behind him. 'Pete!' He staggered across the room. 'Dear God, not another one!'

Kneeling beside the motionless figure, he listened for the sound of breathing. Felt for a pulse. Sighed his relief. Pete was out cold, but still alive.

Tim turned back towards Karakis.

That was when a second, more violent explosion rocked the building.

The Greek stumbled to his feet.

Tim realised instantly, and shouted: 'The fuel tanks! There's spilled octane down there! We've got to get out!'

Levelling the gun at Karakis, he nodded towards the outside door.

But the Greek stood still in the middle of the room, eyes fixed on the steps leading to the store-room below. Already the stone walls were lit up by a flickering orange glow. Then, 'The paintings!' It was something between a yell and a howl of pain. Before Tim could move, Karakis blundered towards the steps.

'No! It's hopeless!'

Halfway down, Karakis turned angrily. 'You must help. They're priceless.' Then he disappeared.

Smoke was already drifting up through cracks in the floorboards. Tim threw the gun aside, bent down, and grabbed Pete's slack, heavy body. Hauling it over his shoulder, he staggered to the door, yanked it open and almost fell down the steep flight of wooden steps. At the bottom he stumbled into George Martin and a police officer.

George gently relieved him of his burden. 'Is he hurt bad?'

'He'll live. Lay him over there on the grass. We've got to go back and get Karakis.'

'But, Major . . .'

'Come on!'

Tim set off round the back of the monastery, and George caught him up. 'There's a door here somewhere.'

Pushing it open, they were engulfed in a choking cloud of smoke.

Tim took a deep breath and jumped through the entrance. The other end of the room was well ablaze; flames were creeping along the wooden racks, greedily grasping at the stacked masterpieces as they advanced.

Tim rubbed his smarting, streaming eyes – and then saw Karakis. The Greek was frenziedly grabbing canvases away from the path of the fire. He turned to stare at his enemy. 'Don't just stand there! Help me save them!'

'It's no good. There isn't time!'

Tim raised an arm to cover his face. The heat was intolerable.

Karakis ran over and thrust a canvas into his hands. 'Don't you care? You must help me save them!'

Tim threw the picture down. By now the fire had almost encircled them. He grabbed the Greek by the arm and pushed him towards the only remaining gap in the wall of flame. But Karakis swung a fist, which caught him on the side of the face and sent him sprawling. Tim struggled up, half dazed, and leaped through the closing circle. There he crashed into George, who took him firmly by the shoulders. 'Come on, Major! It's hopeless.'

Tim turned back. Through the closing curtain of smoke and fire he had a last glimpse of the man who possessed such a total contempt for human life, yet was now dying in a desperate bid to preserve his works of art from destruction. Then George dragged him clear of the building.

The two men fell on to the grass, fifty yards away. They stared, mesmerised by the inferno. Smoke and flame plumed from every window. Part of the roof collapsed.

'We *must* save . . .' Tim took a few steps.

George restrained him. 'It's no use, Major. It's all gone! Nothing could survive that.'

Tim buried his face in his hands. 'Gone up in flames, after all this time. Terrible! Terrible!' It was not the smoke that brought tears to his eyes.

George shrugged. 'Good riddance, if you ask me.'

But Tim was not thinking of Karakis.

EPILOGUE
A public exhibit

There was no time for a honeymoon. Tim and Catherine travelled straight back from the United States to get Farrans ready for its opening at Easter.

Builders and decorators had been in the house for six months: fitting out the great hall as a gallery, turning the solar and library into seminar rooms and the long gallery into a conference venue, refurbishing the dining-room. Tim and Catherine had supervised every minute detail. They had not dared to leave the house until this work was well advanced. Much to her parents' dismay, Catherine had only managed to introduce her bridegroom to them on the very eve of the wedding. Only two days later, they were now back again.

Tim stopped the car at the entrance to the drive, where they both got out to admire the new signboard.

FARRANS COURT
THE
LAPORTAIRE MEMORIAL
ARTS CENTRE

When they reached the house they wandered hand in hand from room to room, admiring, criticising, making notes. It was evening. The workmen had gone, and they had the old mansion to themselves. They emerged at last into the great hall.

Tim squeezed his wife's hand. 'You really do like the place, don't you?'

309

'Darling, I love it. You know that. And what you're doing with it is marvellous.'

'It was one of those ideas that seemed so obvious. A quiet place where artists can come, not just to exhibit but to meet with customers, critics, dealers, talk about their work, explain it, meet with other artists, get together with people wanting to commission paintings or sculptures. And a place where the public can look at the best modern work *and* actually talk with the people who produce it.'

Catherine laughed. 'Yes, darling, I know. I've read your brochure.'

She wandered over to a table by the main door and picked up the pile of mail that had been left there.

'A postcard from Italy. Venetia plans to be here on the twenty-fifth to arrange her pictures for the opening exhibition. She says she can't wait to see what you've done to this ghastly old place. Oh, and here's a letter from Mr Tonashi.' She tore open the long envelope and unfolded the stiff typed sheet of paper. She laughed. 'It's written in his usual expansive style. Listen. "Dear Catherine and Tim, I am sorry I was not able to be present at your wedding. I am sure everything went delightfully. I hope you will consider the enclosed an acceptable if belated present. Yours sincerely, Ichiro." '

'What's he sent? A nice fat cheque?'

'No. It's a newspaper cutting.'

'What's it say?'

'Wait a minute. My Japanese has got a bit rusty over the last nine months. Let's see. It says "A Goodwill Gesture. At a reception last night to mark the arrival of the new British Ambassador, the Prime Minister presented Sir Archibald Raikes with a painting, as a gift from the people of Japan to the people of Britain. The work, 'Adoration of the Magi' by the Renaissance artist Raphael, is to be hung—" '

'What was that?' Tim, who had been only half listening, was now suddenly all attention.

' "The work 'Adoration of the Magi' by the Renaissance artist Raphael, is to be hung in the National Gallery, London, where it is certain to attract a great deal of public attention and admiration—" '

'But that can't be! I mean, how?'

'Do you want me to finish the article?'

'Yes, go on.' Tim listened intently.

' "Thanking the Prime Minister for his generosity, Sir Archibald made special mention of Mr Ichiro Tonashi, the industrialist and connoisseur, through whose good offices the masterpiece was secured." Tim, isn't that wonderful! *The Triarchs* is safe, and going where it should always have been – on public display.'

Tim shook his head. 'Yes, of course, it's marvellous. But I don't understand. Karakis told us—'

'And you believed him?'

'So, if he was lying about it being there in the monastery, he must have already sent it back to Athens in the chopper.'

'Probably couldn't wait to get it packed off to Tokyo and collect his money.' Catherine slipped her arm through his. 'Anyway, does it really matter? The important thing is that *The Triarchs* is safe. After centuries of wanderings, and who knows what trials and tribulations, it's come to rest at last. And you're the one who laid the ghost. You cancelled the evil spell and rescued a masterpiece from obscurity. The world has a lot to thank Mr Tim Lacy for.'

'But, of course, the world will never know.'

She rested her head on his shoulder and gave a long, contented sigh. 'Now it really *is* over. Now you can relax and give your undivided attention to other things – me for instance.' She drew him towards the doorway in the carved screen, lifted the iron latch, and preceded him into the passage. 'Me – and our child.'

'What? Catherine!'

But she had disappeared into the unlit corridor, and only a giggle reached him from the gloom.